I0611596

A Boke of Gests is Copyright © F. Killian, 2021.

All text is Copyright © F. Killian, 2021.

All images are Copyright © F. Killian, 2021.

No part of this book may be copied or reproduced without express written permission from the copyright holders.

9 781735 093413

A Boke of Gests

For Em

Who puts up with this ydyot.

A
Boke
Of
Gests

F. Killian

Contents

The Lady of Salt and Shadows

arly in the sixth century by the reckoning of our kings, or midway through the eighth by the reckoning of the Fermerans who once sailed from the west, there lived a knight in that green land which they had claimed by the name of Pander Travail. Sir Pander was dark-haired and green-eyed, strong-jawed and lyre-tongued. He had done few deeds, but was a renowned warrior and was born of a line then much-loved, but now long-forgotten. It was said that one day he would be remembered as a saint.

These were dark times in what would become our belovèd kingdom. The Sung invaders were some hundred years gone, though their destructive reign was still felt. In Dragonhold the Ferms fought to take land from the Ordals. Great swaths of Segdony were conquered by the Moræls. And the southlands were ruled by dragons and dark, crawling things. Yet in bitter times such as those there is no better time for heroes, and Sir Pander was known even in his youth to be destined for such greatness.

Pander was born in a village on the northern banks of the River Ath, though even the most wizened scriveners of the Great Library would be hard-pressed to tell you its name; today it is but one of many vine-choked ruins under the eves of the Sable Wood. When he was old enough to carry a sword he fought for his village and served the Greening Kings in their conquest of Orden. When he was old enough to grow a beard he took a vow — not to any lord nor lady but to one of his sainted ancestors, who had walked free upon the eastern coast from the boats used to flee ancient Gosiche.

And like his ancestor he wandered. First on boats and ferries down the River Ath, then by foot and horse. From the Greening Hand he crossed the Saintstones and skirted the Knight's Wood until he came to Valmanion, even then a prominent city in that land.

Yet Valmanion was under a heavy pall when noble Travail came upon it; the town was starving, for the men were afraid to tend their fields or to hunt the wood. They were afraid that they would stumble acrost the witch that lived near, for it was said that her beauty was so great as to turn men to salt.

When Pander's great pepper steed rode through Valmanion's stone gates the people knew a man had come to save them. They came to him and he told them of his fathers and mothers, back to before the Sungs came to Gosiche. They applauded him and rewarded him with wines and swords and maidens fair, and he stayed for a time to prepare.

Finally the day came for him to confront the witch, and he rode out amongst great fanfire, a parade following him right to the gates of that town. None accompanied him for they kenned him to be mighty, but the people knew well how the encounter would transpire. Statues, both nude and well-armoured, were completed—begun upon the hour of his arrival—of him hoisting the head of the witch high, gore spilling fantastically. Paintings were hung of her phantasmagorical cave and her vile beauty, struck low by the shining paladin.

Verses were sung and resung, already written as he crossed the orchards outside the walls—a thousand ways of how Sir Pander the Wanderer would ride his mount along the stony path, following the singing of the birds and the whispers of ghosts until he began to see the salt piles that once were good men, cursed by a woman's gifts. From there he would dismount, for the trees would grow thick, and tie his horse to a twisted bough. "I shall return, and swiftly, with my prize," he would warn his ride with love. A fox he would meet by many accounts and query, and the fox point him the way. Forward he would march, his eyes tight shut, guided by the chirruping of his forest friends. At the cave when he came he would cry out and the she-devil come, eager to punish a good man. Yet his eyes would remain tight shut and her beauty would not mar him—not like his sword would her. Once her body was stricken her spell would be broken and her head he would hew from body. His grisly token taken, he would return to his horse then, triumphant, to Valmanion.

These songs were more present even than the crying of the birds, so when the Travail steed was sighted it was with joy the people met the watchmens' cry. Yet joy swiftly turned to horror, as the colour drained from the men on the wall, and they turned not only white, but to salt. And soon the salt turned red and black as blood; the carmine from their veins had drained to their hearts and their hearts had burst, soaking the salt so those terrible statues slowly crumbled like sandcastles and the walls of Valmanion ran with blood.

"These gates I shall open and all those who wish not the same fate will shut tight their eyes," came clear the voice of the witch.

No more were the songs sung, and shrieks of horror rose from hundreds of worried throats. Soldiers ran to bar the door and the heroes that Valmanion held, none so great as Sir Pander, drew their blades and stood with flapping capes in the street at the town's fore.

With a sudden silence born of Valmanion's wailings the

4

gates slid open, pushing the soldiers aside, and in an instant all those who stood against the witch were also made statues of blood and salt. On that pepper steed she rode, letting the fresh blood drain from Sir Pander's severed head along the streets. Her warning rang again and again, and everywhere the women closed their eyes in fear and their children followed, not yet stubborn enough to rush into death.

But the men looked.

All of the men looked.

Some merely did not believe, for what woman had such power? And some could not resist the promise of absolute beauty. But in that last blink of their eyes they were not only struck through with fear, but also with disappointment. For the witch looked no fouler nor fairer than Marie who hung the regent's laundry to dry, or Olena the baker. Her shape was thin but not smooth, blemished and knobbed like a woman, not sleek and buxom like a statue or a lad's tale. Her hair was black and lustrous, but uncut and ratted, and her fingers were calloused from work. Nay, her beauty was not merely physical, but somehow sublime, and when their eyes fell upon her they glimpsed a truth clearer and stranger than what they thought could be contained in the fairer sex.

When she came to the regent's manour she opened the doors there as well and rode Travail's mount up its steps and onto the wide gallery on the hame's second story. There she called and the blind folk of Valmanion came.

"I come not to punish nor with ire, but with desperation. Know me! For I am not merely witch, but woman and Fermeran also, and my name is Abrial. I did not choose what power fell upon me, but I did chose this land. I came to the forests near Valmanion seeking peace, yet ever men came and sought me, damning me for what befell them. No idol am I to be sung of nor sought after, but a woman with as much right to life as any here. This head I hold I shall mount atop the gate so Valmanion may serve as a warning and none more shall fall prey to me nor bother my peace.

"For each of you I give a choice; blind yourself and live in peace beside me, or leave this place and tell all those you meet of the tale of this damned knight who served this damned town."

The women spoke and some left, cursing Abrial for the deaths of husbands, sons, brothers, and fathers. But many stayed. And they lived for a time in their kingdom of the blind, until Abrial died and the children of the blinded children could open their eyes in peace. Even today, the dames of Valmanion wear the sigil of the blindfolded maiden in honour of the first lady of Valmanion.

The Lady of Salt and Shadows.

Old Master Wood

 long time ago, as these stories often begin, in the depths of an old wood so deep and so ancient so as to seem unending to the simple folk of the time, lived an old fellow with a pointed red hat. The man lived in a house of brick and timber with sod rooves which leaned on themselves in uneven, lurching angles like knotty hills. A burbling stream ran past the many-coloured stones of its eastern wall, and on around the south, passing under a quaint wooden bridge carved with knots and flowers and dragons. The bridge was connected to a forest path which led from deep into the holt, over the bridge, and then meandered around small flower gardens and larger vegetable gardens, with little posts every couple yards for eccentric bird houses, where winged mothers chirped happily away in the summer. A pleasant scent always hung over the property, of moss and flowers and honey (for the owner kept a small apiary behind his house), and when he was at home (which he usually was) the smoke from the chimney added its own notes to the comfortable air of the place.

The hermit himself was older than old (yet not so old as the Wood) yet still quite spry, and his only wrinkles were from laughter (and there were many). He was not known to the Men of those parts—leastwise not well—for he seldom had dealings with those who were not his friends, and he only made friends with the animals. Once upon a time he had dealt often with Men, and had lived closer to the edge of the Wood. But he had grown tired of their ways and their pride and their stubbornness and so had retired from the world of Men. For as long as Men cared to tell tales, he had existed as a children's tale, a fanciful jest, or a fool's testament—the old magician who lived in the woods and talked with the animals. Some told foul stories about him cursing widows or baking children into pies, but most spoke of him in jest, as he would have wanted, and a whole family of common jokes existed about his fanciful dealings with the beasts of the holt. No one knew his name, for he was not there to tell it, and perhaps he had forgotten it himself, for he never told it even to his woodland fellows. Surely he had a name—for all folk do—but for lack of knowledge of it he was commonly called Old Master Wood, and this title suited him fine.

Trees move slower than the rest of the world, and so—as Men learned to smelt metal and farm pastures, to build stone castles and wooden halls, to wage war with red swords and pen beautiful gospels with paint of lead and gold—the Wood took the seasons in turn and Old Master Wood smoked his pipe, walked on the forest paths, made beautiful crafts, and chatted with bird, bear, and deer.

Our tale begins late one summer, as autumn's first chill winds kissed the slow stream and gentle fogs settled over the morning lands. Old Master Wood had taken to fishing off the eastern roof of his house in the afternoons, his pipe brightly puffing as he hummed a simple song of his own devising. Occasionally, as he paused to refill his bowl, he would sing the words, which went something like this:

O fa diddle derry

A cool wind blows merry

And here I sit

And swing my feet

8

And cast my line,

Hallooing to all I meet

There were many verses, as each time he began to sing it he made up new ones. As for the fishing, he often caught nothing at all, and sometimes tossed back what he caught after having found a new friend; his diet consisted mostly of roots, berries, vegetables, and other such gentle fare, for he made friends of the animals so easily that often he knew the name of whatever he meant to hunt, and it is a foul soul indeed which would eat his own friend.

On this particular day he had cast his line into the river and sat humming and smoking for much of the evening when he felt a drop of rain on the tip of his red nose. He glanced up only to have another splash near his eye. Laughing with cheerful, white teeth, he tugged on the brim of his broad cap and wound the line about his fishing rod, standing with a huff and trundling down the red-painted ladder he kept near the roof; it was almost dark anyway and he could do with some hot thistle tea. As he came to his front door he found that he had a visitor.

"Why hello, Master Fox," he said, setting his tackle beside the entry. "Would you like some shelter from the rain?"

"Tha' I would, Master Wood," answered the fox, though not in words you or I would understand. "But also I come to ask yer 'elp."

"My help? Why then you must certainly come in and tell me your troubles. And have a cup of tea while you do!"

And so the two went inside and the host hung his blue coat and his red hat on the coat tree as his guest wiped his paws on the mat. After the hermit set the tea on the stove they sat

9

acrost from one another at a small round table near a window facing west, the man in a winged wooden armchair and the fox on a high wooden stool. Whilst they waited for the water in the kettle to boil they spoke of common things—of friends and acquaintances and hobbies they were pursuing—for it simply does not do to discuss serious matters without a warm cup in hand. Old Master Wood talked about his fishing and a queer stone he had found while walking one day, which the Bear of Copper Dell had said reminded him somewhat of the stones of a river some way north where his cousin lived. The Bear of Copper Dell was doing quite well, despite his failing eyesight, and the fox was glad to hear it. As for the furry guest himself, he had taken up bird watching, though often he found himself wishing he was quick enough to gobble them up rather than merely observe them. He had also begun riddling with Willowbrook's Elk, and often brought back the choicest rhymes for his wife, who was pregnant with a new litter of pups.

In time the whistle blew to signal that the tea was ready, and Old Master Wood set out two clay cups and filled them to brimming with fragrant thistle brew. They chuckled one last time and took their first sips, the host gripping his cup between his weathered paws as the rain pattered against the roof and the beast cautiously lapping at his own, bracing himself with two white-stockinged paws on either side.

"So now that we are settled, tell me; what has you so out of sorts, Master Fox?"

Master Fox looked to his tea and took a few more laps before looking up. "Aye, Master Wood, tha' I shall. Ken ye Elderbrake, Washingwood, an' Mintwell?"

"Aye, I do," answered the other, concern deepening on his brow. These were the names given by the folk of the forest to three southerly areas of the greater Wood. Much as we Menfolk name our towns and cities, woodland critters often attach labels to well-known places. Old Master Wood had not often gone to Elderbrake, Washingwood, nor Mintwell of late, for they were too far from the heart of the Wood for his taste, but he knew them to be populous and joyful places, which lived at a certain peace with the settlements of Men nearby. Yet from Master Fox's manner he gathered swiftly that all was not well.

Yipping briefly with dismay, the guest continued, "O woe, friend! For the folk o' those parts—the Menfolk, ye ken—'ave grown greedy an' un'appy wi' their lot, and taken axe to ash an' bow to beast!"

"Men have always logged and hunted game," answered the host, setting aside his tea. "That is the way of things. Yet so too does the Wood take from them, by predator, frost, and rot. Would not Cousin Wolf, who sometimes hunts in those parts, be sore disappointed to see no more sheep in pen and field for easy feasting?"

"'Tis not merely this," spake the fox in desperation, "for I fear even Cousin Wolf may be slain!"

"How would this have come to be? Did he and his band take too much so as to starve a village? If so, perhaps he was deserving of whatever company sought him out to enact justice. Balance in all things, dear friend, is how the Wood is preserved."

"Yet there is balance no longer!" shouted the worried messenger, before calming himself with a few long draughts of tea. When he was composed once more he began to cry. "They are gone! Elderbrake, Washingwood, an' Mintwell all gone! Logged and 'unted and leveled by thoughtless Men! There is naught there now but lumber, stumps, an' mud. Nearly ten leagues it is, undone an' conquered. The folk o' iron an' words 'ave declared open war 'pon the Wood!"

For some time then they sat in silence, save for the patter of rain, the snuffling of sobs, and the occasional cautious sip of tea. At length the hermit spoke once more. "This is not the way of things. There was a time when the kings of Men knew of balance and valued peace with the world. Men are greedy, aye, yet I am loathe to believe that they should forget so sacred a covenant. Stay you here until the rain passes, Master Fox, and after you have left I shall travel north to the hall of King Alimanx, who holds sovereignty over all these lands. I shall speak with him and bring peace back to the Wood."

And so the fox stayed a few hours longer, thanking his host and excusing his tears in endless repetition. Old Master Wood smiled and laughed, but in his eyes was a deep worry. Once his guest had gone—padding through the mud and promising to send regards to his wife—the elder donned his blue coat as if it were as weighty as a penance vest and set his red cap upon his head. With pointed deerskin boots on his feet, a sack of provisions over one shoulder, and his gnarled stick in hand, he set out for the hold of King Alimanx.

II

he lands of Old Master Wood's hame were called Tossley Crook, and he went from there north for a few days until he reached Lifwing Hollow. On his way he met many of his friends, or friends of his friends, and always stopped to share a chat or a game or to lend a hand where it was needed; he was in a hurry, yet even when in a hurry he could not bear to be rude. And though it often took him many days to complete important tasks, he was never too

late, for that was a part of his magic.

Lifwing Hollow was the northernmost glade of the forest which he had crossed in a century or more, yet was still deep enough in the Wood that no man since the elder kingdoms had fallen had made any effort to settle there. A titmouse and her family lived in Lifwing Hollow, and it had been much too long since he had paid her a visit. So here he stopped and offered some twine for her nest. She was much obliged, yet lamented that her young had grown to adulthood and gone on to find their own lives. "But such is the way of things," she sighed. "Life moves on and things change and there is ever a new sadness to weigh on the world."

"But so too are there joys," he said. He did not mention the devastation to the south, though doubtless she had heard of it, as had all his other forest friends he passed. "Tell me, dear Titmouse, where I shall go from here should I seek the kingdom of Alimanx? It has been a few generations since I passed north of your nest, and yet I find myself in need of an audience with him."

Eyeing him oddly, the bird answered, "King Alimanx lives beyond the edge of the Wood, and until late has had little to do with these parts."

"Until late? And what has occurred in recent times?"

"Ye ken the Eald Roads—the ones built afore man had discovered war, yet still after they had made enemies of the trees? Well, some run this way from Alimanx's hame, and on those roads have come his armoured fighting men, in ones and twos and parties of tens. I hear tell they slay dragons and black sorcerers in the mountains and vales of the uplands, yet here they ride with wary glances, and follow dark paths, deep into the Unwanted Depths, from whence they never again return."

Old Master Wood liked little the idea of the king's soldiers parading through the holt, and liked less that they wandered into the Unwanted Depths, which were home to many old things which were best left unbothered. It seemed to him now that the time for visiting was done with, and he asked how he might find these Eald Roads. The titmouse told him the way and wished him luck, and took his gifts to show her mate.

He followed her instructions until, on what seemed the thousandth uncounted day, he came at last to the overgrown grey cobbles of the Eald Road. Where he met it the path traveled in one way northwest—a sun-dappled avenue. In the other it split, with both paths leading into dark and tangled ways where no light reached and only black-feathered birds roosted. "Ho-hum and an unhappiness on those roads," spake the traveler, "I shan't walk that way should I ever help it!"

"Nor should you walk the other," said the trees. "For we know your mission, and do not appreciate your friendliness with Men."

At first he was startled for, though he knew trees could talk, he knew also that they seldom did. "It is a strange Man-friend who does not speak to any of their race for decades at a time! Fear not—you oak, ash, birch, and willow—for I wish only to solve the problems they themselves have brought upon the Wood, not allow them my undivided love."

"The only solution to the Rape of Elderbrake is revenge!" whickered a tempestuous young elm—merely forty years, if that—and the other trees murmured their agreement and angrily shook their leaves down about the diplomat.

Cries of "Revenge! Revenge!" floated along on the wind until, with a huff, Old Master Wood raised his voice to silence them. He knocked his stick admonishingly against a knotty root, rising nearly to his waist out of the soil. "You shall have to move much more swiftly than I have yet seen your kind move in all my years should you wish such a course, for I shan't be your fellow in this. Be happy you have anyone to speak for you at all! Trees may be hot with fury and passion, but so too are they the slowest creatures in all the world." He paused and tilted his head, then laughed. "Save stones. Grandfather Granite would be hard-pressed to best any of you in a foot race!"

"There are things in the Wood much swifter than trees which still hold our hatred of Man," whispered a thick, black-barked oak, but the trees made no further effect to stall the hermit and he continued on his way. In moments he was whistling a gay tune, and even skipping as he made his way up the Eald Road. He did not begrudge the race of lumber their enmity, but he wished that sometimes—merely sometimes— they would allow themselves to think practically.

He made much quicker time once he was on the Manmade way, and it was not two days more before the trees began to thin. Their canopies opened some to let in the light of the summer sun and their trunks grew less wide. Branches grew closer to the ground, and their voices were quieter—for they were nervous of Men, and some had even grown sorry for them and offered easy ways for themselves to be climbed for an attempt at cooperation; some older and more malicious trees, deeper in the Wood near to the Unwanted Depths, would also make themselves appear easy to climb, but this was a trap, meant to wound or kill unwelcome travelers.

At the end of the fourth day since leaving the junction, as Old Master Wood was beginning to consider laying down under the shadow of a mossy rock and resting for the night, he caught sight of two pinpricks of light a ways ahead on the path. "Curious," he mused. "If I am as close as I might figure to the

15

king's border then perchance those are the lit torches of wardens on the road. And if they are not? Well then perhaps some wisp has taken a liking to me and—even should I die—I shall have found myself in the midst of an interesting adventure." (As is the wont of many folk who seclude themselves for great lengths of time, yet still hold some spark of gregarity, he was often wont to talk to himself.) Hoisting his haversack, he blinked the sleep from his eyes and set forth with a font of new energy.

Down the way it was indeed two wardens, newly assigned to this uncared-for stretch of road. One was older than the other, and had a well-trimmed white beard (of which he was very proud). If he had been younger he would certainly have been a knight (or *cnight* as they were sometimes called in this place, amongst myriad other names) for he was quite skilled at his job. Yet, as it stood, knighthood was a recent invention in those days, meant for young men. Besides, the elder watchman was very set in his ways and suspicious of all new things, and likely would have refused the honour if it were offered, even by King Alimanx himself; stubbornness was seen as a virtue by Men in those days, and many even today who now have forgotten the histories of their peoples still adhere to that honoured tradition. The younger watchman wished ever so greatly to one day be made knight, yet it would never be so, for he was a dullard and a fool and would be useless at his assigned station were his partner not so experienced. This one was skinny and pox-scarred from an illness in his youth, and often found his nose to be nearly as wet as the country bog where he had been raised.

These two simple soldiers did not see the hermit until he was almost upon them, and when they did they brandished their long torches at him from horseback and demanded to be told his name.

"I shall tell you my name if you shall tell me yours," he

16

said. And though such impertinence would usually be punished (and rightly so, according to the law), the two complied, for there was a simple magic in the tongue of Old Master Wood.

"Hallmot," said the elder.

"Ern," said the younger. He was very proud to share a first initial with the king, and did not realize that *A* and *E* were different letters. His father, Kinnel, had been possessed of a similar, yet subtly different misconception, believing that Alimanx's given first name was King.

"Well, Ern, Hallmot," he nodded to each as he addressed them, "my name is not something I easily share, but I am sometimes called The Old Man of the Wood or, in more common parlance, Old Master Wood."

Hallmot squinted down at him and sucked at his lower lip. He had heard tales of The Old Man of the Wood—every one bad—and this was not how he had expected him to look. He was not entirely certain what he had expected but it was not a brightly dressed, spry fellow whose face was lined with laughter and whose head would barely reach his chest, should they both be standing and the comical red cap not be worn. Perhaps he had expected a tree which walked. Or a terrible, snaggle-toothed goblin. Or, at the very least, a more imposing sorcerer—with black robes and a wicked white mane, all bedecked in horrid runes and pagan sigils. Yet nay, this Man seemed no more oppressive than a smiling dog lying in the hot sun. It made Hallmot uncomfortable and suspicious.

"Ye carry any proof o' that name?" asked the senior guardsman.

Frowning, Old Master Wood replied, what proof could I give? And what if I am not the same Old Man of the Woods you think I am, but another with the same name? Is not my business more pressing than what I am called by?" He had forgotten how frustrating it was to deal with Men.

This made some sense to Hallmot, but he did not like to be contradicted nor distracted, and he was beginning to realize that the stranger had already done this to him once. "Now ye listen well; I asked ye—"

Even as Hallmot began to speak so too did Ern, and the elder quieted in further frustration at being interrupted. "Then wha' be yer business, Master Wood?"

The hermit ducked his head dutifully to Ern (a motion which made Ern blush with pride). "My business is, in fact, with King Alimanx the Affluent. Know you where I may find him?"

The two riders looked to one another in surprise. Hallmot, his consternation forgotten, answered back swiftly, "What business 'ave ye with our king?" It was very exciting to meet a stranger with business with the King; either he was very important and would be celebrated upon arrival or he was a spy or assassin and would be hung. This fellow looked like neither to the warden's keen eye, but he was aware that both types of visitors often went in disguise.

"I am a diplomat," offered the traveler, this time with a bow towards Hallmot (and a wink which made him anxious), "and I come from the south to discuss the recent aggressions which his people have taken in defiance of the ancient truces." He did not mention from whence he was an emissary, for fear their ignorance would deny him.

The watchmen knew naught of a war in the south, yet both surmised that the world was large enough (and Alimanx's kingdom itself nearly as wide) for thereto be events beyond their ken. They agreed to take him to Hilldell, where the King kept court, and Hallmot ordered Ern to give up his horse for their guest. Ern was quite pleased when Old Master Wood insisted that he preferred to travel by foot; for he was not merely ugly and dull, but lazy as well. They made camp nearby and set out after a meagre breakfast, supplemented by the southron (to the others' delight) with a clutch of songbird eggs.

The way was simple enough, for there were few branches from the Eald Road, and the one they followed was clearly more travelled than many of the others. They passed soon out of the trees and into rolling hills and green pastures, dark and glistening with fresh rain. As they rode, Ern told jokes (many of them in poor taste) and Hallmot scowled and watched their charge suspiciously (though even he had to admit that the emissary was charming enough). For his part, Old Master Wood played along with Ern's foolery, laughing even when the jape was only mildly entertaining, and sometimes sang songs, which he made up as they went. One of these songs, which both wardens though especially catchy, went something like this;

Two men ahorse, ahorse two men,

Their backs so tall and straight,

They ride the Eald Roads dutifully

From Wood to their king's gate.

Two watchmen proud, two proud watchmen,

A sword at each high hip,

Ariding for their king,

Handsome hair 'pon their lip.

And on for many short verses, each complimenting his guides in new and shallow ways.

The land grew hillier as they neared Hilldell, for the village had been named—for shortage of imagination—after both the rising land about it and for the depression in which it sat. At the few poor farms they had briefly stayed at, in barns or on wooden floors, the wardens had bragged of how they were on a mission to greet the King, and had been well-treated by their hosts. So too did Hallmot brag to the other wardens they met deeper in that country (though when he was alone with other soldiers he would speculate on political intrigue and strange sorcery hidden under the stranger's bright clothes). Thus it was that when the three reached the edge of Hilldell they were anticipated and rumours of all kind flew beneath the eaves of the steepled houses (much to Old Master Wood's chagrin).

Hilldell was a settlement of great size (for those days) and held within its valley over thirtyscore Men, women, and children. Wide streets were paved in red stone, angled so the rain would wash the refuse which gathered into shallow ditches to either side. The houses themselves were of sturdy construction, though all of wood—it was too wet in these lands for there to be any serious fear of fire save if a dragon should come down from the mountains in a fury, but so far Alimanx's knights had done a fair job of managing the local reptilian population. At the far eastern end of the village rose the hall of King Alimanx the Affluent, whose peak rose higher than any other building in the town save the steeple of the church and whose façade was adorned with colourful shields and pillars of carven oak. In preparation for the arrival of a foreign diplomat the streets had been newly swept, the beggars forcibly removed to another town, and colourful banners hung from the houses of important Men. Everyone wore their brightest and most well-sewn clothing and guards in pointed helms stood at every street corner. And amongst those bright coats there were also many poor, and it hurt to see. As Old Master Wood looked on he felt a deep yearning for his little stream and his mouth grew dry for want of fresh tea. But if his peaceful life was to continue he would have to confront these self-righteous Menfolk in their crowded halls. He kept a wildflower in his hand to sniff at whenever the stench of civilization hurt his nose too greatly.

He was taken to the gates of Hilldell, such as they were, and introduced by Hallmot in a loud voice, to many appreciative noises from the gathered audience of townsfolk. Hilldell had no wall, and so the 'gates' were merely two tall posts on either side of the entrance to the main street, between which stood two stone-face guards at all times. The guards accepted the stranger and released the wardens back to their duties.

"I fought we were to see th' King!" whined Ern, which earned him a harsh glare.

Hallmot too was disappointed, though he did not voice it. Instead he leaned in to one of the guards and whispered, "He's a charming devil, this one, but a devil nonetheless. Be sure to say yer prayers afore ye sleep lest he lays some curse or other on ye." Then he tapped the iron pendant he wore about his neck twice and took his grumbling halfwit partner back to the Eald Road.

King Alimanx was an old man, and a member of a very old royal line. In his youth he had done all the things which first-born princes were expected to do—slaying dragons, visiting villages, saving princesses, learning his classics and the like. When his father, King Arlan the Magnanimous, passed on from complications of a common cold caught on a rainy day Alimanx had graduated to doing all the things which new kings were expected to do—granting lordships, airing the grievances of his subjects, having statues commissioned, waging great wars, and the like. And as he had grown older so too had his renown; amongst his subjects he was known as being just and wise, amongst his allies prudent yet firm, and amongst his enemies ferocious and willful. And to all of these he was known to be quite rich. His halls were filled with vibrant rugs from the furthest reaches of the east, great tapestries depicting famous battles and fabled loves, rare animals and spices, and gold and silver in every shape and function imaginable. Every castle, court, and manour he owned was as a museum of conquests, geases, and gifts. Yet all of these treasures together paled in his eye to the greatest of all his holdings—the one thing which he could never attach a price, no matter how his counselors begged him to do so.

This magnificent treasure was, of course, the Princess Isadore. Isadore had been born late in Alimanx's life to one of his long string of royal consorts; for all his idyllic virtue and duteous manners, the old king had never taken a wife, instead keeping a steady stream of women of good breeding at his side, each hoping that they should be his choice to wear the spousal crown. Yet none were ever chosen, and each was either dismissed or died in their time. Some said that Alimanx disliked the womanly sex entirely, yet others would point to the fact that he was nothing but courteous to his partners, as well as to the clear love which he held for Isadore. To this, those who first spoke would offer then that perhaps it was truer to say that he had a disinterest rather than a dislike. As for the truth of it, it is likely that not even the King himself knew, for he was not an introspective man. But he did love Isadore, and cared for her in every way he could. Old Master Wood had heard of King Alimanx, and knew his reputation, but not of his love of his daughter, nor even for certain that he had one.

As the magician was led into the royal hall at Hilldell and down the tapestried passages to the King's audience chamber, the little fellow attempted to make simple conversation with his attendants, but they only gave him strange looks when he spoke of conversations with bears or playing at riddles with fish—strange and perhaps fearful. "Where I am from conversations go two ways," he said with a huff. "But perhaps men have grown beyond the need for words." The looks they gave him after this were even stronger.

The audience chamber of Alimanx of the House of Orlo was sealed by two heavy doors, studded with iron nails and painted with green serpents. The hall leading to them was lined with Men in coats of steel rings, and before the gate itself stood a sombre man, his skin stretched taught over noble bones and his spindly fingers locked before him like vines choking an alder bush.

"Min namu beo Engammu. Ic beo First Minister to ur High King Alimanx." He spoke with a voice like dry leaves, and used strange old words and accents. This was not due to where he was raised, but more due to a deep-seated racial arrogance (further inflated by his high position), and Old Master Wood kenned this. "Ic aska eow hwhy eow hafa com. It beeth a lang way by all counts, and eow aur most strange." His cold grey eyes observed the visitor with a morosity approaching hatred. Hatred of the different and the uncontrolled.

But the little hermit was not one to be intimidated, nor discouraged. "I am called Old Master Wood, and I am certain you have heard of me. I come from deep in the Wood to ask why Alimanx's folk have defied the ancient peace and taken overmuch of their forest neighbors."

"The Wudu beeth under the legal holdu of His High-

23

ness. He needs asketh not to enact his will thereon." The hatred in those grey eyes was clear now, and his red-mantled shoulders thrust back stiffly as if the weight of his ire was nearly too much for him to bear.

"That would be a poor thing to hear," answered Old Master Wood, "but if I must hear it I would rather hear it from Alimanx's own mouth. I understand that your king is quite young, and sometimes young Men do not listen to reason unless they are confronted by much older Men. And often not even then! In any case, I would like to present myself in person, even if it is only to be told off."

Engammu was quite taken aback to hear his master called young, and so his manner of false presentment faltered briefly, "His Grace is what? You... I'm sorry..." His grey eyes were wide and his thin lips hung agape, his locked fingers loosened.

"Now see here, Minister," said Old Master Wood, growing tired of the delays, "I have traveled quite a long way on very old and very sore feet and am expected. I have half a mind to give you a lashing with my stick, but considering that that would result in my rapid expulsion from this musty hole (no matter how much I would appreciate that) I have settled for using my tongue. Uproot yourself from that doorstep and announce me, if that be your profession, or, if not, merely be gone!"

The guards in the hallway and on either side of the angry little emissary fought hard not to chortle at the First Minister's embarrassment (though only two or three succeeded). For his part, the First Minister recovered quickly (whilst silently vowing to impose unfriendly duties on those who had been seen to laugh). With a small chirp of a cough, he turned and took hold of the iron rings on the doors and pulled with all his wiry strength, slowly drawing open the doors. Stepping inside, his stony eyes still set on his adversary, he revealed the throne room of Hilldell.

A long hearth was set into the floor, running its length from the door to the dias on which the throne sat. High windows were spaced beneath the roof to vent the smoke of the fire, and yet more wrought arches and fabled tapestries blanketed the walls. More soldiers stood here, as well as a plethora of brightly tunicked and gowned nobles and a company of players playing a soft, majestic melody. The throne itself was old—nearly as old as Old Master Wood himself—and its wooden arms were carved into the heads of serpents and gilt in gold. The rest of the seat was newly upholstered in rich red satin or painted in twisting green knots. A hint of its original simplicity still remained, but it was far overshadowed by the garish additions of passing centuries. And on that royal seat sat Alimanx himself, his robes overflowing his chair and spilling down the steps of his dias in a brilliant waterfall. His beard was long and white and his brows bushy beneath his pointed circlet, but his eyes—the colour of spring clover—were bright and eagre.

"Euwr visitor fromu the Wudu," announced Minister Engammu curtly as he traveled briskly to the foot of the throne, where he sat like an obedient dog.

The King leaned forwards in his seat, one hand holding his golden rod and the other his regal orb. He raised his head slightly, and Old Master Wood took it as an invitation to approach. Thanking his attendant guards for their kind accompaniment (to their mild surprise, for such was merely their duty) he began to stump his way along the side of the hearth; he was very dearly feeling the strain of his journey on that day. As he came, he stopped sometimes to compliment the shade of a lady's gown or to kindly offer tips on cooking, cleanliness, or love. None asked his advice, though all those who followed it later found it most wise and effective. And though all this seems as if it would delay his arrival at the King's feet or frustrate him (or his Minister) it did not, for Old Master Wood had many small magics and these magics ever made it so that he was never late.

At last he stood before the throne, the points of his yellow boots nearly—but not quite—brushing the hem of the monarch's robe. Gripping his walking stick firmly, he swept back his leg and bowed low. "Greetings to you, King Alimanx. Word has reached even my lands, deep in the Wood, of your famous deeds and long reign. I come to your court to seek parlay on behalf of the Woodland creatures who do not speak your tongue."

Clearing his throat, Alimanx squirmed himself deeper into the cushion of his seat. "We have heard tell of thy coming, Wizard. Yet we must admit, we still do not understand the reasons for thy coming. We have no dealings with animals, for to our knowledge they have no kingdoms and make no compacts."

This response irked the kindly recluse greatly, but he managed to smile gracefully, "Then I am sorry to inform Your Majesty that your knowledge appears to be far from absolute." There were many gasps at this and the First Minister scolded him fiercely, yet he persevered. "Yet regardless of your knowledge of these ancient agreements—which I assure Your Majesty surely exist—the fact remains that your people in the south of the Wood have caused much harm to many kind creatures and ancient trees, and I wish to assure that no more damage is done (though I wish what damage has been done could be undone, but alas). I am a being of some knowing and charm—and some few spells—and would put myself at your disposal for any one weighty task, should the taken lands be returned and nevermore disturbed more than is prudent."

Grey Engammu was irate, and whispered to his royal master to expel (or better, imprison) this impudent visitor. But King Alimanx found himself sorely tempted by the offer made. He waved one ringed hand to quiet his aide and leaned forwards once more, "Indeed, Wizard, thou may be of use to us. For our daughter, who is so dearly loved, has been taken from us deep into the dark Wood. Should you venture into those Unwanted Depths and wrest her from the scoundrels what took her we may see fit to grant thy wish for freedom and for peace."

"May see fit, or shall?" said the traveler with a gleam in his eye.

"Shall see fit," said the King, for he loved the Princess Isadore more than aught else, even his many sons.

III

he road back into the forest was lined with curious onlookers who wished to see the strange sorcerer who would perhaps save their monarch's beloved daughter. How word had spread so swiftly when no messenger had seemingly passed Old Master Wood on the way was a mystery, yet often this is the way of things. He was guided on his way once again by Hallmot and Ern, at the request of the little wanderer. Servants of the King had ridden out and told them of their task before they had even left Hilldell, and they had eagerly agreed—for never before had the King himself given them a direct order, even through the lips of a servant.

Ern was eagre to meet the strange little diplomat again (a fact which he had repeated to Hallmot every few breaths until they saw his silly red hat again) yet Hallmot was suspicious, as is the unfortunate wont of wise Men and Men who think themselves wise. The elder ranger decided that there must have been a reason that he was selected for this task (and there was, though he would be loathe to accept that it was the same reason for Ern and that it was merely that they were the simplest and most familiar option), and set himself about discerning what that might be. It was about halfway along the road that Hallmot decided his king must be suspicious of Old Master Wood's motives, and with this in mind he kept a careful eye on the waddling elder at all times, and lost much sleep over his incessant vigil.

When at last they reached the edge of the Wood, the elder watchman was yawning often, his white head nodding in the saddle. The younger, meanwhile, was jabbering incessantly to their charge, as he had the whole way—asking him of his hobbies, his tales, and his friends in the forest (all of which Old Master Wood answered). But all good things must end and, though he enjoyed the company of these men more than he would have thought, the hermit knew that the Wood had no need of any more Men within it.

"It seems we have come to our journey's end, leastwise as a party. The twisted trunks of my home and of my grim destiny loom ahead and I must leave you, my friends." He swept low his cap in a wide bow.

"Oh, aye, I suppose," muttered Ern as his face fell. He enjoyed this strange companion much more than his dour commander did; being closer in mind to a child, Ern was not yet as separate from the ways of the world as most adults are, and was more soft than he was arrogant. He hoped he would see the master again. On the steed beside him, Hallmot snorted, yet did not wake.

"Tell him I admire his dutifulness," smiled Old Master Wood. Ern said that he would. They said farewell once more (for goodbyes are often awkward save amongst close friends) and they each went their own ways—the magician south into the Wood and the rangers north up the road. When Hallmot awoke some time later he blearily asked where their charge had gone and Ern told him that their duty was done. Hallmot fell asleep once more in the saddle and dreamt of a fair lady in a tower who had love only for him, but he was afraid of the height and could not climb to meet her.

Old Master Wood continued under the cover of trees until coming to the fork where before he had been struck by the uncomfortable aura of the deeper path which led into the Unwanted Depths. The trees there knew him, and mocked him for returning, cruelly certain that no peace had been made with Men.

"Quiet yourselves, elders," snapped the wanderer, who was in age a child beside their ancient barks. He was of no mood to be admonished for taking the actions he knew in his heart to be well and good. "I seek a band of rogues who have gan this way, and in their company a flaxen-haired maiden. I imagine the path you will tell me they took, yet I hope my imagination has grown too strong in my aging."

The wind merely whistled and the selfish trunks, so jocular and mocking a moment prior, were made silent. He glared at each, and made note of their patterns; should Mother Rain ever hunger for woodflesh, as sometimes she did, he would know where to direct her lightning-teeth. All things have small hatreds hidden in them, and in the little hermit it was arrogance. To add to this, he was still frayed from having so much to do with Men, even those as kindly as Ern. Mayhaps in a day or an hour his ire would fade, yet in that moment he imagined flames gripping the black boughs which shook in leafy laughter at his confoundment.

"Fie on you then, and may winter come quickly and your roots be made bare." He took his stick and knapsack (still full enough to sustain him, as he always kept an eye out for small edibles) and began slowly to make his way down the thick, dark path upon which he had hoped never to tread.

Soon he could see by the memory of light, and soon after not at all. He had with him two small candles, and he lit one, setting it in a tooled copper holder. The light it lent did little to illuminate his way, yet it brought him some small comfort amidst the choking growth and occasional cawing of darksome fowl. There was little Old Master Wood had to fear in the world, and especially within the great forest he called home, yet he knew that if there existed aught for him to fear it would be found here in the dark heart of the wild. There are few things which hold hatred longer than trees—even the dead forget their ills in time—and here the trees had choked out all that did not hate as fully as them. There is love in trees as well, for the land and for the beasts sometimes (and even, in trees too young to see the ruination of their cousins' corpses, for Man), but that love is far overshadowed in those trees which stood at the dawning of time. Few remain, for fire, village, and rot have all waged their wars. Yet where they remain they remain in tight and terrible communities, plotting revenges which they shall never bring to pass. And through this bitter, barky kingdom strode the hermit, candle outstretched and a whistling betwixt his teeth; he was not frightened yet, and knew the power that song holds in the world (which was much stronger then than it is now). For two sleeps (for there was no measuring of days in the gloom of the Unwanted Depths) he wandered deeper, and his candle burned slower than it would in the hand of any other. Roots soon overtook all cut stones and he followed no paths, and prayed that he would find his way free once his task was done.

It was shortly after his second waking that he heard the cries. At first he thought them to be the shouts of ravens (and indeed there were raven shouts, though they echoed that other sound), but soon he heard more clearly; it was a Man, crying out in fear and panic to be rescued, his voice hoarse and his words almost lost to desperation.

"Mayhaps my journey has ended and I have found the rogues I seek," he mused, though it was only one voice, and not that of a princess. With a fresh breath he climbed over a high-reaching root and began to make his way towards the noise.

Coming about the side of a mighty alder as wide as a peasant hovel he held his light high and glimpsed a fearsome sight. A man's head and shoulders protruded from the tree at a height just above the hermit's hat, and it was he that cried out. The bark about him shimmered oddly in the shadows of the wick, seeming almost to move like the skin of a snake. Above, perched in the shrouded boughs, the greedy black eyes of foul birds watched with interest. Noticing Old Master Wood, the prisoner blinked and cried out, "Man! Stranger! Ye must do something afore I am swallowed whole by this demon-trunk!"

It irked him to be called 'Man,' yet he knew there was no harm in it. Looking up with bright eyes, he asked, "Tell me, fellow, what put you in such a bind? How came you here and with whom? What am I to call you?"

Sputtering and groaning, the man answered, "Call me whatever ye like, so long as I am freed from this doom! I left my company to shut my eyes for but a moment, yet awoke already in the grip of this—ahhh!" His face twisted as if in great pain and he began to drool.

"Company? Was there, perhaps, a lady with you? A princess even?"

31

"Aye, a princess! Damn ye, help me!" He sucked a line of spittle back between his quivering lips.

"Aha!" thought the hermit. "So I am finally proven justified on my path. Unless the Man lies..." But Old Master Wood disliked being witness to suffering on all counts, and so began to croon in the slow, creaking tongue of trees, "Master Whitebark, what ill has this man caused you to instigate such a cruel reprisal?"

The tree did not answer, but moved its branches in a suggestive way, which indicated the uncaringness of Man and hinted at the blind cruelty of nature maligned. Rough knots like puckered eyes stared out at Old Master Wood, daring him to deny the Wood its due. Yet it could indeed prove difficult to locate the Princess Isadore without a guide. And the little hermit, though he shunned company with Men, held no hate for them, nor for anyone.

"I ken that you have been some hurt by this Man's presence," spake the traveler in the tongue of trees, earning a strange glare from the prisoner, "yet I find myself in need of his aid. Should you not see fit to let him free into my care out of kindness, I challenge you to a game of riddles for the life of the Man." This, of course, was both a clever and dangerous gambit, for trees often think themselves wise beyond measure and cannot resist proving such. But trees are not always as knowing as they imagine, and Old Master Wood was full of tricks.

Old Master Wood's adversary mocked its challenger, saying that the wizard was foolish for thinking himself to know more than its ancient lore, but Old Master Wood promised that he could prove it. The tree shook its creaking branches in mirth, but agreed to the challenge, saying that it would not be fair to defeat its opponent too swiftly, and so the challenger should ask first. This pleased Old Master Wood greatly, for his stomach was much too empty to manage tree-puzzles (for he was being sparing with his rations, though he had enough to subsist upon) and he felt confident in his own ask. Leaning on his walking stick, he marked the tempo of his verse with a dancing finger as he recited:

Longer than tree, than rock, than air live I

And joy and fear come oft beside me.

Dancing I go on corpse of all three!

They hate but cannot quell me, for to speak

Is to give me life.

Who am I?

The alder groaned and twisted with the wind, and the brigand yelped and pleaded. A long time the alder thought, its roots tense with concentration. At last it whispered back a thought, and it was wrong. The black birds mocked it and it trembled with displeasure. It thought some long time more and guessed again, though this was not allowed, and still it was not correct. "Tell me, Man-thing!" it shouted in its quiet way, and Old Master Wood smiled at his victory.

"It is the Names of Men. Written upon paper, carved upon stone, and spoken into the air. The Names of Men live long after their deaths, and it is only by forgetting they ever existed that their power is removed."

Shaking with such fury that the rooks above were frightened from their roosts the alder raged against the answer. Against the longevity of Names. Against the unfairness of defeat.

Yet the fact remained that the more forgotten names the tree resurrected, the more memories were given new life. And so, with a shudder and a deafening creak, the prisoner was violently ejected from his prison.

"Aye, Master Alder, should the means avail me I shall never again darken your shade. Now come," he reached down and helped the sap-sticky brigand to his feet, "and help me find those lost friends of yours."

As the two struggled off, deeper into the dark canopy by the light of the lonely candle, Old Master Wood told his astonished companion how he had known the right riddle to defeat that lignin gaoler. How trees think so little of Man so as to deny their many strengths, just as Man thinks little of felling a great oak for timber. The brigand listened and nodded, half in awe, half unsettled, and half already weary with the curious figure in the red hat.

IV

 oldalf was the brigand's name—or merely Dalf to his friends—and he agreed to show the hermit to where his party had made camp. A part of him wanted to cut the stranger down and loot his purse, yet he had lost his wicked dirk in his strange imprisonment and did not think his rescuer looked to be holding a great amount of coin. Another part of him wanted to leave the magician alone in the Wood to fend for himself rather than lead a spell-weaver directly to his band, but Dalf was superstitious and afraid of being cursed. A third, and largely final, part of him was grateful for the service he had been done (however unusual the situation) and saw no harm in the fellow that he and his cruel brothers could not quell. And so he allowed the cheerful old wanderer to

prattle on about trees and birds and stones and heavens knew what else. He did not tell his benefactor that he had sought solitude from his company in an attempt to stow away with a pouch of stolen silver—thirty if he counted aright; Old Master Wood did not need to know of his greedy action, he thought, and he could easily persuade his captain that no harm had been done, as he still felt the hard lump pressed against his breast, between tunic and leather jack.

The campsite, when they came upon it, was empty, however. A trickle of moonlight stole through the impossibly thick branches above, sparkling off the lazy stream which cut through the clearing and dwarfing the yellow light of their candle with its blue. A circle of stones lay scattered about the ashes of their fire, and one of their tents was torn and discarded on the dark grass, which swayed with dark humour in the night. On the far side stood the remains of an ancient stone wall, vine-choked and shadowed by trees.

Dalf stood agog at the serene and chaotic sight. His first thought was that his companions had left him, as he had left them. But then he considered the torn tent, the exposed soil and torn grass, the hurried footprints of a fleeing host. Some dire thing had come upon the camp—of this he was certain.

A dark look on his elderly face, Old Master Wood knelt by the stream and stared into its black-blueness. He knew not what ill fiends walked these dark depths, yet he feared to confront them. Trees may be hateful things to Men, but they do not uproot themselves and attack them openly ("Though it seems they already made an exception for Dalf," he thought with a shudder), so what had fallen upon these Men? Was Isadore yet hale? He smelled blood on the soil; had any died here? He saw no clear animal tracks, but there were many beasts quick or clever enough to disguise their footsteps.

The brigand strode also to the stream, making an effort to hide his discomfort and mounting panic. "Come—their tracks show strongly on the far side. Whatever happened here, they left in some hurry, as should we."

"We shall follow them, but in time," answered the hermit. He cupped his rough hands in the running stream and drank deeply of the cold water. He could tell his companion was agitated, and an agitated kidnapper makes a poor travelling companion, no matter his skill at forestry. "Drink up," he motioned, "we may not find such clean water for a ways."

At first he hesitated, but the refreshing murmur of the water and the kind eyes of his rescuer swayed him. He knelt in the sod and cupped his own handful of refreshment. It slid down his throat smoothly, clearing his cluttered thoughts. Sitting back on his haunches, he gazed off in the direction which the tracks went. Slowly he stood and walked to them carefully. As he did, Old Master Wood made his way to the ancient wall, where he lifted high his light and ran his gentle fingers over the crumbling stones.

"There are tracks only of men," spake Dalf, adding swiftly, "and one woman. Think ye the King's men followed them here?"

"A king, mayhaps. But not Alimanx." Dalf turned towards the other as the magician abandoned his study of the wall and made to join him. "We shall follow them shortly, and find them as well as now they are—this I vow. But first I would tell you of the Old Kingdoms of Men, what reigned long before Alimanx's oldest fathers."

Dalf spat at their feet. "I have no time for tales, wizard. Come or stay, yet think me not so sedentary a fool as ye."

Old Master Wood smiled gently at the swift nature of

Men, which led them to doom as often as victory. "Let me remind you, Master Brigand, of what befell you when last you ventured the dark Wood alone? Wizard, aye, that I am in ways, and I never arrive later than I intend. Would it not be safer to go beside me than without? But I shall acquiesce to your fears; we may walk as we talk. But walk we shall, for I am not made for running. And though you may find my words long and of little interest to a responsible adult, you may find words which may give face to your forest fears."

Mollified, Dalf agreed, though he did not much like being reminded of his defeat by the elder alder. And so they began their walk, with the brigand's eye ever on the path ahead and his ear ever open, despite his pretend aloofness, to his companion's lore-telling.

The tale told was long, though it did not seem that way by the end. A part of its length was due to its age, for all tales of a certain age are long, because the world then is always quite different than the world now and must be explained in greater detail. Old Master Wood knew the story well, though he no longer remembered if he had merely studied it or if he were truly old enough himself to have lived it— he was, after all, very old, and had forgotten a great many things.

The times he told of were those before the wars and animosity between Men and nature, when Men warred only upon Men (for Men seem to have an unshakeable need to be ever at war). When hungry red swords sang in the mists of the before -times and the imaginations of Men far outgrew their knowledge of the world.

"I shall tell you of a king," said the storyteller, "though I know neither his name nor kingdom. Yet this king is as all kings of the time, and perhaps even of this time, and so his story is theirs as well."

Dalf was beginning to tire swiftly of the elder's company—sorcerer or no—yet found pleasure in the bloody words he spun. "I'll bear him another hour yet, mayhaps two," he thought to himself. Old Master Wood saw the thought in the brigand's eye, but hoped it would dispel itself in time.

In the tale there was a mighty king, who ruled his fellow Men in the forest by fear and gold and might. Yet though he ruled a sturdy fortress and a dozen villages he wanted more. The Story-King saw his neighbors with their own fields and treasuries and crowns and wanted to see them subjugated. He trained his armies and told lies to his peasants and hired great singers to tell of his coming victories. And so the Story-King began a story-war and he did indeed win some victories.

But then his enemies, through an ingenuity born of fear, began their own assault on the trees of the Wood, and felled them in greater numbers than ever before to build tall walls and fierce castles, their merlons cutting the sky like the teeth of giants. The Story-King knew he too would need to take trees, and in greater number. Yet he imagined himself a wise king, and had heard tell of more peasants and soldiers of his enemies being felled beneath the cover of the holt. And so he set out to make an ally of the Wood, taking with him his greatest advisors to meet Great King Ash, the monarch of this forest in those days—and some say, even now. After a series of trials, which the Story-King nobly bested, he at last came to the roots of Great King Ash.

"Great King Ash," he spake, "whose bark is as a king's mighty byrnie and whose leaves are as silken cloaks, I come before thee to beg thy aid. What I ask is most fearsome, and so shall I respond with a fearsome payment, shouldst thou ask it."

And so the Story-King asked Great King Ash to sacrifice some of his brethren so that the Story-King could construct mangonels and siege towers to lay low his opponents. The lignin lord had already begun to grow wroth with the lords of Men for the increased lives they had claimed from his folk, yet he still believed that relations could yet be saved between the bark and the blood. Great King Ash agreed, on the condition that the Story-King would plant new trees for all that were felled and, should the war be won, nevermore build homes nor walls of wood, but instead use stone—for, though it was more labourous, stones enjoyed being used for such, and felt no pain at being uprooted. And so the pact was formed.

With the aid of the Wood, he bested his enemies, and one by one the hames of the other kings were burned and they and their families hung from living boughs. The armies of the conqueror swept acrost the land, and soon all villages in a hundred miles owed fealty to one crown. Yet in all this time not a single seed was planted.

Birds came to ask about the planting, and those birds were baked into pies. Deer came to demand the forest be restored, and their heads were mounted above roaring hearths. The trees began to rustle anxiously in the autumn about their betrayal, and were felled to build sturdy longhouses. And so Great King Ash found that Man could not be trusted, and declared a forever war on all who walked upon two legs.

But the Story-King was concerned with other matters, and noticed naught, even as his loggers once more began to fall prey to accident and his roads became choked with root and dammed by fallen trunk. He was instead occupied by the conundrum of a continued line.

For, in his fervour, the Story-King had slain all his enemies and made enemies of all his friends. In his lonely kingdom he had no Men for which to marry his daughters nor women to wed his sons to. In time he found a willing regent who would allow his son to wed the Story-King's daughter, yet it was but a ruse, and the Story-King was slain and his keep burned at the wedding.

All the world heard of the Story-King's fall, and all the world knew that it was by his arrogance that Man would ever war with the Wood. Each Man and each king vowed never to allow the same to befall him nor his people, and yet it happened again. And again. And again forever, for each powerful Man believes that he is too wise and too fated to fail, and so he acts in the same manner as all before him, and is punished in kind.

"And so it was for a hundred kings and a hundred lands," finished Old Master Wood. He looked to his companion, hoping to find a seed of caution planted behind his eyes, yet found only more stubbornness. "Tell me, Dalf, what thoughts come to you?"

"Thoughts? No thoughts, save yet more desire to follow the trail ahead."

The elder harrumphed. "Have you no thoughts on the ways of the old kings? Their mistakes and fall?"

Dalf laughed. "Ye say naught of their glory, yet ye speak long of it. All Men die; is it not better to achieve yer goals and become known afore ye are called to grave? E'en ye spake of the long names of Men to my captor and, though this tale was so long past that e'en those have been forgot, their deeds live on. Were I a ghost of the king what betrayed the trees I would be proud to know my legacy continued. Now come, I hear rushing water ahead."

As the brigand rushed on Old Master Wood clutched

his stick tightly, for before him he indeed saw the shadow of the Story-King. And as for Dalf, he no longer saw a sorcerer of unknown power—so short is the memory of Man and so swift their passion—but a doddering old storyteller, whose greatest accomplishment would be to slow him down.

V

he waterway which they came upon was not terribly wide, but rushed in angry white torrents over jagged black rocks in the moonlight. On the far side rose low cliffs, barely greater than the height of a Man, and against these rattled a small grey boat, bustling and blundering against the hard wall as it was beset by the passionate rapids.

"That skiff must be by what means they crossed," spake Dalf, and defeat fought to be heard beneath his confidence.

"Perhaps," answered Old Master Wood, "Yet how many were in your party? That boat looks as if it could hold three... mayhaps four."

The brigand scowled. "Well, I see no other way, and their trail leads here. See there, where the soil is scuffed and dragged? The boat was brought ashore."

"It must have been moored here when they came," mused the elder. "Mayhaps some of the company followed the shore in search of another ford, and mayhaps we should do the same."

Dalf looked to the scattered remains of the grounding, then agreed. He set his eye to the shoreline and looked for further evidence. Momentarily, he called to his companion and pointed northeast.

As the two set off upstream, Old Master Wood allowed his ear to wander—to hear the whispers of the forest stream. He heard the chaotic, eagre babbling of the rapids. The slap-slap of soft water on rough stone and the miniscule rumbling of shifting sand. The contented swaying of the sward and the gossip of the firs. He whistled in the way the wind whistles, and the cool night air answered back. "It is shallower ahead, and calmer too, in measure," he said to his companion and hurried forwards.

Dalf was surprised at the speed of the miniscule magician as he hopped over stumps and stones and ducked under low boughs and high, thick roots, but he managed to keep pace with him until they stopped beside a break in the roughness of the stream. Wheezing for breath, the other watched as Old Master Wood stepped into the shallow water, his stick ahead of him and his bag (holding his now-doused candle) held high above his head. He stopped when the water touched his knees and turned back.

"I do not think the water goes so very deep, and it should be no trouble for you—and little trouble for me—to cross here."

Shaking his head, Dalf replied, "It shall do no good. The rocks on the opposite shore are higher e'en than those we saw to the southwest." And indeed it was true.

"But look!" Worried of predators and dire enemies, Old Master Wood's voice was too loud for Dalf's liking (though really it was not so very loud at all), yet he followed his outstretched finger. "A rope hangs there against the moonlit stones. This must have been where they crossed. What part the boat had to play in your companions' story I cannot say, yet this is where we may follow their trail."

It took a long moment of squinting to glimpse the hang-

ing braid, yet surely it was there. The outlaw would almost—
almost—wager that it had not been there before (why would the
Captain leave a rope behind?) yet it was there now, as certainly
as his heart feared the magic of the Wood. He began cautiously
to wade acrost the ford after the hermit, catching his boot here
and there on a stray stone yet never stumbling. Soon he passed
his companion who, despite his confidence, was progressing with
even more wariness than the thief.

"Aye! Aye! You go ahead, for I fear the end of the rope
may be too high for me and I may have need of you to lower it
so I may follow after." The water had reached the tip of the
elder's long beard, and this was the depth the ford would hold
until the far side. Yet on Dalf it had not yet reached his hip, and
he was filled with a fiery energy, as if he could see the return of
his fortunes. Old Master Wood could see this in his brisk movements, yet still hoped the Man was strong enough to face his bas-
er urges; there would indeed be no return of fortunes for the
rescued thief should this flame overtake him—of this the magician was certain.

The stream was not so very wide, and so it was merely a
matter of moments before the taller man reached the far side.
Grabbing ahold of the cord with both hands, he glanced over his
shoulder at the struggling figure in the water, who nodded eagerly
and waved with his walking stick for him to continue up. Dalf
felt a brief pang of guilt. Nay, not guilt. It was not that he disliked the hermit (though he would not say that he liked him), but
more that he distrusted magic. Magic was strange and unknowable, and as the hours had passed since his rescue he had begun
to forget the overshadowing gratitude he had first felt and remember that the little wanderer with the red felt hat was more
akin to that hungry alder than to any mortal man. And what
would the others say if they discovered how he had been defeat-

ed by a tree and rescued by an old white-hair? Nay, 'twas better that they parted ways. Men are often like this, and rationalize selfish deeds when times of hardship are seemingly passed.

Old Master Wood continued forwards as he watched the other swiftly climb the rope to the cliff above. His bones were cold, and not merely from the rushing water of the stream. He wished that the thief would chose differently, yet he knew it was not to be so. He called out cheerily as Dalf reached the top, yet Dalf did not even look back before he ran off into the forest on the northern bank, taking the length of rope along with him. The magician stopped then, midstream with one arm above his head, and began to think of a way out of this predicament. The Wind took notice of his concerned frown and asked the matter.

"Oh, simple worries. Silly for one as great as yourself," was his answer. It is always wise, when dealing with the Wind, to compliment it greatly, especially in the summer when the air with which it is always full grows hot. "It is merely that I have no way to cross the stream. Or rather, no means to gain the bank here where the water is calm, and no means to ford the brutal tides elsewhere. I am old, and not terribly tall, and I fear I may drown before I solve my predicament."

Made blithe by his deference, the Wind replied, "I am cousins with this stream by marriage, and if he should calm I may blow yonder craft upriver and guide you safely on it to a landing."

Squinting in consternation—only partially false—Old Master Wood replied, "And how far is this landing from here? I would hate to lose my path, and the Man who left me here is the clearest marker for that path." Yet the markers of mortals are not those of the Wind, and so no true answer could be shared. "I thank you, Lord Wind, and if your cousin would be kind enough to help me I would welcome it greatly."

And so the Wind whistled and the stream roared, and
the Wind whished and the stream burbled, and the Wind sighed
and the stream splashed. Old Master Wood watched as the water calmed and the branches on the shore ceased to sway. A doe
came to observe the odd silence, yet fled as a great gust began to
blow from the southwest. Soon the little boat which the little
master had seen before came bobbing upstream on a great wind.
It passed him, his hat nearly flying off in the gale, then washed
near enough that he could toss in his staff and bag. With some
effort, he clambered aboard and the Wind took him forwards at
a pace far from slow, yet not so swift as to threaten to capsize the
dinghy. Old Master Wood removed his boots and stretched his
sodden socks, pulling them from his feet amidst the spray of his
downstream journey. He flexed his stubby toes as he rode.

At long last the boat slid to a halt on the scrubby shore
of the northern bank, the stream receding behind before resum-
ing its customary raging. Removing his things from the belly of
the boat, the magician bowed (in no particular direction, for the
Wind was all about) and doffed his hat.

"I am poor in many things, and assume (if you are like
to the winds of my home) that you care little for tobacco scent
and have as much of sweet smelling flowers as you shall ever
need. Yet these are the tangible treasures I carry, and you deserve some reward for your kind and selfless aid." This, of
course was only half true, for the Wind always wishes to be com-
pensated and Old Master Wood had clearly seen the dead trees
near the landing—ready to fall on his perilously fragile skull
should he offend his benefactor. "I will sing you a song, and in
that song is a spell, and that spell will keep Men and their acrid
scents from this stretch until next all the planets in the starry sky
align in single order." And the song he sang began,

A whish willow wand'ring

Down black broad bank

Red hat and hope found'ring

On dim dark deed

VI

hen his song was sung, the Wind appeased, and his socks dried, Old Master Wood once more steadied himself to continue his trek. He worried little about the time lost for, as has been said before, time always favoured him in curious ways. He was concerned, however, about becoming further lost, for he knew not where in the Wood he was, nor where Dalf had fled to.

"Men!" he huffed. It was then that he saw a small black squirrel and called out to it. "Hulloo, Squire Squirrel! Know you where can be found a company of rough Men? I seek them and their ill-gotten prize on a mission from a nearby king. Mark you, though! King Alimanx holds no bonds over me and I do it only for the love of my forest friends, who have of late fallen prey to the greed of Man."

"Rough Men wi' prize o' worf?" tried the rodent, rearing on its hindquarters as it looked down on the traveler from a high branch. "Vhere be not many o' vhat make 'round 'ere."

"Yet there are some," prompted Old Master Wood, already questioning his own willingness to engage one of that famously elfin race.

"Aye, some," spake the squirrel. "And vhey I'll gladly

46

guide ye towards. No charge." He clapped his furry paws and scampered to another branch before delivering the directions—a winding path which drove deeper into the most shadowed part of the visible Wood.

Old Master Wood liked little the glee with which the vermin agreed to aid him but, having no clear path, decided to follow the advice, at least to start. He would ask another creature once one was found. Thanking the tittering guide and straightening his hat, he set off on the path suggested.

Yet he did not encounter another living wight before he came upon the clearing wherein he had been told he could find his quarry. A low hill, topped by crumbling black menhirs and fronted by a stone arch, carved in old letters and stoppered with a fearsome granite gate, sat in the centre of the glade. Dead branches clawed at the open air greedily and a chilling memory of an ancient wind dwelt in the space as might an uninvited feast-guest who served a misliked lord. There was no sign of Men, princess, nor camp, and Old Master Wood turned hurriedly to flee from that accursed place.

Yet his way was blocked by two warriors which had stepped with unnatural silence onto the path. They were ghastly frail, and rusted black mail hung on them like sheets of willow fronds. Black helms were upon their crowns and wicked spears in their pale-skinned claws while dirks handled with rotted leather hung from ancient belts too wide for their desiccated hips. Their faces, drawn like old meat, were grim, and their eyes flashed in the gathering fog with a light like the sun glimpsed from beneath an algaed pool.

They stood still, unspeaking and unblinking. He also stood still, gripping his crutch and watching anxiously. He had dealt with the dead before, yet it never sat well with him. The dead are even more bullish and single-minded than living Men, if that is possible, and often they are swift to punish (even if they bemoan their own sins after; the dead revel in their own misery). Silently he cursed the vile squirrel which had led him to this place, before reminding himself that he was the intruder here and not immediately owed kindness; he had not been invited by any save Alimanx, who held no power in this darksome hollow.

"Hail hearthguard," he began. "I mean no ill to your barrow, and would beg be allowed pass. I mean no harm, yet have lost my way whilst searching for others in the Wood." The ancient corpses made no motion, and he glimpsed more fearful eyes in the misty dark of the trees. He began to bustle forwards nodding his hat and saying kind and simple things, yet they only crossed their mildewed arms to block his path and layed baleful gazes upon him. Pulling up short, he cleared his throat. "If I may not pass you must tell me what you wish. Or!" He stepped back with upraised arms as they shifted their spearheads towards him. "You could point me to someone who may. It shall do you nor your curse any good should you merely cut me down, and I have some magics in me which may aid you in your plight."

After an instant's long delay, two green-nailed fingers rose and directed him back towards the tomb-hill, where the stony gate had receded and a darker fog billowed out like a dragon's breath. He thanked his dire hosts and turned, advancing through the thickening mist towards the unearthly lights of the crypt. Here and there he saw bits of mail or broken spear scattered between the rough stones and choking grasses, and when he glimpsed a familiar piece of livery he knew what had befallen Alimanx's knights.

At its gate he hummed a short hum and blew and short breath, clearing some of the grey from his vision with an old and mundane cantrip. His candle flickered and then was put out and could not be relit. A hollow melody of almost-music fled the portal in a necrotic dirge of dead wind and silent moans, just barely unheard under the dreamlike roaring silence of the glade.

"No use in waiting," Old Master Wood muttered to himself as he stowed his doused light. "The dead have waited long enough." And with that he stepped down onto the hidden stair below.

With trepid footfalls he made his way down, blowing mist and fog to less and less effect as his agèd feet fought for stable purchase on the cracked and unstable flight. Each moment the sepulchral non-noise of the crypt grew greater and the mist took on more of the undark blackness of the tomb. The tendrils of acrid air fought past his lips and tugged at his eyelids. He coughed wetly and rubbed the sleep from his gaze, even as he cursed having lived long enough to have had the opportunity to beg Alimanx to give his forest neighbors peace. But Old Master Wood was a kindly wight, and even thinking these thoughts hurt his gentle heart.

"Don't you worry none about your fresh pups, Master Fox. I'll make certain they have a home."

"A heom, a heom... A heom fer a fox..." The voice which answered was far from the quaint chattering of Master Fox. Instead it was dry like cracking autumn leaves and invasive like moss on old stone walls. The stairs had stopped and the still space echoed with the ghostly notes. Two drowned-sun points stared from the gloom into Old Master Wood, and through him. "Thys ys nao heom fer foxes... But a heom fer corses und fer ded Men's baens..."

"Then it is well that my bones do not intend to stay terribly long, for I yet live," replied the magician, rustling in his pack for his pipe. He imagined that the wind he had promised not to annoy with his habit kept far enough from this place that he would not be breaking any vow. And he needed a smoke fiercely.

The voice made a sound like a toad swallowing its tongue, then the twin greeny eyes began to shake in the murk as a mirthful noice like dice falling down a drain, never to be found again, cackled outwards. "Nao Man haf I mat what dear'd tell such flypperies afore myn throan..."

"No flippery was that, but a truth. And if I am a Man I am not as one you have ever met, Your Grace."

"Nao..? Und what surt of Man are ye then..?" The voice was interested now. There had been a boredom in the first threats—as common an emotion in the dead as sorrow or fury—but it was replaced, for the moment, with curiosity. Old Master Wood did not intend to waste that curiosity.

"I am a friend to the Wood (though in far away parts, for I know none of these trees nor beasts) and a practitioner of spells. I was misdirected here in another mission, yet may be of some help to you yet., should I be given safe passage." His eyes were the doe-eyes of the comfortably venerable, and he chewed at the corner of his snowy mustache in imitation of blameless senility.

"Spellsss... Spellsss and corsesss..." hissed the shadow. Old Master Wood sensed the creature's native frustration returning, yet assured himself that he had been right to introduce himself thusly. What other choice had he? "Thur be nao eus fer spellsss here... All here isss corsed already, und soon ye too shall ken yts bayt..."

Braziers, previously unseeable in the gloam, sprang to life in corpse-green flame, illuminating the carven seat flanked by more undying watchmen. Before the dais was layed a black and lichened stone bier, its lid split in two. Upon the honoured stool itself sat the wraith of an ancient king, his knotted beard and matted hair swaying with ghostly vigour as his skin-on-bone claws clamped viciously upon the arms of his chair. He was bedecked for battle, in blackened rings and fiery red mantle, his tarnished crown shining unbrightly above his worry-knotted brow. A black -gemmed medallion hung upon his sunken chest, and rich rings clanked faintly upon his withered arms and wretched fingers. Upon his lap was a shimmering blade, and in his luminescent eyes were a thousand years of hatred.

Yet not all hatred is forever. And the hatred of a Man forced to repay his debts he knew he would one day owe is much weaker than the hatred of one who sees the truth and chooses to disbelieve it to maintain his comfort (or fear). Old Master Wood had met enough dead men to know that most did not choose this for themselves, and often were eagre to mend their mistakes, even should their Man-like arrogance prevent them from speaking as much. The undersized traveler felt confident it was this weaker hatred which he faced that day.

Stoutly he advanced—a feat which even the doughtiest worthy would doubtless have blanched at—and doffed his hat low. "Fair fallen fyrdweard, let not my occupation offend. I know not what warlock, fate, or ill-luck has bewitched you, yet if you will tell me your tale I will do what I can to unmark you."

Thr rotten king looked long at his guest before he answered, his voice low—almost sheepish, "Yt be naot eh teyl y ken haow to tell en the wurds uv lyvyng Men..."

"Then tell it in what ways you know," spake the visitor gently. He had lived a long time and knew many tongues, including many dead. He sat upon the cold floor cross-legged and

51

puffed his pipe as he heard the wraith's lament.

The tale itself was one he had heard a thousand times, witnessed a hundred, and told a score. It was unhappy, unsurprising, and unoriginal—the same woeful prides and payments fallen upon endless wealthies of the folk of Man. Yet to this peaceless corpse they were unique and unfair. Old Master Wood made certain to stifle his yawns; he truly did care to help (even if he thought the common foolishness of Man banal), and it would not do to have his fearsome host think he mocked his pain or found his misery pedestrian. And so he listened as the king told a tale not far divorced from that which he had told to Dalf only that evening.

At last the tiresome telling was complete and Old Master Wood brushed off his knees to stand. "It seems a problem of debts unpaid. A moral and mortal failing in life which damned your corpses to eternal suffering."

The dead king scowled yet responded still, "Aye, that yt seems... Had y but gyven myn bruther hys due, perhaps y wud alryddy walk the halls of the gods..."

"Ah aye, the brother's due." There was little chance of finding the lich's brother, dead even longer than he. Puffing intently at his pipe, the hermit considered the likelihood of instead finding the brother's descendants. Yet nay, that too was likely to be nigh impossible and many years in the undertaking (Time was friends with Old Master Wood—and a generous friendship it was—but even friendship has its limits). "Perhaps a board game?" he thought exasperatedly; unnatural things are endlessly fond of trials of wit and strategy. Yet that risked offense if it was thought too trivial, and he had already promised the use of spells. At last he settled on what he hoped might be a worthwhile compromise. "I fear reuniting with your brother may be beyond my means at the moment. Yet the lands around were once due to him, were they not? And it was for greed that you quelled his breath. I have no need of gold or rings, yet there are many in the lands beyond the black heart of the Wood who do. I believe perhaps our two goals may be pursued side-by-side, and in time the land may forgive you your sins."

"Expleyn..." His tone was not patient, and so the explanation came hurriedly.

"I come here to make peace for the beasts of the forest lands, for Man's ceaseless greed has begun to unhome them. Already I have made arrangements to reclaim their vales (should I deliver Alimanx's beloved daughter Isadore), yet it does no harm to have greater assurance. There are many poor in the near kingdom, and perhaps they would benefit from heavier purses, and be less like to seek for more in the lands of others. And you! Elden Eorl, have been eternally punished for your miserliness and grasping greed. So I propose that what treasures you keep, which I assume to be many, be unearthed and shared amongst the living. Doubtless folks would not be fain to take such gifts from the ghouls of your court—my apologies, but you are all rather disturbing to the senses and common folk are less polite than I—and so I could arrange a mammalian escort of handsome animals to escort your gifts, and I would spread what word I could of their true origin. In time your riches may reach your brother's kin, or mayhaps the great wealth of generosity would alone account for your penance in the curse's eye."

He stepped back then and waited anxiously. The plan itself was clever enough in concept to appease an ancient spell (even enchantments may grow bored of their profession with time), but the dead can be stubborn, as has already been said. As for the idea that an influx of wealth to the lowest class would stabilize Alimanx's feudal kingdom. This was less valid. Yet

Old Master Wood, for all his age and wisdom, knew little of the laws and economies of Men, and tended to assume the best of them, even though centuries of experience should have shown him otherwise.

The barrow-king as well kenned little of the ramifications, but was eagre to be free of his restless ages. And if this red-capped messenger could aid him, he could not convince himself to deny the chance. And so, after a long and painful silence, it was agreed. Two corpse-Men were sent along to guide the living wight towards where Man-blood had been scented (a fortuitous development Old Master Wood had not dared hope for) and the others set about divesting their sodden grounds of their ancient funeral price. Happy to be on the road once more, Old Master Wood struck up a jaunty song as he waved goodbye to his would-be executioners.

In the months to come, the gifts of the ghoul prince would serve to unseat the balance of power in Alimanx's kingdom, and a bloody rebellion would leave hundreds dead. The curse (which only allowed the exchange to continue out of glee for the coming woe) would gloat at the greater guilt brought upon its prisoner by his attempted philanthropy, and the angry dead would ravage the near marches of the land. Yet neither fallen lord nor friendly witch could know that this was to come, and it is beyond the scope of this tale besides to tell all the ill that befell that kingdom.

The road-song the hermit sang began something like this,

A walk, a rock, a stout old stick

I go upon my way

A walk, a rock, a pocket of smoke

To counter days so grey

Say hey! Say ho!

A-travelling I do go

With a walk, a rock, and a stout old stick

And a spirit never (yet ever!) so gay!

VII

ld Master Wood swiftly found the two ghost-guides to make poor conversationalists. They shivered and stumbled as they walked, and would not give so much as a nod in response to any query, comment, nor, compliment. And so he made conversation with himself, carrying on about his further plans for the summer once he was returned from his journeys and musing after what new herbs might be beneficial to his teas. Occasionally the guides would trip or become trapped in a low, claw-like branch (they truly were quite clumsy), and he would have to help lift or extricate them. Here he would always try to engage them again as he fussed over their torn mail and brittle bones (one kept dropping fingers). Yet they remained stoic, and only continued ever onwards. And while they would utter no sound, neither would they slow their progress, until at last they stopped silent and still within sight of a campfire-lit clearing ahead.

Thanking them, and assuring them that he would bring gifts of better-fit boots when next he saw them, the entrepid quester left his escorts. He imagined that they could find their own way back.

In a half-crouch (his knees were not what they once

were) he advanced with slowed breaths. Momentarily he could see that there were some eight or nine Men in the clearing, as well as five tents, a few heavy packs, and a young woman, sitting unhappily by the fire with a wooden cup clutched in her white fingers and her silver-pale hair hung past her knees. The Men, however, were filled with great relish and cavorted about the flames with raised voices and wide gestures. All save one, who sat at the edge of the camp, a mere four paces from the magician, though yet unnoticing of him.

This hapless figure was the thief Holdalf. Since his return he had not been well-treated by the others. He had told them that he had been ambushed in the wood on his watch whilst pursuing a thief (to explain the missing coin, which he still kept close to his heart), and one of the others had helpfully asked if it was by the terrible bear-warg which had attacked their camp. Being chased by a bear-warg (whatever that was) was much less embarrassing in his mind than being ambushed by a tree, and so he congratulated his fellow on his astute assumption. He told of a fierce flight and the fording of the stream, yet never mentioned Old Master Wood—half out of fear and half out of lingering but unacknowledged guilt. The other brigands had been glad to see one of their lost number return, yet the Captain—who was known for his iron-fast adherence to his own law—berated him for the lost loot and encouraged the others to turn a cold shoulder to him until he had repaid his debt. Until such a time, he was due but a third of his usual take, both in plunder and in provender, and was first to be chosen for many menial chores. And so, being too proud and too frightened of the Captain's response to admit he still held the coin, he now sat at the edge of camp on watch once more, half-heartedly sucking on a mealy strip of salted meat.

The rest of the party, save Isadore, was in much higher

spirits, despite their ordeals. After the assault by the fearsome bear-warg and its ghostly allies (where Homart had had his head shorn from his shoulders and Germald had lost a hand before it could be driven off) they had swiftly made their way to the crossing. There they had fortuitously found the old boat, and the Captain had taken two other Men and their prisoner acrost to search for a ford—and indeed they had crossed at the point which Dalf had (though none recalled leaving the rope behind). Their journey after had been fair, and by the time they found a place to settle camp they were once again raucous and hungry for drink, having nearly forgotten losing Homart and Holdalf (who they had assumed to have also been devoured until he arrived at the edge of their camp). Even Germald joked about the golden hand he would buy for his bloody stump with his take from the expedition, with a strong wrist for shieldwork and strong fingers for love.

Isadore was unimpressed by her unasked-for wardens. They were crass and greedy and their gaze was lecherous (though they never touched her in ways more unseemly than a stern grip upon her arm or a heavy hand on the back of her head to keep her moving along the dark forest trails). She liked none of them—least of all Dalf, whom she saw as a selfish alley mutt. There had been a dog like him outside her father's castle for a time, always begging for scraps or helping the other strays to hunt rats, only to take the prize for himself and eschew all pets, playful scratches, or community. And ever he would lose his prize and come slinking back for more, promising he had changed. Yet Men and mutts never change. And she did not believe Holdalf's tale at all. Nonetheless, she found her captivity engaging. They bound her only lightly, and threatened her only gently; alive she was a walking treasure trove, yet dead she was certain doom. She feared little for her life or for her safe return. And if she was not returned, but rather sold to some foreign prince? What of it? She truly did love her father, and appreciated his protectiveness which had so far preserved her dignity (and preserved her perpetual boredom), but longed to be free of his cage, even bedecked as it was in foreign silks. Being kidnapped by rogues and marched through a haunted wood was by far the most interesting thing which had ever happened to her.

Old Master Wood crouched in his hiding place and watched for a time, debating what was to be done. Here was Princess Isadore, yet here too were Dalf who had betrayed him (though out of fear or selfishness he knew not) and his ragged band of fellows. "Surely I cannot best them at arms," he thought, "And it would be unkind (and perhaps unwise) to assume them as dull-witted as others of their career." He knew no spells so great as to banish a whole company of Men (or even one Man, for the more blatant the spellcraft the more impossible its working) nor did he have allies in this part of the Wood save perhaps the hate-stricken ghouls he had so recently left behind. His knees had begun to ache, and so he sat down to think in earnest, his fingers idly playing with blades of the dark grass which grew here in the Unwanted Depths. And as he sat to think, he let out an audible *hmm.*

Looking away from the distant spot of night where his gaze had been unfocused, Dalf swung his gaze towards a nearby cluster of bracken. To his great surprise, there sat the sorcerer he had abandoned. His first instinct was to cry out and draw steel, for he was on watch, and had not he already set himself to betray his former companion? Yet he made no alarum, but stood, quietly, and approached. Perhaps this decision was a result of some protective sorcery, or perhaps it was the guilt which Dalf would never in his life admit to himself he held which betrayed his greed and fear of his Captain. When he stood near, still unnoticed, he cleared his throat, startling the wizened skulk.

"I had not thought to see ye again," he spake softly.

"Through no lack of trying," grumbled the magician from his seat as he tried to pretend he had been on alert and not fiddling with weeds.

This comment hurt Holdalf, though it was in all ways true, for Men often feel most the victim when it is their own faults being shown to them. He did not think it fair for himself to be blamed for a bad decision which he had already rationalized as a necessity. Yet before he could defend himself, the Captain's voice carried into the brush.

"What ho, Wargfriend?" for Wargfriend was the mocking name they had given him. "Do ye address yer pecker always when ye piss, or have we a new guest to tea?"

The hapless thief's mouth hung agape, but Old Master Wood waved to him dismissively, "Worry not, and shut your lips afore a midge flies in." The little fellow stood and called back, "No member I, save of the citizenry of the Wood! I come to treat with you, and mayhaps to share a laugh!" And, though it was the Captain's way to be distrusting and to care little for the lives of strangers, he somehow could not deny the charm of the sorcerer, and invited him to the fireside.

The squat figure shuffled forth from the shadows, followed by the watchman—who wore an expression both cautious and ashamed. Broad grins painted the faces of the company at the clownish character, save for the face of Isadore whose brows beetled over her eyes as if she were attempting to force the newcomer's secrets from him with a glare (and a seemly yet terrible glare it was, much befitting a respected ruler). Old Master Wood held his purse before him as he sat confidently on a log between two stinking, heavily-muscled Men. He made an effort not to let his eyes wander towards the Princess, for fear of revealing his intent, though her glower did force him to restrain a chuckle.

"Tell me, Master Member," chortled the Captain, remaining on his feet, "what brings ye hence to me gaudy hall?" His Men guffawed at aught he said, though whether it was for fear or for lack of humour even they could likely not have said.

"I am a traveler and sometime companion of friend Holdalf here," he waved his hand towards the one he named, whose eyes were wide in sudden anger and distress.

"Oho! So be this the bear-warg ye contended with, Master Wargfriend?" Stammering, Holdalf the Hapless could offer naught in defense afore his commander continued. "Yet yer liaison with me Man explains little the business such an elder has so deep in such dark woods."

Affecting his best mask of a weakened old Man, Old Master Wood began to respond, "I am a person of no proper home, and made to—"

"A wizard be he!" cried Holdalf. "A warlock and assassin! I came upon him as he hunted the company and the Princess Isadore! He enchanted the trees and bewitched my silence, yet he has committed a lie and so I am free! From Alimanx hies he! Slay him ere he sets our very bones afire!"

"Fie," muttered the magician softly. He had hoped either that Dalf's trauma had prevented him from remembering his saviour's purpose, or that the good he had done him had engendered some greater love in his heart. And atop it all, he resented being called assassin, though the accusations of cruel wizardry were not new to his ear from frightened, ignorant Men.

Everyone was on their feet, save Old Master Wood and Princess Isadore (whose expression had become less aggressive and more curious), and weapons were drawn. The Captain, who held a wicked-looking, notched falchion, pointed it at him threateningly. "Explain yerself, witch!" he cried. He would later wonder why he had not merely cut the intruder down on the spot.

"No need for arms," cautioned the quester, "for I myself carry none." At this, he layed his staff upon the ground, though his hand was hardly hale enough to wield it as a bludgeon. "What Dalf says is not all true, that I travelled with him a while this night, though under no bewitchment. I come here with open palms in hopes to parlay for the Princess."

"Open palms and an empty purse," scowled one of the outlaws as he turned the magicians travelling bag over, spilling, mushrooms, herbs, wildflowers, berries, edible roots, a pipe and its weed, and two candles.

"By what means do ye mean to parlay?" queried the Captain, curious despite himself. Isadore herself was also curious, yet voiced no inquiry. "We be Men of the soil, and value coin over sorcery and song."

Old Master Wood, who considered himself much more *of the soil* than these coarse fellows, decided it better not to contradict them. "And I mean not to insult you. But I am a poor fellow of no means, yet was chosen for this task by Alimanx of the House of Orlo." He considered briefly whether to send them in search of treasure near the mound of the black menhirs, yet swiftly dismissed it as cruel to this party and disingenuous to his dealings with the dead king. "And in my effort not to insult you I will assume that you are well aware of the dangers involved in your endeavour as well as in your current environment."

The gathered campsmen glowered for a time at him, until finally their ruler laughed loud and cruel, "Ween ye to challenge us? Speak no more long words, but answer plain."

"Well, I suppose there is nothing for it," thought Old Master Wood with a weighty sigh. "Aye, my intent is to challenge you."

"Ye must fashion yerself a mighty bruiser, Master Member," crowed the Captain, to the delight of his erstwhile audience, "for I see no dirk, dagger, nor bludgeon upon ye."

"None of those do I carry, for in a match of arms I would surely fail."

"Then yer fear of Alimanx must be great indeed for ye to pursue a quest for which the reward was certain death!" The Captain shone now, his chest pressed out proudly; this had become a slaying game, and of all the contests in the world those were his favourite.

"Hardly," rebuked the King's messenger, "for I did not mean to challenge you to combat." He could see the brigands' consternation and hurried his scheme along. "For just as it would be unfair of me to challenge you to a duel of spells, so too is it unfair—unmanly even—of you to challenge me to a contest in which we are not evenly matched."

The Captain did not appreciate any emasculation, especially before his henchmen, and growled as such to his visitor. "And as for honour and fairness, what would imply to ye that we are honourable Men? We are murderers, thieves, arsonists, and rapists; there is no code we follow."

"Ah, no code," replied Old Master Wood. "Yet surely you have pride, and were I to imply I were the greater huntsman—"

"I would gut you where you stood," interrupted his opponent.

"And leave the possibility undispelled? For if I were

dead, Men might say that you felled me out of jealousy of my prowess."

"A dead man has no prowess," came the response, but the magicians breathed easier, knowing he had won. It is a rare Man who does not even pretend at honour, but the Man is rarer still who can stomach having his skills brought into question. The burly forest crook sheathed his wicked sword and spread his arms wide. "What contest do you offer, little one?"

"A huntsman's challenge, where we each venture into the dark of the Wood, and whosoever should bring back the greater prize shall be declared victor and name their prize."

A great, surprised bellow of a laugh greeted this. "Ye carry no bow, nor traps!"

"And none shall I need, nor spells withal, though I do not fault you for taking along your quiver, for my methods differ from yours."

"What methods be those?" asked the Captain, choosing to ignore for the moment the seeming slight against him.

"That I shan't reveal," warned the magician. "First, for fear that you would attempt them yourself, and second for fear that you and your band would mock me as a fool."

"Have no fear of that! Very well, let us be on our hunt, ye by yer ways and me by mine. Minfel, my bow!"

And so they set off on their separate sojourns. The Captain for his part, did not expect to see Old Master Wood again, thinking him to either flee or to be devoured by a darksome predator. Yet, though the hermit felt some misgivings for the challenge he had initiated, they were not for fear of failure but for the consequences on the defeated should his plan—so hastily constructed—prove worthy. He lit the last bit of the candle which had guided him faithfully thus far, bid farewell to the sheepish Dalf, and tipped his hat to the Princess as he wandered off in a direction opposite of the Captain.

It was not long before he stumbled acrost evidence of some great beast. Here in the Unwanted Depths he had no doubt that there were many and many mighty, noble, and fearsome animals and the light of his lonely candle illumined deep tracks in the needled soil, even as his sensitive nose smelled a deep musk. Sniffing, his light held low, he trundled ever deeper until he heard the whuffling, munching sound of a beast supping.

The thing heard him before he saw it, and stood menacingly over its gory prey—unknowable to its former shape for the damage done to it. Small, black eyes sat above a blood-stained snout, and a bristling mane of grey hair rose about its stout neck and behind its pointed ears. Its chest was thick and stout, yet its haunches were taut and coiled as of at any moment it could spring. Agile paws tucked at its prey and a sharp tongue licked at its wicked fangs. No tail was there to see, and the thing was the size of a king's warhorse. It had been a great while since Old Master Wood had met one, yet he knew well enough to recognize a bear-warg on sight.

"Man-thing," it snarled in the speech of Men.

Old Master Wood shivered despite himself, for it was precisely beasts such as this which he had feared when first he and Dalf had come acrost the abandoned camp on the other side of the forest stream; bear-wargs and their kin were known for their cruelty as well as their wit. "No Man-thing I, but—"

"Then what?" Its rancid breath washed over him even from the distance at which it crouched.

"A— A sorcerer of sorts. And I would hope, a friend."

"A friend!" Its laughter was full and deep-throated. "No friend need I save claw, snout, and musk. No beast should fall to thy pink paws. No trail be followed by thy round nose. No she-wife tamed by that weak odour. Nay, methinks thou be more food than friend."

"But!" And up he held one finger, almost regretting what he must do. "Though it is cruel to slay an old fellow in the trees, I am not afraid and—"

"Liar."

"Aye, for it would be foolish to not fear a fierce bear-warg." He mopped sweat from his brow with his blue sleeve. "But I know you, and your kind. I know you hunt alone and feed as much on fear as on meat. I fear you for the death you may bring, yet I know of others who know you not so well. Who would fear your silent stalking and swift shadows and friendship with ghosts. And I think, perchance, you have hunted them already this night." The thing had relaxed its taut haunches some, and listened with interest. "I would offer to lead you to the camp of the brigand-invaders here, and to let you hunt them in your own manner. But you must spare both I and the woman there." He thought briefly of Dalf, then sadly dismissed him; the Man had shown in his fear and treachery to be no greater than the rest of his race.

"Not enough," it snarled. Yet its interest was peaked.

"Not enough? What more would you ask?" The creature had stretched its neck towards him and was snuffling the air with interest.

"A favour." It drooled lasciviously and licked its loose-hanging lips. "To be called whensoever I choose. I shall not be denied."

"Another problem to be solved in time," thought Old Master Wood, yet he agreed. The beast offered to allow him to ride its back but, mistrusting its intentions, he refused and asked it to follow at a distance and come when he called.

"No pet am I," it snarled, even as it slunk into the shadows.

The journey back to the camp was simple enough, and as he neared he could hear the laughter of the Men. It saddened him to know that he should be the end of any merriment, yet he thought once more of their wicked blades and wicked ways and his friends far to the south and steeled himself. Two red eyes winked at him from the black as he ventured back into the firelight.

The Princess saw him first, and her green eyes were sad to see him return empty-handed. She had her reasons to not desire rescue, and did not think Old Master Wood to seem a Man of great pleasure nor resource, yet a part of her had wanted the gentler force to prevail. It seemed there was no justice in peace.

"I am returned, Captain. And it seems a mighty stag you have slain."

Looking up from a game of hand wrestling, the Captain grinned with strong peasant teeth. "Aye, and we have waited to clean it to compare with yer own prey. We had begun to grow impatient, and it seems with reason, for I spy no furred trophy at yer hand."

"Not at my hand, yet at my call," said Old Master Wood, both with confidence and regret, and Holdalf the Selfish was pulled from his stump and into the bracken. Great animal noises contested with his own screams until a terrible tearing noise ended all. The Men were on their feet and shouting, steel and iron sparkling red. "Show yourself," spake the hermit, and the bloody bear-warg lept into the fire, scattering it and quenching all illumination.

The cursing and the clashing were horrendous to the ear, and the trees here conspired to allow no moonlight to aid the assaulted camp. Two red eyes and frantic blue blades battled one-another in the dark and the soil greedily drank the flowing blood as the nightmare beast drank the flowing fear.

Finding the Princess's cold, white hand, Old Master Wood urged her to go with him. She did, for her own mind was so frozen with terror as to not be able to decide for herself and her instincts bade her flee; she had forgotten the distress she had felt when their first camp had been assaulted, and that time she had not even glimpsed the beast. They ran back, towards the cairn of dead men, and some of the band what remained behind fled the other way. Before it turned to pursue, the bear-warg hissed a reminder after the magician, its words licking through the air like tendrils of flame.

"A favour, Sorcerer. Whensoever I choose."

VIII

ho are you truly?" asked Isadore once they were far enough that they felt comfortable slowing their pace.

"A wizard and a messenger of your father," he said. Then, seeing her judging eye, he said, "But those are not the professions I see myself as. I am a hermit, who enjoys little the company of Men. So too am I a crafter, fisher, and storyteller."

"To whom do you tell tales if you mislike the company

of Men?" she asked.

"To my friends in the Wood." He met her eye and smiled kindly. "And my friends are the animals."

She laughed at this, but he realized that it was in delight. "The animals! Much like the legend of Old Master Wood! I enjoyed those tales much when my nurse would tell them me. Do you speak their tongues? Or are they merely as pets to you?" She was eagre and willing to learn and to believe, even though she should have been old enough to decry that which she had no proof of.

"So alike to the legend of Old Master Wood that I may as well be he," he cautioned, and he saw that then she knew the full truth. "And aye, I speak the tongues of beasts, for it is not so hard to learn if one is able to accept that theirs is not the only way."

Many more questions had she, and all these he made an effort to answer as they journeyed in the Unwanted Depths. He found, against his expectations (having so recently and so often been reminded of the failings of Man), that he was enjoying the company of the Princess by the light of his second candle (his first having at last burned itself too low for use). She seemed inquisitive and clever and, though her memory seemed short enough to forget her fear of the bear-warg, she had little of her people's relentless narcissism; she cared more of the world about her than of her own importance in it. Whether this was due to the isolation of her assigned role or a genuine freedom from Mankind's ills he knew not, but he enjoyed the relief the conversation brought regardless.

In time Old Master Wood noted the change in the air—the sick waftings of rot and the chaotic stillness—which signalled a nearness to the barrow-king's lich hill. He held up a hand to quiet Isadore as she mused on the hatred of trees and rubbed his nose. "Your forgiveness, Highness, but we must now confront an unpleasantness. The Unwanted Depths are home to many victims of dire sins—some their own, some those of others—and ahead lies the home of one most upsetting."

"More upsetting than being kidnapped by self-avowed murderers, thieves, arsonists, and rapists?" she chided him. She did like the little wood-tender (moreso knowing his true nature) but he seemed sometimes too cautious, though she sensed that this was born largely out of a kindness towards all things. Still, she knew him to be capable of great harm when needed—as shown by his dealings with the bear-warg—and respected him also for this.

"Mayhaps not, Princess." He rustled through his pack for his pipe, only to find that both it and his tobacco must have been lost in the altercation in the clearing. "Have you ever seen a corpse?"

She frowned. "A few. Warriors slain and set to pyre or bier, my own uncle amongst."

"Nay, I mean an *old* corpse. One which has not known a beating heart in years on end.

"That I have not," she answered, curious. "Do you intend to lead me through a corpse-yard?"

"Nay. Well... Not as such." He did not want to lead her unprepared into the realm of the bone lord, yet knew no gentle way to tell the truth of what they were to face. "You have doubtless heard tales of the unquiet dead, those who yet struggle in this mortal realm though their blood no longer quickens. Well, it is their land which next we enter."

"Then lead on, for I have yet to be greeted by a dead

Man," she announced gaily, and he was struck by the bravery in her breast which is forgotten in the breasts of many Men. "I would be most surprised to find them worser companions than my last fellows!"

And so they came to the hill and its foetid occupants and, though she feared them, she did not shy from them. Old Master Wood watched with something approaching pride as she deftly navigated the cruel maneuverings of the tomb king's conversation (rejecting with grace and laughter an impromptu offer of marriage) and asked after his future plans and living kin. She seemed much more comfortable in the realm politic they now occupied than the weary envoy, and so he sat back against the hill, and shut his eyes for a moment. He knew they would not hurt her, and his back was ever so sore.

When she awoke him it was with a gentle jostling. He had only meant to shut his eyes for a brief moment, but she laughed that he had slept for some time longer than a moment. "Denbolg says that the sun is near to rising, though we won't see it here in the forgotten realms of the Wood."

"Denbolg?" he asked blerily, rubbing the sleep from his eyes.

"Our host. The King Under the Hill." Her smile reminded him of the happy song of a titmouse who has just discovered spring. "He had forgotten it, but it was written on his grave and he helped me to read it."

As he stood, Old Master Wood realized that King Denbolg himself stood by with his attendants, and that he bore what could only be described as a grin (though it was in nearly every way more unsettling than his scowl). "Then it is much later indeed than I had thought. We had best be off. I fare you well, Your Majesty." And he doffed his bright cap to the lord of the little hill.

"Oh no, there is no need for that yet," spake Isadore. "King Denbolg has offered to guide us himself to the end of the Unwanted Depths."

"He has!" Despite his deal made with the skull prince and his general desire for all beings to appreciate and commune with one another he was still quite uncomfortable in the spectre's presence, yet he would not argue the point. For her part, Isadore seemed to have entirely overcome her discomfort with the dead ruler, and Old Master Wood observed with wonder the grace with which she dealt with that forgotten tyrant.

And so they set off—the hermit, the Princess, King Denbolg, and five of the most dexterous of the barrow-king's retinue. As they marched, King Denbolg taught them songs of long-dead Men, though his voice was slow, and Old Master Wood recited poems. The Princess Isadore congratulated both, yet also kept time enough to herself, considering what shape her future should take once she was returned to Hilldell.

In time they reached the point where Old Master Wood had left his well-worn grey boat. The lich offered to have his Men pole them acrost, for they were possessed of an inhuman strength and this suited the two home-seekers well. Once this was agreed, he asked the elder to step aside with him for a moment to speak.

"She be ah spetul thyng..." he droned, and Old Master Wood nodded. "Were I yun-ger and fayrer I am sertuhn I could have swayed her to myn syde... Yet alas... Yet also the better... She ys better folk than many... Und myckle wyse fer her yirs..."

"That she is, Your Grace," Old Master Wood could see in the creature's eyes a humility born of its newfound hope.

"Let her nawt luhrn the weys uf Man... Let her rather learn her own ways..." There was a long silence before the ghost-eyed King spoke again, "She ys better than I..." And if Denbolg could have cried he would have.

At the stream, Denbolg told them he would accompany them no further, for he feared the sun, but he gave to Old Master Wood clear instructions back to the Eald Road. And so they bid him farewell as two hale cadavers guided them acrost the water with strong, dead arms. When they looked back, the grave-wight yet lingered, though his servants slunk back into the depths of the trees. He was but a shadow with filmy eyes by the pitiful light of the candle, but they waved to him and both promised sincerely to visit him again.

"He was quite impressed with you," chided the witch, expecting the royal to be amused, yet she only nodded sagely.

"Denbolg is a sad thing, and I fear his days of villainy are not yet done, but there is hope in him for betterment. A hope it seems few Men have." And in her eyes he saw the glimmer of a silver crown.

Their first glimpse of day (though swathed in black clouds it was) came at the clearing with the burbling brook, where a family of dark-furred stoats played with the remains of an abandoned tent. Here the Princess spoke again, to state that her captors were doubtless dead, and Old Master Wood murmured his agreement. She did not seem sad, but perhaps regretful, and she asked of the traveler's journey with Dalf.

And so he told it, as short as it was, as they re-entered the dark of the Wood and—with King Denbolg's—advice they avoided the captor-alder, though the black birds found them and followed them and cursed them. But their spirits lifted as they moved closer to the end of the Unwanted Depths, and they fed on berries and roots and lamented the arrogance of Man. The black-barked trees too said terrible things, yet it bothered them not, though he taught her some words in the lignin tongue. She was clever and both light of heart and questioning of the world, and she had in her a healthy distrust of the ways of Men. "This is a ruler of folk," thought Old Master Wood.

The blackness of the land seemed to flee with unexpected swiftness, though it was indeed many hours, and in what seemed too little time they came to the Eald Road. Old Master Wood bowed low at the entrance and thanked the place for his success, though it sometimes seemed it did not wish it him.

"Shall we continue?" he asked. "Lead on, handsome Sir Knight," she smiled.

It was not long before they found two rangers on the road, and the magician was not surprised to find that he knew them (though Ern and Hallmot were indeed surprised, both to meet the wood-witch again and to be in the presence of Princess Isadore herself). As the sun set, they made a small roadside camp and Old Master Wood told of his many adventures (accompanied by the welcome sharing of an extra pipe of leaf).

IX

allmot was impressed despite himself at the unlikely success of the magician, yet resolved not to congratulate (nor fully believe the virtuous intentions of) the envoy until the Princess was safely home. Ern had no such reservations, and hailed Old Master Wood as a hero, begging to be allowed to squire for him.

"I am merely an old forest-dweller, and need no squire," he replied. Seeing the boy's crestfallen face, however, he winked and said, "But my shoulder could use a rest, if you should want to carry my pack upon your horse." The pack weighed nearly naught and was equally near empty, yet Ern lept at the opportunity. Isadore smiled.

The entire way back to Hilldell Hallmot could not halt himself from crying out the accomplishments of the wanderer (so great was his excitement, even despite his mistrust), until Old Master Wood reminded him that allies of the original abductors may yet be about in the lands. This made the aging warrior blush and stammer in shame, but he was assured by his fellows that no harm had likely been done. Pleasant weather and frequent meals of toasts and rich jams and soft cheeses made for a pleasant journey, and all present felt as if they had not had so fine a time in many nights. They were almost sad to see the rising land about Alimanx's capital.

They were greeted with much fanfare and, after promising to see the two roadmen again, Isadore and her erstwhile saviour were led to Alimanx's great hall. First Minister Engammu seemed less than pleased at the return of the victor, yet (with many foolish and archaic pronouncements) he introduced them once more to the King.

Alimanx, a vigour unexpected returning to his wrinkled frame, lept from his throne and ran to his daughter, nearly catching his royal robes on the fire of the chamber's long hearth. He clutched her tightly and, with firm kisses and precious tears, proclaimed his love. "Never and never thought we to see thee again, O dearest heart of mine. Without thee there would be nowhere for our love to flow and we should likely have withered and died." Behind him his consort and sons said naught. "And thee, Old Master Wood. Our promise we shall keep. No longer shall the southern ends of the Wood be ravaged, and the ancient compact of which thou didst speak shall be on parchment set."

Waving his hand, Old Master Wood shook his head, "No need, for my sake. Paper and ink mean little to the folk of the Wood. Should you need it to remind yourself or your descendants, so be it, but do not trouble yourself to appease me; your word and action are proof enough." The King thanked him, but the envoy was not yet finished. "I have another ask of you, Your Grace. One which you may at first be loathe to supply, yet which I promise shall be a benefit to all of the House of Orlo. I ask that," he paused to look at the Princess and he saw in her eye first surprise, then assent, "I ask that I be allowed to take and tutor your daughter for a time, and to teach her the ways of the world."

The court was in a moment in an uproar, and grey Engammu cried, "Sedition! Sedition!" in his false airs. At last King Alimanx called his folk to quiet and furrowed his weighty brow, causing his golden crown to tilt precariously. He saw the wisdom in the thing, and trusted Old Master Wood all the more for the delivery of his promise. Yet it is not like a Man to give up a prize so swiftly after having won it. To have a wizard as tutor to one's child is a mighty gift, but this wizard had come from the far reaches of the kingdom, and Alimanx was growing too frail to travel often to see his daughter.

"Canst thou not train her here?"

"Alas, there are ways of this world which may not be taught inside Man's walls. The Princess is bright, Your Highness, and one day will be a great aide to the kingdom. And I would give her all the knowledge I may impart. In addition, I have found myself to be much divorced from the ways of Man—as much as you and yours have bee divorced from the ways of the Wood—and wish (in aid of our reinvigorated treaty) to find how those ways can live in harmony with my home."

With a resignation and a recognition, Alimanx turned to his daughter and asked, "Wouldst thou go with him, and learn as he instructeth?"

"I would, Father."

And so she was freed to go, and after a short stay in Hilldell (which Old Master Wood enjoyed more than he wished, spending much time in the gardens and the larders and telling jests with the royal hounds) they began again on the road. With them happily went Hallmot and Ern, and Hallmot now rode proud as the guardian of both Princess and royal tutor; he enthusiastically complimented his charge on his accomplishments, and assured him at length that he had always known him to be of worthy bearing. Old Master Wood smiled and said, "Of course," and chuckled at the Man's meaningless quest for validation.

The road was long but this time they travelled all as friends, and the journey was fairer even than their last trek together. They came in time to where first the two Men had met the magician, and there they feasted and wined and the Princess asked Ern many things about his life. When again they set their steeds to walking once more they ventured deeper into the Wood. The trees grumbled about fraternizing with Men, and some saplings made idle threats, but in truth they were joyous to hear the news of the treaty's reinstatement, as were the animals (where they met them). In time they reached the titmouse's home in Lifwing Hollow, and the traveler called out a hulloo.

Yet no response came.

He called again and still there came no response. Swiftly, and with a dexterity uncommon in one his age, he clambered up the tree only to see her nest empty, and it seemed for some time. With concern he looked down to his companions. "Could the pillaging have come this far north?" he thought. Yet he did not believe such. And in that moment he noted the clouds which had darkened the sky.

"A favour now I call," came the voice of the bear-warg, and as surely as bees enjoy games of chance there it sat, crouched high in the branches of the abandoned tree.

"It is not sporting to feast on defenseless mother birds," said the hermit, as Ern's horse reared in fright and Hallmot lept from his saddle, lance in hand.

"No sporting beast am I. But nay. Too fast a flight was she," it snarled, licking its snout. Had the sun begun to set? With the stormclouds it was difficult to tell. "Yet her fate has naught to do with the favour you owe."

Hallmot was reaching, attempting to spear the beast, but failing for its height. Ern still strived to tame his distressed mount, and the Princess watched with terror and interest.

"What favour?" asked the warlock with chilled heart.

"A small one I grant. Naught what should burden a heart such as yours."

"Then speak it, creature," spake the squat worthy.

"I wish a child, and find your woman-thing comely." It licked its loose lips once more with great greed.

The thing's voice was quiet enough that those upon the ground could not hear it, but Old Master Wood, in his offense and surprise, voiced, "You wish a child by the Royal Daughter?" At this Isadore and Hallmot gasped in fury and Ern toppled from his steed.

"'Tis but a rut," it crooned, and Old Master Wood's

blood boiled.

Some beasts were as terrible as Man, and some worse. But Old Master Wood could not defeat the thing alone, nor in the boughs of the hornbeam in which they sat. "If a deal is to be made it should be made on even footing."

"The deal has already been made."

"Even so, it upsets my stomach to make arrangements off solid ground. I shall clamber down, and you after, and then we shall speak."

"Not whilst your Men carry arms, nay," it warbled. And Old Master Wood, after he had reached the forest floor, called for Ern and Hallmot to dispense with their weapons, which they did after much complaint, so great was their trust in him.

Once this was done the thing lept down, its powerful mass dwarfing even hale Hallmot. Its unkind eyes met Isadore's and it spoke then to Old Master Wood. "So will you watch or wait?"

"Neither, for it is not my place to choose the actions of the woman and her body." Hallmot balked at this, yet the Thing only sneered.

"So it turns to me to take what is owed." But it breathed not long enough to make good on its deplorable goal. For folk creatures such as dragons and ogres and bear-wargs are often creatures of poetic blindness, and even more prone to the vagaries of language than Men. The assailant had demanded all Men unhand themselves of weapons, and had been mystically blinded by its arrogance when Hallmot handed his lance to the Princess, and greatly surprised when she pierced its heart with it.

The thing fell dead at her feet, and the clouds began to flee the bright sky. Ern once more ran after his mount, and

Hallmot clapped the royal's back proudly as if she were another soldier. She let go the lance's haft and looked to Old Master Wood and the magician smiled sadly.

"Many bad wights end badly," he said, and moved to take her hands. "How fare you?"

She shook but little, and colour already was returning to her face. "I am well, I think. And better than I should have been had your scheme not worked. I am glad that the beast was so unable to see the danger so close to its breast."

"It is a common ailment for beasts, as well as Men," he said. And though he grieved to see death (even the death of one he feared and hated) he was soon set to travel onwards.

"I would send Ern home, if that sits well with ye," spake Hallmot. "He is innocent, and I would 'ave 'im retain that innocence a while longer. But I would travel onwards with ye, if ye would 'ave me, for ye 'ave made me question whether there is not much which I have forgotten as I matured. And I would not 'ave ye face more 'ardships without my spear."

"There is naught further on our trek which I would expect to challenge Ern's innocence," said Old Master Wood with warmth, "and so I would have him follow yet. As for yourself, it thrills my heart to hear you say what you have, for we all may learn from one another (though I doubt you shall have need to bloody your pole again in the Wood). When we get to my home we shall have tea."

And indeed they did. Warm root tea was enjoyed in plenty once they reached his house at Tossley Crook (which had been carefully tended by Master Fox in his friend's absence), and many animals came to visit the newcomers and tearfully thank Old Master Wood (to the great wonderment of the first three and many shushings and "it was no great bother"s from the latter).

Ern stayed the shortest time, for he missed his family and was young enough in mind and heart to still find wonder everywhere, not merely in the heart of an enchanted holt. To him Old Master Wood gave a twin to his own pointed cap, and Ern wore this until he died and it was rich with holes.

Hallmot stayed longer than he would have expected. He had little living family (and less whose company he enjoyed) and found himself enamoured not only with the little magician, but also with the kindness of animals and the calm of the Wood, which before had been so frightening and alien to him. He would practice woodcarving and fishing and play board games with his Princess and their host. He even, in that short time, learned something of the speech of animals. When it came time to leave, he was truly sorry to go, and Old Master Wood also lamented his leaving and called him a good friend. His host gave to him the very pipe he had thought lost in the Unwanted Depths (yet in truth had been trapped in a fold of his satchel) and sent him on his way. When he returned to Hilldell, Ali-manx told him how much it meant to him that he had stayed for a time to guard his only daughter (though Hallmot knew she needed no protection in that place), and gave to him a gilded helm and a seat at the high table on feast days. Hallmot was old, and did not live many years past his time in the Wood, but those what knew him said that he was much changed and was quicker to laugh and slower to anger than other Men. He was married to a woman he had known in childhood before he died, and his funeral was well-attended and an event of great joy.

The Princess stayed for three years, and in that time learned all she could from Old Master Wood. Where he went, so did she, and when she did not understand fully she asked. When Old Master Wood led a parade of animals to King

Denbolg's hill to make good his promise she went with and shared an evening of song and wine with the two venerable wights. Alimanx, her father, visited her once a year, and those times were joyous for all, even as he hid the woes which beset the kingdom for fear of darkening the mood. She learned to question her own prejudices and premonitions and to be both kind and practical in measure, and she delighted in the hidden worlds of nature. Even when she returned to Hilldell she retained a certain peace, which kept her separate in many ways from the fiery race of Men. And this peace kept her level-headed even as Denbolg's coin destabilized the lands of the House of Orlo and his angry dead beset those lands. As her brothers fell to degeneracy, revolutionary violence, or internecine war, she rose and in time became queen herself. It was by her hand that peace was brought once more with the dead, and by her hand that a new, more just order was brought to the kingdom, which lasted into its dying days. Yet by this time she was an old woman, and never again did she manage to meet with her mentor, though occasionally they would trade letters by way of a friendly bird. She was too humble to say it, but her time in the Wood had helped her grow to be better than many a Man.

As for Old Master Wood himself, he was content to remain near home, and never after interfered in the ways of Men. After his initial homecoming he made certain to visit all of his close friends (including the titmouse in Lifwing Hollow, who was quite put out by losing her home but forgave her friend for his part in the matter and later added fur from the bear-warg's pelt to her reclaimed nest). The Bear of Copper Dell was nearly blind, but quite content and he and Old Master Wood Hunted honey together and ate it greedily in the cool shade of an oak. Willowbrook's Elk was eagre to hear his tale, and immediately began recomposing it into a poem. On his visits to the south he found that the beasts were beginning to return to Elderbrake,

Washingwood, and Mintwell, and to rebuild, as best they could. Cousin Wolf was indeed dead, but his brothers and sisters were glad of Old Master Wood's condolences, and he spent a few long nights with them, staring at the stars.

He had delighted in his time with his northern visitors, but also was glad at last to have his home back to himself. Stories were a love of his, and so often he would tell of his travels, yet ever he would end with "And that is why I prefer to stay at home!" The pact between the Wood and Man was maintained in his time and he was glad of this, and when Isadore would send him letters he would joyfully reply (though he begged her not to speak of politics for they interested him little). With the occasional exception (which exist even in the most contented of lives), he returned to his original state of perfect happiness.

"Do ye hate Men fer wha' they did?" asked Master fox once over croquet (which the fox played with his nose rather than a mallet). His erstwhile friend had been allowed an evening away by his wife and litter of young pups, but even though he was glad to have this time with the hermit his talk often returned to his recently expanded family. Old Master Wood did not mind.

"How could I be?" he said, striking his ball gently, only barely missing his shot. "It is in their nature to be foolish, and the world is ever cruel and changing. I think, perhaps, that Man is only different from animal in that he is bored without the constant worries of food and shelter and wild living, and must replace his primal ferocity with unconscious cruelty."

"And I think tha' it is much more complex than tha'," said the Fox, nudging his ball through a curved stick they were using as a wicket.

"Undoubtedly you are right, but it is also not worth dwelling on. Would you like to help me start some beer after this game is done? I have some yeasts prepared which I would very much like to make use of." And his friend said that he would.

The Hat Tree

here was a Hat Tree just on the edge of the Town, just before the Old Road met the Stony Bridge over the Rushing River which formed the edge of town. It was a magical tree, the Hat Tree, and wonderful as well. The children would run out of the village after worship was done and scamper down to the Hat Tree, climbing on each others' shoulders to pick the ripe fruit. Fat Bill would sit on his stool by the Stony Bridge and wink at them with a tip of his flat helm, then look back over the border, his hands resting gently on his spear. The Hat Tree bloomed every day, in felt and cotton and wool. Wide brimmed hats and pointed hennons and funny hats with flappy ear covers in all manner of colours (though many were black or grey or brown). The hats were too big for the children, but they loved them even more for that and would play with them until they were forgotten, and the streets of the town were always littered with forgotten hoods and crumpled bonnets. The mothers and fathers would smile and kick them out of the way, and if the hat was too mussed they would discreetly dispose of it so no child would see them and complain of how much they loved the hat they had not cared for for days.

The Town was small and made most of its money off of wicker-crafts. They did not sell the hats, though they could have—those were for the children. But the Town was known far and wide, and not for its wicker-crafts. They were known for the Temple where worship was held each day, and for the earnest missionaries which traveled as far as they were able from home to spread the word of God. It was often joked that there were more men of the Town outside its walls than inside. The missionaries would go from village to village, sometimes with out-landish hats, sometimes with common ones, and sometimes without any, begging passerby to listen to their gospel. But no one outside the town knew anyone who had stopped to listen to them. The missionaries would wander for weeks at a time, then return home in the dark of night and attend worship in the morning with bare heads. Outsiders didn't come to the Town, for no one had reason to, and this suited the locals just fine—the town was blessed by God and the people there loved Him—that was enough.

Brigid was five years old and lived with Ma and Pa and Tom (her brother) and Millie (her brother's wife). She liked living in the Town; there was always something to do. Some-times she would go down to the Rushing River to wade in the shallows and splash at fish, and on the way she would take a few stones from the Old Road to throw as far in as she could. She never crossed the Stony Bridge (for Pa said God wouldn't like that), but she would always pass the Hat Tree, standing empty after the after-worship frenzy save for a few hats resting too high for any of the children to reach, their brims raw and their crowns holey. The tree had no leaves and no bark, and was as white as Pa's deer bone knife. All of the limbs were short, as if they had been cut—perfect for plucking hats from with little fingers. The top was flat. It almost looked more like a post than a tree. Once she had knocked on the Hat Tree and heard it *thump* like an empty barrel; Tom told her that was the sound that God's heart made, thumping in the sky. *Thump-thump. Thump-thump.* That had made her giggle, and so after that every time she passed the Hat Tree she would thump on it happily.

One day, late in the summer, Brigid was walking down to the Rushing River. On her head was a striped cap with two red strings which Millie had tied gaily under the young girl's chin.

One of the older boys—much taller than her—had grabbed it from the tree and given it to her. Someday she knew she would have to hate boys, but she liked them for now. And she must not have to hate boys forever, because boys became men, and someday she would have to marry a man. She skipped along, her little fists each gripping a little grey rock from the road. She stopped and thumped the tree, and then turned towards the river.

She stopped then. Fat Bill had fallen asleep on his watch, but that was not what made her pause. There was a stranger on the bridge, with high cheekbones and a rugged green cloak. In one hand was a stout oak stave and on his head was a wide, pointy hat. He called out to her and asked her where he had come to, and what was the name of this Town.

Millie liked to quote the priest after worship, and her favourite bit of scripture from Father Quintain's Big Black Book was about strangers.

If ye see them coming

But ye do not know their name

Call to God to bless ye

And run back to thy hame

And so Brigid did just that, shouting to God and dropping her stones and scampering back home, as the stranger called out after her and Fat Bill began to wake from his slumber.

Pa had been very concerned when he heard about the stranger on the Stony Bridge. He had pretended he wasn't, but Brigid could tell. He always huffed more and puffed more when

86

he was upset, and sometimes he would sit in his rocking chair and take out his little brown pipe and huff and puff into that. Tom told her that Fat Bill would talk to the man and help him on his way. After all, the Big Black Book said,

If they be alone

And their path they did mislay

God's men shall guide them on

To Heaven and God's Way

This made her feel better, for Fat Bill was God's man. He watched the bridge to make sure God's beloved people did not get attacked or argued with. Those were bad things. She tried to play the rest of the day and forget about the Bad Man on the Stony Bridge, but it was always just there, tickling her imagination. Was he a Devil Worshiper? A Sorcerer? A Lawyer? A Soldier? A King? All of those were people who would hurt people or argue with people—Father Quintain said so. She played most of the day with her dolls—the one with the nice white apron and the one that looked like a dog—until it was time for supper, when Ma came to get her and took her hand.

Together the family walked to the dining house, where they ate with all their friends and neighbors. Ma slapped Brigid's wrist when the little girl reached for a stick of butter with her bare hand. Brigid cried, but as soon as her mother wasn't looking she snatched a fistful of the yummy spread and licked it up greedily. Father Quintain said a prayer before the meal and after, and everyone ate happily. Brigid mostly ate bread and potatoes; the meat was too salty so she fed it to one of the town dogs, which earned her another slap.

After supper they went home and Pa recited some of the Big Black Book that he had memorized and they all went to their beds. Brigid waited until she could hear them snoring—their big, heavy chests rising and falling as the stars twinkled in through the single window, before quietly tiptoeing out of her cot and going to the door. She wanted to ask Fat Bill about the Bad Man. This late it wouldn't be Fat Bill on the stool, but his brother Good Georg. But their house was under the Stony Bridge and she would wake him up. Carefully she swung open the door, certain not to make a sound and, once she was outside, she scampered as fast as she could down the Old Road, not even pausing to look for stones.

She did pause at the Hat Tree however to knock; it was a ritual she had, as if only she could keep God's heart beating. But before she could thump-thump on the tree she saw two figures on the bridge. At first she thought it must be Fat Bill and Good Georg, but then she saw that one of them had an odd, square-shaped head. She dropped silently to her hands and knees and crawled as close as she could without being seen. One of them—the one with the spear and the helmet—was Good Georg, but the other one was tall with a long cape and boots with buckles that shown in the moonlight. The man with the shiny boots said that someone had not heard the word of God, and Good Georg complimented the man's hat. Brigid realized that the man did not have a square head, but rather a square hat. Which was very odd because adults did not wear hats, unless they were strangers. Ma had taught her that with a rhyme from the Big Black Book.

Do not hide thy head

Lest God thinks ye hide more things

But show thy hair proudly

Unlike heretic kings

Helmets were okay though—Fat Bill and Good Georg always wore them so they must be. Then the visitor took off his hat and handed it to Georg. They both said that they wished the other they spoke of (the one who had not heard the word of God) found God before he got to Heaven. Brigid wished he did too. It was good to be loved by God.

With long strides, the caped visitor started making his way towards town, and Brigid was not fast enough to scoot out of his sight. He came over to her and told her to stand up and she did. Her fear quickly left her when she recognized Tall Oskar—one of the missionaries of the Town. He asked what she was doing out so late and she told him she had wanted to talk to Fat Bill. Fat Bill was sleeping, he said, so she should go home. Tall Oskar offered to accompany her and she went with him. He told her a funny story about a mouse he had made friends with on his travels. Soon she was home and back in bed. Oskar had smirked and put a finger to his lips as he helped her open the door and shut it silently. She promised she would go right to sleep. It was only the next morning, as she put on her blue dress and lacy bonnet for worship, that she remembered why she had wanted to talk to Fat Bill. But there was no time and she quickly forgot again as she was rushed to the Temple.

Brigid did not like worship as much as the rest of her family, but it made everyone smile, even though it was boring, so she endured it. Father Quintain would always start by opening the Big Black Book and reading for a while, and then, when everyone was almost asleep, he would have them all stand and sing songs. Everyone knew the words except Brigid and the other children, but they were learning. After the songs Father Quintain would read more and then say a prayer before talking for some time about what made God happy and what made God sad. Brigid did not want God to be sad, so she always tried to listen, but it was no use—Father Quintain was simply too boring. Then there would be more songs (for which Ma would have to wake her daughter up) and more prayers, and then everyone would shake hands and hug and greet each other before filing out into the Town.

That day was no different, and afterwards she ran with all her friends down the Old Road, grabbing stones for the river and laughing as they wondered what fruits the Hat Tree had today. Finally they arrived and all the little girls and boys began snatching at the low-hanging prizes, or hoisting each other up to reach the higher ones. Brigid laughed and grasped, but she was not fast nor tall enough to reach any of the hats. This often happened, and as was often the case she began to get frustrated. She tried to tug a long, blue hat with bells on the point from another child, but lost her grip and landed on her bottom in the grass. She was beginning to pout and to think that maybe if she cried she could get a new hat today when Fat Bill's spear peaked over the others and lifted a wide, pointy hat from a high branch, carefully balancing it and bringing it down to Brigid's lap. He smiled and winked and went back to his post.

The hat was almost as big as Brigid was, and smelled like herbs and grass and wet wool. Laughing, her frustration forgotten, she put it on her head and let it fall to her shoulders. The spear had poked a small hole in it and the sunlight filtered in. She smiled and called out a thank you to Fat Bill.

Just then she remembered again why she had snuck out to speak to Fat Bill last night. And shortly after this thought came to her she remembered the wide, pointy hat the Bad Man had worn the day before. With both hands she carefully lifted the hat off of her head and set it on the ground. She eyed it studiously. It looked very similar. Almost identical, save for the hole the spear had made. She turned it on its side and gazed inside. Had there been a stain on the brim of the traveler's hat? There could have been—he was very dirty.

Stroking her chin, she looked up at the Hat Tree. All of the lower hats were gone and some of the children had already begun to run back towards town. A crow flew in and landed on the crown of a flat, squarish hat on a high branch, near where Brigid's new hat had come from. A square hat like what Tall Oskar had worn when he told Fat Bill that he wished that the man who had not found God would find Him before he got to Heaven. Could these be the same hats? But how could that be? If these grew on the Hat Tree? She stroked her chin and scrunched up her nose until she remembered a verse Pa liked to say,

Question not God's gifts

For he is wise and mighty

Instead accept his acts

And ever smile brightly

She shrugged and grabbed at the brim of her new hat. The Hat Tree was a miraculous gift of God, and she was only five years old. She should not question it. It was much easier to enjoy the summer when she did not question the doings of God. Or to enjoy any season, really. She smiled and scampered after her friends, dragging the wide, pointy hat behind her in the dust. It would be forgotten in a week and in a month it would be piled in with the waste. But by then there would be more hats. Brigid loved the Hat Tree. Everyone in the Town loved the Hat Tree.

The Beauty and the Beast

A baroque tale of strange love and fearful enlightenment

 very long time ago there was a merchant who had three gorgeous daughters, each more beautiful than the last. Following this pattern, his youngest daughter was the fairest of them all. I was not known to pronounce my own virtues, but it was widely known in the land of my birth that not only was I beauteous and kind, but humble and less affected by my father's wealth than my sisters. I am not quite so humble now.

My father was widely respected as one of the finest merchants in the land—dealing in foreign spices, textiles, and produce. We were never wanting for anything—should we require it, he would provide. My sisters' reveled in the affluence showered upon them, and took many suitors under their wings. I too appreciated what my father had done for me, but I did not allow my thankfulness to turn to bravado. Suitors were not alien to me either, but I kindly turned them each aside, telling them that I was yet too young to marry and that I would prefer to stay with my father a while longer.

In the times that my father was away, I would often content myself with the many pleasures of literature. Neither my sisters nor my father shared my love for the written word, but I reveled in the knowledge which could be found within. My vocabulary has always been far in advance of those around me, thanks to my unending thirst for the knowledge, adventure, and romance within the pages of the many novellas and folios which lined my shelves.

I had long suspected that not all of my father's dealings

were entirely legal, and when he was tried in court and stripped of many of his lands and much of his riches, I found myself single-handedly comforting him while earning a living through my own labor. My sisters would have naught of their father nor an honest days work, and fled to their many suitors, returning home disgruntled and despairing, as their suitors cared not for them when their pockets were empty. Father's supposed friends in the community left him without allies, and I felt his pain at their betrayal. Towards me, the youngest of my clan, the wedding proposals continued to stream but, feeling genuine contempt for the families that had so crushed my beloved papa, I continued to give them the same response as before—that I was yet too young to marry and that I would prefer to stay with my father a while longer.

A small cottage a ways off in the woods became our home for the next year or so, and my father made a living as a woodcutter, whilst I cared for the property. My sisters did little other than pout and bemoan the loss of their pompous past lives. In my naivete I pitied them, and wished that they would learn to live with their situation.

After that year had passed, a message came to my father—who still attempted to retain some connection with his merchant days of old. It appeared that an old partner of my father's had received a shipment of rare spices and was offering them to my father as a first step in rebuilding his lost empire. My father was thrilled, and my older siblings even more so. They begged and pleaded for scarves, dresses, shoes—anything and everything that they had missed in their time away from the city. I, however, doubted the integrity of the deal my father had entered into and, even if his partner were to truly offer him a generous share of profit, I doubted that he would have enough money to purchase all that my sisters begged.

Not knowing my reservations, my father asked me softly, "Béatrice, what may I bring back for you?"

I began to tell him simply, "Nothing, Father," but, thinking that this might make me appear snide and possibly mocking of my sisters, I responded instead, "A rose, Father."

He raised his greying eyebrows in surprise and confusion, but I could see the smile he tried to hide—he knew I was not vain like his other ilk.

"They do not grow here, father, and I do so miss their scent."

"A rose it is, my dear," he said, kissing me on the cheek. He straddled his horse then and rode off for town.

It was nearly a month before he returned again, in which time I alone had to care for the house and for my imbecile siblings. They moaned and whined, hypothesizing the doom of their *beloved* father. I knew they simply thirsted for his supposed wealth, and yet still held little enmity towards them.

After many hard days he finally returned, and to my surprise he trailed behind him a gilded wain loaded with chests full of gold and silver as well as all manner of clothing and finery, their origins mysterious and their threading magnificent to behold. My sister's squealed with sickening delight and raced each other to the cart, while I greeted my father warmly, more relieved at his arrival than that of his gifts. He smiled and handed me a rose. The rose radiated an aura of strangeness, but it was nonetheless the most beautiful flower I had ever laid eyes upon. I was so mesmerized by this magnificent gift, that I almost failed to notice the sadness present behind my father's smiling eyes. When I did notice this creeping sorrow I tried to comfort him, but he would not speak of it. He simply grinned in an imitation of joy and led the household in a raucous celebration of our newfound fortunes. I resolved then to find the subject that so troubled my beloved parent.

Shortly thereafter we moved back into the city and my father began again to rebuild his empire. I noted that in all of his dealings his partner who had helped him that first time was no-where to be found, and also that many of the aspects of the business were handed aside to my uncle, as my father had begun a rather unhealthy habit of drinking. My sisters, predictably, did not notice anything amiss and revisited their old suitors, flashing their expensive jewelry and garments, three times as rich as ever before. My resolve to help my father find happiness in the face of his private hardships was only strengthened by the barriers he constantly kept between us—barriers that had never existed before.

One night, when my father was lost in a drunken stupor, I asked him about the discrepancies I had noticed in his new-founded merchant practice. What he told me I was at first loath to believe.

According to my father's drunken telling, the spices found upon the boat were of a politically volatile sort; his partner had only passed them on to him to transfer the guilt, and there-fore the punishment. My father had been fined and imprisoned, and had barely been able to secure his own release in the short amount of time that he had. By the time that he had freed him-self, his former partner had already fled the city. Penniless and alone, with not even a horse to his name, my father had wan-dered into the woods in hopes of making his way home before he starved.

Here my father stopped his story and looked me right in the eye. In his face I could read pure terror and solemnity—two emotions which he now radiated strongly enough to penetrate the alcohol choking his brain. I was struck dumb by the strength of his dour nature, my empathy crippling my tongue. Sternly, he bade me listen as he recited an old tale.

Deep within the forests of my home, there resides a palace—not a castle, mind you, as it was always meant to impress, never to defend. The existence of this palace was a known fact to me and to everyone in the land, as was the tale my father recited, which is why no one visited that wondrous abode.

It is said that a long time ago, a prince lived in that palace. Some say he was fearful in demeanor, whilst others say that he was the kindest man ever to walk this earth. Whatever the case, the prince was known for his parties—grand affairs lasting days at a time.

One night, a damnable visitor came uninvited to the prince's ball and asked to be allowed entry. The prince refused, and the demon cursed him with a foul shape and a fouler appetite. It is said that every living soul present in the lord's palace that night was devoured in a mad rage. Even now, the people of the surrounding lands claim to often see the fiend prowling the dark woods in search of flesh to eat or fools to ensnare.

That was all that I could glean from my father that night as, after he finished reciting the tale, he nursed his glass of port and fell off into a deep slumber. Still ignorant of the source of his troubles, I nonetheless felt that I had opened an important door, and that soon I could give him my compassion, which he so obviously needed. With the aid of one of the servants I gently brought him to his bed chambers, laying him to rest in comfort before retiring myself.

The next night I again pressed him again about his trip, asking how he had ended up with any money at all, considering what he had told me the night before. He held up one shaking finger whilst he finished his drink. Apprehensively I listened as he began again with a new chapter to his abysmal tale.

He told how he had stumbled and dragged himself through the twisting bark of the endless trees, and how he was soon very, very lost. As he was preparing to give up his life and die on the forest floor, he saw a light ahead in the forest. All around him could be heard strange howls. "Wolves," I offered, but he shook his drunken head. He told me that these were not wolves, and that no canine throat could make these sounds. As he approached the light, the howls grew louder, until he could barely think outside of his need to reach the warm glow ahead. Exiting the thick line of trees, he came into an enormous clearing, and in that clearing sat a great spired palace of grey stone and rose-tinted glass. The ground about the palace was devoid of life, but also was it devoid of snow (as it had been winter when he had made his fateful trip). The palace radiated a dull heat and the hum of the stones seemed to calm the restless howlers. Broken and hopeless, my father approached the massive carven doors and knocked, three times, using a great iron knocker shaped into a mass of thorns.

After a few moments, the doors swung wide, and inside was a magnificent hall, carpeted in red and hung with bizarre and inconceivable tapestries. Two sets of bannistered stairs led up to a dining hall, wherein he found a banquet meant for kings laid out before him. He called and called for the master of the palace, but to no avail. So starved was he that he did not think of the færie tale which spoke of just such a terrible place, and so he eventually gave up his hopes for a host, and sat down in a great throne to eat. The food was strange and unknown to his palate, but it soon grew on him and before he knew it he had devoured so much food that he was barely able to stand. Once he did, however, he found a key laid beneath his napkin, and on the key was written **"Bedroom number 4, seventh floor, easternmost tower."** Delighted at the prospect of a warm bed, he set out to find this room.

On his trek (as that is what it amounted to) through the expansive halls of the palace, he saw many wonders: great halls full of bizarre statues and other works of art, rooms full of floating glass bulbs which glowed and played gay tunes, hidden gardens wherein grew every type of flora available, vast libraries of well-cared for books, and much more. Eventually he reached the bedroom, and tried the key, which fit perfectly. Inside, a four-poster bed hung in red satin and carved of a darkly stained ivory was to be found, and a gown for which to dress himself before retiring. Tossing his wrecked clothes aside, he climbed into the covers and instantly fell asleep.

He told me that that night he dreamt of many strange things, but that when he awoke, he could barely remember any of them. When climbed out of bed he found a new suit laid before him on the footlocker. Donning the new clothes, he climbed down the stairs, intended to set off again as soon as possible to find his home; yet as he passed one of the many gardens, he thought back to my request.

Carefully, he descended down the stone steps into the garden. The rose-coloured roof was made of a tremendous dome of tinted glass, supported by iron girders which crossed sometimes in angles seemingly as impossible, with what was once the top of one becoming the bottom before its end without twisting or turning in any discernable way. The floor of the cavernous room was inset deeply into the ground, and the single stone staircase traced down along the wall for three or four stories before reaching the cobbled paths between the flowers. Occasional oriental trees existed amongst the more traditional flora, all of it blossoming in whites and reds and leafy greens. Papa marveled at the shadows and lightplay from the invisible world outside the glass before plucking the most beauteous of roses from among the patch.

Just as the stem snapped, a tremendous roar echoed through the garden and the ceiling cracked, showering my father in endless shards of rose-coloured glass and revealing the grey and clouded sky above.

Who dares to steal roses from me?

The voice was soft, but bellowing all the same, and seemed to echo for aeons before my father found the resolve to respond.

"I – I did not mean to offend, I simply – "

He was cut off as the hellish voice continued, my father hiding his bleeding face in his arms; *I show you my hospitality—allow you access to my halls and give you permission to feast upon my immortal feed, and this is how you repay me—stealing the greatest of blooms from my greatest garden?*

"It was for my youngest daughter, she asked me simply for a rose."

I shall give you one quarter of an hour to prepare your-self for the punishment to come upon you. Do not be a fool.

My father turned, attempting to beg for his life, but upon seeing his host he was struck dumb. He would not tell me what he saw, despite my pleading, save that it smiled coyly at him.

Perhaps I shall let you go. Would you like that, little man?

The frightened merchant did all he could just to nod.

You mentioned a youngest daughter, implying you have

100

more than one. If you shall consent to send one of your daughters to me, I shall allow you to live. One may even wish to come of her own accord.

My kin was stricken—sitting as he was in a field of broken crimson glass facing a hellish monster many miles from civilization.

You would not want to disappoint me. Now come; tell me of your troubles and I will see what I can do that will be of aid.

He told the thing of his troubles, and of his life, and that he could do nothing to stop his loosening tongue. The creature then sent him on his way, supplying him with a wagon piled high with exotic goods. Two weeks after his return, his partner was found dead, torn apart by bears in the woods along the coast. My father had refrained form telling any of us this gruesome tale, as he would prefer that he died rather than us, but he feared that the thing would come soon, and he wished for me to comfort him.

At first I had not believed him, thinking my father to be lying to me to protect me from the truth, but my opinion was soon changed. The terror in his eyes was all too real, and the story too strange to be a fabrication of his own. A portion of his fear chewed at my soul, now not simply for himself, but for me as well, as I specifically had been mentioned to this creature. For a moment I felt almost repulsed by my father, having dealt as he had with such a devil, but then my signature benevolence took me, and I impulsively promised my father that I would go—that I would save him from the demonic prince of the forest. His eyes grew wide and he begged and he pleaded for me not to go, but I would not hear his arguments. I would not let my father die for me.

We did not speak of that night after that. In fact, my father stopped speaking to me almost entirely, only occasionally giving a passing word. His distance upset me perhaps as much as his fear and sadness had before; I had put forth my life for him, and all he did was shun me for my charity.

The flower which he had brought me had long ago wilted, but I found myself unable to dispose of it. Since my father had not been told how one of his daughters was to join the creature, and he would not tell me the way, I felt a desire to hang on to whatever connection I had to my promise, lest my vow not be recognized and my papa's life be forfeit nonetheless.

One night, after turning aside yet another suitor and retiring to my chambers after dinner, I found the rose on my table, not wilted at all, and in fact more vibrant than it had ever been before. In wonder, I tried to pick it up, and realized that it had grown into the wood of the table, it's roots wrapping through the grain. On of the thorns pricked my finger, and I almost instantly felt light-headed. I laid down in my bed and fell into a deep slumber.

I dreamt of a great black ship, manned by strange men. It came to me in the night, floating in the air outside my window. The men took my hand roughly and guided me aboard, sailing with me high above the towers of the city. I watched, dreaming, as the hull of the ship glided out over the forest and towards a distant clearing. Inside the clearing I saw a palace looking for all the world like the slate-hued abode which my father had described. I felt a pang of trepidation, but the mists of sleep muted my apprehension to little more than curiosity. My captors sailed the ship down through the eddying winds and pulled it alongside a tower window. A plank was extended from the ship to the sill, and I crossed it precariously, entering into a lamp-lit room draped on all sides in glorious curtains. The cool of early spring was not present here, and I was glad of the gossamer gown provided. Slipping out of my clothes and into the lighter silk at hand I climbed over the high frame of the ivory bed, the strange faces inlaid into it seeming to stare and pucker at me. Laying amidst the wisping curtains, I stared above me at endless stars in a black night sky above. I heard the whistling of the black ship sailing away and I drifted deeper into sleep, never once feeling unwelcome in this strange palace.

In the morning I awoke clothed in strange fabrics in a strange bed in a strange room hung in rose. I did not see my clothes about me, and tip-toed cautiously to the ornate door, clutching the extravagant gown about myself. The door I found to be unlocked, and I ventured cautiously forth into the hallway. The halls were carved in relief with portraits of strange beings, and as I descended the stairs I found that the air here felt very much like the odd feeling expelled by my rose. Only barely did I recall then the details of my dream, and so this place held not simply the terror inherent in its architecture and contents, but also that which one finds when awaking in an utterly alien place, for I could not recall how I could have arrived.

After many flights of stairs I came upon a doorway with no door, and beyond lay a vast room full of floating glass bulbs. Each bulb glowed a different colour, and their light combined in various places to create hues which I had been unable to imagine before that point. The ceiling was not incredibly high, and so I could easily reach the balls, which purred with delight as I touched them. I felt a strange, electric tingling from each one, and from each one it was different. I lingered for a time, losing my fear to wonderment until I eventually grew bored of this spectacle and continued further.

In the next room I found a myriad of instruments, some familiar, some strange. All of the instruments were playing themselves, creating a chaotic cacophony of sound which was painful to my ears. The racket almost immediately became too much for me and I swiftly fled this room. Yet whenever I listened closely I could hear these sounds anywhere in the palace, for as long as I stayed there.

Some of the spires of the palace were connected by elaborate buttressed walkways which looked out over the forest. Still reeling with wonderment from the bizarre magics of the last two rooms, I wandered onto one of these bridges, gripping for a moment the rose-tinted marble railings and gazing down at the firs below. The pervading heat seemed even thicker at this altitude, and I found much of the lands around to be obscured by the waves of heat radiating from the foundations. In this moment of relative normalcy I found the fear returning and gripping my mind like the crushing weight of a tree's roots. I told myself that fear would only hurt me here in this strange place, and forced myself to redirect my tumultuous emotions into curiosity once more; I wondered what strange sorcery could be found elsewhere, and marched purposefully towards the next tower, the air thick and choking about me.

When I set foot off the walkway I found myself upon an open balcony, with no rails and no door visible, simply a pink marble staircase descending in a corkscrew fashion down the side of the tower. Nervously bunching the cloth of my covering in one hand, I shut my eyes and began slowly making my way down the stairs, guiding myself with my right hand on the wall. From the landing the stairway had seemed impossibly long, and I braced myself for the journey, but once I had begun it, I almost immediately found my feet meeting the stones of another landing. I stepped off, opening my eyes and gazing in surprise. Looking behind me I found the last landing obscured by the curve of the tower, and this rationale saved me from losing my sanity there on that terraced balcony. Until this moment I had never claimed to be afraid of any altitude, yet I then realized that I had never before reached any height worth fearing. The stairs continued further, but I opted for the door present on this lower balcony so as to remove myself from the sources of this new-found phobia.

The door itself was ornately carved with images of this-tles, roots, and greenery, all wrapped about the menacing faces of silently watching sprites. The faerie stone eyes inset into the door seemed to judge me for not continuing down the stairs, and for a moment I hesitated. Then, summoning up my courage, and reassuring myself of their inanimacy, I pushed at the handle, a rich mahogany lever shaped like the piercing end of a root. I passed cautiously through the doors, making certain not to meet the pressing eyes of the boggarts.

The cavernous room I found myself in must have filled much of the tower, and the amphitheatre seating went down at least a dozen stories at a steep incline. Hung from the ceiling were great twisting cloth fixtures in various shades of red. They spun as if from a slight breeze, yet each at a different speed and in a different direction. At the base of the chamber was a pool of crystal clear water, reflecting the rotating shapes above as if they were wisping tendrils of gore, ever so slowly drifting apart in the motionless pool. I advanced down a few flights, cautiously approaching this new curiosity. The movement about me was almost soothing, and it was not until I was nearly at the pool that the varying winds struck me as odd. I glanced down at the pool and saw not my own reflection, but that of a painted woman, her watercolours running and blending in a bizarre verisimilitude of life. For a moment I gazed at the apparition, before turning vio-lently from her eye. Denying the strange inhabitant of the pond I turned and ran to one of the many exits placed among the seats, figuring myself to at least be close to the ground floor of this vast manour.

Coming through the doorway, I found myself on a wooden catwalk overlooking a great garden of dahlias, chrysanthemums, and poppies. The colours present amazed me, and the whole of it was lit only by the light shed from paper lanterns hung in large clusters about the place. I could see more catwalks spanning the space to the exit, and I paused only briefly to admire the beauty below me. I did not linger on the absence of windows to supply sunlight for the flora.

As I exited the garden of flowers, I found myself in a long passageway lined on both sides in closed doors. Beginning to grow frantic, and wishing nothing more than to be done with my strange adventures, I rushed to the first door and attempted to open it, but to no avail. Many of the doors in this passage were locked, and indeed this pattern continued in many more areas of the palace. I was not especially surprised. In fact, it was more surprising to me that more doors had not previously been closed to me. A large part of me said that I should continue on, but my curiosity won over and I began to peer through keyholes at the spectacles beyond. Many a locked door seemed to hold vast libraries of books, their shelves reaching to the ceiling. I gazed for a time at these catalogues, my heart aching to read their contents, and in fact forgot almost entirely about the strange and unnatural phenomena by which I found myself surrounded.

Eventually I came to an unlocked room and entered. At first I was disappointed to have not found another housing of tomes, but the inhabitants themselves drew my wonder nearly as heartily. Inside were cages upon cages of animals, the likes of which I had never before seen. I stepped cautiously past them, each sitting solidly still save for their watching eyes. Toads as large as a man or hook-beaked fowl as bright as a sunrise, maned

106

beasts with the faces of dogs and long curling tales, or gorillas painted vibrant shades of orange and pale shades of blue. All of these and more sat imprisoned, and not a single one made any move to escape. Cautiously I reached out to pet an especially small looking deer, but it hissed at me like a cat, and the thing beside it began menacingly raking its claws along the bars of its cage. I did not try to free any of them.

I continued on through the palace, exploring and taking in the otherworldly delights and horrors that I found and, after a tangle of closed doors and strange rooms, I found myself on a balcony overlooking a grand entryway. Behind me a great set of double-doors led to a dining hall, from which came the caustically sweet aroma of an unknown banquet. I entered the room and found laid out before me platters upon platters of new and exciting meats, fruits, and vegetables. I suddenly felt very hungry, having wandered through labyrinthine towers all day, and sat down to feast. My fear at the strange abode had long since passed and were replaced almost exclusively with wonder and exhaustion. It was obvious to me that this was the place my father had spoken of, but what fearful thing lived here was the last thought in my mind, enchanted as I was by the splendor about myself.

As I finally sated my hunger, I found that I could sense a presence in the room with me, but at first I could not discern it. My apprehension from my first awakening returned, and I began to agitatedly peruse the room from my seat, too anxious to leave it for fear that something would notice me. When I at last managed to perceive the visitor, I could not understand how I had not seen it, as its terrible form was unlike anything I had ever before witnessed.

Its skin was calloused and grey, reminding me of nothing more so than that of an elephant. It's feet too hinted of elephantine ancestry, being great stumps of hard flesh and knobby bone. Its arms were disproportionately long, and ended in asymmetrical clawed hands. But, of all the aspects of this thing before me, nothing disturbed me more than its *face* (if one could refer to it as such) the only human-like feature was a great grinning mouth full of square, strong-looking teeth, stained with black mildew. Above this gaping orifice the remainder of the visitor's head tapered into one thick tentacle which arced downwards almost to its toes and lashed fitfully back and forth. This latter appendage gradually faded from the grey of the rest of its body to a deep crimson red which seemed only to heighten the fiend's monstrous appearance. It stood well of over eight feet tall and was stark naked, although it bore no genitalia. Its bald head and hairless body were creased and cracked, looking at some points like a piece of clay, cast aside from the kiln for its imperfections. I stared in fascinated horror at the brute before me, seeing now what had scarred my father's psyche so.

The creature stood at the end of the long table, somehow managing to remain largely inconspicuous, even framed as it was against the carmine tapestry behind.

I have brought you clothing.

The thing's voice was just as my father had described it. I watched, trembling, as the thing unfolded one of its clawed hands, motioning towards a crimson pile on one of the nearby chairs. The thing waited expectantly, its speech still resonating in the air.

Cautiously I reached out and took hold of the garments—a magnificent gown and matching accoutrements. As I took the clothing into my lap it lowered its arm.

Put them on.

I hesitated, my cultured proprieties giving me pause

when undressing in the presence of others.

I have no eyes.

Uncomfortably, I slid out of my nightgown and began to dress myself, fearing now for my life, as my father had once feared for his own amidst the shattered glass of that strange garden. I wiped a tear from my face as I thought of my father here with this thing, and another as I thought of my own future here with it.

After much difficulty I finally managed to get the dress situated upon myself and turned around. The beast was standing over me, its hellish grin nearly blocking out the light of the lamps.

How pretty you things are.

I screamed, frightened by its eyeless appraisal, and stumbled back towards the chair. There was no tongue in that mouth, and the fleshy insides simply reverberated with each foul word. The thing sluggishly stalked me, straddling me against the chair. It looked over my head and caressed my skin with one worn hand as it continued to speak.

You are my guest. It is my duty to please you, to care for you, and to teach you. If this does not please you, then you shall please me, which shall be a result nonetheless.

I shifted agonizingly as the thing began to feel me more fervently.

You may join me in the eastern garden should it please you. Regardless, I shall reside there momentarily.

The thing made no motion to vacate, and our contact became increasingly uncomfortable as it explored my form, reading my contours like I would devour a novel. I tried to press its hands away, cringing at the calloused texture of its skin. The strength behind those limbs was apparent, but it did not use the full extent of its power—only enough to suggest that I allow it whatever privilege it demanded. Eventually I pushed past its groping paws and thrashing snout, running for the entryway. I lept down the stairs, three at a time, only to find the door locked at the end.

I cried and cried, slamming my fists against the door in agony until they bled onto the carpet. For the first time my thoughts lingered not once to my father; my anguished tears fell only for me and for my sentence to perdition here in the dark heart of the forest. It did not take long for me to collapse, exhausted, amidst the dry heaves and gushing moisture from my eyes.

After what must have been hours I awoke from my near-catatonic state of anguish and shuffled back up the stairs. The thing was still standing with its back to me in the dining hall, lashing the grotesque appendage adorning its head in a whip-like arc. I fled back through the knotted chambers and spires of the palace, fleeing past countless wonders and terrors until I, by some fortune beyond my conscious understanding, found the tower in which I had originally awoken. I collapsed, spent, on the bed supplied for me, covering my face with the soft sheets and forcing myself to fall asleep so as to ward off the demon below.

That night I dreampt fitfully, still feeling the lecherous presence of my captor. The infinite rooms in the manse weighed on me and I felt nothing that night but a despairing terror of my surroundings. I struggled with my conscience, telling myself that this was neither my father's fault nor my own, but the machinations of the devil below. This was not where I wanted to be.

Eventually my dreams subsided and I descended even deeper into the smothering darkness of slumber.

The next morning I awoke blearily, then screamed again as I realized that I had not simply dreamt of my visit to Hell. I rushed down the stairs, frantically running through the palace until I again found the great front gates, still locked. Resignedly, I climbed the stairs to the dining hall, as I had only eaten one meal the day before. A new and more sumptuous feast had been laid before me, yet I barely touched it, broken as I was by the meeting the night before. I suppose that perhaps the size of the meal should have impressed me, as well as its contents, but I was in no shape to admire the cuisine.

As the day wore on I sat in that room, occasionally chewing some of the strange food or sipping the exotic wines in dejection. I had just decided to finally return to my bed, when the thing came again. It stood three chairs down from me, watching. Just like the time before, I did not notice it until it had stood there for some time, appearing as it seemed, like a phantom.

"What do you want!?!" I screamed, terrified.

I want you to love me.

I spat at it in contempt and fled to my room. Nothing in its detestable form gave me reason to feel any adoration for it.

The next day I wandered the palace once more, trying to find some solace in its wonders. To my chagrin I found the libraries still barred from me. Turning from the pursuit of literature, I attempted to visit some of the extravagant gardens. I say attempted, for when I made a motion to enter one, I noticed *it* standing amidst the flowers. This was true each time I tried to visit any of the myriad gardens. Even in the garden of broken glass, where my father had once met the thing, I found my terrible host waiting.

That same night, at dinner, it visited again, this time in a different position at the table. I ate in silence, ignoring its presence.

Do you love me?

I ignored it, surmising that it knew full well my answer.

Do you fear me?

I glared up from my meal, too taken by anger to avert my gaze.

"Of course I fear you! You are nothing but a damned and detestable beast!"

To my surprise, I found myself feeling less terrified than bitter. This thing thought it could mock me—thought it could wear me away with its terrible visage and uncanny presence. Then the fear returned as its grin widened, revealing the moldering flecks adorning its teeth.

Do you know me?

I did not know what it meant by that, but I could feel the marrow in my bones turning to ice as its inhuman voice echoed through the hall. Keeping my eyes firmly affixed to my food, I answered meekly, telling it truthfully that I did not understand it.

The next few weeks progressed much the same—each day with me exploring new wonders of the palace and each night the thing visiting me and entreating my love. Eventually the castle became everything to me and my terror of my new-found home overshadowed my memories of the home I had left. Despite its usurping of my past home, I still despised it; how could I love a place as strange and impossible as this? I fretted constantly, fearing (or perhaps hoping) at every turn that one of the treas-

112

ures herein would suddenly turn deadly. My appearance in the mirrors was drawn and pale, but healthy nonetheless due to the rich diet. Stress had worn on me unduly.

I came to fear my host less and less as time wore on, even losing some of my anger towards it; I saw it then as no more than another tenuous horror of this palatial maze. Our conversations over supper were still rather curt, but once it had asked those first three questions, the answers to which were always the same, it sometimes would ask other questions. It would ask me if I had seen a particular room, or it would ask me about my dreams, my desires, and ultimately my fears. At first these questions frightened me as much as its usual ritual, but with time I learned to answer them, and we were known to hold brief conversations on occasion. Of this I was grateful, as never once did I find another sapient being within those confining walls.

One day, while cautiously exploring my surroundings, I found a great library whose tomes stretched farther than I could fathom. To my surprise I found the door unlocked, and I entered the library and began to explore. The books were unfamiliar to me, as were many of the languages they were transcribed in. I spent hours in there, just gazing at the spines, my thirst for knowledge again revived. As I was finally resolving to find my way out again, I turned a corner and found it standing amongst the shelves, a great ledger in hand.

I approached it and inquired as to the nature of its read, asking it the first question I had ever ventured. It tilted the volume towards me and pointed with its claw.

This book is far older than even I. This passage here might be of especial interest to you.

Written in that aged script was a lengthy passage—a history of sorts. It spoke of the lands around the forest, and of the

113

cities of man. From there it became much more specific, detailing the lives of a small merchant family. With a start I recognized the names of myself, my father, and my sisters, and found a more detailed summary of my person than even I could have provided.

I begged it to explain this trickery. Never once had I told it my name, and never had it asked. Being no stranger to the written word, I also found myself enthralled by the apparent authenticity of the book's age.

There are many things written here which are truths— truths that cannot be learned elsewhere in this world.

driven by my fear, I begged it to show me more, and it agreed. It continued to narrate and guide me, explaining the nature of not only the book, but the library, the palace, the land, very time itself. For days I neither ate nor slept, simply digesting these horrid and majestic truths. It was not long before I had learned more than I felt I could handle and remain sane. I was overjoyed with my newfound breadth of knowledge, yet I was also overwhelmed and exhausted. My mentor sensed this, as in this time we had actually become quite close.

Do you love me?

It had been a very long time since the thing asked this of me, and I did not know how to answer. Eventually I shook my head. It had supplied me with so much, and been so kind despite its fearsome nature, but I did not feel any compassion towards its calloused form.

The thing seemed almost sad—the first emotion I had ever read from its featureless visage.

Do you fear me?

I nodded. The sadness seemed to disappear from its

aura almost immediately. There was still a lingering trace within me of trepidation; despite its compassion and generosity it was still a fiend, and terrible to behold. Beyond its appearance, I found its wealth of knowledge imposing, and I knew I had only learned but a piece of it.

Do you know me?

I shook my head. I still found myself far from understanding what it was or why it existed. I wondered often, but never once did I find myself even close to comprehension.

You may still come to love me, but I have taught you all that I can at this point. Now you must teach yourself. You may leave whenever you are ready. Simply put on this ring.

It handed me a carved leaden ring, engraved with countless intertwining faces, which I had never before noticed that it wore.

Should you ever wish to return, simply leave this ring on your bedside table.

Speechless, I took the ring. I gazed at it in confusion and something approaching sadness—I had come to feel comfort in the constant terror of this otherworldly prison, and was not certain that I wished to leave it. When I looked up, my instructor was gone.

It did not appear for the next few days, and I was surprised to find myself fretting as to it's well-being. I scolded myself and told myself that now I had a means to go home, yet still I lingered. It was another month yet before I finally donned the ring.

I awoke momentarily in my bedroom in my father's mansion. A rush of joyful feelings flowed over me, as I remembered fondly my feelings for my original home here amongst the rational. I rang the bell next to my bed, and a maid entered, screaming and falling into a feint at the sight of me. Barely feeling any sympathy for her after my lengthy alienation from human company, it took me a moment to gather myself and come to her side. She came to and stuttered out a deference, begging my forgiveness.

"I wish to see my father," I told the poor woman, helping her to her feet.

She stammered to me for a few moments before finally answering with simply, "M'lord's been dead some time now, Miss." She looked at me caringly, finally coming to her senses. "I'm so terribly sorry."

In shock I sat upon the bed, staring blankly for a time at the polished floorboards at my feet.

"And of my sisters?"

"Oh! They are still here Miss! Shall I fetch them?"

I nodded dourly and waited a while in thought.

Upon reuniting with my sisters I found that I had been gone nigh on three years. In my absence my father had drunken himself to death and my uncle had taken over management of the household. I was saddened by the loss of my father, but I managed to lift my spirits slightly with the idea that perhaps I could impart some of my new-found knowledge unto my siblings. I tried to tell them my tale, but they would have none of it, scolding me for trying to frighten them with outlandish stories and blowing off my insight into the world as so many fairy tales. My conversations with my uncle fared no better, and I soon learned to detest those that I lived with.

My family's minds were simple and their interests worldly. They had no interest in knowledge, and would not face their fears that perhaps their understanding of the world was wrong. One cannot evolve if they do not accept that there are greater truths than those taught from the lectern of a priest or common scholar.

Word of my return was quickly overshadowed by the rumors of my malevolent demeanor. The horde of suitors which at first appeared swiftly dwindled. I soon suspended myself from leaving the manour, as I found the people of the city too disgusting to bear. Not one person with which I had spoken had accepted my gifts of knowledge, and most had shunned them outright as blasphemy or madness. There were some who said I was a witch, and others who called me insane, as they believed my papa to have been at the end.

Barely two months after I returned I left the ring on my bedside table, awakening to the low hum and dull heat of the castle. Ecstatic at the prospect of once again speaking with someone as open-minded and willing to embrace learning as I, I rushed down the stairs, calling out for my host—calling to it by dark names which I knew not whence I had learned. Eventually I found it, in the garden of broken glass, feasting upon a lowly woodcutter and his family. At first I was disgusted by the carnage before me, but then I saw the irrelevancy of my feelings—why should I fear for them? They were already dead, and it was surely a fate the imbecilic countrymen deserved. For a moment I was offended by my own callous rationale, but this too I realized was a simple-minded crutch; I could not hider myself with caring for those who would not traverse the dark alley-ways of discovery as I had begun to.

It glanced up from its meal and greeted me simply. It knew I was there, and I it. I stood in appreciative silence as it finished its gruesome deed, feeling as I did much like a student observing the strange and unknowable ways of the adult world.

When all was finished I took its hand and we returned to the dining hall. It watched me as we feasted, sometimes coming near and stroking me—exploring again the human form. I did not mind—even reveling in the foul arousal which it brought me. I told it of the idiots who populated the land and of my contempt for all that did not relate themselves to its truths. I laughed as I fed, marveling at my lost naivete; this was where I wanted to be.

When I had finished it told me of its prey, saying only,

They feared me, but they would not know nor love me.

I offered my agreement, caressing its foul skin and gently planting kisses. It asked me if I should want to learn more, and it asked me if I loved it. I laughed louder than I have ever laughed before or since.

"Yes! Yes! I love you! And I shall only love you all the more if you should continue to teach me!"

And with that it took me. Amidst the beauteous rising chorus of chaos from the music room I had encountered when I had first arrived we intertwined. A carnal dance, so alien to any experience I had ever had, yet so familiar as to bring me closer to my mentor than I had sometimes even felt to myself. It was impossible, this intercourse, to be had with any other being, and it was equally impossible to copulate with the demon in any earthly way. In this first taste of eternity I celebrated and bayed with joy.

After we had expended ourselves we retired to one of the magnificent locked libraries I had found before. It stood aside and allowed me to open it myself, and as the tumblers turned I felt a rush of adrenaline as the knowledge within pressed at me to obtain it. In the pages of those studies I learned more about my host, and of its brethren. It appears that this was not the lost prince of long ago, but the demon who had come to the prince's party. And it was not any fallen angel named in any sacred text, but something far more terrible, and more beautiful. For it is not my host's duty to field the sins of man—although it occasionally does fill that role. No, my host instead finds greater pleasure in plumbing the minds of men for their greatest secrets, and bringing them to light—feeding them to the roiling chaos at the center of existence.

In the endless times that have followed I have learned to appreciate its beauty even more—I would not love it so were it not as perfect as it was. The physical form is not what is so appealing in this creature, but the knowledge that it guards. It is all that is wrong with the world, and all that is beautiful, and for that it must be known and loved, for without love its existence would indeed be dark. I do not why it chose me over my father, but I am glad. My adoration has destroyed me, but brought me so much closer to perfection. Truly bestial are we that deny his beauteous chaos.

A City Man

ive hundred federal notes.

Bring him back to Chancellor for five hundred notes, six if alive. Dead or alive, he was coming back to Chancellor.

Ernest Boragne was focused. Utterly focused. As the train rattled along its tracks through the dusty badlands beyond civilization he repeated his quarry's price again and again. Five hundred notes, six if alive.

There was another passenger in the car. A fat old fellow with a bowler cap and a frayed suit. He had fallen asleep with the latest issue of the *Chancellor Post* across his face, and the thin pages fluttered as he snored. The passenger had already been asleep when Boragne boarded, and he had no intention of waking him. The dust on his shins made clear that he was one of the fools hoping to make a fortune in the west. Boragne knew how good it was to live in the city where it was clean and you didn't have to break the law just to get by—he had never felt the urge to leave it behind for fantasies of new frontiers.

Boragne was gaunt and his black hair, slicked back into a sharp peak, had begun to whiten at the roots. He bore a few days' shadow on his cheeks and was dressed in a crisp grey suit, complete with new bow tie and long jacket. His bowler cap sat on his lap with his fingers laced over it as his brown eyes stared at the sleeping figure and through him, unfocused on the world. Focused only on his thoughts.

Five hundred federal notes.

She had said it wasn't enough. Six if alive, he had re-minded her. But it wasn't enough. She said he should be done with this life. But where would she be without his money? Where would she be if he didn't take these contracts?

The train rattled and creaked as it pulled into another dead-end stop. Out here the towns were little more than the stations themselves. No brick buildings. No industry. No cul-ture. Just wooden fronts behind which were bars and bordellos and bally poor moneylenders. The frontier was for dreamers and the doomed. Boragne reached into his pocket and checked the time. His watch was silver and embossed with small flowers. She had given it to him for his fortieth birthday, just after his fa-ther had died.

With a snort the paper slid off the other passengers' face as he sat up, listening to the whistle blow. He rubbed his piggy eyes and brushed out his thick grey mustache. He looked to be older than Boragne by at least ten years.

"My apologies. I suppose I was a tad more tired than I assumed. I didn't notice you board. I'm er... Name's Todd. Benjamin Todd."

"Pleasure to meet you, Mr. Todd." But Boragne did not look at all pleased. "I am Ernest Boragne. I boarded at St. Amon. I transferred from the J. L. Montegue line out of Chan-cellor."

"A Chancellor man? My, my. We don't get many city boys out this far West. What line of work're you in? Me, I'm in investments."

Investments. Most likely he was in land, selling dry plots to prospectors with promises of silver and gold. Boragne was not a boy, nor did he like the sound of this man's palaver. "I'm with the Acquisitions Union." He looked out the window, willing Mr. Todd to cease his prattling.

"A Functional? Well, isn't that exciting!" He leaned forward, but only so far, since his great gut quickly got in the way, straining the buttons of his cream-coloured shirt. "Tell me, you hunting some great villain? Some fugitive fled from the pen? Anyone I know? Was it in the papers."

Boragne was done answering the investments man. Aye, he was a *Functional* as the common folk called him, though *she* didn't like it. Pursuing wanted men across provincial boundaries where the federal marshals could not go. Each contract paying his way to the next.

Five hundred federal notes, six if alive.

She was worried about his health. Five men in his family dead by fifty of Rugor's Dementia. What few years he had left he should spend at home. He was fine, he had told her. Always told her. The last time she had said it he had hit her so hard she cut her lip on the counter before he left for the station.

He had forgotten his contract and the neighbor had caught him just in time.

But he hadn't forgotten his gun.

He had heard that it got cold at night out in the desert, but by the days you wouldn't know it. He was glad to leave Mr. Todd when he disembarked at Gilestown, but he had feigned regret. It was important to be polite. He scowled as he noted the dust already forming on the ends of his coat. Boragne had no bag and so left the train to find the local constable. As he walked the bare, un-paved street he thumbed at the small writing pad he kept. His leather gloves shielded him from the filth. This was the last place where there had been word of his quarry, sent by a federal auditor named Wiles who remembered the villain's face from the *Post*. The Functional had to work quickly if he wanted to net the payment before a public bounty was posted.

How much would they offer? Two hundred? Three? Certainly not five, six if alive.

A low roof, crooked and buckling, topped the jailhouse. Silhouetted by the afternoon sun, a lone vulture cawed from the rooftop. A wizened old man in an impractically wide-brimmed hat sat in a rocking chair beside the door. His skin was as grey as the uniform he wore, and a tarnished brass star was pinned to his breast.

Boragne stepped forward and tipped the brim of his own cap. He introduced himself and held out his contract, which the man squinted briefly at before dismissing it. "You are the constable, are you not?"

Nodding, he answered, "Name's Ames."

The Functional told the lawman the name of his quarry. Ames said he had seen him when he came through town, but he had caused no trouble. Boragne tipped his hat and thanked the constable, turning to leave, but turned back and asked in what direction the man had traveled.

"I just told ye he took a coach toward Millings. 'Bout four days ago." Constable Ames eyed the visitor strangely and spit. Boragne scowled and went on to hire a horse. It cost him thirty federal notes.

The last contractor had followed the quarry to Vincent's Wake, on the edge of Pendleton Province, where the criminal had killed two farmers. He hadn't had time to do to them what he did in Denbridge or Lossen. Or what he had done in that northern Chancellor burg.

Horrible.

Five hundred federal notes worth of horrible, six if alive.

The horse he'd hired was sturdy and spotted. The stableman said its name was Nod. A local guide had offered to accompany him for five notes, and he had given him three. Three notes was enough money for the Dovanri wanderer.

But five hundred wasn't enough for her, six if alive.

Valio—that was the guide—said that Millings was only two hours' ride from Gilestown, or four by road, since the road followed the cliffs. They would take the shorter ride, to beat the bounty. T o save time. *She* didn't think he had much left.

They set out across dry bluffs between Gilestown and Millings, the rocky ground and Nod's gait doing no favours to Boragne's rear. He did not even remember how long he had been in the business, but he had never taken a liking to horses. He would much rather chase his quarry through cobbled streets than in the dry open air of the counties, but five hundred notes was nothing to scoff at. Unless you were her.

He had loved her once. Hadn't he? She must have looked so beautiful in her youth. But now she was old like him. Her skin had begun to sag and her hair had lost its luster. She worried too much, ragging and moaning about the cost of the doctor one moment and begging him to retire the next. She didn't understand. If he wasn't there to catch degenerates like this, who would? And if he wasn't there to collect the five hundred federal notes, six if alive, who would?

They did not ride hard, for the sun was still high and they were saving time by avoiding the road. Valio, his scarf bright about his neck despite the dust that coated him, offered some dried meat and pickled greens, but they were spiced and Boragne knew after one bite that they would upset his aging gut—he was nearly as old as his father had been when he died. He would eat after Millings. The Dovanri spoke for much of the ride, telling stories and watching the clouds. The Functional did not care for Valio's anecdotes of ghosts and friendly thieves, but he remained largely silent.

Entering Millings, Boragne growled low in his throat. If he had not seen the sign outside of town he may have mistaken it for the town they had just left. The same cheap flaky-painted boards and flat roofs greeted him, and the same wan faces, dried out by the sun. The same bally bordello and the same bally general store. His toes curled at the thought of the dreary lives the men and women of this town must lead. Nothing to do but stare at the dust and muse about when they were going to strike big.

They tied their horses before the tavern where, through the batwing doors creaking slightly in the wind, could be seen an empty common room save for one lone drunk and a sad piano player. The untuned piano played the same old song every piano played out here in the west, much too jaunty for the dreary deserts and sandy bluffs and full of wrong notes and clanging keys. The guide went to join the drunk, hand already gripping the notes just given him, and Boragne left him to find the constable.

Opening his pad again he scanned his written notes from the last lawman, but he was distracted by the heat and had to stop and read them again. Two times he read them before his eyes focused and his mind settled. She would have panicked and told him it was the Dementia, but it was only the sun.

Constable Myers was younger and talked more than Constable Ames, but the roof of the jail still needed work, and there were still a few crows hanging about, just like before. This time the lawman took the contract and read it thoroughly, being certain of the crimes contained.

"Horrible," he muttered.

"Horrible," Boragne agreed.

Myers asked what the man looked like, and when Boragne described him the lawman swore – the uncultured dog. There was no need for that type of talk. The man had come and bought supplies at the store in town. Supplies for cooking and camping and prospecting. Prospecting wasn't good around Millings, but he wouldn't listen, so they had pointed him in the direction of the small mine north of town, abandoned two years previous by the Mint & Denning Mining Company. There were families up there. Women and children of other hopefuls who refused to believe the mine wasn't worth the effort.

"Help them," begged the constable.

"Aye, no harm will come to them if I can help it."

Before he could leave the man stopped him with a hand on his arm. The hand was layered in dust. "Have you ever seen a heat storm, Mr. Boragne? Oh, well be careful then. We get them around this time of year, 'specially up in them hills. Lighting struck one of the miner's hutches last year. Burned all night. Damn hot too. Fierce as a spooked nag and strange as Hell."

"Mind your tongue around me, Constable."

He could bear this awful place for five hundred notes, but he would not be party to profanity. She was good about that. She never swore, even when he forgot to come home at night.

Valio did not want to go further without more notes, and he

would not allow himself to be underbid again. Three more notes to travel to the M&D mine. The drunk had been called Isaac and the pianist Boris.

"It's too rocky for the horses, Mr. Boragne. I know these hills. We must walk, so sorry."

It was not so far to the mine, and Boragne angrily regretted paying Valio for work he could have done himself; a rusted iron scaffold was visible above the hills from just outside of town, and they merely followed it until the sun began to set. The mine at first looked to be set within some low hills, but as the two crested these the Functional saw that M&D had built a pit mine here. So much money wasted on land dry of minerals. Camps were visible dotting the floor of the mine, even in the setting sun. Some featured cheap shacks and careful workstations to siphon the loam. Others featured a tent and a sieve, and sometimes just a bedroll with a shovel and a waterjug. On the far side was a black mark where Valio said the lightning had struck as Cosntable Myers had said, but a new hovel was already built over the ruins of the old. If life in Millings and Gilestown was sparse this life was as near to true misery as Boragne had yet seen. He mumbled a prayer to Saint Lorraine for steadfastness in his quest and absently thumbed the hilt of his sixgun, bright and unblemished inside his long coat. The chamber under the hammer was empty to avoid accident. His suit was ruined and it had been barely a day. Filthy and wind-scarred. But he could buy a new one once he was paid.

Stumbling down the rocky side of the mine, they eventually found solid footing near the edge of a greying hut which sloped dangerously to one side. Valio had wrapped his bright scarf around his face and so was not beset by the same fit of coughing that betook his employer. The door to the hovel slammed loudly open on the other side and a balding man with a white beard came cautiously around the corner, long gun in hand.

"Who're you? What're you doin' 'ere? This's my claim. Get yer city boots off my tract. Oy! Dovy! Hands where I can see 'em!"

But Boragne's contract was enough to assuage the man's fears, though he still would not lower his weapon from the guide.

He and his brothers manned this plot—two whole acres— and had since the mine closed. They had been employed there, but now the Nolan brothers were operating on their own. They had made twenty-three notes selling gold in those two years, but they knew a big break was coming; no-one else had found any-thing yet, which meant their plot had the greatest chance of scor-ing. At least according to them.

Boragne was once more glad of the few hundred notes he would make, more if his quarry lived.

Herb, the Nolan who had greeted them with his rifle, told them that his brothers were sleeping. He would not have invited them, "in in any case," he assured them, just so they were clear where they stood with him. He knew the man they sought and had seen him working another plot.

"Those damned Emersons down on the east side."

"Watch your language, Mr. Nolan."

Herb Nolan made a face and spit.

Traveling to the eastern side they had easily found the Emerson plot. Not one, but two shacks stood here, both sturdi-er than the Nolans' and freshly painted in a bright shade of blue. As the light died men were leaving their sieves and shovels and brushes and picks where they lay and gathering about a fire. A few brief questions confirmed that the Emersons hired plenty of labour—they were rich and barely visited the site themselves.

"But isn't the gold gone?" asked Valio.

"We ain't diggin' gold 'ere," answered Mitch, one of the workers, his face stained, "We're mining coal. Some o' the other plots 'ave caught on as well."

"Is there a Mr. Emerson here?"

"No sir, Mr. Functional, sir."

He asked them if they knew a man who matched the description in his contract, and they all nodded aye. He could see by their eyes that he was not well liked. Unsurprising, for a man so soulless so as to do such awful things to his own family. And the victims in Denbridge and Lossen, to say nothing of the farmers he had slain near Vincent's Wake.

She had wanted a family. Or he had. It all got muddled after she started worrying over his health. He forgot so many things in his anger with her. Why wouldn't she believe him when he told her he wasn't losing his mind? There was no mania to dull his senses. No fugue to prevent him earning a few hundred notes, more if he did well.

They asked if the man had a bounty yet and eyed him evilly when he told them no. Boragne resolved then to hurry in case they disbelieved him and made to apprehend or kill his prey before he could find him. The quarry had beaten a man named Jules yesterday morning and been forced out by the foreman. Foreman Walsh said he thought he'd seen the fugitive working with some small camp on the north lip, but he wasn't certain.

"I knew there wasn't no good in that man."

"Why didn't you go to Constable Myers?" But the look Walsh gave him told him that to them Myers was of the same world as Boragne, and that world and theirs did not mix.

At least they were agreed.

It was very warm and the labourers mused that a storm might be coming.

"The heat will drop with sunset, and then it'll pick right back up and burn like whistlin'."

"There's no protection if the lightning comes for you," chirped Valio.

"None save prayer."

Boragne nodded at the man who had spoken. Prayer was always safe, even if you didn't remember all of the words.

As they walked to the lip of the mine Valio chewed absently on his rations. All the men here were grimy and caked in dirt, and what few women and children he saw seemed even worse. None of them appeared to have ever bathed and their breaths all stank of alcohol. Boragne did not drink. He used to, but the doctor had told him that he needed to quit. At least that was what she said, but he couldn't clearly remember what the doctor had said to him. She worried when he said that. But no one listens to doctors. Not closely.

"Why are you still with me, Mr. Valio? You're job is done and I am paying you no more."

"I'll leave soon enough, Mr. Boragne, but I don't intend to head back tonight and I would appreciate the chance to see a Functional arrest such a vile criminal. You did not tell me before how deplorable his deeds were."

An arrest. Or a gunfight. It was a few hundred federal

notes one way, and more the other. Either way it was good money.

At the northern ridge they found a half dozen camps, but the first they came to was empty. The coals of the fire were cold, and in the dusk Boragne could not see a trail. He led Valio to the next tent, luckily finding the man awake, but he had not seen those campers for much of the day. They visited another plot and a jolly man named Lon said he didn't know them. At the following camp the man looked confused and said he had not seen them for much of the day.

Valio eyed his employer strangely. "Do you not remember Benny, Mr. Boragne? It can't have been ten minutes."

Of course he remembered Benny, he had merely needed to make certain. One can never be too careful when such a violent man is concerned. In Denbridge their intestines had been entirely removed and their ribs splayed so the heart and lungs could be taken. At Lossen all that was left were the bones and the blood. Sometimes Boragne thought she was as frightened by the things he must see, the people he must catch, as by the imagined Dementia she cried over and berated him about. He had never felt an inclination to be violent with her before her paranoia about his health.

Finally they visited a tent where a man named Casper told them through his muskrat whiskers that they had left for the deeper hills with their new hired hand around noon. He had expected them back, for they had left their tent. There were two of them—a father and son both named John. Casper pointed them toward a bluish plateau some ways distant. There was supposed to be silver there, but the natives talked of spirits, so he had never gone. These country folk were superstitious and foolish. But he thanked the prospector and let him return to his beans, which he had offered and been denied. Boragne's stomach rumbled. He had forgotten to eat in town. But beans in brown sugar was not a decent meal and he had no intention of facing his quarry with the upset a meal of beans would cause him. He would eat later that night. Or tomorrow.

More walking. His boots were sturdy, but they were scuffed now. They were not the garish high boots the men wore out west here, but sensible boots. Boots you should pay to have shined. His spurs jangled in the dust. He hated spurs, but he had known he may be riding and the horses in these parts were likely to be green. The horses would have been useful now.

Valio had returned to his talk of ghosts and desperadoes and promiscuous farmers' wives. Nonsense. But it was better than the silence of the desert. Barely. Boragne walked in silence as the sun set and the temperature fell.

One tale did manage to catch his attention however and he asked the Dovanri to begin it again. The wanderer's dark eyes lit up and he began once more. Telling of the Wendigo and its hunger for flesh. A spirit walking in the form of a man, but the man would not know those he loved and they would not know him. Like a wild dog it would begin with those for whom its heart had once beat strongest, and with each life it took it would become less human and more predator. Hunting and killing. Killing and eating. Eating and eating. Eating until there was nothing left of it but the haunt within the man and it could stand no longer in the world. But the Wendigoag could stay in this world for centuries before their tastes pulled them else.

Boragne shuddered despite himself. Shuddered at the cold.

"Where did you hear of this, Mr. Valio?"

132

"From a Peruwac hunter in Gaff County. He said that his uncle had become Wendigo and slain their entire village. He had only survived, Mr. Boragne, by reasoning with the last of the humanity in the Wendigo. He offered to show me the site of his village, but I declined. I have never met a Peruwac hunting alone before or since." His eyes were still bright with the tale, but he looked strangely frightened as well. "His face was long and grey, and his nose flat. He was young, but his cheeks hung low and his ears were long on the top. Never have I seen so strange a man, Mr. Boragne."

"Many Peruwac are ugly." The childish fear Boragne had felt was gone. "It was a good legend, but the theatrics at the end weakened the telling. Next time leave them off, Mr. Valio."

He was glad that Valio did not voice the same thought that had come to him at the telling of the story. Had Valio chosen that myth on purpose?

It was cold but Borgane had worn layers. His hand sat restlessly on his sixgun as they neared the earthen monolith.

Towering into the young night sky, the wall of the plateau was not as sheer as it looked from afar, and craggy paths spiraled up its sides. Not as sheer, but taller still than it had ever looked from afar. It was hot. Had it been so hot on the walk from the pit?

Boragne stopped to gaze dumbly at the stars twinkling dimly in the inky blue sky. Something rumbled in the distance. That sky and those stars. If those could be seen in Chancellor he perhaps would spend more time out at night. Nights spent out on purpose. Not wandering because he had not thought to go home. Would she still worry then? Of course she would. She was paranoid. So paranoid she could not even see how good it would be to be paid the notes for this contract.

Dead or alive, some hundred credits in his hands.

"Mr. Boragne," the Dovanri called. By the starlight Boragne could make out a dark stain, which Valio was touching gingerly. They should have brought a lantern, but it had not occurred to them as they left. "Had we brought a lantern as I suggested we could see more clearly, so sorry to bring it up again, but I think this is blood. It is cold and dry, but the sun has not yet bleached it away." The Functional did not need to be told that it was blood, nor that it was from today. He glared at the back of the Dovanri's soft cap. Valio turned his head to meet his eye. "I am not a fighter, Mr. Boragne, and I do not wish to die. I will wait for you here."

"You come all this way just to leave now?" Boragne was incensed, despite the usual lonely manner of his profession.

The guide shrank back, his hands raised. "I do not wish to die, so sorry. I will wait here and call for you if there is danger. Call like an owl. I know many sounds, Mr. Boragne."

Red-faced and sputtering, the Functional looked up past the brim of his cap at the stony tower above him. "Do you at least have a gun to defend yourself?"

"No, Mr. Boragne, only my knife."

Bats flapped about the path as Boragne struggled up it alone. He must have knocked a stone loose or made some terrible sound to disturb them so. That would make it much harder to surprise his prey. One of the foul things had even shit on his new coat. It was ruined now. But he would buy a new one with the bounty. It was so hot, but he refused remove his coat. He didn't want to lose it.

Why didn't she want the money?

He took care of her, and he made good money hunting fugitives. She was ungrateful. She didn't care. This was his life. When he returned home he would tell her how things would be. She wouldn't berate him for his choices. She wouldn't complain about his late nights or when he was absent-minded because his work had been tiring. It was for her, and she didn't understand.

A few hundred credits to kill a cannibal.

He could do that.

Halfway up the slope he found two canvas shoulder bags and a pile of tools. Sieves and shovels and brushes and picks. The bags were stained black. Blood. He had thought he would find blood. He had known it, somehow. The blood trailed up the path, toward the summit. Drawing his sixgun, he spun the cylinder so the empty chamber was no longer under the hammer. There was no moon, but the stars glinted silver off his holy arm, and he muttered a half-remembered prayer as he began stalking up the path.

Along the sides of the cliff were old native drawings. He passed a trio of old huts built into the hill, made of dark stone or clay. Lines and swirls and incomprehensible scribblings—his eyes came unfocused when he looked upon them. But he was not here to look at history. Sweat beaded on his brow. He stopped and angrily scrubbed at the stone with his sleeve, but the writing would not be undone. Somewhere a coyote howled and he barked back at it, wordlessly.

Thunder shook the sky and a flash of lighting followed swiftly after. Stepping back, he blinked and looked at the wall, then down at his frayed jacket. It was ruined. He would have to find a way to pay for a new one. But now he had to kill the cannibal.

Weapon in hand and shoulders hunched, he resumed his cautious stalk up the hillside, his spurs rattling like snakes with each step. Closer and closer. Thunder rumbling. Lightning burning the distant dust. Closer. Soon he could see the crest, the starlight and the lightning ricocheting off it so it seemed to glow and flash in the dimness. As he neared the top he could hear a noise. A humming. Or a whistling. Some small noise among the crashing of the storm.

"I'm coming home, Helen."

The top of the plateau was smooth and black, darker than the stony paths below. Tall stones stood or lay scattered about and the stars were mirrored in them darkly. The heat trapped itself in the stones and filled the peak with choking warmth. The humming was greater here and he cautiously set one food forward, afraid for a moment he would somehow trip and fall into Hell. But his boot met dark sand and he continued on. The storm split the sky and rumbled like deep laughter. He looked about, watching for movement. A part of him sang out to look back, for he could surely see the lights of his home from here. But he must be vigilant.

He nearly fell over the corpse. Looking down, he paused. His gaze lingered for a long moment at the face of the boy illuminated in the crashing lightning, his dead jaw frozen open in fear. Did he know this boy? Where would they have met? The boy's stomach was open, and his ribs cracked. His insides were gone—nowhere to be seen—and bestial toothmarks were visible along his arms and near his groin. Black blood pooled thickly in his open throat and the cavity of his chest. Boragne began to hum along to the unearthly tune.

He called the cannibal's name and fired off a shot at a fleeting shadow, then two more as he spun, unsure. Bats flew up in clouds then, spiraled back to their routines. The coyote howled and Boragne barked back.

Pacing between the stones, he soon found another staring death in the storm. This man was much the same as the boy, but his fingers too were gnawed and his wound reached deep between his thighs, empty. Boragne wondered if lightning could do such damage. He stood above the corpse and stared at it and through it, unfocused on the world. Focused only on his thoughts. What had he forgotten? He hummed to help himself remember. Why was he here? Where was here? He felt his fingers loosening on his sixgun as he realized the humming had stopped and he gripped it tightly, spinning and firing again.

The bullet skimmed one of the black rocks near to his face as the storm crackled and dust flew into his eyes. The Functional cried out and swore, pawing at his face, his gun still gripped firmly in one gloved hand. His eyes ached with the rock dust and stung at his eyelids. The gloves he wore were too bulky and he threw them to the ground, gasping as he blinked in agony.

There was a shape above him and it offered him water. Thankfully he rinsed his eyes with the canteen, blinking until he could see. See the cannibal before him. He raised his gun, but the fugitive lifted a blackened hand and warned him, "You don't know what else is out here. Shhh..."

He lowered his weapon and nodded. He did not want to attract anything dangerous. He was from the city and did not know what dangers this mesa could hold. The man looked different than the photograph he had seen in Chancellor. It had been an old photo. People change. This man had less hair, and it hung in straggling strands. He had jowls and a flat nose and his ears drooped, almost to points. And his teeth. Long teeth with small gums. Sharp teeth. Sunken eyes. And he hummed. That was the humming. It was the man with the water.

"I am supposed to find you. My name is Ernest Boragne."

"Aye, that seems right." He eyed Boragne and his black orbs reflected red in the lightning. "Tell me, Mr. Boragne, are you ill?"

Boragne nodded. What was he doing here? "I think I'm dying."

"That is too bad, Mr. Boragne. Come, sit." He followed the man to a small fire and sat beside it. He loosened his collar and slid out of his jacket, dripping with sweat. A rich smell came from a skillet resting on the coals. It seemed hot enough to cook without a fire. "What are you dying of?" His voice was low and guttural, but he spoke so well. Like a city man.

"Rugor's Dementia." That was right, wasn't it? "I forget things." He took the plate he was offered gratefully. He did not remember the last time he had eaten.

"What sorts of things?"

He could feel the slow tears on his face, cold in the heat. What didn't he remember? His gun was still firmly in his grip and his finger twitched on the trigger, the metal burning on his skin. "Everything."

"Do you want a fork, Mr. Boragne?" He nodded and thanked his friend as one was set on his plate. Friend? No, he didn't know this man.

"You don't have to die, Mr. Boragne."

"I don't?" He could not grab the fork because he was holding his sixgun. It glittered in the starlight, then flashed in the lightning.

"No." The man was eating and drooling, his long face canine in the ghoulish flickering of the flames. "All you have to do is eat."

Boragne's mouth watered as he looked upon the meat, pooling in ripe juice, and his finger twitched on the trigger.

At Eternity's Gate

or the first time in millenia it is my birthday. That's the problem with time travel; besides the fact that you can't really build meaningful relationships or ever settle down. I have no idea how old I am. Looking at myself in the mirror when I wake, I sigh. There is a streak of grey through my beard and up through my hair; perhaps I'm approaching sixty, or maybe I'm still nearly thirty but the strain of my adventures has worn on me (which it has).

Shoving the down comforter aside, I briefly glance at the naked form beside me. My head hurts. I don't remember her; she's just another in a long list of women. As I stand in front of the mirror, naked and bleary, I run my thumb and forefinger along the scar down my chest and try to remember how I got it; time travel does things to your memory—makes you forget.

I walk across the studio apartment to the kitchenette and open the freezer, the fridge, the cupboard—does bacon need to be refrigerated? I have no idea. I settle for cereal with milk, but the milk is sour. No, not sour, goat. I hate goat milk. I hate goats.

I hear a slight moan from the bed; she's waking up.

How old *am* I? I was born in the twenty-third century—no, scratch that, I was born in the year 1200 AD in the town of... Fuck; I really am a mess.

The girl is awake. I smile at her and try to remember her name. I fail to recall even what names are appropriate to my current environment, and motion to the cereal. It's okay—I think she's more hungover than I am. The tension across the table is awkward, her hunched over her cereal, unnoticing, and me gazing at her as I try to remember where I am.

Her name is Artemis. She works for the Ministry of Artistic Expression. I tell her I lost my license in the war. She seems to understand, and agrees to pilot me to the registration office for a new one. I'm very careful not to say *what* war it is I lost my license in, as I don't have a clue.

She really is quite beautiful. As we glide through the atmospheric metropolis of New Brunswick, I can barely keep my attention off of her. I brush her hair out of her eyes and she giggles in surprise.

She's nervous. I was unusual for her. My heart drops as I realize she was hoping I was a dream. She doesn't want me to stay. I could stay anyway; I'm comfortable in my charisma, but I don't feel like manipulating someone like that. Not today. Not on my birthday.

At the office I kiss her on the cheek and bid her farewell. She is surprised. Damnit! She doesn't want me to be there but she didn't expect me to leave. How do I read this? How do I let her go?

I chuckle and assure her I'll see her tonight. She smiles, but her emotions are still confused. I tell her I'll take the tram back.

I won't take the tram back.

Wandering into the office, I have no papers and no plan, and I'm fairly certain my clothes are at least a century out of date, but I continue on. I always make it a point to pick up a license.

If there is one thing I am especially good at thanks to my travels it is lying. I lie well. I lied myself onto a throne once—although I'll admit that wasn't the best plan; I knew I'd be leaving inside of a week.

I've tried to examine my travels, but I can never remember whether I'm forced to leave, or whether I choose. I know how I leave, just not why. Sure, sometimes I'm being hunted, or got too deep into politics (or once or twice I contracted a disease incurable in the current day), but sometimes I'm perfectly happy. I rub my hand over the ridge in the back of my neck as I talk to the licensing officer. I don't even know what I'm saying. I'm too preoccupied with my own brand of problems. Sometimes I'm the hero, sometimes the villain, sometimes the victim, and sometimes not even part of the story at all. But whatever the case, I'm tenacious in my endurance.

They take my prints. *We'll have your license momentarily, Mr. Balthus*, they say. I must have been here before—I'm in the computer, but the name is a lie. I chuckle silently.

I take my license and exit the office. I walk to the curb, intending to leap down to the next platform and set off into the city, but Artemis is waiting for me. It is my turn to be surprised.

She tells me she got off work early, obviously forgetting that she told me this morning that today was her day off. She is nervous, unsure—she hasn't decided what to do. I suppose I'll stay for a while; it *is* my birthday after all.

Sometimes I pretend I'm mad. I pretend I'm sitting in a madhouse. When I do this I visit psychologists. I pretend they are all the same person and that I am simply imagining different forms for them.

I tell the doctors everything, crying and making myself appear weak. The doctors stroke their beard and ask me questions. I answer with half-truths, lies, and full-truths. The doctors write reports and adjust their glasses. Sometimes I laugh and make their bald head sweat. Sometimes I try to convince them of the truth, and they nervously play with their ponytail or stroke their hairless chin in interest. They tell me to come back next week on some day ending in Y. I tell them I will come back so that they can help me.

But I never come back.

If I wasn't drifting down through the levels of New Brunswick I'd probably be talking to the doctors—it amuses me. As it is, I sit next to Artemis and watch the city float by. She glances at me throughout the ride. I can feel her unease.

My perception of time is warped. As I look at my felt overcoat and my white lace shirt, I consider the possibility that perhaps my clothing is more outdated than I had first surmised. I ask Artemis to stop at a clothier's. She looks at me, confused. I stumble and rephrase my question. She nods and takes a left.

The store is large and all of the checkouts are automated. I have a card. Everyone pays with cards these days. The only difference between my card and everyone else's is that mine never runs out of money. I put off using counterfeit currency for a very long time, but eventually I realized how necessary it was to someone in my position; there's no way in Hell I could hold down a job. I buy some clothes and, with Artemis's permission, change in the back seat. When we return to the apartment I burn my old clothes in the disposal—I don't need them and I can always get new clothes.

Later that night I ask her about her life. She's a nice girl with a nice life. Now, by nice I don't mean she doesn't have

143

problems, I just mean that her life has no violence, very little instability, and no time travel. She was engaged, but her lover fled. That was two years ago. I have been the first man in her life since then. She says I look familiar. I know why; people often tell me I look like a famous painter. He committed suicide and painted a lot of flowers. I'm not big on the art world. I know that I am the worst man to be her salvation, but I let her kiss me.

That night she cries. I feel as if I should be more compassionate, but I know that on the outside I appear the epitome of caring; I am a very good liar. While she sleeps I ponder; I should leave right now. I'm no longer human—I am a parody, a satire, a mockery. I have too little feeling to be human. I decide to stay with her. I will pretend to be human and pretend that I am not something less. To live one's life consecutively is a blessing.

As my birthday ends, I drift into sleep. I know I am a monster, but as long as everyone's having fun, what's the harm?

I live with Artemis for a year. She was happy, but I think she sensed my distance. I hope she finds a good man. I fake my death—a shooting. I pay the man well. Then I visit the doctors.

I am in a very devilish mood today. I walk into their office and am led to the chair. The doctors give me their usual spiel and I respond like a madman. I have learned nothing in my travels but callousness. I hesitate in my story and consider returning to Artemis. I am somewhere else.

Literally.

I wander under the stone arch, the bustle of the market following me. I do this sometimes, revisit my past lives. Mind you, I don't talk to them, but I like to see myself from a different point of view. I am a king. A bad king. I can see the gallows, full of carrion, and the sewers, full of shit. I'm an asshole. Maybe I should see a doctor. For real. I might be depressed. From what I understand it's not healthy to focus on one's defects. I can see myself being carried on a throne over the crowd.

I leave.

I have a hard time remembering who's famous, I once quoted a very intelligent man named Geoffrey Hudson and was met with no recognition then, when I attempted to plagiarize the wordage of an acquaintance in conversation I was complemented on my knowledge of Twain. That wasn't his name.

A bank hired me some time ago and I have worked as a teller since then. The pure quantity of currency passing through my fingers amazes me. Before this I was a pilot in an intergalactic war... or a naval battle; I wasn't really paying much attention. War bores me; why do humans rush to end their existence so surely when they have so much to live for? The progression of a human life appears not dissimilar to the chapters of a book to me; one thing happens, and then another, and later events are effected by earlier. Humans have the ability to learn from their mistakes, if not the will; I do not.

Finally I understand the concept of learning from my mistakes again (I had forgotten). But it simply doesn't apply to me; my relationships are transient, my problems have no bearing, and everything I do becomes the problem of the current inhabitants of the timeline.

I don't understand how the timeline works, and I don't pretend nor try to. I simply travel. I shouldn't have left Artemis.

Artemis is by no means the woman I have stayed with the most, nor the woman I have most cared for—but she is the woman I have been the cruelest to. Perhaps my year of pretend emotions had succeeded in retraining my brain a bit, for I regret my decision. The customer asks for an item from their vault. I tell them I will get it and leave.

I don't think I'm in the right time, but I make my way through New Brunswick anyways. The lights spark and creak, hanging from their foundations, and some of the platforms drift at a lazy awkward angle. No one lives here. A starcraft rests on the ruined remains of the upper city. Maybe I did that. I just assume I had a hand in anything that confuses me.

Outcasts and the refugees become my companions. The last of the human race. Or, more probably, merely the last of the people of New Brunswick. But I pretend they are the last of humanity. I wonder whether humanity drifts towards barbarism or kindness in its last days. The people of New Brunswick give no indication.   They are dead. I live amongst them regardless. I can't deceive the dead.

I travel too far and spend some time on a train. The traincar is transporting goats. I don't know why. I hate this place. I leap from the train.

The hospital is clean. That's nice. Most hospitals I've visited have been war hospitals. They would have amputated my legs instead of splinted them. I wait to recover.

Sometimes I think back to when I think I started traveling this way. I remember being young and excited. The prospect of time-travel excited my imagination. I probably volunteered for some hair-brained experiment, because I know I don't have the brains to invent a time machine myself, nor the dexterity to implant it. I was a fool; I could have been human. What is the human reaction to relationships called? I don't remember. That's a bad way to describe it, I think. I resolve to read a dictionary.

Love. The *emotion* is love. Damn, I'm rusty. Also, bacon should be frozen for storage. Good to know. Artemis helped me with the second bit.

Today on my way to work I watch myself get shot, and then rise again to pay my co-conspirator. I pay him double to forget the whole ordeal. Artemis will understand the missing money. I'll tell her it was part of the vehicle bill. I get in an accident.

Artemis knows I'm foreign. She doesn't recognize my accent. I tell her I'm from Luxembourg, the only nation I've never visited. I don't even know how to place my accent, mixed as it is between every place I've spent time. She hugs me as we watch the vehicle being repaired. She came to pick me up from the mechanic's. I will stay here. I will not set a time limit. I will try to love. After all, it *is* my birthday.

We embrace.

Artemis asks about children. I tell her the truth. She understands. I leave out the portion of the truth which explains *why* I am not in contact with any of my children. I also avoid revealing the number of them. She is my life now. Maybe I'll meet this child; stranger things have happened.

The painter's name is Van Gogh. He cut off his ear for love. He was a madman. I dislike him. We are too similar from what I can tell. I tell Artemis that I would love an original Van Gogh.

I hate looking at the sky below me and long to stand on

solid ground, so I go on a business trip and bring my hiking boots. The Himalayas are beautiful in the past. I wonder if mountains live life like me. Doubtful.

As I travel I make friends with fathers and mothers and sons. I learn what a family means. I think perhaps I may be human again.

I return from my business trip in under a week. The merger fell through. I let her console me. My job means a lot to me.

No matter how hard I try, I cannot imagine living with a pregnant woman. I make jokes. I grit my teeth behind my smile. The doctors tell me it's nothing to worry about. I write a book while I am in office. I have a chapter about being a father. I am not going to run for re-election. I don't pay attention to how well the book sells. I am still using my counterfeit card.

Artemis takes me out for dinner. She truly is beautiful. I think I might be close to loving her. Our wedding was almost as gorgeous as she is. I still cannot think linearly despite my new life. I try to paint. I am terrible, just like Van Gogh. I hate him almost as much as goats. Artemis thinks I am from Luxembourg. I no longer find my lies amusing. I had a cold heart, but I am gradually feeding its fire.

I have never stayed with a woman this long. I can feel my bones pressing against my skin. It is my birthday, and all I know is that I am old. Artemis is old as well, but not quite as old. Vincent is a strong young man and Ilsa is a good wife for him. Artemis named our son after my favorite painter. I hate Van Gogh.

I am considering my death. It is still many years off, but it is a subject I have never considered before. Artemis's death is also something I consider. We could live forever, if I used technology from another age, but that would be cheating. My grandchildren would probably cry. I do not have grandchildren. I kiss Artemis and go to work. I make an honest living.

I am a doctor; I am smarter than I thought. I no longer take pride in my scars. In fact, I had most of them removed. I no longer play madhouse with the doctors; I am only a small monster. I feel the bump in the back of my neck. Does it age as I do, I wonder. I told the surgeon it was an experimental cure for paraplegia. He told me I looked like Van Gogh. I told him he looked like a goat.

I am in space. It is cold. I am basically dead. Thoughts move faster as you die. I smile at Artemis and we kiss. There is no cure for her disease. She is beautiful. We are old. I am about to die a happy man. My grandchildren will probably cry. I have grandchildren.

Words are impossible and unnecessary. The sky is beautiful. Van Gogh wasn't that bad of a painter. I was. I chuckle. Artemis embraces me. The Earth has not been formed yet. We exist before time. Time is a terrible thing, and everything else is beautiful. Everything is beautiful here. Artemis knows my secret. No one else ever has or ever will. We will die in each other's arms and we will be happy. Forever. That's what forever means—time unchanging. Time doesn't change for the dead. We have led good lives, and I have led bad ones as well.

My last words are *Thank you*, and hers are the same. We saved each other from ourselves. For the first time I am happy that I traveled as much as I did.

This perfect moment is my favorite birthday gift I have ever received.

The Chalice and the Noble Blood

HAT FOLLOWS IS a tale of a time that never was. A time when the isles of the North Sea were no longer Brittony, nor yet England. When men wore plate and coat d'arms and professed in Latin and French hundreds of years before Guillame the Bastard and the Battle of Hastings. A time when magic reigned and chivalry was far from myth. In short, 'tis the time of Gramarye of which I speak, and of its king, Arthur Pendragon.

But this tale is far from a joyous one, for far gone were the days of gay feasting and noble quests. Arthur sat long upon the throne of Camelot, and all good things must come to an end; the faithless Queen Guenevere had fled with Lancelot du Lac and that treasonous friend had declared war upon the Round Table, convincing many to join him; Arthur's one true son and nephew, Mordred of Orkney, had risen also against Pendragon, and his *Thrashers* (as the Mordredites were known) ravaged the countryside. And amidst it all the sovereign—England's greatest lord, had grown despondent, and left the ruling of his realm to a steward. Acrost the land lords had sworn to one pretender or another—in the East 'twas said that Sir Lancelot would return the court to its former glory and return the Eye of God, mentioning not once that 'twas he himself what made God swear ill 'pon Arthur's lands. In the North, Mordred sat in Orckney, sending black knights acrost the borders and down through Northumbria to bring back the cruel fist of Fort Maine. Aye, some men still belonged to Arthur in heart and soul, but they were often those too stubborn to be changed or too hopeless to see a better future and many of them were slain by the Thrashers or imprisoned by the blind but well-meaning knights of du Lac.

In this time of shadows, in the west of Gramarye, in what would later be called Wessex, there was a manour by the name of Winterbourne Stoke—much different than the lands which now bear that name, though not far distant. The lands held by the House of Winterbourne Stoke—whose members were called the Twombleys—would seem of no great size now, but in those forgotten days they were indeed large. So large, in fact, that the Lord of Winterbourne Stoke had been given the title of earl in the days of Arthur's father, Uther. At the time, the Earl of Winterbourne Stoke had kept six bannerettes (or lesser lords) beneath his rule, but in the time of our tale—the time of the fifth Earl of Winterbourne Stoke—there were but four lords in the land: Sir Driant—the Earl himself, Sir Herawd—his eldest living son and the Count of Badenshire, Sir Maurel—another son and the Sheriff of Colham, and Sir Galardoun—the dour, crippled Sheriff of Goring and brother to the Earl who claimed to have been maimed at the battle of Towney, though in sooth had not been there at all. Of these men only the Earl and the Lord of Goring still held their lands, for the Twombleys had refused to betray their king and so had been beset by Mordredites, who deprived them of their northernmost holdings.

As our tale begins it is Whitsun in Winterbourne Stoke, and Sir Driant and all his sons, uncles, and cousins have come to remember together the birth of the Church and the many Gifts of God. But the festivities had been grey and the beer soured and now, as a black storm raged outside the hall, they feasted as the Apostles after the Crucifixion. The Twombleys had long been at odds with the nearby Nettles of Berwick St. James, and with the rise of Mordred and of Lancelot the occasional illegal taxation or brief imprisonment had given way to total war. The Twombleys were not entirely innocent, but—they were sure to remind themselves—at least they were not Thrashers. Not two weeks had passed since the Battle of Gallows Marsh, in which the previous Earl (also named Driant) had perished. And though they had won the day, the death of the Twombley patron hung heavy upon all.

At the head of the table sat Sir Driant l'Ours. He was not so large a man as his name implied, but his melancholy glower and deep, commanding voice were enough to cow many lesser men. He wore a blue tunic emblazoned with a silver chalice, and in his gloved right hand he held a twin to that sigil, full to the brim with sweet summer wine. From beneath his greying brow he observed the hall—the flutes and harps seeming somehow sad, the jesters too old, the priest too young. His kinfolk bickered quietly, naively assuming him too ill-at-heart from his father's death to notice the disquiet between their laughter. But though Sir Driant l'Ours was indeed ill-at-heart, 'twas not for sadness but for fear of conspiracy. Or of reprisal. For it had not been Nettle arrows that felled his late father, but Twombley, and his own fingers had let fly the shafts.

"Mulgeatis, infernus manaque!" cried Sir Maurel l'Audace, second heir to the Earl. *Drink Deeply, Hell beckons!* Nearly fifty drinks were hoisted high, amongst them the silver chalice of Sir Driant. Near the other end of the long table which sat at the head of the hall, Sir Galardoun noisily drained his mug, wine spilling in his beard and dribbling from his mustache. He spat and chewed, working a loose piece of gristle from his teeth, then muttered some blaspheme beneath his breath and weathered the direful stare of his son.

"To speak such upon a holy day, Father! My good Mother surely would be ill."

L'Nain, for that is what men called him, shifted his use-

152

less left arm and scowled, "No man wote what thy mother would do, for thy mother is dead these ten years. And fain am I of that, for thus she needs not see how far our noble blood has sunk." Had the arm nearest the boy been well he would have struck him, but it was as ill as his brother-earl's heart and so he reached for yet more wine.

About the hall these same quarrels sprouted like mushrooms in a færie circle, and never a man, woman, or child was untouched by ire in that long night. Save perhaps Sir Maurel, who had made the toast. Sir Maurel, in a colourful jerkin of purple and gold, with black along the seams and dark fur in the collar, joked and laughed as if all were right in the world. He sat with Herawd, his elder brother, and talked excitedly of the old quests of Arthur's knights and of what questing could yet be done in Gramarye. He flirted coyly with the servants—and even with his brother's blue-eyed wife—and kicked his pointed boots in dance as he took a serving maid from her platter. Even those most beset by worry and sorrow—Sir Driant by far amongst these—could not help but smile at his antics. 'Twas said that if Sir Maurel had been born in the time of his grandfather he would perhaps have grown as great as Gawain or du Lac and sat at Arthur's Round Table. But he had not been. And so his family often shook their heads in pity and whispered that he should be lucky to die in his bed rather than be taken by the time's dire enemies, only to smile again as he passed.

It was as Maurel was with the serving made, behind a pillar with flagon in hand, that the first of the troubles came. Sir Maurel was telling the lass how her hair reminded him of the hills of the Midlands on a spring morning, "soft and lush and rolling with the joy at what mysteries they might conceal." The maid, who was quite enjoying the attention despite her embarrassment, asked, "But what of my eyes? Surely something must be said of them if thou hast so much to say of my locks?" He threw wide his arm, sending a splash of wine hissing into a lit torch, "Ah! Thyne eyes! What magnificent clear pools. So like the waters of Eden what washed Adam and washed Eve in the time before their trouble." The lass's brow furrowed at this and Sir Maurel, unused to such consternation upon a pretty face, asked the matter. "My eyes are brown."

But Maurel was saved his embarrassment by the knock upon the door the hall's great entrance, so near to him that he dropped his drink in alarm and the servant cowered in his ready arm. The knock came again and Sir Driant demanded to be told who begged entry. Bryn, the bastard brother to both Herawd and Maurel, asked Herawd if it could be the men he had sent to stable the horses for the storm, but those men had been led by Driant's brother, Dylan, and had returned once the priest had finished the Whitsun Feast prayers. "Per'aps 'tis Sir Eoric, come to apologize," called a young cousin, referring to the Nettle who had commanded—and died—at Gallow's Marsh. "Per'aps he comes not to apologize," spake l'Nain grimly. For a long time none moved as the thunder crashed and the knocking rose. Finally it grew too much for Sir Driant; he did not believe in ghosts, but if they *did* exist and had come calling 'twas for him they would seek. The Lord of Winterbourne Stoke stood and unsheathed his sword, bellowing in his bear's voice, "Open! Open yon gate and let us have done with our judgment!"

As if 'twere Moses himself setting the Red Sea to part the tables stood—to a man—and faced the stout oaken door. Mothers herded children for the stairs. Blades were drawn and pages were sent for shield and helm—knowing that there would be time naught to don them if an enemy waited outside (and in those days an unexpected visitor was more like than not to be such). For some mad reason the minstrels played on, piping to the

154

twisting night. Bryn, bastard son of Driant, took seven men and approached, passing without noticing Sir Maurel, his blade in one-hand and the brown-eyed lass in the other. But as Bryn's hand touched the iron ring that furnished the door there was a thundering like the pagan hammer of the old gods and the gate flew wide with such force that Bryn and his seven men were thrown upon their backs. The sounds of the thunder and of the slamming doors shook the stones of Winterbourne Stoke and awoke a family of thrushes in the rafters which swooped and chittered through the crowd as children screamed. The wind howled like a mourning Scott and the rain poured inwards with the force of God himself. In an instant all the torches and candles were blown out and cries arose from terrified throats—men and women alike. Only brief flashes of lightning showed the tattered figure which stood alone in the opening, silhouetted and dressed in Death's own rags. Two fierce horns rose from the thing's head and in his hand was a blade surely wrought in Hell's own forges. Half demon and half willow, it swayed as it walked, willfully stepping past Bryn's men as they moaned and hurried to push shut the door. In terror, Sir Driant stood at the hall's far end, his sword loosening in his grip. The ghost of Driant the Elder, for surely it must be, had reached the end of the table nearest the doors. It took one more ponderous step, then spun on its heel as Sir Driant dropped his blade. Then spirit fell, its head clanging against the wood of the table as the gates of Winterbourne Stoke were finally shut against the storm and all was lost in a black pall.

O nce the candles in the hall had been re-lit, Sir Herawd Twombley and his youngest brother, Emlyn, leaned over the still figure in the flickering light, holding a wick close to the thing, whose chest rose and fell heavily. It made a terrible growling sound, and all the gathered Twombleys and their men frantically crossed themselves to protect against evil. But Herawd could now see that this was no beast, and breathed easier for it. What had seemed a terrible horned head, black like the pit of hell, was instead a battered iron pot helm, fitted on the sides with blades, bent upwards at the midpoint. Resting beneath these forge-wrought antlers was a bent and tarnished golden crown. The grill of the helmet was closed and latched, and naught of the man's face could be seen. A tattered surcoat of yellow and green (or perhaps blue) hung tightly about the man's thin frame. He wore plate which may once have been fine, but now was bent and scarred and missing in places – a few stills from the gauntlets, the left shoulder strap to the breastplate, more than a few rings from the mail. The badge on his breast bore a golden hunting horn.

"'Tis no demon nor haunt," announced Herawd, already forgetting his fear of moments before, and hating his family for not realizing sooner. "This here is a man. A knight, though to whom he belongs I know not."

"A knight traveling alone on such a night? I think not," growled Galardoun, pushing through the crowd. "There's more than a mite strange in the air this Whitsun and I won't have us taken for fools by some trickery. Rhodri, Yorath, take ten men and search the grounds!" He motioned to his son and to his bastard brother, whose mother had always been kinder to Galardoun than his own. "And don't think ye of returning until ye've found from whence this cretin crawled."

As Herawd turned to argue with his uncle and admonish him for sending good Twombley men to be soaked in the storm, Bryn the Bastard reached out with his sword and flicked open the small grate which hid the knight's eyes. The hinge shrieked as it moved, and quieted those nearby, though those too far from the scene to clearly see continued to speak in low voices. Two pale, grey eyes gazed out – unfocused – from the opening. Slowly, some light began to fill them and the man grunted, perhaps in fear. He reached for the black sword stuck in his weathered belt – unshielded by scabbard or cloak – but Bryn rested a black boot upon the visitor's chest and his arm relaxed.

Up to this point, Earl Driant had not gathered the courage to approach, but had heard his son announce the benign nature of the guest, and his borther crying foul. He had stood, first in the dark, then in the flickering candlelight, just before his high seat with one hand resting heavily on the stout table before him. His breath had come as heavily as that of the collapsed knight, his eyes wide and his mind resettling. In the moment that the door had opened, Driant had resolved himself to death; he had not been shriven since that morning, and even then had still failed to admit to his great sin, but Hell would surely be a fairer prison than the cold, stone walls of Winterbourne Stoke, where undoubtedly there waited a knife – or worse, a truthful tongue – behind every unopened door. Once his breath had returned and his heart had begun to beat its familiar rhythm, the Lord of Winterbourne Stoke motioned to a page to hand him his sword from the ground and joined the excitement, holding his weapon high and bellowing until a path was made. "Unhelm him," he commanded once he was near, and Bryn did.

As the helmet was unlaced and pulled – with some difficulty – from the knight's head, a great ocean of tangled, black hair was revealed. With the permission of the castle's lord, the visitor clumsily untangled his mane from his shaggy beard and once more stared up from beside the gathered company's feet. Still he remained silent.

"By what name are ye called? What master do ye serve? From where do ye hail? Who is king of all the land?" demanded

Lord Driant, lending his own sword to those of his sons, awkwardly posing over the prostrate form.

"Name? I..." The man's voice was sonorous and deep, but his speech was slurred as if awoken from slumber.

Sir Maurel, having abandoned his most recent maiden quest after the excitement caused her to faint, squatted low and spoke forcefully into the knight's wide, grey eyes. "Where are ye from?" From somewhere nearby someone proudly cried Sir Maurel's name and he smiled, waving a hand absently.

"I am..." Screwing up his face in thought, the prisoner answered. "Fallowbrook. I come from Fallowbrook." None present knew of a place called Fallowbrook, and Galardoun soon said as much to the floor. "I do not know where it is, only that I came from thence."

"And why came ye here?" pressed Lord Driant. He was still not entirely convinced that this was not some trick sent to test him by the wise God above.

"I know not, sire. I remember little of my journey."

"What of thy journey do ye remember?"

"Dead forests. Barren shores. And," his face contorted in an eddy of exhaustion and fear, "demons." At this a gasp traveled through the crowd and someone near the stairs cried out in a high shriek (it was determined later that this had been the chapel priest). "I have been pursued and tortured by demons and dreams since I left my home in Fallowbrook." (It was at this point that the chapel priest fainted dead away and would not awaken for some time.)

"But tell me, knight," continued the Earl, his knuckles white about the hilt of his sword and his mouth dry, "What is thy name?"

"I do not remember," was all that could be offered, and eventually the knight was taken away to a tower chamber, to be seen after by the chirurgeon and the apothecary and the chapel priest (once he was feeling up to the task), and kept within until something could be decided to be done with him.

In time the chaos subsided and the cups and spoons were cleared away and the men spoke long into the night of war and crowns and rumours of a nearby force loyal to du Lac. Sir Driant, drowning in his wine, had almost forgotten about their strange visitor as he stumbled to bed. He disrobed and set his jewels in a small chest lined in red velvet on a small table painted in vibrant scenes of questing knights before sliding under the heavy quilts beside his wife, whose name was Fflur. They kissed briefly and turned their backs to one-another. Yet before sleep took them Fflur commented on the strange man in the tower, and how he had heard neither of Arthur, nor Gramarye, nor even the Catholic God.

That night Lord Driant slept restlessly, and dreamt of the crypts beneath his manour. In the dream he stood over the open tomb of his father. There was no light save what filtered down from the open stairwell, but he could see well that the elder Driant's eyes were open—watching—even as the rest of his face was deathly grey. Driant the Younger, his lips parched, whispered in the darkness, "Tell me, Father, have ye sinned?" The corpse made no reply, but a red-yellow light began to fill the room and a deep voice offered from behind, "His sins will not save us." Driant turned to see the Knight of Fallowbrook silhouetted in the door, a blazing torch in his hand.

Herawd, the eldest Twombley heir, also had such a dream, alike in all ways save that it was he, Herawd, standing above the open tomb of his own father, Driant the Younger. The Knight of Fallowbrook came also to him, answering the same question with the same, strange answer.

Neither father nor son told the other of their dream upon waking.

The next morning saw the fears of the late night war council realized, as riders approached the walls bearing bright banners and announcing that they came from a mighty host, whose commanders sought audience with Lord Driant. L'Ours consulted his uncles, all old and wise with grey beards, and they cautioned him against defying so great a host; inside the walls of the manour were sevenscore and five fighting men, but the army which waited a short ride east numbered almost eight hundred men. And so Driant l'Ours let the messenger carry on that he would greet the commanders in his audience hall as soon as they could arrive.

Once the riders set out the halls of Winterbourne Stoke exploded with activity. There was truly very little which could be done, but men often have a need to feel useful, especially men who own expensive weapons. And so the Twombley knights shouted and waved their arms about, whetting their blades and examining their armour and coats and sending squires and pages on all sorts of mundane tasks which were given sudden urgency by the restlessness of their masters. Only Herawd, who held no especial hatred for du Lac and his adherents, managed to keep a level head, and spent the morning trading stories of Camelot's glory with his young son, Afon.

It was nearly midday before the enemy arrived at the gate, and so there was time enough for the inhabitants of the manour to eat their morning meal. The meal, however, was meager, for the servants had been as distracted as the knights by the news, and had failed to complete many of their chores, including the gathering of eggs. Sir Maurel had commented to Herawd and his wife Efa that even the apostles ate better fare than cold porridge. Herawd had ignored his brother whilst his wife tittered and in a short time the meal had been cleared away, barely touched. The knight of Fallowbrook was fed in his tower, and kindly thanked the young boy who brought it him.

Horns announced the coming of the knights-commander, and eager watchers—Sir Maurel amongst them, his lips close to the ear of the maiden's sister from the night before—stood upon the walls looking east. The horns blew brightly as some twoscore men rode over the tumbling hills, their banners snapping and their lances held high. "Is that Lancelot? I hear he is handsome, even now," asked Maurel's companion, and the Sheriff of Colham glanced down from his attentions. "Nay, Lady," he answered, glad that he would not need to compete with the famed traitor for the eyes of any maidens, "Those banners fly for Sirs Govendral, Murs, and Palthenor. Ye ken," his eyes lit as he bit gently at her neck, "they call Palthenor *le Dragon*, but I doubt he can set me alight quite as ye do." And so Sir Maurel was not present to greet the visitors.

Sir Govendral led the knights to the gate, and when humbly invited by Sir Herawd, rode his charger into the bailey, wheeling to address the gathered watchers, his shaven face handsome despite his age and his long, white hair bound in a tight braid behind his back. Sirs Murs, squat and bearded, and Palthenor, gaunt and cold-eyed, sat ahorse and scowled behind. "Fair knights of Arthur! Though our loyalties run tangent, I am certain thy hearts beat true. We have come a long way, and, aye, our swords are sworn to du Lac, yet we have been beaten and bruised by Thrashers and are in no right shape. We shall be fain to pay arrears once our means arrive ashore, should ye allow us rest 'pon thy lands. We entreat ye 'pon the very laws of hospitality laid down by thy King Arthur in the glorious dawn of Camelot. We swear by our titles and our heads, however much these mean to ye, that no ill shall befall thy men or lands by our means if ye should shelter us. We need only rest for a few short days, and then shall move north to find shelter amongst allies so ye may not be accused of harbouring enemies."

Sir Driant, who had come to his window at the sound of the horns, called down from above. "Though I would have enjoyed thy speech better had it been held in my audience chamber, I appreciate thy oath." Driant was known well for his hospitality, and was loath to deny it to any who asked, even an enemy as despised as du Lac's swords. "Ye may make camp on my lands, should ye cause no trouble, and also may ye and thy noble soldiers join our feasting. We have few chambers here, but what we can afford, we shall give."

Nodding his head in thanks, Govendral accepted the invitation to use the family's lands and to feast with Driant, but admitted to preferring to sleep nearer his men when on campaign. "Thy gifts shall be well remembered," he called, and rode out to collect his forces.

Once Driant had descended to the rapidly emptying bailey, his eldest heir congratulated him, "'Twas fairly done to offer what little we could to so fair a visitor—even though his loyalties run contrary to our own. Perhaps someday we may see a reward for our kindness. Beyond the coin he promised." But the Lord Bear had little interest in further rewards.

Midday was almost three hours past when Govendral's camp began to be erected in the green field before Winterbourne

Stoke Manour's gate. Dour Sir Galardoun announced that he meant to survey the grounds, and Driant gave him leave, though he knew there was little his brother could do, even should he find something amiss. And so the Sheriff of Goring took his son and a few other Twombley knights under his command with his eight men-at-arms and marched imperiously out the front entrance and down the gentle slope into the forest of multi-coloured tents. He was dressed in freshly shined mail with a thick, sleeveless black doublet over, his forearms guarded by plated leather gauntlets, and a cape of white damascene silk upon his back, his wide belt proudly displaying his long sword and wicked dirk, and a brooch of diamonds on his breast.

Galardoun spent much of the afternoon marching this way and that with his men, watching imperiously and occasionally harshly questioning those they encountered which l'Nain saw as weak, or imposing arbitrary restrictions on where tents could be placed. For their part, the du Lac knights took this pestering fairly lightly and allowed the crippled knight to lumber about where he pleased.

But Driant's brother was not as bullish as he put on, and he made a point to listen carefully to what was said by those who stood and gossiped and to hear the whispers between the words of those who smiled and bowed as he bellowed. It seemed there were a great many Thrashers in the parts around, and rumours ran that Mordred himself flew his black banner above a mighty force intent on sweeping through the west before hooking east towards Camelot. Some men spoke of missing France or Saxony (a foul place filled with foul folk, whose presence here Galardoun liked but little), but dared not travel the same seas again, for fear that Merlin would once more summon fearsome serpents to sink their fleets, as he had seemingly done on their approach; Galardoun knew of the wizard Merlin, and had heard many tales of his fearsome magics, but he had not met a man who had seen the sorcerer in nigh on thirty years, and he hoped the loathsome Celt was not merely absent, but dead. The serpents were likely superstition, yet even so he ground his teeth at the thought that such magics might be used to defend Arthur's sacred kingdom.

Govendral had gone to the feast hall to meet with Galrdoun's kin, and so Galardoun asked sometimes after Murs and Palthenor, learning soon that they too had gone to the castle. But there was another name he heard whispered—a fourth commander of the force, though never was his name spoken easily. Olgwydh. Olgwydh the Dreamer. Olgwydh the Bloody Goat. The Sheriff of Goring took his men and followed the nervous fingers which pointed towards the northeastern edge of the camp. There they found a golden tent, and before it a handsome knight in fine black robes embroidered with stars on the sleeves and black hair and a sharp, salted beard. He looked to be no older than Galardoun himself, and sat on a stool, sharpening a wicked long knife on a leather strop, the far end held by a blonde-headed boy. "Sir Olgwydh, I surmise," announced Sir Yorath, the Sheriff's bastard brother. Looking up at his name, his eyes a brown so pale as to almost be yellow, the knight's hand slipped and the page yelped briefly. There was a spray of hot blood and Olgwydh blinked. All present looked to the dusty ground where the youth's thumb rested peacefully.

The boy began to wail and Olgwydh stood quickly, shouting for a physician. Once empty, the clearing before the Dreamer's tent filled quickly with panicked energy and men and boys rushed frantically hither and to, looking desperately for aid. Galardoun, himself above caring for the wellness of an enemy servant, stood still and waited. He saw Olgwydh kneel in the dirt and grab the boy's shoulders, speaking softly to him, and scowl and cuff at a dog that came sniffing after the digit. The digit which Galardoun clearly saw in Olgwydh's hand for a blink of his eye, and then was gone. Galardoun had no patience for delays, and less still for sorcery. Growling low, he took two long steps forwards and towered above the black-garbed stranger.

"Stand, Sir," he commanded, his good hand resting on the hilt of his sword. The blade was forged with silver, and blessed by the pope in Rome; no servant of darkness would withstand its biting edge. Olgwydh complied, wiping the blood from his brow with the same hand with which he had pocketed the boy's finger. Behind them a physician was overseeing a large moor who was carrying the ghost-faced boy off to the surgeon's tent. He asked in soft tones how he may serve. "Ye may serve by returning what ye took. I shall have no heathen rituals on my brother's soil." But Olgwydh claimed no knowledge of the thumb, save that he had handed it over to the physician when he had come. Galardoun knew this to be false, but could gain naught from the softly smiling Welshman but a burning frustration. He allowed his temper to be curbed – temporarily—and asked the knight his lands and kin.

"No lands have I, nor kin," said he. "I am the only one of my line what still lives."

"Bear ye any relation to the Olgwydh of Uther's court?" asked Galrdoun, for he knew some little history of Arthur's father, and recalled now having heard tell of a man named Olgwydh who fled the justice of his liege, never to be seen again. He also had born a blood-red goat upon his badge.

"I am he," said the knight, and Galardoun gaped. Were this truly the same man he would surely be over a century old, and there could be little denying his witchery. But what could valiant Galardoun do here, deep in the enemy camp? Feeling suddenly very small, he resolved that he must retreat, and bide his time until he could deal with this sorcerer as befit his sins.

He bid farewell to Olgwydh, his face white, and gathered his men to continue the tour of the camp. As they made their way towards the encampment of the hated Saxons, separate from the main force and partially under the eaves of the forest to the west, the Sheriff's son bemoaned the wounding of the young boy. His father was quick to remind him that the boy was as damned as his master, and the younger Goring was too cowed by his father's gaze to ask further what was meant by this.

The Saxon camp was much more barbaric in appearance, with rougher fabrics and pagan charms hung in every place. Long-bearded men with great big arms and wicked axes wandered about, eyeing the visitors. The thegns joked loudly in their native tongue and sang strange, haunting songs that flowed over the Twombleys like the waters of a cold stream, chilling their bones and reminding them of dead things and of past failures. Galardoun did not lead his men between these tents, but after watching for some time led them back to the manour; he had seen enough of the enemy and the folk they consorted with.

As Galardoun set out to make his presence known in the camp, the castle's halls were filled with high spirits, for when knights come visiting it is often a joyous time, even if they are enemies. Throughout the hall servants rushed to and fro as minstrels tuned their harps and lyres and ladies and maidens tried on their finest gowns. Rich smells of salted meats and sweet wines drifted through the corridors, and healthy laughter cut through the air, splitting foul tempers from their masters like soft roast from the bone.

Knight-Commander Govendral arrived early in the

evening, and Driant made certain to provide his full attention to his guest, smiling as they downed cidres and ales and rhenish beside the roaring fire. Herawd joined them for a time, but soon left for the camp to seek out Murs and Palthenor, leaving his father alone with Govendral's rich tales of chivalry-of-old and his own anxieties and fears. Driant said little, and heard less of the charming old knight's reminiscences, instead measuring the dire straights of his demesne when surrounded by so many enemies. And the weight on his soul. And who was this Knight of Fallowbrook, still locked in his tower? A spy for the Nettles? For Mordred's vanguard? For God?

In time the tables were laid for the feast and Galardoun returned, but Driant was too drunk to be sensible, and he spoke little over the feast, allowing Maurel to officiate for him. Eventually he excused himself and made his way to bed, humming a strange tune which had come into his head as he considered the intentions of his noble guests.

That night there was no restful sleep to be had in the manour, and the guards on the wall whispered that a moon so high in the sky should not be as yellow as this one was. The only noise which broke the cautious silence was the low singing of the Saxons in their cantonment. All throughout the camp and up in the castle, knights and their companies tossed and turned in their beds, always on the edge between nightmare and waking. Always, that is, until the roar came.

A terrible animal bellow, as of a bear the size of a mangonel, shook the stones of Winterbourne Stoke and made the grass cower in fear. In an instant men were on their feet, shielding their kin and grasping for swords.

In Maurel's chambers his blue-eyed tryst shrieked and

he quieted her with a kiss, even as he donned his byrnie; "I have not yet slain a dragon in my life, but I have always felt that I someday would." When he gained the eastern wall his brother Herawd was already there. In interest and alarm Sir Maurel noted, as his men had, the colour of the moon, but also that there was not one but two of them hanging in the black and cloudless sky.

"At last ye are awake, Brother," spake the elder son. "Some witchery is afoot."

"I have gathered as much already, for I am a wakeful man, Brother, and would not allow myself to sleep on a night such as this. Not with so many of my loving family in need of care."

Herawd ignored his brother's impish smile, and grabbed for a saucer-helmed guard, eagerly fleeing for the walkway into the castle. "Hold, and tell me why ye and others abandon thy places."

"Abandon? Nay, I merely meant—" But the Twombleys knew the lie in his wan face and shook him until he answered aright, telling them of the terrible giant which had been seen stalking the bailey. "Tall as five men, aye, and clothed in black! 'Twas it what bellowed, 'fore it climbed o'er the wall."

"Which wall?" demanded the heir to Winterbourne Stoke.

"The West, Lord."

And so the brothers let the terrified man go, calling to what men would still listen to gather themselves and their arms and to open the gates. Herawd and Maurel hurried down the stair which led into the bailey and mounted their frightened horses in haste. As they prepared to ride forth, the gate slowly lower-

168

ing and some twenty men inelegantly gathering behind, their crippled uncle called to them from the steps of the hall.

"Nephews! The fiend has flown! A pox upon us, for the sorcerer and his fallow familiar have infiltrated our towers and taken our blood!" It was a long moment before Maurel and Herawd could convince Sheriff Galardoun to speak his mind simply, yet when he did the truth he revealed chilled their blood; the knight of Fallowbrook was gone without a trace, the guards set to watch them being found wandering the pantry searching for sweet samplings. And worst of all, Lord Driant himself was equally as absent, and poor Fflur was no wiser as to his location, though they had shared a bed. L'Nain was adamant that he knew the culprit, and that his name was Olgwydh. "Qui sciens occisi homicidum!" cried he, as he led the charge through the gate, his shining sword held high. *Those who are slain know their murderer.* His kin behind were hard-pressed to follow.

In the camp below, resting in a wide dell which preceded the dark forest to the west, they could see fires lit and torch-bearing bands of men scampering between tents, shouting into the night. "It seems a giant the height of five men would be difficult to lose," muttered Sir Herawd, yet indeed there was no sign of a giant in the camp.

They were met by a party of men afoot, and at their head was Knight-Commander Govendral. He hailed them, yet drew his blade when, in a fury, Sir Galardoun on his black horse bore down on Sir Olgwydh with his silver sword. "Stay, Uncle," bellowed Twombley's heir, and a hint of his father's boldness came to him and brought his white-caped kin's wrath to yield.

"That sorcerer, Sir," said l'Nain, waving with his weapon. "Ye will surrender him, and as well our kin and captive, should ye be party to this disgrace." But Govendral seemed ignorant of all happenings, even to the angry eye of Goring. And as for Ol-gwydh, it seems he had been with Govendral the night long, discussing what path should be taken away from Winterbourne Stoke when their health was returned. Olgwydh began to give many details about the nature of their potential paths, but the Twombleys quickly silenced them.

Before they could question the invaders further they were interrupted. Somewhere west a cry had gone up of "Saxons! Saxons!" and almost beyond their own volition, the men of the manour had spurred their steeds to action. At the edge of the Saxon camp they found trampled fires and torn tents, yet not a Saxon man nor Saxon blade to be found. Sir Ogwydh joined them soon with a mounted company, and told them that his master had went to search for the other two captains, who had not been seen for some time.

"Was it not true that ye sought them last night?" he asked Herawd, but Herawd shook his head, annoyed that the Briton had knowledge of his intentions the night before.

"I spoke only briefly with them," he said with a wave of his fair hand, and his brother eyed him strangely. Maurel was a lustful man, and easily distracted, but if there was a man whose movements he knew near as well as his own it was Herawd's, and Herawd had not returned home from his visit to camp until many hours after the sun had set.

"Thy father and thy mysterious visitor both are missing, and so too our Saxon horde," continued Olgwydh, suddenly unconcerned with Herawd or the missing officers. "Six dozen thanes do not disappear without trace, yet also have I known barbaric folk to travel swiftly when they think to be hounded. Arm, men! Arm and mount! To the woods! We hunt the Saxon men!"

And once more the Twombley heirs were thrust in a flurry of fate into a mad ride. Deep into the dark forest they went, plunging faster into the untamed wilds than any there save perhaps Sir Olgwydh would have liked.

No banners flew, and each man still shook sleep from their eyes as they held their unfastened helms to their heads. The wood was as a dream, haunting and oppressive. The wood, in fact, felt so alike to the unhappy sleep they had each awoken from that many men startled at shadows or cried out at trees rising from the night. Herawd and Galardoun prayed loudly, one clutching a silver crucifix and the other a silver sword, whilst Maurel hollered for Saxon blood and shook his torch, laughing in gallant glee even as those about him shuddered in fear.

For hours they rode, this way and that, over roots and under branches. They followed phantom sounds and ghost-tracks, the dark and angry bark of the wood pressing on them like a tomb. Galardoun would lead for a time, then Maurel as he dashed after an imagined giant, then Herawd as he called them back. An eternity they spent in the brake, leaping from imagined prey to feared battle and back again.

Finally the grey light of morning began to colour the trunks, and even Maurel could feel his eyelids drooping with sleep. Some men, it seems, had already given up and ridden back to camp (or been eaten by a giant), and their party numbered little more than it had when they rode out from the gates of Twombley Manour. Herawd and Galardoun had dourly agreed in low voices to return, when Olgwydh (who alone among them seemed unpained by a sleepless night) pointed, with one long white finger from his starry robe.

"What is there?" And where his finger led they saw a low hill, its borders fenced in black iron.

171

"A barrow," answered Galardoun. "From ages long past. It has sat in this wood since before my father's father and all his fathers I could care to name sat in our hame. We leave it be."

"We have been everywhere in this wood, yet not there," continued the Welshman. "Could it be that the Saxon villains found solace in the tomb?"

Though the suggestion seemed unlikely—and even perhaps a trick to trap the Twombleys in some further curse—to Goring's Sheriff, his nephews lept at it, and soon they were dismounted. The other knights waited cautiously at the edge of the fence, as Galardoun, Olgwydh, Herawd, and Maurel approached the heavy stone which marked the gate. Faded runes and old pagan etching adorned the door, and a carving—like an X but with only three legs and curving in on itself—was cut into the stone. "What does it say?" demanded Galardoun of the Bloody Goat, but their guest claimed he could make no sense of it.

Maurel put his ear to the stone and told that he heard some sound, like wind from inside. Like wind, or a song. Herawd pulled back, and stood some ways away, praying and pacing, but the other three set to work on the stone, calling others to help. They thrust and pushed, levering stout trunks under the grey weight and swearing at the strain, yet in the end even ten men could not move the stone.

"No man has passed this way in many lifetimes," said Herawd at last, watching his companions sputter and sweat.

Olgwydh smiled then strangely and set one finger to the side of his nose, "Or ever perhaps."

"A secret door!" cried Maurel, not to be undone by a long-dead architect, yet no such door could be found, and in time they hung their heads and rode their horses home.

The night's troubles were not lifted with the sun, however, but multiplied. Riding out of the southern edge of the wood, the Twombleys rode with Olgwydh back towards their manour and the du Lac camp before it. Making swift time, for their sleepy heads sought the comfort of their beds, they stopped only briefly by the tents to return what knights that were not theirs still rode with them before riding up the hill to their open gates. Sir Olgwydh bid them adieu, and assured them that he would keep them well-informed should any sign of the giant be found at camp.

The wind whistled, and at first it seemed that it whistled to a strange rhythm; both Maurel and Herawd found themselves swaying to its haunting harmonies. But Galardoun knew it to be more than the wind, and swore to wake them from their stupour. "Wake, fools! 'Tis no weeping cloud sound ye hear, but a Saxon dirge, and there upon the steps to our very hame kneels the villain what sings!" And indeed, upon the front steps of the manour knelt a man, his arms spread wide, and it was from his direction which the eery dirge flowed.

Drawing their swords and leaping from horseback, the frustrated knights and their men behind bounded up the stone steps three at a time. It was just as they were gaining the landing that the doors to the castle opened. A bleary-eyed servant shrieked in alarm at the figure kneeling before them and fell to the ground in a faint. The Twombleys halted then as well, skittering to a stop and bumping against one another with a clattering of steel and toned fighting-flesh. From behind they could see that the figure wore magnificent plate—well-made, but stained in blood and dented and cut. But also could they see that his spine had been rent; a black iron stake had been thrust between his shoulderblades and down, through his twisting muscles and out through his tailbone, before being driven into the hard stone of the entry. His head was leaned back, his plumed helm balanced against the stake so his head would not fall to his chest. A matching stake had been driven through his arms, extending them in a ragged and gory mockery of the Crucifixion. "Those stakes are alike to those about the barrow," whispered Maurel, and his elder brother whimpered briefly despite himself.

Amongst those gathered perhaps the least offended by dire sights, for of dire sights he had seen his plentiful share, Sir Galardoun sheathed his silvered blade and stepped slowly about to the fore of the thing. And when he had done so he gasped and bit at the leathern gauntlet of his good hand. Before him, dead, lay Sir Govendral le Patriote, eviscerated and left in a most barbaric fashion. And betwixt his teeth were strung his own gut-strings, and as the wind played through them they sang like Saxon thegns.

It was at this very moment that Lord Driant's strong voice called out behind him. "What has befallen the house? All the men and women on the grounds are in disarray, and doors and armouries lay open as if we had been looted. And here, my eldest sons and brother stand with armed soldiers even as the sun rises. Here! Who is that kneeling there?" He stepped around his larger brother and immediately fell to his own knees with grief, Sir Govendral's empty eyes staring above him. *And so my sins bring low everything my fathers have built. However shall we save the Twombleys now?* Yet he did not allow his despair to show in his voice as, still staring at the phantom, he delivered orders, "Herawd, take Maurel and fetch the other commanders of the du Lac host; they must know as honestly as we may provide what has befallen their fellow. Ye, nephew, fetch the chirugeon from his chambers and turn him to the examination of Sir Govendral." The Twombleys swiftly set to their patriarch's orders, and he was left to watch the corpse in despair. His bastard, Bryn, came soon with more men and helped him to his feet, but Driant would not let the body be disturbed until the chirurgeon had examined it.

It was not long before Herawd and Maurel, both dangerously drowsy, rode back through the gates in the company of Sirs Murs and Palthenor. Murs's face was tomato red, and his knuckles white about his horses's reigns, but Palthenor showed no emotion, save perhaps an even greater distaste than when last he came upon the manour. Both dismounted—Murs with surprising alacrity for his frame—and hastened up the stairs. His first bellows were mighty indeed, but were staid by Bryn's upheld hand and dire stare. "Listen ye," he said to them, his voice proud but practical, "for a great sin has been laid upon our step, and ye should hear of what has occurred."

And so Bryn told of the giant in the courtyard, and the strange astrological happenings in the night sky, and Murs and Palthenor and Driant all listened. To Driant, who recalled only fitful dreamings, this was news indeed, but he dared not interrupt and seem improperly omnipotent for a lord (though already he found himself under-dressed for the occasion; it alarmed him especially that he was not to be found himself in all that time). *The curse, it grows. And it brings doom upon us, for surely there is no forgiveness these captains may give for the slaughter of their fellow. And to what fey realm was I pulled? And by whom?* His thoughts strayed to Fallowbrook in the tower, to his dream of the night before, and to his own red visions that night afore he forced himself to abandon his fearful ponderings. At length Bryn had finished telling of the castle's defense and the search of the camp (which Driant thought Murs and Palthenor seemed as reticent to admit their knowledge of as he of his nocturnal experience), and Maurel told of their discomfiting ride and their return to the step.

Sir Murs guffawed once the tellings were done, blowing spittle and waving his fat fingers in frustration. "Ye think us fools? That we should believe ye had naught to do with the giant nor this gory travesty? Nay! What ungodful things ye wester-men do have lived long enough in the sight of feckless men, yet those days are at an end! Ye craven! Ye betrayer! Ye prayerless host! Prepare thyselves, for there shall be no more peace 'tween du Lac and Twombley. Tomorrow at noonsun, on that very field where our camp now sits, shall red blood be spilt!"

"Hold, friend!" cried Lord Driant. "My son speaks in truth! There is no Twombley hand in this assault, and were I to be proven wrong ye may rest thyself assured that that hand, nor its twin, should remain attached to Twombley wrist!" But Murs and Palthenor were not to be dissuaded, and rode back through the gate with the bearings of knights happy with a hunger for vio-lence, yet also with haunted looks, as men what have seen the very punishment of Heaven.

"And so it is to be war," said Herawd, and though he made to hide his own battle-pleasure, it shown brightly in his breast.

While Maurel told of the Saxons—who had set a fire to burn some two score dead yet would not speak of what slew them nor where—the eldest Twombley heir stole away to sleep, content despite the absymal events. With great sadness and per-vading guilt, l'Ours prepared his house for their final battle. The Knight of Fallowbrook had not been found.

That evening however, a scout returned to the manour with yet more dire news; Thrashers to the north in great number, greater even than the du Lac band. Murs and Palthenor were yet too proud to meet with the lords of the manour, but Olgwydh came, and with him a semblance of hope.

Yet that hope was tainted by the dour nature of Galardoun. Ol-
gwygdh came with an offer of truce, leastwise until the Thrashers
had been defeated, but the fearsome Sherrif interrupted him
even upon his arrival, demanding that "this sorcerer snake," be
thrown from the hall. Galardoun was rested now, and surrounded by friends, and so felt more comfortable challenging the warlock, though the spell-weaver's nearness caused his wretched arm
to itch. But his foolish brother would have naught of his warn-
ings, and welcomed the Welshman to drink and to speak.

"I thank ye, for ye have been most hospitable in all this.
Or," he paused, affecting an air of concern, "thy house has. For
ye were not to be found all through this last fearsome night."

"I am cursed," said Driant l'Ours, "to walk the halls
while sleeping."

"A dire curse indeed," purred Olgwydh. Twombley's
kin said naught, though they knew him never before to have
been stricken with such a condition. Yet what other explanation
was there to be found?

"As I said," continued the Bloody Goat, "We are wont
to join forces against the Thrashers, and revisit the singular mystery of the murdered marshall and the absent Arthurian. Our
scouts estimate that the horde should reach us near that same
noontime that my companions had named for our own battle—
that of ye and I - and so we shall have our camp dissolved much
before then. Ye may consult with myself and the others, if they
shall meet thy eye, afore we ride forth. But tonight we must lay
what plans we may and I shall relay them to goodly Murs and
friendly Palthenor."

And so the plans were laid. The knights of the house went off to find their rest or stand their vigils, and the lords of the house waited about the fire with wine and maps of the hills. Galardoun spake little, save to contradict each plan set forth by the black-robed ancient, only to invariably proposition the same plan some time later. Herawd, adversely, was quite vocal, though all his plans seemed ill-devised—despite his ardent defense of them—and they were dismissed for fear of spreading too thin the force or confronting to great a flank of the Thrashers. Maurel in time grew bored and, slapping his father's sinewed shoulder, declared that he trusted the wits of older men, but for his own sake would trust in his heart and in a warm bed; he japed that Lady Efa must have kept Herawd's bed warm, unknowning that he would be up at council till the high hours, but he was dismissed with a waving of weary hands.

In time Driant himself grew too weary to plan further, and begged Olgwydh's leave.

"Of course, dear host. May thy rest be stationary, and if not, may ye be found afore thy absense becomes a worry once more."

And so each of those four commanders went their ways. Driant to his bed and Galardoun to his, Olgwydh to his tent, and Herawd away beyond the gates and beyond the sight of watching eyes. The Count of Badenshire swore to return for his wife and son once his business was done.

That night, once all were abed, though some for barely an hour, the terrible, animal bellow came once more, and in the sky shone two moons and one was high and yellow. No beast could be found on castle grounds, yet neither could Lord Driant, and still was no trace found of the absent Fallowbrook knight.

And wherever Driant walked, his dreams were red. It was dark, in his dreams, save the yellow glow of two dead eyes. They towered above him in the cavern in which he lay, frozen upon a stony alter. The thing—a giant in black rags—spoke curses and accusations which tore at the Earl's heart and ran its cold fingers along his chest. His clothes it tore from him, and a strange sign it carved upon his stomach. It grinned a deathless, joyless grin.

Yet then a great sound, as of the crumbling of a castle wall to mangonel stone, brought with it a new, paler yellow light, and before it the red light of torches. Rough men, in furs and chain bellowed through their blonde beards in Saxon chants. Their steel shone in the eery dream-light, and their shields clamoured against one another as they filtered into the lair of the beast. Driant could not move, but heard their cries—of glory, of fear, of pain—and saw as pieces of them were torn free of their skin by claw and by terrible blade. He felt the patter of their blood upon his pale skin, and the weight of their guts as they were tossed upon the altar. At last the shouts turned to whimpering as l'Ours succumbed to shock, even in the midst of the dream. As his vision faded he looked once more towards the yellow moon, revealed in the open door, and saw the giant hold out its hand towards a figure silhouetted there in horned helm and with blackened blade.

When Maurel was awakened by the roar on that second night he had only just gotten to sleep. In the chaos which filled the manour grounds he found that not only had his father disappeared, but so too had his elder brother. With the aid of Bryn and Emlyn, he secured the grounds, and Olgwydh came with news from the camp. Knowing his uncle's dissatisfaction with the black-clad knight, he sent Galardoun to lead a party after the

Saxons—who once more had vanished en masse—to discover whether they had aught to do with his father's mysterious disappearance on two consecutive nights of their own wanderlust. The Welshman told that no beast had been seen, but the remaining Saxons had fled into the wood with torch and fury and bared blade. "Perhaps if thy father were here he would have some insight into the affliction what besets these lands." But Maurel had his duty to perform, and ignored the knight-commander's insinuations. It was nearly dawn before Winterbourne Stoke was again at peace, other than the scouts which had been sent to find his missing kin, and Maurel slunk back to his own bed for the first time that night, confident that he had done what duty he could. *Someone must lead the army at noon, and I am it seems, for the moment, the heir.*

In the woods, Galardoun rode the night long, only near morning daring to approach again the haunted barrow deep in the holt. The wild tracks of the angered Saxons had led towards it, but he dared not confront black sorcery under cover of black night. Yet as the first red rays of the battle day began to pierce the tree canopy they found no signs about the lich-hill of the Saxon warband. The Sheriff dismounted there and, his blessed sword before him, approached the tomb. Yet there was no disturbance there, and no footprints (not even those he himself had left the night before, he noted with superstition and alarm). With one last look at the runed gatestone he returned to his horse and, defeated, led his company back towards home.

But it was as they left the brake that his son, Rhodri, pointed to another figure leaving the cover of the trees, red with blood and unclothed. "Surely a Saxon berserk," he suggested, and his father agreed. With a cry of "Qui sciens occisi homicidum!" he led the charge across those few fathoms, only realizing as he was almost upon the disoriented wanderer that it was, indeed, his brother.

With great force he called his men to halt, and lept from his saddle. Driant was naked, and soaked to the bone in gore. A man's entrails drooped about his shoulders and a flap of white skin fell over one arm like a cape. "Brother," he said, laying his great mitt upon his sibling and brushing off the horrid mantle. L'Ours ceased his progress, but made no notice of Galardoun, nor the horrified men what surrounded him. His eyes were vacant and unseeing, and his fingers grasped at air. "Driant! Driant!" He shook the man and crossed himself and shook the man some more. He was pleased at least to see that none of the blood appeared to Driant's his own.

At last a light returned to the Earl's eyes. "How came I hear?" He asked, and shivered at the morning cold.

An anxious look traveled from each man to each other in the gathered crowd, and Rhodri muttered about the Beast. Hearing this, Galardoun, who had been unbuckling his grand cape for which to cover his lord, took one long step towards his son and, with a mighty heave, thrust him from his saddle. "Speak no superstition of thy betters," he said, though in his own heart he feared as well a curse on his noble lord's head. "And surrender thy horse to the Earl. Come," he turned to Earl Driant, draping him in silk where once he had been clothed in gizzard. And as he threw his cape about his shoulders and helped him atop his regretful son's steed, he noted a scar upon his stomach, as of a spider with but three legs. He crossed himself and turned his eye to God, but said naught of it aloud. "Ye are home and safe, and if ye know where came ye from, ye may tell us now or at the manour."

"I was dreaming," said the Earl, but he would not say what he dreamt of, for surely now he knew himself to be haunt-

ed for his sins. And he mentioned not the strong arm of the loz-
enged knight with the grey eyes who had helped him from the
holt.

Once Earl Driant was washed and the other great men roused
from their short and restless slumber they met all in Winterbourne Stoke's hall. A pall was on the company, and each
looked on the others as a corpse pitying those soon to join him
in the dirt. The Saxons had all fled in the night.

"My heir is gone, ye tell?" asked Driant thrice, with
greater sadness each time. His hands shook as he gripped his
bare blade.

"And no man slept this night, for fear of the saftey of ye
and he," said Maurel to the first ask, though his merely shook his
head after. He had begun to fear that his elder brother pursued
ill aims.

"The plans Olgwydh relayed to us seem fair enough,
and I shall gladly lead the fore," offered Palthenor nobly, his
disdain replaced by a fatalistic love of battle. The camp in the
dell before the gates had nearly been dissolved.

"And I the rear, it seems," said Murs. "I would not have
our host appear a coward on his own lands." The Thrashers
numbered eight-hundredscore, and would be arrived in two
hours, perhaps more, perhaps less.

Galardoun entreated his brother-lord, "My Lord, forgive
me but ye are unfit, such trauma in thy nightly voyage have ye
seen. Let me lead our force, so ye may rest and live. Maurel
even, though he seems as much l'Audace as ever, winks with
sleep." He did not mention his hatred for Olgwydh which all
knew well, nor his distrust of Murs and Palthenor, but his con-

cerns were waved away and forgotten, despite his persistence.

"It seems almost as a dream. How unlikely this meeting, and this three-way war. How strange the vanishing knights. It is almost as 'twere a punishment of God—handed down in fable—so grand is all the misfortune on this hall," spoke Olgwydh. Lord Driant shuddered at his words and Galardoun saw his brother's skin turn white as fog.

Little was decided in that awful conference, and less was ate or drank. And when noontime approached and the great host of Mordred's vassals stood upon the northern ridge, the haggard host of Winterbourne Stoke stood ahorse to meet it. Dark clouds rolled over the green fields as the first horns were blown, and as the beat of hoof and drum caromed off ear and helm it began to rain.

Sir Palthenor led the vanguard, veering west to assault one wing of the Thrasher army at the last moment, and Sir Driant's force, supplemented by men from du Lac's, smashed into the front line. This was as intended, but the enemy forces did not seem as surprised nor disarmed as they had hoped by the changing charge. Young Emlyn was struck beneath his gorget be an arrow bfore his lance could meet the enemy, and Sirs Dylan and Talfren (younger brothers to Galardoun and Driant) were trampled when their mounts were upended by grounded pikemen. But the other Twombleys fought on, and fought well. Galardoun, bearing a fresh white cape, swept through with shining sword and resounding prayer, severing heads and crushing skulls, even with but one good hand. Bryn the Bastard and Maurel l'Audace fought side by side, their loyal men behind them as they thrust deep into the formations of their foe. Driant too fought, though his eyes were drawn ever to the weeping heavens, and his voice resounded more than his blade.

The initial push seemed a success against all odds, and the spirits of the striving knights were lifted by the advance of Murs's rearguard as they cut their way ever deeper into the black-clad ranks of Orkney. Yet as Murs came, his riders gathered speed. And as they gathered speed they too lowered lance. It was too late when Galardoun's son cried out that they were betrayed, and he was skewered even as he made to warn his kin. In surprise, the defenders were undone, and Palthenor's own wing came west again, swinging axe and firing arrow into the men of Twombly and those who had not been a part of their plot. For it was to the Mordredite camp where they had gone, whenever they could not be found. "Betrayal! Betrayal!" wailed those betrayed, and the du Lac men turned to find Olgwydh and ask his order. But Olgwydh only smiled, though he fought now an impossible battle with his gilded sword.

"Fight on! Fight on!" came Galardoun's shout, and beside his bastard sibling, Sir Yorath, he rode thick, straight into the heart of the line, seeking the commander of that vile host. Water flowed off shining plate, and bright capes turned black as the mud fed on blood. The defenders fought fiercely, though they were now surrounded on all sides, and lighting crackled in the distant sky. Yorath blew his noble horn, and Galrdoun showed his might, but too few had followed him in his worthy gambit, and soon he was separate even from his honourguard. His fervour turned to desperation, and he fought not for victory but for life. His dead arm ached, remembering when it had been free and wishing it could aid him—if only he had not sold it for his hubris in youth. Yorath's leg was cut and he was unhorsed, crying yield as vicious men approached with upraised clubs, and Goring's lord could see others too who were now afoot in the crush of foeman's fierce assault. One figure still was ahorse however, his coats dull and tattered, and it was as he gazed in wonder at that horned helm what came to his defense that a heavy lance struck his own helm and forced him from his seat. As Galardoun looked up at the master of his defeat, his blood turned cold to see that pristine kit and blue and silver feathered armet.

"Et gladiu et in caestu!" called Galardoun's eldest nephew, and horns were blown that he knew to be Herawd's men. *By sword or by guantlet.* "Yield, Uncle," he said with unbecoming pride. "Father is dead, and I am made lord of thy lands."

"I shall not believe this till his own empty face I see!" came the response of Herawd's brother Maurel, who had followed his uncle as best he could, and now found his treasonous brother above that selfsame kinsman. "What brought such black will to thy bright heart, Herawd? Ye needed no host to sit upon the seat of Winterbourne Stoke, for it was thyne by right!" Behind him, Bryn came riding swiftly, standing his horse above Galardoun—who lay in a daze—his arms ready to defend against any assault.

"But what right has the servant of a defeated king?" laughed Herawd, wheeling his steed to face his brother. "Camelot has died, and it lies only now in rot. Whoever sits the throne next shall not be Arthur, but his rightful heir, Orckney! Murs and Palthenor know this as well, and it was with them I conspired to save our house!"

"To save our house? Nay, ye have damned it!" shouted Maurel through his tears. "Our kin lie bleeding and split about this field, and ye have naught of thy own to follow thy steps. I have sinned in my time, but I regret not the love I gave, nor the son I begot of Efa, thy wife! Take up thy sword and match me! No yield may there be between us brothers two, but death only take the weaker!"

Enraged, Herawd lifted his glittering sword and rode swiftly to Maurel. But Maurel dodged his swing, shield above his head, and cut a gash in the chest of his brother's mount, so deep the thing could walk no more. Herawd tumbled from his horse, who broke its neck as it fell, and landed full in the red mud, his visor filling with earth and gore. He turned, lifting his visor so caked with soil, and found his brother above him afoot. Badenshire rolled to the side and snatched for his sword, feeling the heavy weight of a weapon falling on this back. He moved his steel to block another strike as he stumbled to his feet, and Maurel pushed on him with his shield, striking him back against a heap of corpses. The traitor swung and slashed, cutting only once between his foe's mail. Maurel Lord Colham, meanwhile, put the full of his weight behind his shield, keeping his brother pinned; with his free hand, gripped about the pommel of his sword, he began to strike—fierce, blunt blows about his kin's exposed face and the unarmoured pits of his arms. Again and again he struck, ignoring the feeble swings of the architect of their family's fall. At last Herawd's struggles ceased, and he looked up through a bloodied, broken face at a morass of fury and sorrow.

"Ye slay me brother and there shall be no more Twombleys."

"There are no more Twombleys," intoned Maurel as he let drop his shield. "And aye, ye shall die. But I shall first make good our father's promise. That he of our blood what slew Sir Govendral should not retain the hands with which the deed was done." And he began to tear the metal gloves from Herawd's unresistant palms.

The doomed heir choked out a laugh, for his fear of a

moment past was gone and he could see only the humour in his end. "'Twas not I what slew that noble knight, but Murs and Palthenor—though I think his crucifixion beyond their work, and perhaps the doings of the craven Saxon men."

"Ah," growled Maurel, having removed the gauntlets, as Bryn watched grimly on. "So ye were not the one to wield the blade, yet held the coats for them that did. So I shall do ye a kindness and not take all of either hand." And he thrust his brother's hand flat against the breastplate of a fallen knight, and in one fell stroke cut the fingers from that limb. As his elder screamed and drooled in surprise he did the same to the other hand.

Galardoun had managed to struggle to his feet, though his vision still swam, and had called a man to aid him to his horse. About them the battle raged, but there was a calm here, as in the heart of a storm. Once ahorse he looked to the tragic scene of two brothers, both betrayed, "Leave him, Maurel. He shall bleed to death or catch a rot from the wet. Do not burden thyself with having pierced the heart of thy brother."

After a brief hesitation he nodded and remounted, knowing that he had pierced the heart of his brother already years before, when he took his brother's wife to bed. They gathered themselves and, arms ready once more, strove back into the battle, towards the doomed host of which they were servants and commanders.

Elsewhere too tragedy flowed like water, and amongst it all sat Sir Driant (who was not, indeed, dead). His arm had grown weary as his woe had grown heavier, and he sat ahorse now deep amidst his struggling men, and Sir Olgwydh beside. Olgwydh had sheathed his blade, and the Lord of Winterbourne Stoke held his own rested acrost the neck of his destrier. "Ween ye to see another dawn?" asked the Earl without hope.

"I ween to see many more dreamful nights," responded the Welshman. About them men died, and the red grins of the Thrashers could be seen more and more betwixt the thinning helms of the friendly bondsmen. "But look, for ye need not fall here in this storm of steel," and one of his black-robed arms (for he wore no mail, even in battle) stretched out southeast, towards the manour.

There, amidst the rain and crackling lightning, a black shape lurched over the manour walls. Once over, pooling first like liquid shadow, it stood and began its march north. Driant's eyes grew wide as he beheld the terror which had haunted the grounds the last two nights: a giant, five times the height of a man and clad in ragged black robes like a funeral shroud. It bore a great coat of grey mail, and in its hand was a weighty blade which glinted yellow in the light of the moon, risen now even though it be yet day. From its back there rose a long shaft, and even at such a distance the Lord Twombley could see the glint of its yellow eyes.

"Go to it. Confront thy fate," said Olgwydh, tapping l'Ours's elbow so he raised his sword.

"Fate," whispered Driant Twombley, and began a slow trot through the warring fighters. They moved aside as if unseeing, and there was naught to halt his advance. The creature grumbled low, and it seemed to shake the earth. Some few others noted it and fled, but most seemed unawares. Olgwydh rode beside, whispering to Driant of fate and dreams and strange, yellow roads.

Deeper in the battle, Maurel and company had nearly rejoined the force, when a deep and familiar voice at his shoulder called his attention. "There!" said the Knight of Fallowbrook. "What devilry is this? Is that not thy lord father?" And Maurel saw that it was so. Saw his father being led by the Bloody Goat towards a towering nightmare fiend.

"The sorcerer!" cried Galardoun, and raised his silvered sword once more with a cry to God. Hapless, Maurel and Bryn could do naught but follow, and the defenders were left without captains.

Fallowbrook rode beside them, and even in their charge, l'Audace called to him and asked to where the knight had gone. "Away," he said in a voice used by men who have seen no happiness in their life. "Away and back, along dead roads. I know some of what has been forgot, and I know that the doom brought by Mordred will be naught compared to the doom of the yellow moon." And on they road the swifter.

Driant too had begun to charge, and Olgwydh beside, silent now, but smiling. And as he neared he saw that the shaft in the giant's back was a great, wicked arrow, fletched in fleeting shadows. And the fiend's cloak too flowed like darkness flees a torch. And the face of the thing he saw as well. "Father," he gasped, and his heart was choked with fear. *I have done this. I have brought this doom.* And he called out in latin in a roar like an avalanche and charged full-speed at the thing with his father's face. Olgwydh left him then, and rode for the wood.

Galardoun and Maurel, reclaimed lances set, were yet too far when Driant met the beast. They saw his horse rear with gallant poise, and his sword flash in the lightning. But the giant's sword, which it had drug in an ugly path along the ground, was faster, and the Lord of Winterbourne Stoke fell to the soil in two bleeding halves. The sword swung back and so too was his horse slain. The Twombleys roared and spurred their steeds, who roared in equal anguish to their riders, and two heavy lances struck through the creature's mail. They did not see its face, so blind were they with vengeance. One lance stuck, the other broke, and the heavy blade swung in an arc, knocking Maurel from his seat and sundering his plate. Fallowbrook and Bryn rode in as well, their swords sweeping and their horses kicking. Galardoun and Bryn and Fallowbrook rode in circles, cutting at the thing's arms and riding out beyond its terrible reach. It glowered, but was silent as it struck to kill. Behind them the slaughter raged as the Battle of Winterbourne Stoke continued its terrible work. At last the thing fell upon its knees, and Bryn, bastard son of the last Twombley lord, lept from his horse to the things great shoulders, gripping the arrow shaft with one gauntlet and cutting fiercely with the other. Fallowbrook and Goring too rode closer, stabbing upwards at its stomach. Atop the thing, Bryn found his footing loose, as finding footing in a swift stream on smooth stones; the cloak was like cold water, and it lapped bitterly at his boots as he struggled. But in three mighty hews, the bastard took off the head of the thing and it tumbled to the ground atop its sword as the two knights below fled its collapse, its cloak pooling once more about it and the grey head rolling aside.

Bryn ran then to Maurel, and rested him upon his knee, and Galardoun looked to the thing's great nob. Maurel was grey as the sky, and slick blood spilled redly from his open stomach, down his leg. Yet his mouth still worked, and he tried to rise.

"Brother," he said, though he had never called Bryn such before. "Go with haste to the manour, and take Efa and Afon far from here. For I have sinned, and they should not pay for what I have done to Herawd."

It was then that Galardoun gasped and stepped back in horror from his father's face, and looked to the arrowed corpse of the giant. He could think of no reason for such a terrible ghost to haunt this folk, save if the Nettles held great sorcery (which he knew them not to have) or if there had been some ill done to their father for which payment had not been had. He thought then of his brother's grey face after the Battle of Gallows Marsh, and how grey it had been e'en afore news came of their father's death, laid low by cruel archery.

"The wizard flees," called Fallowbrook, his horse nervous. "Even now he runs within yonder brake, and should he reach some hidden gate I fear his ill weavings may yet return."

"My son," sobbed Maurel.

"We cannot hold!" replied the mystery knight.

Galardoun, somber in gaze, had ridden his horse near to his nephews. "I know something of witchcraft," he said. He raised his terrible, dead arm. "For in my youth I thought it better than love of God. We must do what we may to keep this land safe for the worshipers of Christ, and that means we must swiftly after that black-hearted necromancer go." He frowned with truthful sorrow. "Thy sin was not so great as Herawd's, I ween. But we must not risk the health of Christiandom for our own sakes, or that of those we love."

Sitting up in Bryn's arms, Maurel nodded with his own great grief. "There are no more Twombleys."

"I have my misericorde here. Should I dagger thy heart, Maurel, so ye die not in such pain?" asked the bastard.

"Nay," winced, Maurel, resigned to his fate. "I shall ride."

"Thy horse is dead," warned Galardoun.

"Then he shall ride with me," declared Bryn grimly.

Once all were ahorse, the anxious Fallowbrook knight

tugged at his reigns and made for the forest, calling, "Follow!"

And they followed. And behind them died their kin upon the hill.

Back they road into the oppressive dark of the wood, as the sun began to set behind. The battle had been fought for many hours, though it had seemed all that calamity had come at once. Bryn rode in the saddle behind his brother, and his arms were about his bandaged stomach. Maurel grinned with pain and gripped at his blade tightly; he could feel his soul fleeing his body, but he meant to see Olgwydh dead. They had failed to defeat the invaders, and could not save their kin. But they could see a wizard dead. He glimpsed the same grim determination on his uncle's face.

They rode swiftly in the wake of Fallowbrook's knight, and he followed a path none of them could see. At last he stopped, and they found that their mounts stood before the dreaded tomb at the forest's heart, and that the runed stone at its maw had been slid aside. The air was full with the same haunting tune which was plucked from Govendral's morbid harp-strings. Fallowbrook dismounted and looked about, then raised the grill of his helm as he helped Maurel down. "I know not what we go to face, but I ken this man to be a consort to demons and a walker of terrible roads to other lands. My name, as much as it matters now at our journey's end, is Gargond, and I shall stand with ye in that cavern. On my way here I begged help from friends, though I know not if they shall arrive."

"What friends?" asked Galardoun, but their guide did not respond.

"Can ye stand?" Bryn asked of Maurel, and Maurel demonstrated that he could. He grinned and spake their father's name, one hand clutched to his side. There was no colour anymore to his skin, and his boots made wet sounds as they soaked in his carmine waters.

"The wizard waits," intoned Gargond of Fallowbrook, as if in some morbid ritual, and together with swords upraised they entered the sound-sick burrow. The inside was dark, but they could smell the stench of spoiled meat, and a wet feeling hung in the air. A narrow step led down, and Sir Gargond took one pace, then retreated, observing by the forest light the black blood upon his sabaton.

A low chuckle echoed from inside the hill, and soon Olgwydh's unhappily pleasant voice echoed forth. "I apologize, but I had not expected visitors. Let me light thy way." And a torch was lit in his white hand, illuminating the stony hollow beneath. At its centre lay a stone altar, large enough for a man. But the walls were what drew the knights' attention, as they were painted red and hanging with the guts and bones and hearts of many men. The floor was full to the wizard's waist with black, putrefying gore. Near to the door a blonde-bearded head bobbed to the surface, and Galardoun knew that they had found the missing Saxons, slain in their quest to slay a sorcerer and his familiar; Goring's Lord vowed then that, should he live, he would never again judge the Saxon's for their faith, for it seemed they hated and feared the dark arts as greatly as any God-loving man.

Pushing past his fellows, Maurel waded into the horrible pool, unnoticing. "Have ye had thy fill of blood, wizard? For I mean to let ye of it."

Olgwydh smiled gently. "If ye mean to do this, I would warn ye watch thy step." The others cried out in alarm as, in an instant, Maurel l'Audace slipped and fell beneath the black surface of the bloody sea. The other knights then roared forwards, their swords upraised, and Sir Olgwydh too drew his sword.

Fallowbrook paused near where the heir to Winter-bourne Stoke had fallen, but saw that Bryn already had leaned low to search for his brother's corpse. His uncle, meanwhile, had thrust ahead. Galardoun was a large man, and far from slow, yet he had but one arm, and even his pope-blessed sword could not reach the warlock as he defended himself with torch and blade. Steel rang on steel in the dank chamber of terrors, and Gargond lunged at the sorcerer's back, but the wizard was ready, parrying both knight's swings in a single stroke. He smiled as he fought, but did not laugh again. Bryn began to pull his brother from the muck, not yet dead but vomiting the blood of other men, now two days old.

"Think ye that this is real?" taunted their foe. "Is this not more dream than truth? In what world would ye find thyself in measure with a necromancer in a room of blood." Their ter-rible dance led them in a slow circle about the barrow's wall.

"In this world, it seems," growled Galardoun, lunging forwards, but Olgwydh stepped back and the silvered blade only narrowly missed Gargond. As he tried to stand again, his legs wide for balance in the viscous ooze, he felt a cold hand on his neck and his strength began to leave him. He struggled to keep his eyes from fluttering, and fell back against the alter. At last, knowing that his legs would fail him, he clambered atop the stone table so as not to drown in the remains of men. Beyond, Fallowbrook and Olgwydh traded blow for blow, their sharp sounds resounding about the cave.

"Let me be, for I can stand," snapped Maurel, but Bryn, trusting him not, dragged him to the same altar that their uncle lay upon and leant him there. Bryn had dropped his own sword in the rescue, and so he snatched Galardoun's holy weapon as its owner snored fitfully on the grisly table.

Ducking under a hanging intestine, Bryn swung the shining arm in two hands, his teeth clenched in terror and determination, and he struck the first blow upon their enemy, cutting at the hand which held the gilded blade. In surprise and agony Olgwydh dropped his steely brand and raised his flaming one. The light which flared from the torch was blinding, and Gargond stumbled back against the steps to the tomb. Bryn was blinded, but did not fall until the torch struck him hard upon his swordarm and he felt the searing fire spread swiftly along his limb. It burned his skin, traveling under his mail and crawling upwards towards his face like a terrible worm and, unthinking, he plunged himself into the gore to douse it.

"If only this were a dream," came Olgwydh's haunting lilt. "And ye children could awake. But the moon's terrible master sleeps on, and there is no truth which remains. Thy sins drew me, but thy passions kept me. Sing, dreamers, for now ye die or ye dream forever."

Maurel, leaned weakly against his uncle's stony bed, yet still gripping his sword as if it were his very life (and to his mind, it was) noted a figure standing on the stairs above Gargond. A figure in a helm adorned with wide antlers, and a coat of yellow-painted mail. As Olgwydh ranted and sang his madness, Maurel looked to the strange figure, and the figure looked back. This was Fallowbrook's friend, he knew, but he was as frightened of him as he was of the dream-mage, perhaps more. The figure held a battered blade, and beckoned with its free hand for him to come, and another—womanly—figure in its shadow, her hair raven dark and eyes a fierce fire, mirrored him, but Maurel turned towards the burning spell-light in the Welshman's hand instead. He had already known he was set to die, and he had not the strength nor courage to follow that painted knight and his fell

195

bride to whatever road he led. Lurching to his feet, he bellowed the enchanter's name and lept acrost the altar, ignoring the blindness brought by the light. He lept fully atop the knight-commander, his sword falling, falling, falling even as the black-robed body was carried under the surface of the pool, and he himself was lit afire. As he died and as he slew, he whispered the names of all his kinfolk slain, and he whispered the name of his brother's wife, and of his son.

All was dark when Galardoun awoke. He was prostrate upon the grass outside the tomb, from which a foul stink arose. Turning his head to the side, he saw Bryn and Gargond seated near a small fire. "Maurel?" he croaked, but they only shook their heads. With some effort he sat up, shaking his head in pain and begging for water. It was then that he noted the other figure, standing still in the shadows in an antlered helm and yellow-painted mail. He asked who it was.

"This is my friend," offered Gargond, brushing his black mane from his face. "I know not his name, but he has aided me on occasion, and those who know him in my home of Fallowbrook fear him greatly."

"That introduction does not instill confidence," growled Galardoun. "What of Maurel? How did he die?"

"I did not see," said Bryn, "but I found his body. Burned and black, and clutching this," he passed his uncle the holy sword. "Our God has killed a terrible servant of Hell this day, I ween."

They sat in silence for a time, as the sun trickled sparsely through the trees. The new knight said naught in all this time.

"What shall ye do now?" asked Gargond. And the two

men thought. They thought of the terrible slaughter on the hill. And of the strange magics which undid their family. They thought of Driant the Elder's ghost, and Herawd's betrayal. Of their abandonment of the women and children and elderly in the castle. Of Maurel's sacrifice and of Galardoun's shameful sorcery in his younger days. Galardoun even found himself regretting the poor ways in which he had treated his only son before he was killed by Murs's charge.

"What may we do?" answered Bryn. "Should we return home, we should be put in shackles or slain. We have no allies living to help us retake our lands, and we two men are not enough to overthrow hundreds upon hundreds of victorious Thrashers. And should we leave, then we live with guilt forever, and shall be destroyed by it."

"Would ye do good whilst ye can?" replied Gargond of Fallowbrook, glancing back at his strange companion.

"What good would ye think us capable of?" cautioned Galardoun.

"There are more like Olgwydh. Here, and in other lands. And my friend knows the way. Come with us, and help us stop elsewhere what tragedy befell here. I think perhaps that was why I came, though my failed memory prevented me from saving thy hame. My friend can show us roads where our swords can cut down more mages, and make certain their evil may not spread."

Galardoun and Bryn looked to one another, and each looked to their sword, Galardoun to his silver and blessed one and Bryn to the gold-etched one he had stolen from the corpse of Olgwydh. To Galardoun it was sinful to leave what remained of his kin behind, yet sinful also to allow sorcery to roam free in the world. He could see the same conflict in his nephew's face.

Closing his eyes, he asked God for answer, but his head hurt too much to decide. In either case he would live in pain forever, and in either case many more would suffer. "I cannot decide," he breathed.

"Nor I," said Bryn.

And the antlered stranger held out one leather-clad hand, and in it was a shining, golden coin. And so it was decided, by fate alone (if you believe in such things) that they should walk the roads that Gargond walked, and they should fell what wizards they found. And they walked behind the painted knight off of Arthur's land, and beyond the stars, and saw worlds and pains they could never have imagined outside of dreams. And in Gargond they made a mighty friend, and that friendship lasted as long as their hearts held true.

And once the Battle of Winterbourne Stoke was finished with, the Thrashers took the manour. And Herawd, who had survived despite his maiming, returned to his wife and his brother's son. And there was a sadness in him and a regret at all he had done and at the loss of his kin, and so he loved them as ever he had. And he wore golden fingers, whose leather straps made terrible welts on his hands. And when Arthur died and Mordred died and the land fell into disarray he saw the failure of all his hopes and he died unhappily, long after Afon and Efa had passed on from the plague.

And in time, Maurel was right, and there were no more Twombleys.

The Hole Under the House

he knife came down.

Down.

The knife came down and the blood came up.

The blood welled up like milk from a teat.

Me blood welled up and left me and I cried out, even though I had chosen this. They had asked for someone to serve the gods and I had said I would. Even though I knew it would mean the knife would come down and the blood would come up. I had hoped he would smile as he did it. Hoped his lips would say he had felt the same as I had. But he were grim. Grim as a priest should be. When I cried out the pain were in me heart, but it were not wholly real. It were mainly in me soul.

And now me soul is all that remains.

They wrapped me in cloth, so tight I would not have been able to breathe, had I still been able. Me eyes were dug out and replaced with coins, and a cold knife laid on me breast. The knife cut like fire, even though it lay flat. It burned and it burned but I had called all I could ever call. Silently screaming, they set me in the hollow beneath the house and shoveled black dirt over me as I tried to writhe, tried to cry for help.

Cry for love.

I never saw him again. He did not even hold a shovel as the soil rained down, thudding against me wrappings like rain on me cloak in the cold springs. Cold springs I would never feel again. And even those cold rains was hot compared to what I feel now. Only cold.

Cold.

Cold.

Cold.

Down in the hole there are nothing but rodents and spiders. The rodents chew on me toes and skitter loudly in me skull, but the spiders are gentle, crawling softly under me wrappings and apologizing for their little feet, which I cannot even feel. I try to wiggle me fingers or lick me parched lips, thin as onion skins, yet I am frozen still, the knife burning a brand in me chest, filling me heart with pain and fire. I have been here a long time. Longer than all the lives of all me grandfathers. I know this, though I cannot watch the sun. Me silver coin eyes shift in their sockets as heavy rat paws press on them in their frantic tunneling. They live in me belly and chew on me guts.

Mayhaps the rats have eaten me heart.

Sometimes I hear voices above, distant and muffled. The spiders tell me the land has moved on. Iron and steel have grown like creepers acrost the land and choked out the forests. White picket fences stand where once there was Roman roads. Men are too afraid to die to carry a knife. Instead they carry fire in their fists. They speed along in great metal wagons on metal roads, breathing dragon-smoke. They are too impatient to pray. Not nearly as patient as I. I who can do nothing but wait. Wait in the dark in the hole under the house.

The spiders tell me that the men are gone that once lived above me. Grandchildren of grandchildren of the men who emptied me heart. They grew old and died because they could not bear to see the world change. Mayhaps they too rot under the earth, pining for the pain of life. The house is empty for a very long time. Empty like me chest. I can hear the rats gnawing on me rib cage.

Me heart is surely gone.

More spiders come and live in the wood and soil and they sing to me. Moulde grows above and slowly crawls down, down, down until it rests beside me. It asks if it can home inside me with the rats and I cannot say no. The rats do not like the moulde in their house, but they cannot fight it, and so we live together in the dark—the rats, the moulde, the spiders, and me.

In time the spiders come again and tell me that there are men above once more. They think there will be more danger for their kind and they prepare to be driven out. I am sad for them, but I know I cannot follow; I am wrapped up and trapped under the foundation, pinned here by the cruel steel of the knife me priest laid upon me. The spiders fight against the newcomers, but they are like the rats and the moulde—they cannot win. Many die and some leave, or dig deeper down beside me. The rats are killed when they go up to poach for food. It is one man, and for his many murders they call him Cruelty.

It is just me and the spiders and the moulde under the house of Cruelty, and we are happy. As happy as we can be. The spiders are few and frightened of the surface world. The moulde cannot think but only grow. And I am dead and me heart eaten ages past by dead rats. I am not certain how happy that can truly be. But we are happy.

Until the roaring comes, and the hammering, the chiseling, the chopping and the pounding. They are crushing the house and razing it. Digging it out and filling it in. The house is being expanded, destroyed, remade, and confused. The spiders flee and the moulde cries out as its brothers are slain and I lay still, grinning me hollow, rictus grin. A great metal beasts tears through the foundation and thin bands of sunlight sparkle on me silver coin eyes. Me wrappings have rotted and I can almost see the world once more. Almost see the shovels and the hole I rest in as they dig, dig, dig. They are digging me up. Bringing me back into the world. Soon I shall walk once more.

But no, the beast belches steam and shovels soil with its steely trunk, pushing me, unseen, aside. Lumping me in with a pile of other unwanted refuse. I fall and am buried again, still unseen, me rotten cloth peeling away.

And the cruel knife falling.

Falling down.

Down.

And me chest rising up.

I breathe cold air with cold lungs and wait for the sounds to die. I am free from the hole, free from the knife. I am free to walk and laugh and sing and love.

But as I pull meself from the soil, the thick, wet clumps clinging to me bones and piling in the hollow of me gut, I look down on me reflection in a muddy pool of rainwater, lit by the moon. That is not me. That is not a man. Not a free thing. What stares back with silver coin eyes is blue and grey and skeleton-thin. The skin peels and stretches thin and a black cross sits deep in its chest where the knife once lay. I run me fingers, thin and sharp, over that hole, and watch me blackened teeth chatter and chitter. I reach inside me empty stomach and reach up, feeling around, hoping to find an heart.

But I am dead.

I howl to the moon and make no sound, falling to me

knees and shuddering in sorrow. What good have I done the gods in me eternal torment? What can I do with no blood in me veins? I am worthless and friendless.

Save the spiders. The spiders was me friends. And the moulde. And even the rats who ate me heart. And the man and his army of shovels and axes and hammers killed me friends. Broke me home. Brought me up into the cruel moonlight. I gaze about and see that the house still stands, or perhaps another house in the same place; silver coins are not much good for seeing. I will find Cruelty, and make him pay. I was happy once—or as happy as a dead man can be, with his heart eaten by rats—but that were taken from me. Just as I were happy once before, but that were taken from me with a grim face and a falling knife.

Me quiet rage bellowing from me absent lungs, I lurch towards the house. Cruelty shall know cruelty. It is a long way, me legs unused to walking, but I urge meself onwards. For the spiders. For the spiders.

I come to the door, old and thick and claw uselessly at it. It does not move. I push and tug, but I can feel meself coming apart at the seams. And so I drag meself back and look up with silver coin eyes at the moon and then at the house again.

There is a window, open to the cool breeze. I clamber through it and stand in the dark of the house. The house which stood as me gravemarker for so long. Someone snores, shaking me skull with its harsh sounds. I follow them, me bony heels sliding on the wood. Scraping. Scraping. Soon I come to the stairs and climb them, me hands wide so I do not fall. Were I a man me heart would be beating loud, but I have no heart and it is only Cruelty's snoring which fills me. That evil, wicked man who took me life from me. I can never repay the man who took me first life, but I can repay Cruelty.

At the top of the stairs there is only one room, and at the far side, under the moon in a pointed window, he sleeps. A lump of blue blankets slowly rising and falling. Rising and falling. Welling up like me blood and falling like me empty chest. Scraping acrost the floor, I come to him. Scraping. Scraping. Standing above him, I growl, loud as the night. Me claws reach down and grip him, turn him on his back to face me.

And he is beautiful.

I know then that the rats did not take me heart when they ate it. Only hid it away. Safe, so no one could claim it. All of me malice is gone in an instant and I remember what it were like to be a man. What it were like when I first met the priest. What it were like to touch meself alone as I thought of him. The sound of his laugh and the thought of his hands on me skin. Me claws tremble and I step back. His hair, blonde and curled, falls away as his eyes flutter, but do not open. I love again and at once fear again.

I am alone and he can never love me.

How could any man love me as I am when they could not love me when I were alive? I weep mouldey tears and crouch in the corner of the attic, beating me fragile skull against me hands. Woe! Woe! And I have nothing to give him, nothing but me love. The love of a dead man. With a cry I burst to me feet and make to run for the stairs. Until I remember what I do have.

Returning to his bed, I reach up and pluck out one of me silver coin eyes. Gently, I lay it on his breast above his heart, and his hand atop it. His fleshy plump fingers curl around it and I smile, shivering as I watch. That is for him. And this—I tap me remaining silver coin eye—is for me.

I return to me dirt pile outside the house, burrowing

deep and crouching there as the shovels return, careful not to go near the knife which imprisoned me. I can feel warmth now, but only in me chest. The warmth of love. Cruelty is too unkind a name for him, but it is the name I have known for too long and so it stays.

In time the new cellar is finished, and the dirt is laid out in a garden with a pretty little pool. I live in that pool, and watch him when he does not see me. Me one good eye shines in the sunlight and the moonlight, and I often see him playing with me gift. Does he know I am here? He must. He must know. All the little things I do for him. All the little gifts. Keeping the white picket fence fixed and scaring away the rabbits and deer so he can grow his vegetable garden. Taking the spiders and giving them an home far from his bed. Singing to him as he sleeps. He may not know that he loves me, but I think he does. Sometimes he leaves small gifts on the fencepost at the end of the stony path he made—bows of yarn and little carvings. I take his gifts and treasure them at the bottom of the pool and smile as I think of the two of us together, living our lives as one.

The priest took me heart from me, the knife took me life. The rats took me guts from me and the shovels took me home. But Cruelty took nothing from me. Everything he has of mine I gave with love. And now I live and laugh and love with him, he in his house above the hole, and me in me garden pool...

Y Knew Robyn Hode

y, y knew Robyn Hode.

A gode man ſome would ſaye, a vyllayn others. Yn tymes we were cloſe, but often y gayn'd great ſhame frome hys wylde wayes, and ſo y ſhall tell ye of the Lorde of Barneſdale Wode. Lythe[1] ye to myn[2] tale and remember, though y found hym often to be a wycked and uncouth man y found hym also to be a compaſſyonate man yn ways and a belyever yn the God of our fathers yn hys owne man-ners. Nowe yn myn olde age y ſometymes thynk myn dyſtaste fore Robyn Grenewode's ardour fore lyfe maye have bene myſplace'd. Who can a man truely judge that our Lorde yn Heaven cannot foregyve? ſo lythe and judge ore lythe and love, but lythe ye and knowe what y have knowne.

When fyrſt y met the ſylvan kyng of that Yorkeſhyre foreſt yt was a bryghte daye yn June. The rayn had wet the grene, grene graſs the nyghte before, but now the ſun ſhone happyly though y mynſelf was ſorroweful. The robyns and the thruſhes ſange as y rode ſouth frome Yorke, myn ſon beſyde me nurſeyng the hand the ſheryff had hurte. Myn beard was more grey than when we had ſet forthe, and unruly fore lack of a razore, and hys eyes were downecaſt fore the whole longe ryde.

We came, us two, to the edge of Barneſdale Wode and loked on at that ruſtlyng grene holte[3]. Were myn ſtrayts not so dyre y ſhould have lyke'd to loke some tyme on the beauty our

1.   Listen
2.   My
3.   Forest

God had made of thoſe ſtout trunkſ and thoſe ſhapely leaves what hyd the joyeous caperyngs of the Kyng's dere. Myn ſon complayn'd of a payn yn hys wryſt and y ſylently bemoan'd the length we ſtyll muſt go before we reach'd our ſturdy hame[4] at Veryſdale. 'Come ye, boye, fore the road ys not ſo very longe yet,' y lye'd wyth love. He hyd hys broken hand then frome the damp.

We had left the Roman road of Ermyne ſtrete—whych Harold Kyng followe'd afore he fell'd the Norwegyan kyng and the exyled Earl Toſtyg—and followe'd nowe the ſymple path whych went yts waye nowe depe ynto the darke wode. Our ryde was ydyllyc and, though the wyde boughs of the trees wet our humble tunycs, our ſpyryts were lyfted ſome to ſee the blythe[5] manner yn whych the ſun ſemed to play betwyxt the leaves and chaſe the ſquyrrels and the flutterbyes as yf yn some gaye dance. Yn thys bryef joye even our heavy hearts were move'd to ſonge, and our voyces range wyth ballads whych oft we had ſung yn leſs unhappy tymes.

Yt was lykely by the ſounds of thys mynſtrelſy that y came to knowe Robyn Hode.

As we rounded a bend we found ourſelves met by three bolde men. One was ſtout and blonde wyth longe hayr and a noble beard, lokeyng every part the Daneyſh vyllayn. Another was well-dreſſ'd yn red cloth and ſmyle'd lyke he had juſt tolde a jeſt. The laſt was a darke-browe'd dwarf wyth thyck muscles whych ſtrayn'd hys common coſtume. All three bore ſharp ſwordes and the dwarf bore alſo a ſturdy woden ſtave. Yn dayes and years to come y would come to knowe them each, but on fyrſt meteyng y ſaw only lawleſs men.

4.   A house or home
5.   Happy

'Who comes to the Grenewode wythout yts lorde's leave?' aſk'd the tall one yn a voyce drowne'd yn northern accents. The red companyon laugh'd and added, 'Ay, who?'

'Y am a pore knyghte, and thys myn only ſon,' ſaye'd y.

'A knyghte!' they cry'd, and fell upon theyr knees. 'Honour'd are we to mete ye here.' Then ſtode the blonde yeoman[6] and motyon'd wyth hys hand. 'Y am call'd Lyttle Jon fore myn ſyze, and thys ys Wyll ſcarlocke and Much the Myller's ſon.'

Y greted them each and bowe'd myn head tyl Wyll ſcarlocke laugh'd yn a fryendly waye and wave'd hys ſcarlet arm. 'Ye ſeme a decent man, and he a decent ſon. Our maſter has bade us ynvyte all godely men what walk hys lands to feaſt wyth hym beneath the Tryſtyng[7] Tree.'

'And who ys thy maſter?' y bade hym.

'Our maſter,' anſwer'd the ympyſh Much, doubtleſs named fore hys ſyze as much as was Lyttle Jon, 'ys Lorde Robert of the Wode, whome ſome call Loxſley and others Robyn Hode.'

Myn heart froze then, fore y had often heard travelers what came to Veryſdale[8] by thys waye ſpeak of the fearſome ban-

6. A yeoman was often a servant of a noble or churchman or, in a later context, a landholding commoner. Chaucer writes of yeoman in the 14th century as following the former pattern, though describes multiple examples of yeoman as foresters dressed in green and well-learned with the bow. This is likely due to a medieval law in England forbidding yeoman from practicing with any weapon save that.

7. Derived from Scots, it originally meant an appointed place during a hunt, but later came to mean a secret meeting place.

8. Though Verysdale is mentioned consistently as the home of Sir Richard, no such place is known to exist. Hints to its site exist throughout the text, but its exact location is unknown.

dyt call'd by thoſe names. The gaze gyven me by myn ſon prove'd hys breaſt was alſo afflycted wyth cautyous and heavy trepydatyon. ſcarlocke ſtyll gryn'd bryghtely, but the ſhape of hys fellowes' mouths remynded me more of hungry wolves than fryendly hoſtes.

'Y maye be pore, but y ſtyll a be gentle and could not refuſe the ynvytatyon of a lorde, e'en ſhould y wyſh yt.'

ſmyrkyng Wyll clap'd hys hands and ſpun upon hys hele. 'Then praye followe, 'tys not far.'

And ſo we followe'd, myn ſon and y, prayeyng ſoftely as we were led through the Grenewode. Thys was but the fyrſt of many tymes yn whych y was afear'd fore the lyfe of mynſelf and myn famyly yn the tyme y knew Robyn Hode, though thys tyme y dyd not yet fear fore myn ymmortal ſoul.

After a tyme followeyng theſe three as they ſang bawdy ſonges we came to a clearyng depe yn the holte. At the ſyghte of yt y gaſp'd and bryefly forgot myn fayth, utteryng an oath whych brought me no pryde. Here at Barneſdale's centre was an oak taller by twyce even than myn caſtle walls, yts trunk wyde enough to block Ermyne ſtrete at yts wydeſt forke. All about yt the trees were hung wyth banners of all hues and drape'd yn rych cloth. Gaye fluteyngs and poundyng drums accompany'd ſtrumyng lutes and voyces rayſe'd yn a dozen ſonges. Merry men prance'd and caper'd 'neath the great Tryſtyng Tree yn well-made grene jacks, mantles, hode, and hoſe. Women there were as well, as loud and coarſe yn theyr revels as the menfolke, and ſome dreſſ'd much too ymmodeſtly. Y ſtruck myn ſon's pu-nyſh'd arm to ſee hym gawk. Tables as yn a feaſtyng hall were ſet upon the ſward[9], wyth an hyghe table ſet wyth trenchers upon an earthen mound. Rych ſmells of ale, of wyne, and of ſun-

9.   Grass

coke'd[10] game fyll'd myn noſe and, were yt not that the jeſters and foles had bene replace'd by the feaſters themſelves, y maye have bene convynce'd that thys dyoneſyan farce was yndede a noble meal.

One of the few bandyts not arraye'd all yn foreſt grene was a man yn rych golden capes and great weather'd gloves lyke thoſe of a falconer, though he ſtyll bore the grene mantle. Much went to fetch hym frome the mayden upon whych he ſemed to me to have made hymſelf too famylyar. When he turne'd y ſaw hys doublet to be black wyth grene leaves lyke thyſtles yntrycately damaſk'd[11] upon yt. A ſylver'd baldryc[12] fell acroſte hys hale cheſt. He ſmyle'd as he came thyther towards us, and remove'd hys gauntlets, whych Jon toke, to reveal ſylver ryngs. Hys hayr and beard were browne lyke honey and he ſmell'd of flowers, bread, and drynk.

'Ye muſt be the famous Robyn Hode,' y ſpake, un-wyllyng to dyſmount though ſcarlocke bade me to.

'ſo y am call'd by myn fryends yn the foreſt,' ſpake he, hys eye atwynklyng. 'As well as by myn enemys what dwell yn halls of ſtone.' He laugh'd wyth a voyce lyke ſylver bells. 'And who are ye? Thy clothes be rych yn colour but pore yn care, and ye carry weapons and ſhyelds to overburden thy palfreys[13].'

'They be a knyghte and hys heyr, Lorde,' offer'd Lyttle Jon. 'We found them alonge the path and thought theyr bellyes

---

10. Sun-cooking was a medieval method of preserving meat and killing harmful bacteria, which involved leaving the meat out in the sun for days at a time before serving or packaging.
11. Decorated in a particular and variegated style, the fashion originating in Damascus
12. A belt meant for holding a sword, worn over one shoulder and extending over the opposite hip
13. A riding horse most often used for short distances and by women

loked to be wantyng.

'Ay, theyr bellyes and theyr rayment,' added Wyll ſcarlocke yn mockyng.

Yn haſte, to perhaps avoyd ſome further courteſy of theſe wodefolke (though yt avayl'd me naught), y ſpake, 'Y had no yntentyon of begyng on thy hoſpytalyty, Maſter Robert, but ynſtead meant to make myn waye to Blyth ore to Doncaſter by the nyghte and there ſeke lodgeyng and rere-ſupper[14].'

'Avaunt[15]!' laugh'd the robber kyng, 'Ye muſt nedes ſtaye here and have a proper ſupper ynſtead, by the grace of our Lady.'

'Gramercy,' y ſpake then, yn defeat.

'Whych one ys the Lady,' aſk'd myn ſon yn ydyot won- der as he gaze'd upon the crude harlots of that hoary wode. Robyn and hys men laugh'd at thys, but y was ſhame'd and ſtruck hym.

'He means to ſpeak of Mary Magdalene, the conſorte of the Lorde,' y hyſſ'd through myn tethe. He bluſh'd and was fyll'd wyth remorſe.

'Come, and take myn ſeat at the table,' ſpake Robyn.

And ſo y went, and through hys rych table—ſet wyth pheaſant, grouſe, as well as dere and all other manner of yllegal game[16]—began to knowe Robyn Hode.

Once we were ſeated yn our hyghe ſeats Robyn ſtode before the table, hys hands claſp'd before hym. At fyrſt y could

14. A meal often eaten quite late at night and marking the final meal of the day
15. "Go away!" A common exclamation
16. All game in English forests were the property of the reigning monarch, espe-
    cially the Roe, Fallow, and Red Deer as well as the wild boar, meaning these
    could only be hunted by the King and what nobles he gave permission to.

not gueſs hys yntentyon, but all too ſone myn curyoſyty turne'd to horrore as he began to delyver a ryght whych bore more than a Paſſyng ſemblance to the Uſe of Yorke[17]. Yn aſtonyſhment we two pyous knyghtes ſat and watch'd thys heretyc maſs. When bread was offer'd and communyon wyne we croſſ'd our arms as yf we were unbaptyze'd. Wyll ſcarlocke mock'd us, but we could not take thys false Eucharyſt and ryſk our ymmortal ſouls fore the pryde of Robyn Hode. Y would have left yf y were able, but yt ſtruck me how lyttle we had eaten ſynce we left Yorke and the arryval of the banquet bewytch'd us.

The fode was freſh and largely free of moulde, yet ſtyll there was plenty of ſalt and garlyc to dyſguyſe what was there. Y dare'd not queſtyon how ſuch affluent fare fell ynto the hands of Loxſley. The wyne was hearty and full, the ale wonderfully ſour, and the water as pure as yf yt had bene drawn juſt frome the wells of Eden. Y drank, but not yn exceſs (does not the gode boke ſaye, 'et nolyte ynebryary vyno yn quo eſt luxurya ſed ymple-myny ſpyrytu[18]?'). Myn ſon, however, ſtaye'd lyttle hys gluttony, and y ſaw hys gaze growe ſtupyd wyth drynk. Y marvel'd that he could drynk and eat ſo myckle[19] wyth hys ynjure'd arm and hys eyes caſt ſo lecherouſly about.

Maſter Robyn and hys man Jon ſerve'd us wyth theyr owne hands. Y beg'd the Wodelorde halt fore myn emba-

17. The Use of York was the variant of the catholic liturgical rights practiced in northern England prior to the reign of Henry VIII—which most certainly should not be performed by a layman such as Robin.

18. Ephesians 5:18 (as set forth by King James in 1611): *And bee not drunk with wine, wherein is excesse : but bee filled with the Spirit.* It seems that, whether by misunderstanding, misteaching, or willful ignorance Sir Richard here misuses the passage, misinterpreting it to imply one should drink wine, so long as they do not overindulge, rather than a more common interpretation which would be to avoid wine entirely, as the Holy Spirit can supply fully for God's people.

19. Much

raſſment, 'Are ye no noble? Thy men call ye Lorde, yet theſe lands belonge yn myn knoweyng only to our Lorde ſheryff.'

A darke loke paſſ'd on Robyn's face, but wyth a jolly chortle yt fled hym. 'No noble y, but a yeoman be. Myn men love me as a lyege, yet 'tys all yn jeſt—ſhould a true maſter of theſe trees come callyng we ſhould all bend a knee, and y fore-moſte.'

'And ys not the Kyng's man what wears the badge of Nottyngham maſter of theſe trees?' Even to thys daye y knowe not what overcame me to challenge hym ſo, but y have bene lucky yn myn lyfe to have ever bene a favouryte of that grene rogue.

The loke agayn paſſ'd hym, but he chyrrup'd bryghtly, 'Y knowe the man not, but knowe better that he has never yet ſet fote yn Barneſdale Wode. Yf ever he does y ſhall have to judge fore mynſelf whether y fynde hym a lawman ore a knave,' and caper'd offe to tend the gather'd flock. Hys lyghte nature to-wards the man what ſhould be hys maſter ſat unwell yn me, but y had lyttle more tyme to ſpeak wyth hym untyl the ſun had be-gun to ſet.

As the gloamyng[20] ſet upon the clearyng, an half dozen more butts[21] were produced and tap'd to the cheres of the revel-ers. The foreſt's ſtrange benefactor ſtode atop them as they vomyted forthe ſtronge drynk and gave a prayer (whych ſemed to me more jeſt than worſhyp) before thankyng the Lady Mary Magdalene and fyllyng hys owne horne. Yt ſeme'd to me then that he held an eſpecyal apprecyatyon of the gentle apoſtle, and yndede yn all the years y knew hym y found myn aſſumptyon unchanged'd. Thys ardour ſeme'd to ſpread acroſte the whole

20. Twilight or dusk
21. An English measurement used by brewers, equivalent to 491 litres

of the womanly ſex, and though y have heard ſome prayſe yt y have ſene too much of hym and hys comporte wyth maydens to conſyder yt much greater a vyrtue than a myſchevyous lechery.

Hys horne ſloſhyng over hys leathern gauntlet and hys muſtaches whyte wyth ale, he came to us agayn as the torches were lyt and the mydges and dragonflyes began to buzz. 'Marry[22], fellowes! How fare ye at the feaſt?' he cry'd moſte boyſtrouſly.

He toke a ſeat near to us and hys three ruffyans what had taken us alonge the path joyn'd alſo. Y had begun to yma-gyne an eſcape, but wyth our captors returned y was reſygne'd. Myn ſon ſpake yn reſponſe, too much joyeous yn tone, 'Gramercy fore thy kyndneſs, Maſter Robyn, fore y am much ſatyſfyed!'

Y gave an eye to myn ſon ſo he would knowe how yll yt had bene fore hym to ſpeak ſuch—and before hys father had ſpoken. 'Ay, gramercy. Yt has bene ſome wekes ſynce we have eaten ſuch fare,' y ſaye'd. Y added, knoweyng y muſt ſhowe courteſy, even to thys vagrant yeoman, 'ſhould ever ye paſs through Veryſdale ye can be aſſure'd of as fyne a meal.' Y hope'd never to be call'd upon to make gode upon myn promyſe, but the Lorde forces all oath-takers to be proven honeſt yn tyme.

'Y ſhall remember thy generous offer when next y wend that waye. But that tyme ys not nowe, and ye have ſup'd full well. Ys yt not ſtyll more common yn England fore the knyghte to paye the yeoman fore ſervyce than fore the yeoman to ſupply unrewarded?'

Y felt then the nearneſs of hys lyeutenants, and remem-ber'd well the ſhene of theyr ſwordes and fear'd then the blackneſs yn theyr breaſts. Myn heart was certayn then that y knew the truthe of Robyn Hode. 'Holde, y beg!' y cry'd urgently. 'Y am but a pore knyghte and have naught but ten ſhyllyngs yn myn pack.'

'We ſhall ſee the truthe of that,' cry'd Robyn wyth excytement, ſpyllyng ale. 'Jon, go to the gode man's palfrey and count the contents of yt. ſhould thy myſfortune be tolde true, ſyr Rychard, y ſhall do all y can to relyeve thy payns, but ſhould there be but a ſheckle more y'll have yt all 'fore y ſend ye on thy waye.'

No choyce remayn'd to me but to nod dumbly and to watch as Lyttle Jon lumber'd to where myn ſtede was fetter'd, hys great Nordyc paws hungry fore yll gayns. Y knew myn truthe to be tolde well, yet y began to ſweat and to hope myn count had bene aryghte. Loxſley's arm was about myn ſhoulder, and ſcarlocke's about myn ſon's. They gryn'd and jape'd wyth Much the Myller's ſon as Jon laye'd out a cloth upon the graſs. Hys arm went yn myn ſaddle bag and—empty as yt was—he quyckly found myn purſe. The coyns clynk'd forlornely as they tumble'd frome theyr home, and wyth one thyck fynger the ſaxon counted myn meagre holdyngs twyce. Once thys was done he rayſe'd hys hayry head and noded to hys wynkyng patron. 'Ten ſhyllyngs y count, and nary more nore leſs,' he ſaye'd, hys voyce ympoſſyble to read.

Myn ſon and y bothe jump'd as our backs were ſlap'd as yf by fryends and Robyn lept to hys fete. 'Ye knowe lyttle howe glad y am to fynde ye an honeſt man, ſyr Rychard—though y would as much have enjoye'd a treaſure cheſt,' ſaye'd he. 'But our Lady provydes as ever ſhe has and y would lyef[23] hear thy tale. Tell us howe yt came to be that ſuch poverty fell upon ſyr Rychard at the Lee.'

23. Gladly

Y knowe not what came upon me then—nore perhaps what left—but though theyr faces had not change'd y found them ſuddenly the careyng vyſages of fryends. Fore the fyrſt tyme y glympſe'd the godely hearts whych dwelt wythyn theyr black breaſts, though whych was truer y have never bene certayn. Myn tongue began to ſpeak and y could not halt yt, as yf y were bewytch'd.

'Myn ſon here and y bothe rode yn great ſpyryts to the lyſts[24] at Yorke. As ye can ſee, he ys an hale boye of twenty years, and ſo he rode the jouſt fore our famyly as y reſted myn olde bones. And he rode well, and wyth honour. He won by ranſom[25] much coyn, wyth whych we meant to returne and do well by our lands yn Veryſdale. O that ye had ſtop'd there, ye foleyſh ſon! Y wyſh nowe that y had not gyven ye myn name, that only one Rychard ſhould be ſo dyſgrace'd! He went, thys foleyſh boye, to joyn the melee, lorded over by the ſheryff John. The boye's arm was ſtronge, though not ſo ſtronge as hys wrath and ſadly ſtronger than hys wyt. Whyle he fought that playeful war he found hymſelf the target of a fayr knyghte of Lancaſter. The lyon knyghte fell upon myn ſon yn full fury, hys ſquyre cloſe behynde. 'Twas clear to all that young Veryſdale's ſkyll was greater, yet ſtyll the other would not relent. Would that myn lackwyt ſon had but bene gentle yn hys vyctory, ore even gyven yyeld! The ſhame brought by loſeyng face ys naught to the ſhame he earn'd. When hys opponent would not concede, fore the arrogance of hys blode, a rage unſemeyng yn a Chryſtyan man overtoke myn only heyr. Wyth blodey ſtrokes he cut downe the knyghte of Lancaſter and turne'd too upon the ſquyre. Wyth two cadavers at hys fete, y cry'd to ſee the ſyn. Yn

24. A field where a joust was held
25. In a joust, the losing competitor's armour and horse would be forfeit to the winner, and they could purchase them back by paying a ransom to the victor.

216

anger ʃheryff John, the maʃter of the games, demanded geld[26] fore hys ʃlayn kyn and ʃet hys ʃervant to crypple the hand whych bore the guylt. Fore all hys faults, myn ʃon flynch'd lyttle when the ʃheryff's rod fell harde upon hys arm. But fore the geld we were ʃore ʃpent. We paye'd all we had earn'd as well as all we had brought, and ʃtyll we owe'd four hundred pounds ʃylver. Yt would have bene Yorke's darke dungeons fore us bothe had not our neyghbore yn the churche—the Abbot of ʃaynt Mary's—offer'd to lend us the coyn the vyolent act had loʃte us. We toke the abbot's kyndeneʃs, though we had lyttle hope to returne the ʃylver. Yn a whole year pore Veryʃdale could ʃcarce gayn the coʃte, e'en ʃhould y tax the peaʃants ʃore. Yet ʃhould y fayl to repaye the Abbey by year's end y ʃhould loʃe all that land whych belonges to myn ryghte.' Myn beard was wet when y had fynyʃh'd, and myn ʃon hung hys head to ʃee hys father's tears.

The others noded ʃagely to hear myn ʃad tale and the Wodelorde offer'd me a drynk of hys horne. He ʃoftely ʃpoke, 'Truely 'tys ʃad to ʃee ʃo ʃwyft and ʃo far a fall. Tell me, gode ʃyr knyghte, were ye made knyghte by battle ore by gode ʃervyce—as yeoman ore the lyke?'

'Neyther, Robert, but by myn father and by hys, and on fore an hundred years and more. The houʃe at Veryʃdale has bene knyghted ʃynce the days of the fyrʃt Norman kyngs,' y anʃwer'd.

'Where ʃhall ye go, ʃhould ye not repaye the loan?' he aʃk'd.

26. The wergeld was a price put on each living being and piece of property, which was to be paid on the event of that individual's death or destruction. Its usage here is curious for the fact that the use of wergild was increasingly uncommon after the 9th century, and had nearly disappeared by the 12th, with capitol punishment being the more common result. This, perhaps, implies the greed of Sheriff John rather than the common course of legal proceedings.

'To the Levante,' y ſaye'd, unplan'd. Y decyded then the path myn lyfe ſhould take when the Abbot of ſaynt Mary's toke myn anceſtral lands. 'To the Kyngdome of Jeruſalem and to Calvary to ſee where our Lorde was crucyfy'd and mock'd, and hys ſyde ſplyt by the Holy ſpear.'

'That ys a longe journey fore an eldyng man and hys famyly,' ſaye'd Robyn ſomberly. 'Have ye no fryends nore kyn on whych to call? No lenders who would be more kynde to ye?'

'Y am the laſt of the Veryſdale lordes—no kyn remayns to me ſave wyfe, ſon, and ynfant daughters. As fore fryends y have only our God what dyed on tree,' y ſpake.

By then yt was not merely y and myn ſon what cry'd, but Jon, Wyll, and Much as well. Y could ſee that they knew well the troubles y had gayn'd.

'Fye!' bellowe'd the Hode, throweyng hys horne and ſhakeyng the table wyth a kyck. 'Fye and befoul! That one who clayms to ſpeak on our Lady's behalf ſhoulde be ſo cruel to ſo fayr a man!' He came back and ſtode over me yn myn ſeat, hys eyes fyerce and hys fynger ſhakeyng. 'Howe much dyd ye ſaye ye owe'd the vyllayn? Four hundred pounds ſylver? Thys y ſhall lend ye eaſyly, and ye ſhall repaye me as ye are able, wyth no threat to thy demeſne, domayn, nore heyrs. 'fore ye leave Barneſdale Wode ye ſhall be fyt wyth a cheſt to bear thy pryce, and men to ſee ye ſafe to the other ſyde. Worry not fore ſuryty, fore all ſuryty y need ys our Lady's love.' Y was ſpecheleſs at ſuch generoſyty. 'Gawp not, but followe, fore ye ſhall ſtaye at Robyn's lodge thys nyghte. Ha! Ye dyd not thynk that gode Loxſley of the Wode ſlept yn the dyrt, dyd ye? Up on thy fete and followe!'

Y ſtode and followe'd, myn ſon behynde wyth hys wound hyden, and we were joyn'd by Wyll, Jon, and Much. All three loked on me wyth ſuch pyty that y was bothe comforted and ſhame'd yet more. 'Y am ſorry that the Churche has wronge'd ye, and ſorryer ſtyll yf we have fryghten'd ye. But Robert ys gode to hys worde and a fryend to all who are unfayrly tax'd,' ſpake Much.

The lodge was quyte near to the Tryſtyng Tree, but hyden by a brake of wyllowes. Yt was a longe, woden hame yn the ſtyle of the olde ſaxon manours before Norman culture decyded the country's myndes on ſtone. Yt had a longe, lowe rofe and eaves carve'd wyth horſes, dragons, and heroes yn poynted helms and brygandyne mayl[27]. Grene banners hung frome the ſagyng eaves, decorated wyth arrowes, fetters, croſſes, and ymages of ſaynt Mary. Ynſyde yt ſmelt of ſwete wode and herbs and moulde. Revelers laye on benches about the hall, near ſlepe ore already ſnoreyng. Robyn ſhed hys yellowe cape at the dore and led us deper ynto hys ſanctum. He brought us to a ſmall chamber, wyndoweleſs and darke, but well-ſupply'd wyth candles and rugs (though they loked and ſmelt quyte olde). Two ſturdy woden beds ſtode near the walls and a croſs upon the table.

Yt ys a wonder that myn fear dyd not returne, fore deſpyte the candles and the the furs thys could eaſyly have bene a cell. Yn the months whych dyrectly followe'd myn fyrſt meteyng wyth Robert Loxſley y wonder'd ſome on whether he was ſome enchanter ore devyl—akyn to Morgan le Faye and a ſervant of Lucyfer's ayms. Yet though he was wronge yn many of hys manners and fryghtenyng yn hys occaſyonal charms y knowe Robyn Hode to have bene no more ynfernal than the cat whych lyves yn Veryſdale and ſometymes ſteals fode frome the table and other tymes yowles at the mone, but wyll gladly reſt yts head yn peace ore allowe ytſelf to be pet ore ſcratch'd behynde yts ears as y am

27. An armour composed of cloth or similar material lined with steel plates, riveted in place

doyng nowe (though thys ys not to ſaye Robyn was not full of many terryble syns, one of the greateſt of whych y was woefully made wytneſs to).

'Howe came ye upon ſuch a well-mayntayn'd olde place?' y aſk'd.

'Yt was left here and forgotten, lyke the compaſſyon of Chryſte yn the hearts of Norman byſhops. When fyrſt y came to the Grenewode here y found yt abandon'd and overgrowne. But, wyth the help of the fryends y gather'd, y reſtore'd what y could of yts former glory,' anſwer'd our hoſte. 'But come, ſyr Knyghtes, ye ſhall be kyted fore thy journey.' Wyth that he ſhut the dore and left us.

Y lyſten'd cloſe fore the clyck of a lock, but there was none and ſo myn ſon and y fell ynto a ſtrange ſlumber. That nyghte y dreamt. Y dreamt of Robyn Hode, dreſſ'd yn a cloth-of-golde mantle and a ſylver crowne. At hys arm walk'd ſaynt Mary Magdalene, aglowe wyth the love of God. They laugh'd and blew noyſyly betwene theyr lyps at Nottyngham's ſheryff, who was there as well. Hys hands were red frome blode and hys face was red wyth fury as he ſhouted back at them. There was a ſmall cut upon hys neck, whych grew ſlowely as he bollowe'd. Nearby, a dwarf wearyng a lyon's head prance'd naked, waveyng a dyrk above hys crowne, yts very poynt wet wyth gore. He ſang, 'Quy reſponderunt ſomnyum vydymus et non eſt quy ynterpretur nobys dyxytque ad eos Yoſeph numquyd non Dey eſt ynter-pretatyo referte myhy quyd vyderytys[28].'

When y awoke y was yn a ſweat, and y was glad of the baſyn y found ſet before the croſs fore whych to waſh myn face

28. Genesis 40:8 KJV: *And they said vnto him, We haue dreamed a dreame, and there is no interpreter of it. And Ioseph said vnto them, Doe not interpreta-tions belong to God? tell me them, I pray you.*

wyth. Y woke myn ſon, though he complayn'd, and ſet out to fynde Robyn. The ſun was already hyghe and myn ſtomach beg'd fore ſuccour. Yn no lengthy tyme y found the lodge's maſter, ſytyng and ſyngyng gaye ſonges beneath the Tryſtyng Tree as a woman paſſyng fayr ſat upon hys lap, accompanyyng hym wyth harp and playeful voyce.

'Gode morrow, ſyr Rychard!' cry'd Robyn when hys ballad was done, but made no efforte to ſtand, nore to dyſentangle hymſelf frome the flaxen-hayr'd mayd. 'Have ye met Clorynda? Yf y be the Kyng of the Foreſt (yn jeſt alone, of courſe) then ſhe ys the Quene of the ſheppardeſſes.' He kyſſ'd her fully and ſhe laugh'd and y recognyze'd her as the gyrl y had ſene hym moſte oft beſyde the nyghte before.

'Y have not,' y ſaye'd.

'Truely, ſhe has more claym to tytle than y! 'Tys ſaye'd her father's fathers bore the blode of ſaxon kyngs. Gyve them a command, Lady, fore they muſt obey a pryncefs, e'en one dyſgrace'd,' he ſpake.

ſhe hyt hym playefully and turne'd back to me, ſayeyng, 'The only command y would gyve ye, gode ſyr Knyghte, ys to enjoye thy tyme yn the Grenewode and to make thy waye ſafely home to thy wyfe, daughters, and ſerfs, who y am certayn are ſyck wyth love and worry over thy abſence.'

'Y ſhall make haſte as well as y myghte,' y tolde her.

'ſyt, and break faſte,' ſhe ſaye'd then, fynally leavyng her rogue's lap.

We ate freſh ſcones and umble pye[29] and drank hot mead and lyſten'd—and even laugh'd—at the jeſtyng of Robyn and hys fayr companyon whome y dare'd not watch too cloſely leſt

29. A peasant dish made from the innards of animals, in particular deer

221

myn mynde betraye the love of myn lyfe. Myn ſon had nede to be remynded of hys proper vyrtues—and of hers—thryce (much to the amuſement of Loxſley and of Clorynda). The ſummer ſun wynkyng through the branches ſeme'd to ſhowe the fo-leyſhneſs of myn fears the nyghte before. Myn comforte then beneath the Tryſtyng Tree was the ſtart of a tyreyng pattern throughout the tyme y knew Robyn Hode—fyrſt offended wyth hys ways, then charme'd, then back agayn.

When we had fynyſh'd, our hoſte lept up and held out hys hand. 'Come, fryend,' he ſaye'd, 'and let me fyt ye bothe to travel on to Veryſdale.'

He led us around the trunk of the oak to where our horſes ſtode beſyde a cart of red cedar. Leadyng us alſo around the cart, he lyfted the grene coveryng to reveal a ſtrongebox bound yn yron. Produceyng a ſmall key no larger than hys ſmalleſt fynger, the ſmyleyng yeoman prynce open'd the cheſt and reveal'd a glytteryng wealth of ſylver coyns.

'By the ſaynts,' ſwore myn ſon and, though y was as ſtrycken as he, y held myn tongue frome blaſphemy.

Loxſley preſſ'd lock'd the treaſury and preſſ'd yts opener ynto myn palm. He crowe'd to me, "Tys as y alwayſe ſaye—our Lady provydes! Knowe ye that there ys neyther more nore leſs than four hundred pounds yn thys holde, fore y would not have ye ſhorted nore unknoweyngly bear a greater weyght of re-payement. Paye me as ye are able, and worry not on the tyme yt takes—y would have there be no ſpecyal preſſure on ye nore on the peaſants of thy land. And nowe, theſe men are fyt to bryng ye home.'

'But Robyn,' ſpake Lyttle Jon, who had only juſt ap-pear'd, 'we maye not ſend hym hence yn ſuch arraye. Hys coats are threadbare and wan, as too are the young Rychard's.'

'Ye ſpeak aryghte,' agrede hys maſter. 'Y am roughly of the ſame ſtature as the elder, and ſo he ſhall have a ſet of myn clothes, and hys ſon, beyng meaner yn ſhape, ſhall have a ſet frome Wyll ſcarlocke.'

'He ſhall?' ſaye'd the name'd man, chokeyng on hys breakfaſte beſyde Jon.

And ſo we were garb'd—myn ſon yn jolly red and mynſelf yn well-ſewn grenes whych ſmelt of yncenſe and wodeſmoke. To us as well were brought four boltes of cloth—a ſylk, a wole, and a lynen yn grene and a lynen yn red—fore whych to make ourſelves fyne clothes agayn. Fore thys gyft Robert Loxſley would not be refuſe'd. At Jon's ynſyſtance alſo were we gyfted haler horſes, and the burly ſaxon beg'd to be allowe'd to ſquyre fore me a tyme. Thys too y felt unable to refuſe, though y ſeldome regreted hys ſervyce.

We ſaye'd our farewells and ſet back on the path. Much the Myller's ſon, mounted atop a pony, led a band of a dozen outlaws. They eſcorted us and Lyttle Jon not only to the border of the foreſt, but ſome waye further ſouth and eaſt to the very edge of Veryſdale, where we met men who bore ſworde and ſpear fore me. Y thank'd the dwarf, and he me—fore as we journey'd we had found a fryendſhyp yn our common gruffneſs.

'And fryend Jon,' ſaye'd the ſmaller man, 'Ye ſpoke truely of thy wyſh to joyn wyth Rychard over Robyn?'

'Y ſhall always be Robert's man,' he reply'd, 'but y would ſee the wyder worlde agayn, and y would do what y maye wyth myn heavy hands to bryng weal to ſuch an unlucky and godly man.'

The Myller's ſon noded ſagely. Lyttle lean'd lowe to Much and ſhoke hys hand. We ſaye'd farewell agayn and made our waye home to Veryſdale's hall—the caſtle name'd Ryverſmotte by myn anceſtor, though the ryver had longe ſynce run dry and a ſmall holte replace'd yt. Myn wyfe, Edyth, and myn daughters Margaret and ſarah were by the gate to ſee me, and once we were ſettle'd and they had met Jon properly y tolde them what y knew of Robyn Hode.

Lyttle Jon was not yn myn ſervyce fore longe. Thys ſuyted me well enough fore, though y found hym to be loyal and capable yn all thyngs, y could not help mynſelf but wonder as to whether he ſpy'd upon myn fynances fore hys outlaw patron. Yt was ſome four months after y repaye'd the Abbot (who was none too happy to recyeve hys payement) that ſquyre Jon went up by ſherwode waye to Nottyngham Towne fore to compete yn a game of archery before the ſheryff. When he returne'd to Veryſdale he tolde me that he had ſplyt the wand^{30} each tyme. ſheryff John had bene ſo ympreſſ'd by thys that he had call'd the man forwards and aſk'd hym what was hys name and where was he borne.

'Y ſaye'd to hym that myn name was Reynolde Greneleaf, and that y came frome Holderneſs,' he tolde to me. 'Do not chaſtyse me fore lyeyng, ſyr, fore y fear'd he maye knowe myn name and remember myn outlawery, though myn byrthplace was no lye. He aſk'd me to joyn hys ſervyce and offer'd me twenty marke more per year than e'en ye offer. Y ſaye'd y ſhould nedes aſk ye and he gave me leave, ſayeyng y ſhould ſerve ye fore twelve monthes more, after whych to be made a deputy of Nottyngham, fore ne'er before had he ſene a bowe pull'd ſo well.'

The ſheryff was a powerful man—more powerful e'en

30. A common (and difficult) test of archery involved thin wooden rods (or wands) stuck in the ground. Here it is said that Little Jon split each of these in two with his shots during the contest.

than olde Wyllyam de Wendenal, who ſerve'd the gode Prynce John Lackland whylſte hys brother languyſh'd yn the pryſons of the Duke of Auſtrya. Hys law fell yn thoſe dayes acroſte Nottyngham, Derby, and even great Yorke. Fore thys reaſon y could not deny Jon hys requeſt. Y held no hatred fore the Hyghe Sheryff (though myn ſon would not hear hym ſpoken of), fore y knew hym to be juſt and powerful, e'en yn hys ambytyon, and he dyd not holde the kyndneſs towards the Jews whych hys dyſtant predeceſſore dyd. And ſo Lyttle Jon ſerve'd me yn fayth fore a year and four monthes (though ne'er yn the dealyngs of myn coffers nore taxes) before leaveyng to ſerve yn Nottyngham.

On the ſubject of myn coffers they were much ymprove'd and yn two years' tyme y had ſave'd enough exceſs coyn to paye back myn benefactore. An healthy harveſt and gode fortune at local games had led to a rapyd returne of myn former ſmall wealth. Y had made an hundred fyne yew bowes, wyth fyne cedar ſhafts fletch'd wyth peacock and ſylver goſe to fly frome them. Fore thoſe hundred bowes to holde y rayſe'd an hundred men, all dreſſ'd yn red and whyte and ſat them upon fyne horſes caparyſon'd yn lyke colours and hung wyth bells. Wyth thys company y meant to returne to Barneſdale Wode to repaye myn debt and ſhowe Robyn the fortune whych hys gyft had allowe'd me.

But myn departure was delaye'd by the fetters of hoſpytalyty. Two dayes before y meant to leave, a vyſytore came to Ryverſmotte—one ſyr Roger of Doncaſter. All clothes he owne'd were of depe ſanguyne, and hys black beard was fynely cut.

'Why have ye come to Veryſdale?' y aſk'd of hym when he came to myn ſturdy gate on hys hyghe black horſe.

'To ſhare yn thy hoſpytalyty and Chryſtyan charyty and

ſup on ſalt and bread,' ſaye'd he.

And ſo he was a geſt yn myn houſe, where he ſtaye'd fore nyghe on a weke. He was gode company, though hys humour was darke and he praye'd only when myn wyfe ore a pryeſt was preſent. Though none was expected, he offer'd fayr gyfts yn the forme of a carven croſs frome ſaynt Cuthbert's Abbey, a blue ſylken ſcarfe fore Edyth, and rattles fore our daughters. Fore myn ſon he brought no gyft ſave hys fryendſhyp, whych myn heyr gladly accepted. The two ſpent longe dayes together yn the foreſt and longe nyghtes yn converſatyon by the fyre, ſpeakyng often of theyr wyll to joyn the Cruſade yn the land of God[31].

Eventually came the eve of ſyr Roger's departure. We ſat at table and, as the duck was ſerve'd, y ſpake to hym, 'Ye have bene a fayr geſt, but have ſtyll not ſaye'd what bryngs ye to thys ſouth country.'

Hys anſwer, when ſaye'd, froze myn blode. 'Knowe ye Robyn Hode?'

At fyrſt y toke hys queſtyon to be an accuſatyon, and fear'd what vyllayny Loxſley had ymplycated me yn. But ſone myn mynde returne'd to me and y knew hys queſtyon to be as ynnocent as y. Myn mouth full, y made as yf to ſhake myn head, but myn oaſyſh ſon ſpoke over me. 'Ay, we have met hym, we bothe.'

ſyr Roger's darke browes roſe yn genuyne ſurpryſe, yet ſtyll y watch'd hym lyke y would myn enemy. He aſk'd us then, 'Howe came ye to knowe that robber?' and y held myn hand to

31. The crusades in the levant, by most accounts, were ended (and lost) by 1291, so it is unclear what conflict this would refer to, unless an earlier version of this text exists which sets this story not in the 14th century, but in the 13th. Regardless, it is evident from this reference and others of a similar nature that the text as it came into my possession is a later transcription of an earlier account.

ſtaye myn chylde's tongue.

'We met hym two years gone on returne frome the lyſts of Yorke. He offer'd us hoſpytalyty, as we have ye, and left us well to journey home.'

'Ay, y have heard of Hode's generoſyty. Many a fryar, monke, and pylgrym have fallen prey to hys Chryſtyan charyty of late.' Yndede y had heard tales of Robyn's actyvyty ſynce we parted waye's, but y had praye'd (evydently yn vayn) that yt was untrue that Robert o' the Wode had fallen upon many clergy that paſſ'd through Barneſdale and ſet the ſame trap fore them as he had laye'd fore me but, fyndeyng them lyars, had ſtryp'd them of theyr godes and (yn ſome caſes) theyr frockes as well. 'Y am a lover of the Mother Churche and wyſh to ſee what yll truely reſts yn Barneſdale Wode. Y wode not have evyl lyve yn the lands of Nottyngham.' He pauſe'd then and ſet hys mylk upon the table. 'The lyſts of Yorke two years gone? Were ye wytneſs to the ſlayeyng of the Kyng's couſyn? Y heard of yt only frome thoſe what knew thoſe what were there that daye.'

Myn ſon hung hys head then and beg'd me yn ſylence not to betraye hym to hys fryend. But y would not make falſehode of our dyſgrace. 'ſaw yt and wept. Not only fore the couſyn of Edward what was geſt of John, but alſo fore the man what dealt the blowe, fore that glayve[32] was held by a Veryſdale hand. But we have paye'd the pryce twyce over fore the wronge done. Yf ye have ever fought yn war, mayehaps agaynſt the ſcot, ye knowe the accydent a man's fyrey humours maye do hym.'

ſyr Roger noded gravely. 'Ay, y am ſorry and un-derſtand. Howe unlucky that ye ſhould have bene ſo befoul'd by thyne owne vyolence and by force'd peace wyth outlaws. Tell me though, nowe that thys yll ys paſſ'd, what knowe ye of Robyn

32. Sword

Hode.'

'Lyttle more than ye have ſaye'd. He lyves a yeoman's lyfe wythyn the wode and feaſts wyth others of hys band.'

'Howe many yn that band?' he aſk'd.

Recallyng frome myn tyme y gueſſ'd, 'ſeven ſcore at leaſt.' At thys he ſpat hys mylk and aſk'd agayn, but myn anſwer was the ſame.

'Y thynk perhaps the daye ys yet far that y ſhould ſeke the vyllayn Robyn at Barneſdale,' ſaye'd he. 'Fore yt ys wyſe to choſe one's battles. But marke myn wordes, fore lyttle gode comes to thoſe what mock the men of God. When the chyldren ſaye'd to Elyſha, "Go up thou bald head, go up thou bald head," yt was the wyll of the Lorde that they be gyven theyr puniſhment[33]. And alſo of the Wanderyng Jew—what reward dyd hys myrth get hym[34]? Y ſhall awaye to Doncaſter,' he pauſe'd, 'ore Perhaps to Kyrklyes fore whych to fynde the love of our Holy Churche beſtowe'd upon myn weary organs.' He ſmyle'd then and y knew not why, though yn the years whych followe'd the death of Robyn Hode y fear'd to thynk y maye knowe the truthe of ſome of the moſte foul rumours.

Once he had left fore Kyrklyes Abbey y agayn ready'd myn ſoldyers. Myn ſon as well was horſe'd, tyl y tolde hym to dyſmount. 'A man muſt ſtaye at home whylſt y am ſo far afyeld, fore to protect our land and kyn.' Loudly he proteſted, but y

---

33. II Kings 2:23-24 KJV: *And he went vp from thence vnto bethel : and as hee was going vp by the way, there came foorth little children out of the citie, and mocked him, and said vnto him , Goe vp thou bald head, Goe vp thou bald head. And hee turned back , and looked on them , and cursed them in the Name of the LORDE : and there came foorth two shee beares out of the wood, and tare fortie and two children of them.*

34. A common medieval legend told of a Jew who taunted Christ on the Cross and was cursed to walk the earth until the Second Coming.

would not be move'd. Y knowe not whether myn concern was as y ſaye'd, ore yf y begrudge'd hym fore hys wordes to ſyr Roger. Ore even yf a part of me ſtyll thought back to hys unvyrtuous gaze whych he wore at Robyn's table. But y left hym home—and well y dyd! Fore y can not ymagyne the worry that ſhould have fallen 'pon Edyth ſhould bothe her cloſeſt kynſmen fall ynto the myſchyef whych Loxſley had yn ſtore.

Y had thought y had knowne Robyn Hode—fore hys wyckedneſs and hys charme—but y dyd not knowe the depth of hys chyldlyke evyls untyl y came that year to Barneſdale.

We wended our waye northe untyl we came to the edge of the Grenewode. On our waye we paſſ'd by Wentſbrydge and there found a wreſtleyng match. Fore pryze had bene offer'd an hale whyte bull, a ſwyft courſer[35] complete wyth brydle and ſaddle burnyſh'd yn golde, a payr of gloves, a ryng of red golde, and a pype of wyne—a fayr wynyng yndede! Here we ſtop'd to obſerve the game, and had fayr enjoyment of yt. Y am glad that y toke thys daye to delaye, fore once we met the edge of Barneſdale we were beſet by the darkeſt of Loxſley's ympyſh ympulſes.

Unfortuneately fore our gode chere, the folke of Wentſbrydge dyd not take kyndely to the vyctore—a ſtronge man frome Fayrburne. When he beſted the laſt comer, hys thyck arm about hys neck, a cry came frome the crowde. A man came forthe as the vyctore toke hys pype and daſh'd yt upon the ground. At thys all the men of Wentſbrydge roſe wyth murderous yntent. But myn men as well roſe, wyth fyerce arrowes and bryghte ſwordes and won back the man hys ſpoyls. No blode was ſpyll'd and y paye'd hym fyve markes fore hys loſte wyne. Then, fore theyr hatred, y order'd the unhappy men of that unhappy towne to tap a caſk of wyne fore any who would drynk.

35. A warhorse

Even thys upſet lyfted myn heart more once yt was ſettle'd, fore y had done the Lorde's charyty. But myn hyghe ſpyryts laſted lyttle longer, fore ſone we arryve'd at Barneſdale Wode. We rode wythyn, ever our eyes alert fore movement yn the brake and bruſh. But ſome tyme we rode before we ſaw anythyng more threatenyng than a fox. Yt was as we ſlowe'd ſo y could gayn myn bearyngs and attempt to remember the waye back to the Tryſtyng Tree that two fygures lept frome the bruſh, dyrks yn hand. They growle'd fyercely and ſhoke theyr ſwordes. There was a pauſe and then myn men began to laugh, and the aſſaylants as well.

'Jon!' cry'd one man. 'Yf ye claym'd to be lyttle before ye have no ryghte nowe. Ye loke to have eaten all the ſheryff's larders!' And Lyttle Jon yt was, wyth a wartey, wyde man beſyde whoſe bald head glyſten'd wyth ſweat, though the breze was cole.

'As well y could have, Wyllum! Fore not too longe gone y beſted the butler and after made fryends wyth thys here coke,' he anſwer'd. 'ſyr Rychard! Ye have come to repaye our Lady's gyft, methynks?'

'Ay, y am,' ſpake y, obſerveyng hym yn careful manner. "Tys gode to ſee ye agayn, ſquyre Jon. Howe goes thy ſervyce to thy maſter? Yt ſemes perhaps not well yf ye have battle'd wyth hys butler and ſtolen hys coke.'

'Myn ſervyce goes fayr yndede, ſyr Knyghte! And better come evenyng y ymagyne. Do not men have bouts yn jeſt? And y have ſtolen no coke, fore he comes alonge of hys owne ac-corde.'

Y knew Jon and knew hys heart to be gode, fore a crymynal, yet found there to be ſome untruth yn hys wordes, though of what y could not tell. 'Where, then, ys thy maſter?'

'Ahuntyng yn the Wode!' he laugh'd. 'ſhall we go fynde

hym?'

Robyn and the Hyghe ſheryff yn the Wode together! Y knew no gode could come of thys, fore bothe were proud and ſtronge of heart, and bothe laye'd claym to Barneſdale. 'ſees he no danger? Ne'er ye mynde—ay, let us fynde hym, and ſwyft! Y would not wytneſs a ſlaughter thys daye!'

And ſo we rode downe the foreſt road, eager and anxyous, wyth Jon and the ſheryff's coke yn the wagon whych held the ſylver. Yt was a wonder we were not heard, fore all our hofebeats and our bells. But ſone we heard other ſtedes and a chorus of huntyng hornes, and through the thycket, much as Jon Lyttle had (though ahorſe and greater yn number), came ſheryff John and hys company, ſurrounded all around wyth hounds and theyr maſters.

The ſheryff rear'd hys horſe and yt turne'd, pranceyng. He drewe hys longe ſworde and ſhoke back hys black cape, lyned yn whyte fur. He bore thyck black hayr whych fell about hys ſhoulders lyke water. A fur'd coat, whyte and ſpoted wyth golde rondels rychly cover'd hys ſtronge frame. On the breaſt of hys grene damaſcene doublet was the ymage of a ſtag rampant. Hys botes, belt, and glove were of rych black leather, and hys yellowe brytches were as bryghte as the call of hys horne. Wyth hys golde and ſylver ryngs and ſhyneyng chayn about hys neck he loked a fyerce myrror to Robyn hymſelf. Brandyſhyng hys weapon and alloweyng hys ſtede to land on yts fete once more, he poynted to me, fore y was clearly the moſte noble of the company. 'Who are ye what come ynto myn wode wyth ſo great an hoſte? Mean ye to take me? Knowe then that y am favour'd of the Kyng and fought wyth hym at Eveſhame[36]. Edward ys a fyerce fryend, and payes no ranſome when he can wet hys blade. Come ye, knave, and try thy arm at the capture of Nottyngham's

36. 4th of August, 1265

ſheryff!'

'Holde, Lorde,' y beg'd, unbuckleyng myn baldryc and throweyng yt to the ground. 'Y mean ye no harme, though y have done yt yn unfayr wayes at Yorke. Y am ſyr Rychard at the Lee, father of the Kyng's couſyn's foe. Y come thys waye wyth ſylver-cheſt to paye a debt y owe. Would a vyllayn ryde ſo bra-zenly, wyth bells and banners and an hundred clangeyng ſpurs?'

ſheryff John ſcowle'd but ſheathe'd hys blade. 'A longe waye ye come fore a debt to be paye'd y wager. Y heard ye bor-rowe'd of ſaynt Mary's Abbey to paye thy kyn's blode debt. But that was two years gone and the Abbey ys nearer Veryſdale than here. Ys the Lorde of Veryſdale ſo yll wyth money that he ys ever yn debt? Who ownes thy coffers, Rychard?'

Y could neyther admonyſh hym fore hys nedeleſs ſhameyng nore admyt the truthe of whome y ſought, ſo fore a moment y ſat, open-mouth'd upon myn horſe's back. But myn punyſhment was lyfted by the ynterventyon of Lyttle Jon, who ſtep'd forwards betwene us, 'He goes towards a fryend of myne, Lorde ſherryf. ſyr Rychard ys a noble gent, and thys debt ys more a gyft. The two had made a wager of ſortes, and nowe thys gode knyghte means to make gode on hys defeat.'

The loke on the Hyghe Sheryff's face turne'd frome confuſyon to joye, and he laugh'd blythely. 'Reynolde! Ye wry baſtard! Howe came ye to be about yn Barneſdale Wode, and yn the company of thy olde maſter?' Y dyd not much lyke the lye whych Jon had tolde, nore the ſudden abſence of the rock-face'd coke.

'Y ſhould have aſk'd thy leave, but y came fore to vyſyt myn brother, who has bene ſyck wyth gout and lyves yn Fayr-burne. And on myn path y happyly met ſyr Rychard! Y aſk'd to joyn hys merry company, fore though y am a great ſwordesman

232

and a better archer y am no match fore a determyne'd band of brygands.' The brute pauſe'd and motyon'd conſpyratoreyally to hys maſter, who lean'd downe yn hys ſaddle, ſmyrkyng, to hear. 'Have ye heard that Robyn Hode haunts thys wode?'

ſheryff John's laugh nowe was as loud and ſudden as thunder. 'Robyn Hode! Y have bene ſheryff fore nyghe fyftene years and ever lyttle folke talk of Robyn Hode. "The Champyon of the Tax'd," "The ſcourge of the Abbey," "The Kyng of Watlynge ſtrete." But yn all myn tyme never have y bene gyven reaſon to thynk hym real. Theſe are myn wodes, and myn knyghtely company can eaſyly defend 'gaynſt the common outlaws whych crawl beneath these boughs. Marry! Yt maye even be greater ſporte than the conyes and grouſe whych ſeme to fyll thys holte ynſtead of dere!'

ſquyre Jon made hys face to loke embarraſſ'd (though he wynk'd to me where the lawman could not ſee). Y ſylently curſe'd hym fore engageyng me yn hys deceptyon and praye'd fore the wyſdome to free mynſelf before y was made outlaw (O howe fear can prove oracle). 'Ay, y have bene foleyſh. Y was merely enforcel'd by the ſplendour of thys grene place. Truely, God left ye a gyft yn theſe browne trunks yn thy lands. Yt ſemes ſo unfayr that ſo faye a place as thys ſhould belonge to any man, and ſo ye are a fortunate lorde,' ſaye'd the conſpyratore. 'And of thy ſmall game; yf ye ſhould tyre of hares and byrds we have ſene a great ſtag wyth many tynes and fur of grene.'

A ſparke alyt yn the ſheryff's eye and he loke'd to me. 'Ys thys true, Veryſdale?'

Myn tongue was ſtyll dumb and Jon mock'd me fore yt, 'He ys ſtyll yn ſhock frome the beauty of the beaſt and the noble fygure thy grace makes. We muſt hye ſwyftly yf we are to fynde yt agayn.' He turne'd to me. 'Fryend Rychard, y fear ye muſt

233

leave many of thy men here—an hundred bell'd horſes are lyke to fryghten the harte[37].'

'Ay, ſyr Bryce ſhall dyſmount and ye ſhall have hys horſe, whych ys devoyd of bells,' ſpake the Hyghe ſherryf.

'Hys horſe does not knowe me as myne does,' y offer'd lamely.

'Rychard,' ſpake Jon ſoftely yn a tone only y knew to be a threat, 'Would ye have our ſhare'd fryend knowe ye were unwyllyng to go ahuntyng wyth Edward's honour'd ſervant? Certayn am y that he would underſtand the opportunyty ye are beyng gyven. And who knowes who elſe ye maye yet mete yn the Grenewode?'

'Jon ſpeaks aryghte,' ſaye'd John. 'Do not ynſult me, ſyr Rychard.'

Y could not ſtaye myn tongue frome expelyng forthe the Lorde's Prayer—and yn vulgar Englyſh. Y bluſh'd at the glares y earn'd as y mounted ſyr Bryce's ſtede. Another mount was gyven to Jon and we ſet out, leavyng myn men and a part of the ſheryff's party to make camp on the path. Myn man Wyllum knewe our true dyrectyon as well as y, and as y bade hym ſtryke the tents there was a wan pall of fear upon hym.

As we left behynde myn cavalry and coffer y felt a chyll as y fear'd that y knewe the mynde of Robyn Hode.

We rode depe ynto the wode, and every hofebeat ſeme'd as the breakyng of one of Revelatyon's ſeals, but there were not ſeven but a thouſand-thouſand. The hornes were as Heaven's ſoundyng trumpets. The laughter as ſatan's call.

There were perhaps a ſcore of us. Y rode wyth the ſheryff at the head of the force and Jon rode further ahead, hal-

37. An adult male deer, especially a red deer over five years old

looyng and bloweyng hys horne—alwayes juſt out of ſyghte. Myn heart was thunderyng wyth the terryble choyce y found. A part of me envyed ſolomon, fore when he was gyven the judgement of the two mothers he made the terryble rulyng whych ſhowe'd theyr true hearts. But there was no thyrd choyce yn that wode. There was no terryble ruleyng whych would free me frome guylt yn all eyes. Yf y betraye'd Jon and Robyn y would be at theyr mercy, alone yn theyr petty kyngdome. But yf y ſhould betraye John and remayn ſylent y maye be knowne as an accomplyce to outlaws. Yt occure'd to myn cowardly heart then that perhaps the ſteward of Yorke maye condemn me deſpyte myn loyalty. And ſo yn myn dyſtreſs y fayl'd to ſpeak untyl after Lyttle Jon cry'd to have found the dere.

'Haſten hence! ſheryff! Here! The crowned Prynce of Barneſdale!' beckon'd Jon the Falſe, and John the Hyghe hye'd hys horſe o'er an hedge and downe a dytch—out of our ſyghte.

Yn an ynſtant we were caught up wyth the ſheryff, and y made myn beſt attempt at a cry of ſurpryſe. Y knowe not howe convynceyng yt was, fore Loxſley greted me then by name. He ſtode on a great fallen tree beſyde Wyll ſcarlocke and about hym dozens of bowes were vyſyble, pekeyng frome the trees and over ſtones. The hounds barke'd and lunge'd, but theyr handlers pull'd at theyr leaſhes. The Yeoman Prynce was dreſſ'd yn well-ſewn but ſymple grene wole, wyth a poynted grene hode and archer's gloves. The only marke of ſplendour upon hym was hys glytteryng baldryc. Lyttle Jon ſtode on the ground afore the tree.

'Ye have betraye'd thy maſter!' cry'd the lawman, hys face red. 'And ye, Veryſdale; y knewe aryghte when y met ye here that ye were of foul heart.'

'Y have never betraye'd myn maſter, Lorde ſheryff, fore

y have ne'er valued any above God, and Robyn just belowe. And e'en were y not the Grenewode's man, ye gave me lyttle satysfactyon yn thy employe.'

Rydeyng to sheryff John's syde as the ranger spake, y try'd to stammer myn defense, but was sylence'd. 'Tell me, outlaw, what ye yntend wyth me and myn men?'

'Chere thyself, bytter gest! Y mean only to showe ye the generosyty of myn wode.'

'Thys wode ys myn, not thyne, Hode, by worde of Edward Kyng!'

'Then he can tell me y am wronge,' smyrk'd cruel Robyn.

And so we were led through the summery forest, and the cole breze of the holte fell on our faces lyke tears. John of Nottyngham would no more talk to me than feast wyth hys hounds, and y could not bryng mynself to laugh at scarlocke's japes. Y regret often what befell the Lorde of Yorke, but so too can y not help but condemn hym, though the hatred he earn'd frome me was selfysh. Yet dyd not the Kyng also foregyve hys fell dome? Was Robyn's spell so great so as to seduce e'en God's chosen Englysh kyng?

Yn tyme (whych seme'd an eternyty fore myn woeful thoughts) we came to the clearyng overloke'd by the Trystyng Tree. The smells, syghtes, and sounds whych greted us were so alyke to what y had encounter'd when last y came to Loxsley's demesne that yt seme'd harde at fyrst to remember what tyme was the present. Y wonder'd bryefly yf y had not fallen aslepe yn the outlaw's cell and dreamt the ynterveneyng monthes. But the clearyng was too full, and not merely wyth the men of the Wode. Myn owne men were there as well, and the remaynder of Nottyngham's—the two men what had surrender'd us theyr stedes.

236

And the ſheryff's yre was too apparent to be a dream.

Fore the fyrſt tyme ſynce we were taken the ſheryff rode beſyde me. 'ſyr Knyghte,' he ſaye'd, 'there are many brygands here, but not ſo many that we maye not defeat them, we lordes two. Ye brought a myghty force, and combyne'd we muſt nearly equal the forces what holde us.'

'That we maye,' y anſwer'd cautyouſly, 'but 'twould be yll to do harme when we maye be mere geſts.' Y knewe even as y ſpake that myn wordes were porely ſaye'd.

'Mere geſts?' The ſheryff's bellowe was as a a clap of thunder. 'He has taken a ſworne offycer of the Englyſh Throne and force'd hym—'

'To attend a feaſt?' Myn fear made me bolde but O would that yt had not. Would John have lyve'd to bear an head of whyte had y not ſat ydle? Perhaps y ſhall have an anſwer of ſaynt Peter when y holde rede[38] afore Heaven's gate; that tyme ys not far frome me nowe, yf the aches whych have tremble'd myn fyngers, ſpyne, and bowels theſe laſt three wynters maye be taken as a ſygne.

The lawman hyſſ'd and brought hys ſtede to hele before me. Hys face was reder than the creſt of myn feather'd helm but hys voyce was lowe and courſe. 'Ne'er thynk to ynterrupt me agayn, ſyr Knyghte at the Lee. Yf y tell ye to fyghte theſe folke ye ſhall fyghte them. What ys thys defyance yn thy face? Treaſon? Naye. Fear. What ſpell or vyllaynous plot does thys wodeman holde o'er ye? Yf yt be thy famyly ore thy godly lands y ſwear by Edward's Crowne that y ſhall dryve theſe vyllayns frome them. Naught can he do 'gaynſt ye that maye not be undone by myn offyce.'

'And what yf yt be neyther, but a debt ynſtead, whych

38. Conference

honour demands y paye?' y aſk'd.

'Honour? Debt?' Hys browne eyes narrowe'd. 'Howe ſaye'd ye that thy debt was ſettle'd after the murder of ſyr Bard of Lancaſter?'

Myn hands were ſhakeyng and myn tongue was large yn myn mouth, but y was ſave'd by the call of one of the foreſt men. What was y to have ſaye'd? Y could not well enough betraye ſo great a lorde fore fear of myn ryghteful tytles, but neyther could y fayl to repaye the debt y had accrued yn gode fayth—even to ſuch a rogue as Loxſley—wythout ryſkyng punyſhment frome God above? But the man's cry ſave'd me, fore a tyme (and per-haps too longe, fore myn problems were made more foul 'fore y could conſyder a ſolutyon) frome thys dylemma.

'Dyſmount, lordes, and make merry, fore ye have come to our feaſt, where ye ſhall be treated as thy ſtatyon ys ac-cuſtome'd, but yn the beauty of our wode!' He was a man y had not before ſene, wyth a ſharp noſe and wavey black hayr paſt hys ſhoulders, and he ſpoke French well. Hys handſome ſkyn was darke, ſave fore hys hands. Y thought at fyrſt they were gloves, but ynſtead ſaw that hys ſkyn there was merely as whyte as ſnowe. He caught myn gaze returnyng frome hys gryp on the ſheryff's brydle and wynk'd. 'Myn hands are a gyft, ſyre, and made me ſomethyng of a favouryte wyth the ladyes of the contynent.' Y dyd not knowe what to make of the man, nore dyd y knowe the yntentyons of Robyn Hode, but y followe'd hys advyce.

The ſheryff and y were led together to the hyghe table and he was ſat yn Robyn's ſeat. Before y could be ſhowne myn owne place y notyce'd Wyll ſcarlocke near me and claw'd at hys coat.

'Man,' y ſaye'd to hym, yn ſome unyntended urgency.

238

'Y would speak wyth Robyn swyftly, fore to be done wyth myn busynefs.'

scarlocke shoke hys head and yt jangle'd, fore there was a brafs bell tye'd to one twyfted lock of hys hayr. 'Tut! Gode syr, the Lorde Robyn has ayms to entertayn ye. Shall ye not allowe hym thys small favour?' Y could see that Wyll senfe'd well the terrore yn myn breaft, yet he merely laugh'd as y was guyd'd away once more to the table. Of all the band Wyll was perhaps to be trufted leaft—yn all myn years y have never knowne hym to do a purely godely thyng unlefs yt made hym laugh.

Very shortely the clearyng quyeted some as Robyn toke hys place ftandyng before the loamy ftage on whych we fat. Y heard hym remarke to another that 'Our Lady provydes' before he once more began hys hated Grenewode Ufe. Expectyng thys, though y had sene yt but once, y was not as blatant yn myn affrontery as was myn noble better, who had only juft fynyfh'd argueyng wyth the whyte-handed man.

As the fyrft syllables of latyn, tynged wyth Loxfley's Yorkefhyre lylt, reach'd hys ears and he realyze'd what he was hearyng, John of Nottyngham shot to hys fete as yf he had bene bytten and shouted yn shock and outrage. Wyll, who fat on hys ryghte syde whylfte y was on hys left, pull'd hym bodyly to hys chayr, furpryfeyng hym so thoroughly that he quyeted before he could fynde wordes. After thys, the scarlet man saye'd somethyng yn the warden's ear whych ftaye'd hys tongue fore the length of the herefy even as yt fet ftormeclouds upon hys browe.

When the unpleafantnefs (ore at leaft that whych ryfk'd our ynvytatyon to fyt at Chryfte's ymmortal table) was fynyfh'd, and the falfe Eucharyft refufe'd, the fode was called fore. Y had thought the tyncture of the sheryff's face was fryghtenyng when y denyed hys call to betraye the Forefte Lorde, but at the syghte of

239

what was brought forthe he turne'd ſo purple as to be almoſte black, and only by gulpyng hys wyne—at Wyll's ynſyſtance—dyd he regayne hys breath. The fode was ſerve'd not on the common dyſhes of myn laſt vyſyt, but on elaborate ſylver, fancyfully ynlayd and well-ſhyne'd. Y was yn mortal awe of the dyſhes, but as they were ſet downe a knyghte ſat beſyde me gaſp'd.

'What troubles ye?' y aſk'd. The fode yndede ſmell'd ſplendyd, but yt was hys eyes what flare'd, not hys noſtryls. The game was ſurely poach'd, ay, but what elſe would he expect of the outlaw Robyn Hode?

'That man there ys Lorde John's coke,' he ſaye'd as he motyon'd to the man what had bene wyth Lyttle Jon before, who laugh'd and boaſted wyth the other foreſt folke, 'And thys hys fyneſt ſylver!'

Juſt then Robyn appear'd to us wyth Lyttle Jon beſyde. Jon ſerve'd a plate to me—the byrd upon drape'd yn thyn, crack-leyng ſkyn to make myn mouth water—and hys maſter wayted perſonally on the lyege of Yorke.

'Here be our fyneſt game byrd,' he ſaye'd to the Hyghe ſheryff wyth a ſmyrk, 'gyfted by our Lady and ſupply'd by our beloved Kyng. What? Ye do not enjoye yt? Perhaps ye are on ſome holy faſt, denyyng thyſelf meat as the templars claym'd? Ore ys yt the dyſh? Ah, the dyſh then. We are but pore rangers, fryend, and cannot afforde the rych ſervyng toles one ſuch as thyſelf muſt be accuſtome'd to. ſurely ye can foregyve us.' The vyllayn's eye twynkle'd. 'Ore ſhould y daſh the offendyng traye ſo yt maye no longer harme ye by yts meagre nature?'

The whole whyle that Loxſley ſpake the ſheryff was ſtruck ſpecheleſs by hys audacyty. When fynally hys tongue began to worke agayn he bellowe'd wyth full force, ' Have done wyth me knave Robyn, and cut myn head and ſhoulders. Taunt

240

me no longer, but end myn humylyatyon forever.'

'O dear ſheryff,' cluck'd Robyn Hode, 'Fear ye not, fore thy lyfe ys ſafe and ſacred, by myn Chryſtyan charyty and the love whych Lyttle Jon bears ye, O John the Great.' Wyth that he ſet downe the platter and laugh'd as Wyll ſcarlocke tyckle'd the lawman's belly before they bothe ſcamper'd awaye. Y doubt there was truely much love to be had frome Lyttle Jon, but the captyve quyeted and ſat yn ſullen gryef untyl the meal was done.

As the laſt dyſhes were clean'd awaye under the hateful eye of our noble lyege the ynſects of the wode began to ſyng, and ſone after followe'd the broad voyce of the Whyte Hand, who y had learn'd was name'd Gylberte. Gylberte ſang a loud, ſlowe ſonge about a knyghte of the Prynce's Cruſade whoſe fayth carry'd hym frome Acre back to Rome. The weyghty tones of the Frenchman cover'd the clearyng as our captore-hoſte returne'd and aſk'd of us what we thought of the meat. Knoweyng myn place, y defer'd to myn lorde before y made to ſpeak.

'Ye have had thy fun, Loxſley,' ſaye'd ſheryff John. 'Nowe free me and myn men ore have done wyth us. Y ſhould have lyke'd to gyve ye fyghte, but the coward knyghte beſyde me ſhall not rayſe arms.'

'Rayſe arms?' balk'd Robert the Hode. 'Why ſhould he rayſe arms agaynſt a fryend (as y ſone hope we two maye be as well)?'

The eye of John of Yorke was fyre then. He loked only bryefly to me, yet y could fele hys hot poker of dyſdayn pyerce myn heart and cleave myn ſoul. Here y was reveal'd fore myn comporte wyth outlaws once more, and yet more bluntly than e'er before. Y began to ſweat and y could ſee that Robyn Hode knew what he had done me. Y hated hym then, but fear'd hym more, though y had an hundred men. Mayehaps y was a coward, but who that yet lyves can saye fore certayn? When y am dead y shall ask of Charlemagne, of Constantyne, of Davyd; perhaps one of these great commanders of Chryste's legyons has sene me and judge'd me, though y cannot.

'Not a coward but a traytore!' announce'd Yorke. 'Ye had bothe best holde the knyfe what slayes me, fore y shall see ye bothe hang'd should y reach Nottyngham, and all thy men besydes! A fyeld of gallowes—a forest of corpse trees—shall cover the hylls and the lands shall stynk of carryon untyl Chryste's Mass!'

'Tut, John!' saye'd Robyn, shakeyng hys fynger. 'Ye speak so awefully that ye shall fryghten Much.' The dwarf, whose nose only reach'd the table's edge, agrede mockyngly. 'Much, y shall save ye frome thys man's devyl tongue. Yf he ys to be a gest of Barnesdale he must loke the part. Go fetch hym a mantle grene and gyrdle, blouse and all. Gode Jon! Take hym and see he knowes howe each buckle, tye, and sleve ys fyted and—synce he shan't nede them longer—take hys pyed[39] coat and hys furs, fore they shall loke fyne as gyfts wythyn our closet.'

The heavy hand of Lyttle Jon was tyghte upon our hyghe master's shoulder and myn heart beat swyftly. The Yorkeyst knyghtes near to us were whyte, theyr eyes sharpe and angry. But y could see the gleam of daggers near to Jon, and the greater John's men must have sene the danger as well. They went wyth, even as y was grace'd wyth another hateful eye.

Robyn turne'd to leave and y stode and spake hys name; yt was tyme to have done wyth myn duty.

'What ys yt, fryend Rychard?' Hys tone betraye'd no knoweledge of the yll he had done me, though y knew Robyn Hode to have spoken knoweyngly agaynst myn ynterest (and that

39. Consisting of multiple colours

of myn neck). But had y not alſo acted agaynſt mynſelf yn takeyng money of the bandyt? Yn takeyng Jon to ſquyre? Yn returneyng thyther and yn refuſeyng myn better's call to arms? Would y have bene better fyt fore myn ſeat above had y abandon'd myn lands and made the harde trek to Jeruſalem? ſurely the Gode Boke has ſome ynſyghte, but y knowe too lyttle Latyn and remember too lyttle of the teachyngs to recall any paſſages ſo dyſtynct. Y ſhall beg ſome ynſyghte of the pryeſt what takes myn laſt confeſſyon, however ſone that comes.

'Y came here to Barneſdale to fynally make ryghte the gode ye have done me,' y ſpake.

'Well, welcome once agayn, gentle knyghte,' anſwer'd he wyth a joyeous embrace. 'And worry not that yt has taken ye ſo longe, fore thys was to be expected.' Y bluſh'd at the ſlyghte agaynſt myn honour, though perhaps well-meant. 'And have ye thy land agayn?'

'Ay, Maſter Hode, before God y do.'

'Then thank God, and thank too our Lady, who has ſene fyt to paye thy fee, and more beſydes,' he laugh'd.

'Paye'd myn fee? Our Lady?' Y was agog.

'Ay, ye gapeyng knyghte,' he ſpake wyth obvyous glee, 'Fore her cellarer came frome her abbey and brought to us a myghtey cheſt, fyll'd all up wyth ſylver. Thy borrowe'd coyn ys returne'd home, and there ys plenty beſydes—the Lady has ſupply'd well fore us all thys year. Y have ſene fyt to add another cheſt of equal weyght to thy wagon, the contents of whych to be uſe'd fore the betterment of thy lands and loyal offycers.'

Certayn was y that the cellarer of ſaynt Mary's Abbey had not brought hys cheſt to the Grenewode wyth the yntentyon of offeryng yt to the Lorde of Loxſley, and neyther had any of

243

the other ſuppoſed couryers of that bleſſed apoſtle. But Robyn would not be move'd, eyther to take the coyn y had brought hym nore to reſcynd hys bounteous gyft. And ſo y lye'd to mynſelf and let mynſelf belyeve yt fayr to uſe thys coyn fore Veryſdale. Y dyd not regret the comforte yt afforded me, but alſo dyd y not ſlepe well untyl myn coffers began to hurt once more—and even then y had new problems cauſe'd by myn cloſeneſs to Robert o' Hode whych dyſturbe'd myn peace. Y aſk'd mynſelf e'en as y accepted the generoſyty of the Grene Prynce why y had defended hym frome ſyr Roger, thus alloweyng mynſelf to fall wythyn the ſmyleyng bandyt's trap of guylt once more. Why y had not ſtode up and joyn'd wyth the Lorde Hyghe ſheryff when he had aſk'd.

And what of the ſheryff? What was to be done wyth hym? Though y dreaded to do ſo, y aſk'd myn hoſte of thys.

'Yt ys too late fore ye to ryde tonyghte, ſyr Rychard, e'en ſhould ye wyſh yt. ſo ſtaye and fynde thy anſwer on the morrowe,' he ſaye'd. 'But there are too many of us fore the hall, and John's boke ſayes, "Amen amen dyco vobys non eſt ſervus mayor domyno ſuo neque apoſtolus mayor eo quy myſyt yllum,"[40] and ſo we ſhall all ſlepe under the ſtars.'

And ſo y ſlept on the harde ground beſyde myn men, ſtareyng at the ſky. ſomewhere nearby y ymagyne'd the ſheryff ſtruggleyng and complaynyng. Y wonder'd yf he was afrayd. Ynſects would ſometymes crawl acroſte me ore tyckle myn ears. Y was moſte unhappy that nyghte.

But y ſlept, and dreamt of fyre yn the Holy Cyty of Jeruſalem.

Y was awoken the next daye by the yrate ſhoutyng of the

---

40. Iohn 13:16 KJV: *Verily, verily I say vnto you, the seruant is no greater then his lord, neither he that is sent, greater than hee that sent him.*

Lorde of Yorke, obvyouſley revytalyze'd by whatever ſlepe he manage'd to take. Myn bones were ſore—much as they are nowe—but y roſe and followe'd the noyſe.

As y approach'd, ſtyll bruſhyng the ſlepe frome myn eyes, John the Greater was berateyng John the Lyttle as Much watch'd. He was complaynyng about the aches yn hys back and the graſs yn hys hayr. The ſaxon ſquyre was merely ſmyleyng.

Y arryve'd a mere breath afore Robyn, who came up behynde me and ſtartle'd me greatly. He ſmyle'd and aſk'd howe the ſheryff had ſlept, whych drove the Kyng's man once more to red-face'd ſylence. Our hoſte merely ſtode and watch'd wyth unhyden glee untyl wordes agayn came to John of Nottyngham; y have never knowne a man to take ſuch pleaſure yn dyſcomforte as Robyn Hode, nore to take ſuch joye yn aydyng thoſe he favour'd.

'Thys houſeyng ys by far the worſte y have ever knowne,' ſaye'd John Yorke.

Gaſpyng yn mock offenſe, Robyn anſwer'd, 'Thys ys the houſe of our order—that of the Grenewode Tree.'

'No worſer order have y ever met, of anchoryte ore fryar. Were y paye'd every marke yn Edward's England y ſhould not ſtaye here another moment of myn owne volytyon.'

'Then ye are ſet to be dyſappoynted,' gryn'd Barneſdale's lorde, 'Fore y yntend to kepe ye here fore twelve monthes ore more—however longe yt takes ye to learn to be an outlaw.'

'An outlaw?' balk'd bothe y and John together.

'Ay, an outlaw. Fore ye ſhall be myn greateſt fryend and confeſſor, and at myn ſyde dyveſt all the abbots of England of theyr wealth.' Y could ſee that Loxſley was ſore pleaſe'd wyth hymſelf, yet y knew not howe ſeryous hys ſtrange threat was meant. Yndede, ſtyll y do not.

The ſheryff gryp'd hys ſworde then. 'Y have ſaye'd yt to ye once and y ſaye yt agayn; ye muſt nedes ſmyte myn head frome myn ſhoulders 'fore y playe at thy games yet more.'

'ſuch a pretty head,' remarke'd ſcarlocke.

'Yf that be thy wyſh,' ſaye'd Robyn Hode ſadly, lyftyng hys owne blade as Lyttle Jon held ſolydly theyr captyve's arms and the foreſt men drew ſtele on the ſlepey men of Nottyngham.

The lawman blanch'd and try'd to ſtep back, yet he could not. ſmall claſhes rang under the Tryſtyng Tree, yet none featureyng myn men; they ſtode as tranſſyx'd as y by the terryble ſcene before me. Jon puſh'd downe on hys noble once-maſter's ſhoulders and Nottyngham's prynce could do naught but obey, fallyng to hys knees yn the wet graſs. Loxſley ſtep'd forwards and playefully aym'd hys weapon at hys captyve's thyck neck. Only when the bryghte blade touch'd hys heaveyng ſkyn dyd ſheryff John cry out.

'Mercy! Mercy!' he cry'd wyth wet eyes, 'Let me go and y ſhall be a better fryend than e'er ye could have hope'd. No greater ally ſhall ye have than the Lorde of Nottyngham and Yorkeſhyre bothe. Merely pleaſe to ſet me free. Y would not ſpend another daye on thys moſſy flore, nore ſee myn head ſhorne free. Pleaſe, ſyre Robyn, Mercy!' After thys he fell to wordleſs blubberyng.

'ſwear me then an oath,' ſaye'd Robyn. 'By myn ſhyneyng ſworde that ye ſhall ne'er awayt to do me yll, by land ore by ſea. And ſhould ye fynde any man of myne, be yt nyghte ore daye, upon thyne oath ye ſhall ſwear to help them yn any manner ye maye.'

Humylyated, the ſherryf repeated thys foul oath, and kyſſd Loxſley's threatenyng blade wyth tear-ſtayn'd lyps. Once thys was done Robyn ſet us bothe upon our waye. John Yorke's eyes were full of hatred and defeat and myn heart was as full of fear as myn cart was full of coyn. Fore y knew that what Robyn Hode had done that daye bode porely fore us all.

After y returne'd home frome Robyn's fearſome kydnapyng of ſheryff John of Nottyngham y ſtaye'd longe yn Veryſdale and ſeldome travel'd northe of Huntyngdon. Rumours and wylde ſtorys travel'd ſwyftly of the gaye and terryble dedes of the heroyc Lorde of the Grenewode, and y made content to stere clear of bothe them and the progreſſes of the Lorde of Nottyngham. Myn ſon left ſhortely after myn returne to ayd yn the retakeyng of Jeruſalem and, though y am glad to God that he has ſervyce as an holy warryor of the Croſs, y often wyſh that he had ſtaye'd, fore yt has bene ſome years nowe and he has not yet returne'd to claym hys byrthryghte.

Yt was yn thys tyme—yn whych y cower'd and lamented ceaſeleſſly—yn whych Much the Myller's ſon paye'd me an unexpected vyſyt.

The dwarf came unattended and ſhould lykely have bene turne'd awaye had y not chance'd upon hym argueyng wyth the gate guard on myn returne frome a vyſyt to myn neyghbore to the eaſt[41]. He was dreſſd gayely yn rych, red cloth wyth a feather'd red hat atop hys wyde head. Y aſſure'd myn erſtwhyle bondeſman that y dyd yndede knowe the odd traveler before

41. This chapter opens with multiple references to the location of the elusive Verysdale, while still providing frustratingly little true detail. We know that it is south of Huntingdon, but little else. Who is this neighbor to the east (who is mentioned again when Robin visits next)? It is likely we may never know for certain.

ſmyleyng cautyouſly downe and aſkyng Much hys buſyneſs.

'Years paſt ye offer'd a meal alyke to that whych we gave ye 'neath the Tryſtyng Tree.' Myn heart ſank as y remember'd myn promyſe. 'But as y forgot to announce myn vyſyt, y ſhall ſettle fore whatever ye have avaylable.' He gryn'd and pyck'd at hys tethe as y dyſmounted ynſyde myn walls.

'Y ſee the lyon on thy breaſt. Have ye turne'd ſquyre as once Jon dyd?' y aſk'd, reſygne'd to myn taſk as hoſte.

'Naye. Y was gyven thys by a young page what came upon our buſyneſs wyth a brother. Pore pup had no more uſe fore yt y'm afrayd.' Y ſwallowe'd to ſee hys hand reſt gentley on hys ſworde's pommel; y knew Robyn's men to be ſcoundrels, but yf theyr fun had turne'd to the murder of boyes? Y dyd not aſk Much why the boye no longer neded hys clothes, and perſuaded mynſelf that y was too untruſtyng. Yet as the years have growne longe y have often wonder'd and regreted. Would not the horrore of the moment have bene worthe the eventual embrace of God at ſaynt Peter's gate? But alas, what ys done (ore not done) ys paſt and y maye only praye that the Lorde's heart ſees the gode yn myne.

Much ſtaye'd longe at Veryſdale—three wekes ore more—before makeyng hys waye onwards. He ſpoke often of Loxſley's many ſchemes to cheat the Churche ore ſhame the ſheryff and y pretended courteſy. Myn geſt often ſhowe'd remorſe at the wanton chaos of hys ſyre, yet y could not fully truſt hys regret as y loke'd upon the chylde's doublet he wore. ſtyll, y could not deny the gode he dyd the lands about by denyyng the grede of the clergy. Y would aſk foregyveneſs fore ſayeyng ſuch were yt not true that the churches of England fed gredeyly on theyr paryſhyoners, yn much the ſame manner that the Abbot of ſaynt Mary's fed on me after myn ſon's myſfortune yn Yorke's lyſts.

When the daye fore Much to leave had arryve'd—a cole ſummer daye whych teaſe'd the comeyng autumn, though yt was yet wekes awaye—y ſhare'd a cup of hot cydre wyth hym afore myn roaryng hearth (yt ys alwayes neceſſary to kepe yt burneyng yn thys drafty hame—even as y wryte thys on a ſwelteryng daye yn June y am wrap'd tyghtely yn furs yn myn ſecluded ſolar[42]). Ydley we playe'd at Nyne Man Morrys[43] as we ſyp'd our ſpyce'd drynks. Much had juſt fynyſh'd ſyngyng a ſonge he had learn'd of a young mayden when y made myn only attempt on hys vyſyt to quyet myn ſubtle fears.

'That was well-ſung, Much,' y ſaye'd. 'Yet tell me, what thynk ye of Robyn's games wyth Yorke? Are hys yntentyons purely juſt? Thynk ye that he means yll of the ſheryff? Thynk ye the ſheryff maye fele a nede to take actyon agaynſt hym?' Ore agaynſt hys allyes, y dyd not add.

The dwarf loked ſolemnly at me and ſhoke hys head. 'Y aſk few queſtyons of God and fewer of man and y am an happy man fore yt.' We playe'd yn ſylence then untyl he made to leave.

He bade me not ſee hym offe, but made fore the far dore, pauſeyng bryefly before he had croſſ'd half the hall. Turneyng, he ſhoke out hys cap and turne'd back as he place'd yt on hys myſſhappen head. 'Ye and y bothe knowe Robyn Hode's myrth too far outweyghs hys mynde.'

And ſhortly he was gone.

---

42. A private room, often in an upper story and more exposed to the sunlight than other chambers in the home
43. An English game played on a grid with white and black pebbles

Autumn had nearly come when next y heard tell of the doyngs of the Lorde of Barneſdale, and y heard tell yn a moſte alarmyng and dyſcourteous manner.

Y had heard that there was to be an archery conteſt yn Nottyngham, wyth the offer'd pryze of a ſylver arrowe fletch'd yn red golde. Myn hands recently bother'd by great payns, y had foreſworne the chance to compete (the ſame aches, yn fact, whych payn myn hands to thys daye). But y have no nede to tell ye of Loxſley's love of the bowe nore hys relatyonſhyp wyth the ſheryff of Nottyngham (nore myn owne ylls wyth the ſame), and ſo y wayted yn fear of what myſchyef he myghte make.

The daye of the conteſt came and went, and the next daye there was news that Robyn had won the game, but alſo news that a force of arms march'd downe Ermyne ſtrete beneath the banner of Yorke. Wyth anxyous antycypatyon y awayted theyr paſſage. Two nyghtes y wayted and praye'd—bothe fore the men of Yorke and fore the men of the Grenewode. Thoſe dayes moved ſlugyſhly, wyth grey rayns and longe hours. Y dare'd not ſend men after more rumours, and ynſtead ſtaye'd ynſyde and read letters of myn ſon's exployts yn the Holy Land untyl yt was too late to read by anythyng but candlelyghte, and after that y praye'd agayn.

Unable to ſlepe on the fourth nyght y wander'd the halls of Veryſdale, humyng hymns and tapyng myn fyngers yn relentleſs rhythms. Y knew not what y wayted fore, only that y wayted. The mone ſhone hyghe and bryghte when fynally y reſolve'd to retyre, but yt was then that the page came. The boye, no more than eleven, tolde me yn wyde-eyed whyſpers that a company of rough and wounded men had come to myn gates. Y neded not aſk to knowe yt to be Robyn Hode.

At the gates were roughly two dozen men and at theyr

head was theyr ſmyleyng, grene-hoded lorde. Behynde hym were Much and Wyll ſcarlocke, and yn theyr arms the ſlepeyng carcaſs of Lyttle Jon. To a man they were blodey'd and bruyſe'd, and myn heart ache'd to ſee men ſo ſorely hurte, and ache'd more to thynk of thoſe who had not made yt to myn dore.

Loxſley ſpoke many wordes to me at myn ſturdy gate, but foremoſte amongſte them was that damn'd curſe—"ſanctuary." Y had no wyll to engage yn the war whych had begun, but leſſ to deny myn owne Chryſtyan charyty. And ſo, as ys ryghte when aſk'd, y granted them forty dayes yn myn walls, and as theyr muddyed botes tramp'd paſt y whyſper'd farewells to a peaceful end to myn dayes.

Y had myn ſervants ſhowe the men to barracks yn whych to gather ſome reſt. As y ſtode and watch'd them myn wyfe awoke. Y aſſure'd her that all was well and ſent her to care fore our daughters—y would explayn all yn the mornyng. As ſhe unhappyly left, Robyn came to me and thank'd me.

'And nowe y ſuppoſe ye would hear our tale?' he aſk'd and, though y rather would have not, myn curyoſyty overcame me and y led Loxſley, ſcarlocke, and the Myller's ſon to the chamber where y had laſt entertayn'd Much. We ſat afore the fyre and y produce'd a bottle of ſpyryts gyven me by myn neyghbore to the eaſt, who had only bene fryendly once myn coffers were yn order. Then the bandyt lorde began hys tellyng, 'Heard ye ſurely of the ſheryff's game?' Howe he could ſtyll ſmyle whylſte hys men were ſo ſorely hurte y dyd not knowe.

'Y dyd. And alſo of the pryze.'

'Ah, the pryze,' ſaye'd ſcarlocke, 'Howe beautyful yt was. But alas, yt was left ahangeyng frome the Tryſtyng Tree.'

'O ho!' cry'd Robyn. "Twas not! Fore bravely dyd y wade back through the fraye as our defeat was made certayn, and

251

toke back by sworde what y had won by bowe.' And frome hys baldryc he produce'd a sparkleyng sylver shaft, fletch'd and headed yn yellowe golde. Yt felt bothe lyght and heavy yn myn hand, yts workmanshyp so fyne y scarce belyeve'd yt was made by human craft.

'Was thys before ore after Jon was struck so mortally?' ask'd the dwarf wyth a sour loke. Scarlocke as well loked yll at the syghte of the arrowe. Even Robyn's fryends knew hys trycks to have gone too far.

Theyr master ygnore'd them and press'd on, 'But y am before mynself. Afore y went to Nottyngham y gather'd 'bout myn Trystyng Tree myn men—some seven score—and tolde them of myn yntent to wyn frome loathesome John hys pryze. They chere'd fore me and beg'd to knowe myn plan.' By the lokes on the faces of hys two companyons y doubted they would chere hym nowe, e'en had they done so then. 'And so y call'd fore all to hoyst theyr bowes and joyn me on the road, but only syx fore to shote wyth me (fore y am a sportyng man); those syx would be scarlocke and Much, Godeman Gyles, Tod of Myntz, Lyttle Jon, and gode Gylberte.' At thys lyst of names Wyll choke'd as yf stab'd and, as Much touch'd hys hand, y saw hys eyes were wet. Robyn paye'd no mynde; fore all the gode he dyd hys neyghbores, the Lorde of the Grenewode was selfysh above all else. 'The rest and theyr bowes would be alonge to assure me 'gaynst all harme.

'We came to Nottyngham yn hyghe spyryts and were well receyve'd. The game fyeld was grene and the crowde joyeous. The other competytores blanch'd to see so fayr of competytyon.' Y wonder styll to thys daye howe fully he be-lyeve'd yn the love he tolde that others gave hym. 'All the arch-ers there were fayr yndede, though none so fayr as those y brought. Save Gyles and Tom.' He frowne'd as he thought of

252

hys leſs able'd companyons, then contynue'd, 'But Gylberte and y were beſt, e'en 'mongſte theſe. Each tyme we ſhot we ſlyce'd the wand, ſave the laſt, when he ſlyp'd yn the fynal ynſtant and ſhot hys wyde. 'Tys a ſhame. He could have beat me.' But not fore a moment dyd y belyeve Loxſley would have abyded that. The ſheryff gave me the pryze, ſmyrkyng to hyde hys ſhame, and we rode ſwyftly home.

"Twas not longe after we had left that we learn'd the godely ſheryff purſue'd us, wyth blode on hys mynde.' Robyn pauſe'd and eye'd me evylly, 'No fryends of hys came thys waye, dyd they? And ye dyd not, nore would not, ayd them, ay?'

Clutchyng myn goblet tyghte, y aſſure'd, 'Y do only as ys requyre'd. Quy fydelys eſt ey quy fecyt yllum ſycut et moſes yn omny domo yllyus.'[44]

Laughyng ſharply, lyke a crowe, the Brygand Lorde ſpake that yt was no matter, fore he knew us to be fryends. 'Excuſe me nowe, dear hoſte, fore y have not relyeve'd mynſelf fore ſome tyme. And,' he laye'd an heavy hand upon myn owne, 'hoſpytales ynvycem ſyne murmuratyone.'[45] Wyth that he left, whyſtleyng Grene ſleves[46] and kyckyng hys fete.

We ſat yn ſylence fore a moment, Wyll, the dwarf, and y. Then Much ſpoke, hys voyce lowe, "Twas a ſlaughter, ſyr Knyghte. Lyke naught y nore many of us had ever ſene.' ſcarlocke began to cry. (Thys ys the cloſeſt y ever ſaw the crymſon caperer to human regret, and never dyd y ſee yt agayn; y learn'd later that Wyll's brother Gyles had dye'd as a reſult of

44. To the Hebrews 3:2 KJV: *Who was faithful to him that appointed him, as also Moses was faithful in all his house.*

45. I Peter 4:9: *Vse hospitalitie one to another without grudging.*

46. It is unlikely that *Greensleeves* was composed prior to the 16th century, thus introducing a curious anachronism. This is, perhaps, less curious when one considers the apparent fascination with Robin Hood held by King Henry VIII.

thys myſchyef, and ever after dyd he only take part yn vyolence when he was certayn of total vyctory.) 'They came upon our revels yn the wode. Twyce the men we kept yn our company they brought, all bowe-trayn'd and garb'd yn mayl. We ſtode bravely, but were ſore preſſ'd. Many of us were wounded, Lyttle Jon amongſte.

"'Maſter," ſaye'd he, hys eyes a-rolleyng yn hys ſkull, "fore all the love of Chryſte on Croſs and all the love ye haſt ever borne me, as mede[47] fore myn ſervyces to ye and the free men, let not the ſheryff fynde me alyve. Take up thy blodey ſworde and ſmyte ye offe myn head. ſtryke me! ſtryke me! Deal me wounds as depe and wyde as the Northern ſea ſo there be no hope that y ſhould lyve!" But Robyn would have none of yt, and bade me carry Jon upon myn back as we fled. Many a tyme had y to ſtop, fore though y am ſtronge and hale, but lyttle y be, and as y reſted y fyre'd back at the ſoldyers what followe'd us. Yn the chaos many men were found, then loſte, untyl we came to the edge of the Wode, where our commander met us once more.' Y could near taſte the reſentment yn Much's wordes, and found the ymage of the dwarf carryyng the gyant to ſafety more tragycal than comycal. 'And ſo frome thence came we, untyl we found thy caſtle and hoſpytalyty.'

He ſtop'd and y noded and there was naught to ſaye. ſombrely we ſat untyl Loxſley returne'd, croweyng of the thryll of the battle, as yf any there had ear to lyſten.

Yn haſte y excuſe'd mynſelf and went to prepare the caſtle; ſurely John Yorke would wayt no tyme to come upon myn walls, and here y was beholden by myn Chryſtyan duty to gyve ſanctuary agaynſt myn lawful lorde. Y had no doubt that, ſhould Nottyngham turne yts ſwordes agaynſt me, not even the twyn dytches whych encyrcle'd Ryverſmotte would protect me frome

47. A deserved reward

them. O howe y cry'd that nyght, and myn wyfe was no comforte to me.

Clothes and armes and beds were gyven them, and yn myn love of Churche y gave them ſafety fore forty dayes.[48]

Y neded not wayt longe, fore wythyn an half a daye the ſtronge army of the noble ſheryff ſtode arraye'd before Ryverſmotte. That whole nyghte longe y had barely ſlept, and y had ryſen before the dawn. Deſpyte myn complaynts, Edyth had accompanyed me as y pace'd the halls and prepare'd myn men fore ſyege. Howe gode ſhe has always bene to me, and howe fayr a love we bear. Y ſhould lykely not lyve to wryte thys thys daye were yt not fore her, and y am ſad wyth guylt at the thought y ſhould dye before her and leave her alone wythout even myn ſon to care fore her. Knowe that y love ye, Edyth, ſhould ye read thys, and ever have, e'en as y fell prey to the charmes of Robyn Hode.

Yt was past none when y was call'd to the wall, fore Yorke would have rede wyth me. Once there y ſaw clearly the noble Law, dreſſ'd yn ſhyneyng armour wyth a black ſtag upon hys breaſt and the blue and golden flag of Yorke flyyng above hys head. Wyth hym was a myghtey hoſte, greater than y had even fear'd, and myn heart ſank to ſee the end of myn lyne.

'Greteyngs, ſyr ſheryff, and welcome to myn lands,' y call'd. 'Y would ynvyte ye yn, but yt ſemes ye bear me the ynſtruments of yll wyll.'

John Yorke, hys vyſore rayſe'd, call'd back, 'ſyr Rychard

48. Forty is a number commonly given in the bible, and was the length of time where sanctuary could be sought in a church.

at the Lee, ye traytore knyghte, by kepeyng here the Kyng's owne enemy ye betraye thy faythful vowes. What ye have done goes well agaynſt all lawes and ryghtes, and markes thy name yn red.'

'Y cannot deny what ye accuſe, and yet alſo cannot yyeld, fore veryly y am a true knyghte and two promyſes nowe conflyct. Greatly would y love to followe the wyll of myn one true ſyre, had not y taken a Chryſtyan vowe, and bene bound to ſhyeld hys flock. Wend ye forthe, ſyrs, on thy waye, and do unto nore threaten more to Veryſdale tyll our Kyng's wyll ys wyt[49].' E'en frome the dyſtance o'er whych we ſhouted y could ſee the Lorde Yorke's dyſcomforte.

'What vowe ys thys what overrydes thy love of Nottyngham? Were ye any other man y would be ſore aſtounded, but y knowe aryghte the heart of Rychard Veryſdale,' came hys reſponſe, and myn heart wept to be ſo reproach'd by myn lyege lorde.

'Theſe men are hurte and ſore afryghted, and have beg'd myn godly love. Fore forty dayes they ſhall wythyn reſyde, and after frome theyr bond am y free. Go ye ſwyft to London Towne and beg fore Edward's wyll—fore only he ore the Pope yn Rome could tell me y have done yll,' ſaye'd y, myn voyce bolder than myn breaſt. And ſo Nottyngham and hys many banners ſet offe ſouth fore London, and y was left yn further fear.

Myn wyfe noted thys fear when y joyn'd the houſeholde fore the myddaye meal and gryp'd myn hand tyghtely. All that y wanted was to retreat to myn ſolar and medytate on myn croked promyſes—to God, to Kyng, and to Robyn Hode. But after we had eaten—myn daughters bothe fryghten'd and enthrall'd by Robyn and hys rough men, who laugh'd and tolde bolde ſtorys loudly—ſhe toke me aſyde and kyſſ'd myn cheke, ſayeyng, 'Ye

49. Known

256

are a gode man, Huſband, and only faulted by beyng too dutyful. What ys to come wyll be dyffycult, and lykely dangerous fore us all, but yt ys not fore the yllneſs of thyne heart. Ye are a true knyghte, and neyther kyng, nore God maye deny that.' Her eyes were fylmy wyth uncry'd tears, and y ſaw then that there was more to fear than myn honour. Edyth would ſupporte me yn myn ſelfyſhneſs, but y neded alſo to thynk of myn daughters (and of myn wyfe yf ſhe would thynk not of herſelf). Y reſolve'd then that y ſhould break myn promyſe and returne Robyn to the Wode, ſanctuary be damn'd!

But fortune once agayn ſmyle'd upon me, as even yn that terryble moment dyd Maſter Hode come upon us, and ſpoke of a moſte wondrous reſolutyon, 'Y thank ye, Knyghte Ry-chard, fore thy bravery 'fore that vyllayn, and fore the generous gyft of thy hoſpytalyty. But y fear we muſt wend ſwyftly home, myn men and y, fore our buſyneſs to further attend. All ſave Jon, who y fear ſtyll maye be unfyt to fote, yf that does not ympoſe; yt takes more than a nyghte of reſt to mend an arrowe'd knee.'

ſpecheleſs was y, and myn wyfe beſyde, untyl myn tongue agayn gayn'd lyfe, only to betraye me once more yn yts braynleſs defenſe of tradytyon. 'Naye, gode Robyn, thynk not that ye ympoſe. ſtaye thyſelf under Veryſdale rofe as longe as ys neded; y have made myn promyſe,' ſaye'd myn devyl lyps.

But the devyl yn grene was adamant, and uncharac-teryſtycally ſofte wyth hys wordes. 'Ye have made a choyce, and a gode and Chryſtyan one, but y ſhall not have ye lyve by yt yf yt bryngs ye harme. Y cannot aſk ye to accept yt wyth wordes, only wyth thy heart. Me and all myn trope ſave ſquyre Jon ſhall de-part wyth next mornyng's lyghte. And knowe ye that ever ye have a fryend 'neath Barneſdale's Tryſtyng Tree.'

And so yndede they left, and y ſaw ſtronger than e'er before (ore lykely e'en ſynce) the charyty ynſyde the ſtorme whych was Robyn Hode. Y wyſh'd them luck by the Lady ſaynt and he wyſh'd me the ſame and they were gone o'er the brydge and ynto the country grene. Beſyde me yn the muſty bayley Edyth gryp'd myn arm, her eyes wyde and blue as ſhe watch'd the hauntyng clouds glowe tawny wyth the ſun. 'Thys ys not over, Huſband. The worſte has but begun.'

And yn myn breaſt y felt her wordes ryng true.

Yt was not longe before Jon was alſo on hys fete agayn, though he walk'd wyth a lymp. He bore the arrowehead whych had yn-jure'd hym on a corde about hys neck and fynger'd yt when talk turne'd towards Nottyngham and the Grenewode. 'Twas ſaye'd the ſheryff had gone to London and returne'd, and once more fayl'd of ſeyzeyng Lorde Robert of the Wode, and thys news fyll'd myn ſaxon geſt wyth an hunger fore the road. Ten dayes frome when fyrſt y open'd myn dores he made to leave, and y dyd naught to ſtaye hym. But y dyd ſpeak quyetly to hym afore myn gates, and aſk'd hym howe fare'd hys love of Loxſley.

'Undymynyſh'd, fryend Rychard. Fore, had yt not bene fore hym y ſhould have bene bled on a fyeld ore bound yn dun-geon, yet nowe y am free,' ſpake he.

'But were yt not fore hys antycs would ye not never have bene ſhot at all? And dyd not Much ſtrayn hys back, not Robyn, to carry ye hyther?' y offer'd.

The blonde's eyes grew ſad then and he bruſh'd hys fyngers on myn arm. 'Y had thought ye knew Robyn Hode as y do. Fore Much am y grateful, ay, but ever more fore Maſter Hode. He loves ye, Rychard, as much as he loves me ore Wyll ore the Lady Magdalene. Quy confydet yn dyvytyys ſuys corruet

258

yuſty autem quaſy vyrens folyum germynabunt.'[50]

Wyth that he left, a ſtout walkyng ſtyck yn hys hand and hys blynde adoratyon hys ſhyeld. Y thought hym a fole then, yet was y any dyfferent? By myn vowes and myn ſtrange weakneſs to thys man y fear'd? Had y knowne then the power he had o'er even the greateſt of men y maye not have deſpyſe'd eyther mynſelf nore the ſquyre Lyttle ſo dyrely.

Yn that tyme myn wyfe worry'd oft after our daughters, but y beg'd her to kepe fayth. All thys tyme, however, myn own heart grew heavyer as y felt mynſelf dryftyng ever cloſer to dyſaſter. Who could y truſt to care fore myn daughters ſhould y fall prey to the Lorde's plan? Would our kyng foregyve me fore what y had done? Y toke to hawkyng alonge the banks of the Gwaſh as y ponder'd theſe ſorrowes and myn owne tyes to Robert Loxſley. Rumours flew that Edward Kyng was prepareyng to make hys waye northe, and thys dyd lyttle to ſettle myn mynde.

Two dayes after Lyttle Jon left y was out wyth myn men alonge the ryver, when myn hounds began to baye and growle. Thynkyng yt perhaps a bear whoſe fyſhyng poſte we had dyſturbe'd, y call'd them back, and aſk'd myn fellowes to ready as we made our retreat. Yet no bear came forthe, but the lyvery'd men of Nottyngham Towne, and yn great number. Theyr maſter bore a wryt frome hys (and alſo myn) maſter; y, ſyr Rychard at the Lee, was to be taken to Nottyngham forthewyth to be ympryſon'd, try'd, and executed at the pleaſure of yts lorde fore the cryme of haveyng knowne Robyn Hode.

There could be no argument, and y would not ſlaye men loyal to the Crowne, even had y the numbers to oppoſe them. And ſo y was taken and myn wryſts bound. Y beg'd myn

---

50. Prouerbs 11:28 KJV: *He that trusteth in his riches, shall fall : but the right-eous shall flourish as a branch.*

knyghtes to ſend myn fynal wordes of love to Edyth, Margaret, and ſarah, and—ſhould he ever returne—myn noble ſon as well.

As y was led awaye y cry'd to remember howe all had once bene, and agayn to ymagyne myn punyſhment.

But y had more fryends on Earth than oft y allowe, and yt was fore love of me that y was ſave'd, much as yt was fore love of Robyn dyd he ever and always eſcape John Yorke's graſp. And glad as y am y of myn lyfe, y wyſh only the pryce had not bene ſo hyghe, and that the Prynce of the Grenewode had ſought ſhryveyng fore hys ſelf-appoynted heroyſm.

What y mean to laye downe next has bene tolde to me—many tymes—but y was not preſent, fore at the tyme y languyſh'd yn John Yorke's dungeon.

When myn men returne'd to Veryſdale wyth news of myn fate, y would have expected Edyth to be ſtrycken utterly uſeleſs by gryef, yet ſhe was not. As ſone as worde reach'd her ears ſhe dreſſ'd herſelf as ſympley as ſhe myghte and toke to horſe deſpyte all wordes agaynſt. Rode ſhe eaſt towards Barneſdale, accompany'd only by two ſtout men and her faythful heart. Theſe men ſhe toke alonge had bene at myn ſyde when y had fyrſt met Lorde John yn that wode, and ſo ſhe hope'd they maye guyde her to the Tryſtyng Tree.

Once under the boughs ſhe was ſtrycken, much as myn ſon and y had bene two years before, by the beauty of the trees, though yt was autumn nowe. Under thoſe red and golden leaves her ſtede was gyven thankful reſt, as her ſwyft gallop became a trot and the ſounds of the quyet foreſt match'd the ſounds of her beatyng heart.

After ſome tyme, as the ſun duck'd lowe and depe duſk

ſettle'd 'pon Barneſdale, ſhe call'd her fellowes to halt. 'Y had hope'd to fynde Maſter Robyn's hall afore nyghte, yet nowe y fear myn plans are all undone. Unleſs eyther of ye knowe the waye?' But they dyd not, and none had brought tent nore bedyng, ſo great had bene her fervour when they had ſet forthe. Dejected, ſhe fear'd the wylde wode, fore even wyth two ſtout knyghtes at her ſyde ſhe knew that a lady ys far frome ſafe yn a foreygn holte paſt darke.

They rode a ways further, jumpyng occaſyonally at the crack of leaves ore the ſkytter of ſmall paws yn the bracken. The horſes began to ſwaye wyth exhaustyon, and deſpyte myn love's objectyons they were force'd to ſtop and to dyſmount. 'We muſt nedes yet fynde ayd fore myn huſband,' ſhe pleaded, but myn men what followe'd reply'd, 'And theſe anymals muſt nedes have reſt yf they are to ſurvyve the nyghte.' And ſo they began a ſlowe ſearch on fote fore ſome ſhelter.

Yet no ſoner had they begun theyr exploratyons when an hyghe whyſtle was heard, and a dyſturbance came yn the trees. Three men lept downe, all hoded and maſk'd yn Lyncolne grene. Each had a wycked-ſhene'd dyrk yn theyr fyſt and grey capes to match the glome. Myn wyfe, ſo brave yet ſtyll ſo gentle, cry'd out and ſtep'd behynde the knyghtes and they theyr ſwordes dyd bare. But behynde as well were the brygands, and ſone coarſe hands were on her fayr arms. Her men fought bravely well, yet outnumber'd and darkeneſs-blynded were they; ſwyftly was one dealt a ſore blowe and the other brought to yyeld.

'Tell me, Lady, yf ye maye, what bryngs ye here ſo late? Thys wode ys greneman land, and dangerous yn full lyghte,' ſpake one, hys eyes one blue and one grey.

'Myn husband, ſyr, ys what bryngs me hyther, hys ſafety

261

fore to earn. ſheryff Jon has taken hym, and holdes hym yn dungeon. Y knowe Robyn Hode frome ſtorys and frome table, and would have hym lend what ayd he were able,' ſhe ſpake bravely, her head hyghe.

'Y praye ye tell who ys thys man, what aſks ſo much of our dear kyng?' was ſtated the reply.

'ſyr Rychard at the Lee, ys he, and none too happy ſhall he be at the receptyon we receyve'd. Y ſhould hope ſyr ſamuel's arm can be bandage'd well, leſt ye wytneſs myn lorde's yre.' Y wyſh fervently that y were half the man myn wyfe had cry'd me to be, yet as myn age growes, y fear, ſo too does myn cautyon. And yn that tyme y was a vyctym ever to the wants of the Grenewode's captayn.

The acoſter's eyes then wyden'd, and he fell upon hys knee. Pullyng lowe hys ſcarfe, he kyſſ'd Edyth's whyte hand wyth hys rough lyps. 'Foregyve us, Lady Veryſdale, we knew not who we came acroſte. Y ſee nowe the famylyar lyvery, once clouded by the nyghte. Had y but ſene more clearly y would ne'er have laye'd upon ye ſo fouly.' There was fear yn hys eye and, though y knowe not whether y have met thys certayn vaga-bonde before ore synce, y knowe hys fear was not of me but of Robyn Hode.

They three were unhanded, theyr weapons returne'd, and myn wounded man's arm bound tyghte. The man what ſpoke offer'd to lead them to the Tryſtyng Tree, where they were aſſure'd that fyres ſtyll burne'd and fode aplenty could be found. Followeyng yn ſylence, theyr nervous horſes on leads, the three of Ryverſmotte found many paths whych theyr eyes maye never have ſene, no matter the tyme they ſearch'd. Edyth was bolde of heart and determyne'd of yntent, and tells that the whole walk there ſhe held her head hyghe, and flynch'd not once at the fryghtenyng ſounds of the wode; of thys y have no doubt, fore myn wyfe ys a maſter amonge maſters of the art of the publyc face. O howe y wyſh y could have bene there to wytneſs her ſtoyc march!

Preſently they came to the edge of that great clearyng that twyce to that poynt y had feaſted wythyn. Three of the hodes toke the exhausted ſtedes to care fore them, and the man wyth two-colour'd eyes led myn wyfe to a bench beſyde a fyre, ſhooyng awaye the ruffyans there to make ſpace fore Loxſley's neweſt geſts. 'Wayt ye here and y ſhall ſwyftly fynde myn lorde.' And wyth lyghte fete he was offe ynto the depe of the crowded glade, full deſpyte the loſſes Robyn muſt ſurely have taken 'gaynſt Yorke's ſtronge arm.

Myne wyfe ſat yn ſylence, head hyghe though her ſurroundyngs were moſte fearſome. All drynk ſhe deny'd, though ſhe accepted bread when offer'd. ſhe knew not howe longe ſhe wayted, ſave that the ſun had fully ſet but the fyre near whych ſhe ſat dyd not yet nede tendyng. Often has myn wyfe tolde me of the fearſome deparavyty of that place, though ſhe found yt more amuſeyng than ever y dyd. Thankfully ſhe toke no part, but merely watch'd the revels.

When her wayt was ended yt was not by Loxſley, but by a fayr woman. 'Hayl, vyſytore, and well met,' ſaye'd Clorynda (fore that faythful bryde of Lorde Robyn ys who thys was). 'What bryngs ye hyther to the Grenewode ſo late and yn ſuch great dyſregard fore thy ſtedes?' Yt was then that myn wyfe broke her ſtoycyſm and tolde all ſhe had heard, begyng to ſpeak wyth the maſter of the outlaw band. Clorynda, who had only near the end of the plea made knowne her name and nearneſs to Robyn Hode, laye'd her ſofte and gentle hands on Edyth's and ſpake once more. 'Robyn ys currently yndyſpoſe'd, hys joye at repellyng hys enemy once more thys weke haveyng weaken'd hym to drynk. But y ſhall rouſe hym and turne hym to thy—to our, yf y maye—cauſe. Myn Rob has lyttle love fore the dyſcomfyt of England's faythful landholders, and feles ſtyll una-venged of Lorde John's betrayals. Juſt thys morne news has come that Nottyngham offers an hundred pound to he what bryngs hym Robyn Hode; the vyllayn hopes to prey on the weak myndes of the peaſant caste to bryng lowe England's fayreſt de-fender! Come, and wayt beſyde the hall whyle gode Robyn ys rouſe'd.

They went then, Clorynda, myn wyfe, and myn two men, to that antyque hall hung wyth banners and lyt wyth merry-ment. Many of thoſe yn the clearyng had begun to bed downe, but the wyndowes of the lowe hame ſtyll ſparkle'd wyth candle-lyghte and ſpyll'd forthe laughter. The Quene of the ſhepherdeſſes bade Edyth wayt outſyde as ſhe enter'd to crys of her name. Yt was thankfully not too terrybley longe afore the dore was once more open'd and out ſtep'd bothe Clorynda and her lorde.

Robyn was dreſſ'd yn a grene robe, yts puff'd ſleves ſlaſh'd wyth golde, and fyne golden hoſe. A black blouſe hung open to hys cheſt, ſpyllyng curleyng hayr, and upon that breaſt laye the golden chayn of offyce whych had bene taken frome the ſheryff at hys humylyatyon. Yn one hand was a ſylver goblet, doubtleſs alſo taken frome the unlucky Maſter Yorke, and on hys head was a dropeyng red cap. Edyth knew hym only frome myn ſtoryes and frome hys bryef vyſyt, yet frome theſe was conſcyous to be cautyous wyth hym. Hys eyes were unfocuſ'd and hys ſmyle croked, but hys lady on hys arm ayded hym to come to hys mynde. Wyth the Lady Veryſdale's ayd, Clorynda tolde hym anew all that had tranſpyre'd. When all was ſaye'd, Robyn toke one more ſyp of wyne, belch'd loud, then excuſe'd hymſelf.

'Y mean no harme by myn ympropryety, Lady Rychard. Ye have merely caught me at the heyght of celebratyon.' He pauſe'd and knytted hys browes, concentrateyng harde. He then handed hys chalyce to Clorynda. 'Ye ſaye our foe has taken thy huſband?'

'Y ſaye the ſheryff of Nottyngham has taken myn huſband,' anſwer'd myn wyfe wyth care. The outlaw laugh'd at that, and the Lady of Barneſdale ſmyle'd ſoftely. Y beg ye, gode Robyn, and all thy folke, by the love of our Lady grant me one bone. Let not myn lorde be ſlayn and leave hys wyfe and chyldren empty of claym. Has he no ſon yn England to defend hym, and no faſt fryends ſave ye. Y praye ye Robyn, to take up thy ſworde fore love of Rychard as hys ſon toke up the Croſs fore love of Chryſte!'

Nodyng, the Foreſt Kyng ſpake. 'Ay, ye and he ſhall bothe y ayd, though fyrſt y muſt reſt myn head. Fyrſt let me laye mynſelf downe ſome hours few, then myn men y ſhall lead to Nottyngham wyth ſwordes held hyghe. Ye ſhall ſtaye here and have myn chambers, and thys very nyghte y ſhall ſend Much and company to gather thy daughters.'

'Myn daughters?' aſk'd myn wyfe.

'What Rob yntends maye have dyre conſequences. Yet yt muſt nedes be done to ſave thy man,' offer'd Clorynda, and only here do y holde myn wyfe at fault; had ſhe but aſk'd further much ſorrowe maye have bene avoyded and our chyldren nede not have bene gather'd by the dwarf yn dead of nyghte. And Nottyngham maye not have met ſuch payn. Yet ſhe relented and allowe'd herſelf be led ynſyde as Loxſley ſought ſotheyng water and a fyne bed of moſs.

The furnyſhyngs of Lorde Robert's bedchamber ſurpryſe'd me lyttle when Edyth tolde me of them—y have knowne Robyn Hode oft to be vayn. ſylk hangyngs and lavyſh tapeſtryes of ſaynts, golde-bound cheſts and a toweryng bed ſet

265

wyth downe coveryngs, a wryteyng deſk of exquyſyte conſtructyon, and an yvory waſh-baſyn. Myn wyfe was much pleaſe'd by the accommodatyons, and eſpecyally by the well-ſtock'd hearth, and ſo ſlept ſoundly. A longer reſt ſhe toke than oft ſhe would, and when ſhe roſe the Prynce of Barneſdale had bene true to hys worde and had ſet forthe fore Nottyngham wyth moſte of hys fyrd[51] before the ſun. Only Much and an handful of wodemen remayn'd, alonge wyth a party of fyfty of myn men and bothe myn daughters, who were frantyc wyth joye to ſee theyr mother.[52]

'Worry not,' offer'd Much as Edyth fretfuly aſk'd after Veryſdale. 'All ys well as yet, and ſone Lorde Rychard ſhall knowe the freedome brought by Robyn Hode's ſworde.' But Much ſmyle'd not as he ſpake of ſuch happy thyngs.

The men what toke me brought me to Nottyngham Towne and, paſt the gable'd roves, downe to the dungeon beneath the caſtle. Alone and fearful was y, and draughts whych fylter'd betwene the colde ſtones chyll'd myn bones to yce. Yn the darke y could not ſee yf the other ſhapes held there yn manacles were alyve ore dead, and myn mynde paynted bryghte ſkeleton vyſages on theyr ſlump'd forms.

ſome days y languyſh'd there—perhaps two, perhaps a dozen. Yn that tyme y fear'd fore myn wyfe and chyldren, and wonder'd after theyr fate. Occaſyonally a ſlouch-ſhoulder'd

51. A form of English feudal levy, here likely used metaphorically as Robin has no right to raise a fyrd, as Richard would know. Additionally, the use of a fyrd was a Saxon tradition, not in use in the centuries after Norman occupation.

52. Further confusing the location of Verysdale, it was stated previously that their horses were nearly killed riding to Barnesdale for a whole day, yet in a single night Much has ridden to Verysdale and back!

gaoler yn browne coyf would come wyth ſtale bread and thyn porrydge, he ſomehowe ſmellyng worſe than the pyt yn whych y was confyne'd. But one daye he brought no fode, but a ryng of clatteryng keys.

'The maſter calls fore ye. ſome trouble on the road frome Blyth.' And myn hands and fete were unchayn'd only to be bound once more wyth leathern corde by the ſoldyers whych wayted above the dungeon ſtayrs.

Y was led, a ſpearpoynt at myn back, ynto the wyde ſtretes of the towne. Blynkyng to ſee the ſun, y dyd not at fyrſt knowe the mounted ſhape of ſheryff Jon frome that of the gallowes he ſat near to.

'ſyr Rychard at the Lee, a pleaſure to ſee thy face agayn.' But y knew by hys voyce there was no pleaſure to be had. 'Yt ſemes y gueſſ'd ryghte yn the love thy fryend holdes fore ye.'

'Myn lorde?' aſk'd y, yet ſlowe to thynk frome ſo longe beneath the Earth.

'Even nowe Robyn Loxſley marches up Ermyne ſtrete wyth ſeven ſcore outlaw bowes. Y ymagyne he comes to reſcure ye, fore no coaxyng nore ſtronge arm has proven worthey of bryngyng hym forthe to me.' Hys gaze was colde and harde and y knew that, no matter the judgement of the Lorde, myn lorde on Earth had judge'd me foul. 'Myn men ſtand ready and the gallowes are ſtronge. 'Fore nones[53] ye bothe ſhall hang.' Juſt then a loud horne blew and the bells of the towne began to ryng. 'Ah, the vyllayn comes!' The ſheryff then ſpur'd hys horſe and motyon'd hys men to bryng me thyther; y could not reſyſt. We ſtode then at the end of the wyde ſtrete afore the gate, the ſcaffolde ſome yardes behynde us, and watch'd as Robyn's grene

53. The sixth Catholic hour, or the midafternoon prayer, taking place around 3pm

-clad army approach'd the open avenue ynto Nottyngham. 'Ye ſhall bothe hang together. Yet worry not, ſyr Rychard—ye ſhall hang fyrſt. Ryverſmotte ſhall be a fyne addytyon to myn hold-eyngs.' The ſheryff ſmyle'd evyly and y whymper'd wyth deſpayr.

The ſheryff's archers ſtode cautyous upon the walls and downe the ſtrete as Loxſley ſet fote upon the cobbles. Many fyngers laye tenſe on many fletchyngs, and the ayr was ſtyll as early mornyng. About us, locals fled to ſhadowe'd eaves and ſhutters clack'd ſhut yn fryghte. Myn legs began to ſhake wyth worry as myn bladder dyd complayn, but ſone grene Robyn left hys men and ſtode a wayes ahead.

'Abyde, proud ſheryff,' he ſaye'd, 'Abyde and ſpeak wyth me. Y would fayn[54] hear what news of Edward Kyng. Comes he up the Roman Road[55]?'

'The Kyng?' aſk'd Yorke, unbalance'd by the query. 'Thys buſyneſs be wyth ye and y, though Edward ſhall appear. He comes not though to paſs hys judgement, but to approve myn owne.'

The Wodelorde gryn'd and bowe'd then. 'God hymſelf as wytneſs, y have not run ſo faſt on fote yn nyghe on ſeven years as hyther y came todaye. And on vowe to that ſame God y promyſe ye, proud ſheryff, 'tys not fore thy gode.' And faſter than y had thought a man could draw, he fyre'd a ſhot frome hys lythe bowe whych ſtuck, aquyveryng, yn John Yorke's breaſt.

Y cry'd out and fell upon myn knees. Arrowes flew and ſtele ſang and myn lovely lorde fell craſhyng on the ſtones. Tears fyll'd myn eyes to ſee myn lyege's death, and all about

54. Happily
55. While there are multiple Roman roads in Britain, it is likely that this is yet another reference to the famous Ermine Street.

were fearful dyeyng ſhryeks and cruel laughter. The walls of Nottyngham rang wyth ſhouts of 'Robyn Hode' and myn heart broke at the tragedy, though the murder'd would have ſene me dead.

ſwyftly—ore yn an age (myn mynde was far frome knoweyng)—Loxſley ſtode above me and, wyth one fell ſwyng of hys brygand blade, ſmote offe the ſheryff's head and wet me yn hys blode, sayeyng, 'Lye ye there, proud ſheryff, thy evyl all bene done. Myghte every man ſynde ye more truſty nowe than e'er when ye drew breath.' Behynde hym hys mens' ſharpe ſwordes cut lowe what guards yet ſtode and had not turne'd craven. Lokeyng downe he ſmyle'd agayn, and myn ſtomach churne'd anew. Wyth ſhyneyng edge he freed myn hands and myn fete, and yn myn hand he set a bowe. 'ſtand, fryend, and ayd us yn our flyghte. Wyth me and myne come quyck to Grenewode's eaves, through myre, moſs, and fen. Awaye go we to Grenewode's breaſt, where wayts thy wyfe and daughters fayr, tyll y have gayn'd the gode grace of comely Edward Kyng!'

And though yt ſycken'd myn heart and fyll'd me ſtyll wyth fear, to the Grenewode dyd y go.

Back to the Grenewode hye'd we, through myre, moſs, and fen. All that tyreſome waye, though we rode ahorſe on ſtolen fleſh and truely not ſo longe a ryde yt was, much fatygued was y. And who would fault me fore myn tyredneſs? What godely knyghte would not be ſtrycken, as yf by an arrowe through the heart (alack, to remember Loxſley's fell ſhot), to ſee hys feudal prynce laye'd lowe at hys fete? And by a ſelf-avowe'd fryend beſydes! Others yn the trope alſo wept, but ne'er when yn Robyn's ſyghte; once a man made thys myſtake and was ſmote frome hys ſeat by our yreſome guyde. 'Cry not fore thoſe what tax unfayrly, but

269

fore thoſe whom are unfayrly tax'd. Yf ye muſt cry, do ſo fore fryend Rychard, and then only fore the joye he has attayn'd.' Y could not mete any eye when thys woeful thyng was ſaye'd.

When at laſt we breach'd the eaves of Barneſdale, and ſwyftly came 'pon the Tryſtyng Grove, y ſhouted wyth joye to ſee Edyth and myn chyldren unharm'd and held them to myn breaſt. 'ſo wan are ye, and thy rybs ſo large; yn what yll waye were ye kept? And what of ſheryff John? Howe came ye free of hym?' ſhe aſk'd, but y kyſſ'd her ſylent; y would fayn not ſpeak of what terrore had befallen Nottyngham, ynſtead to relyſh myn love. To God then turne'd myn thoughts and to the Pſalmes— 'Confundantur et revereantur quarentes anymam meam avertantur retrorſum et confundantur cogytantes myhy mala.'[56]

Myn joyeous reunyon was upſet by myn wyfe's ſcream, after whych ſhe hyd myn daughters' faces on her hyp. Turneyng, y felt myn byle ryſe as y ſaw Robyn ſtode upon a table. Yn hys hand was the noyſome head of John of Yorke, produce'd frome yn hys ſaddlebag. Hys black hayr was plaſter'd about hys face, and even on ſo ſhorte a ryde he had begun to bloat, but Nottyngham's ſheryff yt ſurely was.

'Free men! Lythe ye nowe to Robyn Hode!' call'd he. 'That foul ſheryff what rul'd theſe lands ys dead by myn fayr hand! No proud law rules us nowe ſave London and Edward Kyng!' The cheres what followe'd drowne'd hys laughter and he was borne awaye by loveyng hands. No cheres however came frome me, and myn wyfe ſhe echo'd myn Pſalme frome a moment pryor. *What was to become of us?* What retrybutyon would the Crowne bryng on us? What could y have done to reſcue Maſter Robyn's vyctym? Could God foregyve a wytneſs of ſuch a cryme? Y nede not have worry'd—leaſtwyſe of the mortal

56. Psalmes 34:4 KJV: *I sought the LORD, and hee heard me ; and deliuered mee from all my fears.*

concerns; though that next year was ryfe wyth uncertaynty and an unhappy choler, y am nowe a bleſſed and uncrymynal man, wantyng only fore myn ſon abroad.

News came ſwyft of the Kyng's arryval, and of the great hoſte he brought—nyghe as great, ſome ſaye'd, as what was brought agaynſt the ſcots at Dunbar[57]. ſettle'd he yn Nottyngham and a pryce he place'd on all 'neath Barneſdale's boughs. All lands of Veryſdale he ſeyze'd yn worde (though Robyn's myſchyef kept hys governores e'er frome her marches) and offer'd them entyre to any what ſhould do the deed and ſtryke offe myn very head. Fore Robyn the pryce the ſheryff had ſet mayntayn'd, though ſome ſaye'd yt yncreaſe'd by fyve, by ten, ore even by an hundredfolde. 'Twas ſaye'd the Kyng was ſore wroth alſo fore the dearth of dere, fore Robyn hunted ſo enterpryſeyngly. Fore ſyx monthe and more Edward Kyng lyve'd at Nottyngham, and y—yn fear—wyth Robyn.

At fyrſt y lyve'd merely yn the Grenwode's hall wyth myn famyly and dyd not go on expedytyons, yet ſone y found y could not mayntayn thys ſtate; Robyn and hys men teaſe'd me fore myn ſuppoſed cowardyce and regale'd me wyth tales of theyr adventures (ſemeyngly unaware that y dyd not relyſh myn outlawry as they dyd theyrs). Much the Myller's ſon worry'd after myn ſanyty beyng ſo ſecluded, and myn owne Chryſtyan vyrtues ſone cry'd out at takeyng ſo much generoſyty and returneyng none. What more could y loſe, y aſk'd yn prayer, and what Hell awayts the ungrateful? And ſo, ſyx wekes frome myn reſcue—mayehaps ſeven—y agrede to engage as one of the foreſt men (as already some of myn ſoldyery, fled frome Veryſdale, had done).

Y went wyth them to hunt the Kyng's dere and (woe!) to

---

57. This is seemingly a mention of the Battle of Dunbar in 1296, placing this story (if this amongst all of the historical references in Richard's tale is to be trusted) in the last decade of the reign of Edward I, who died in 1307.

wayelaye rych men (though myn blade ne'er y rayſe'd). A poynt made y, however, ne'er to accompany Robyn on hys queſts agaynſt the clerycs. And on the tymes whych he brought thoſe capture'd Chryſtyans home y toke myn famyly awaye and we praye'd yn the wode, at a place where the foreſters had erected a ſymple croſs, and ynſcrybe'd at yts baſe the wordes of Marke 16:9[58].

And all thys tyme longe ſtoryes ſtyll flew that Edward Kyng ſought us heartyly, yet never—e'en on occaſyonal forayes ynto the Grenewode—dyd he fynde the Tryſtyng Tree, fore ſo well-hydden was yt. Y had no hope of hearyng worde of myn ſon, and no hope alſo of regaynyng myn land, though yt was yet ungovern'd. No longer a noble, nore e'en a true knyghte, y cry'd often and thys was much to myn ſhame. Myn famyly adopted the lyfe better than y, and myn eldeſt daughter was gyven a poynted hat by Robyn whych ſhe would wear at all tymes—and whych ſhe cheryſhes e'en to thys daye.

One daye, yn early fall, Much tolde me that Robyn wyſh'd to ſpeak wyth me, and ſo y went, each fotefall full of trepydatyon. Y found hym by a ſtream, ſewyng torne tunycs wyth Clorynda. When they ſaw me, the ſhepherdeſs toke her leave and Loxſley offer'd me a ſeat beſyde hym and the gur-gleyng ſtream.

'ſome tyme yt has bene that ye have lyve'd 'neath Gre-newode's boughs, ſyr Rychard.' Y noded only. 'And ſome help ye have bene on the hunt and yn the tranſporte of moneys. Yet thy ſworde ye rarely bare, and ſwyng yt never. And oft when we ſearch ye out fore an adventure ye are nowhere found, and when we returne there ys a ſofte terrore on ye, as a man come frome maſs.' Hys eyes were ſearchyng, though he ſmyle'd kyndely.

58. Marke 16:9 KJV: *Now when Iesus was risen early, the first day of the weeke, he appear'd fyrst to Mary Magdalene, out of whom he cast seuen deuils.*

272

Though we had never ſpoken of yt y knew then and knowe nowe that Robyn Hode knew the truthe of myn heart. 'Y wyll not ſhame ye to aſk yf thy arm yet remembers to ſwyng a glayve, but alſo ſhall y not take naye fore anſwer thys daye; a noble ab-bot frome ſome northern ſee rydes Barneſdale waye wyth but fyve brothers, and y mean to teſt hys fayth. Go ye then wyth me thyther, ore gyve ye the anſwer y have tolde that y wyll not take?' Yt was clear there was no optyon before me, and ſo y aſſented. Wyth jubylatyon Robert o' Wode clap'd myn back and crowe'd wyth joye. 'Go ye, ſyr knyghte, and don thy byrnye[59], fore ſwyftly we ryde fore Ermyne ſtrete!'

And ſo y gather'd myn mayl (gyven me by the free men after a robyng of a rych knyghte on hys waye to the mydſummer fayr), baldryc, helm, and ſworde and made ſwyft progreſs to-wards where we were to departe frome. Edyth was yll-pleaſe'd when y tolde her fore where y went, but y could neyther lye to myn wyfe nore deny the fearful ſummons of our jolly hoſte. 'Our Lorde protects thoſe what honour hys death on the Croſs,' y remynded her and went. And well that y dyd, fore of all the abbots to mete on the road none could make as fayr an encoun-ter as that one.

The godly men had come downe through Nottyngham and we wayted—Jon, Robyn, Much, Gylberte Whyte-Hand, and y—yn that ſame place where ſo longe ago y had fyrſt bene waye-laye'd. More archers wayted yn the wode, and myn hand was wet wyth ſweat upon myn blades hylt; y would not draw on Chryſte's men, but yt ys ever a great comforte to a knyghte to knowe he holdes ſtele near to hym (e'en ſhould hys hand ſhudder at odd tymes as myne ys prone).

Yt was nygh ſext[60] when we heard hofebeats comeyng

59. A chainmail tunic
60. The fifth Catholic hour, taking place at roughly noon

ſlowely and a great, depe voyce rayſe'd yn a jolly ſonge. Loxſley, wyth a wynk, ſtep'd alone ynto the road. ſhortely about the bend came ſyx men mounted, wyth ſome half dozen ore more ſumpters[61] comeyng behynde, overladen wyth godes. Y could fele the excytement yn the ayr at the ſyghte of ſuch an heavy load, but myn blode roſe only yn hopes that the abbot made no attempt to deny Lorde Rob. Thys holy man was dreſſ'd much as hys brothers, yet more rychly and wyth a wyde hat and ſtyff black botes. 'Twas he what ſung ſo loud.

Myn hoſte—and, though y hated to admyt to yt, yn many wayes myn maſter—ſtep'd forwards and, as the ſynger's voyce falter'd, grab'd the reyns of hys horſe, ſayeyng, 'ſyr Abbot, by thy leave, y fear ye muſt nedes abyde here a tyme. We be foreſt yeo-men of thys wode; we make our lyveyng on the Kyng's dere and have no other means nore land. But ye! Ye have churches and rents bothe, and ſurely great plentys of golde. Gyve us ſome of thy coyn, out of holy charyty and thy gracyous heart.' ſo bolde was he that y fell frome myn crouch, landyng unkyndely on myn rear yn the wet leaves.

ſpake the abbot then frome hys handſome beard, 'Y brought no more here but forty pounds; y reſyded ſome tyme yn Nottyngham wyth our kyng, and there ſpent much on hys noble fryends and theyr heyrs. Y have but forty pound and no more. Had y an hundred pounds y would gyve full half to ye, but alas, y am made pore by myn love of Edward Kyng.'

'Come men,' laugh'd Robyn, 'fore thys man ys ſo weary frome hys exceſs that he knowes not that he gayns no love by ſpendyng Churche golde on unchurchely thyngs. Relyeve hym of hys ſylver!' And we came out of the trees, all of us yn a pack. Y could ſee the monkes were aſtounded, yet they dyd naught to

61.   A pack horse

ſtop the gredey hands whych ſearch'd hys bags. Theyr maſter had a noble bearyng, but hys face was ſhadowe'd by hys broad hat. However, another monke, wyth black beard and black eyes, loked ſomehow famylyar to me. And yndeed he ſeme'd alſo to be conſyderyng me yn that ſame manner and ſo y loked awaye.

When all the coyn was gather'd 'twas laye'd upon a cloth and Jon knelt downe to count. 'Forty pound,' he ſaye'd at laſt, and Loxſley clap'd yn glee.

'Take thys here,' he motyon'd to one half the pyle and ſpake towards Lyttle Jon, 'and dyvyde yt fayr 'twene all what wear myn grene. The reſt y gyve gratyouſly to me.' And wyth ſwyft arm he ſwept twenty pounds ſylver ynto a waytyng ſack. 'Fore thy generoſyty, gode abbot, y gyve ye thys gyft—that ye maye paſs thys waye unbother'd, ſo as to hopefully come our waye agayn.' And wyth that he ſtep'd out frome the road, and we companyons follewe'd.

The abbot toke thys all yn ſtryde, and thank'd us fore paſſage, 'Gramercy, y ſaye. 'Tys kynde we were not harme'd, and kynder ſtyll fore what y bear.' He poynted wyth one ryng'd hand and a monke produce'd a proud, red ſhyeld, marke'd wyth the lyons of Edward Kyng. There was an awe upon the party, and Robyn laugh'd once—perhaps yn ſurpryſe ore e'en yn nervouſneſs. 'Our great Kyng, of Plantagenet borne, ſends thys profe, that ye maye take ynvytatyon and come to Nottyngham fore wyth hym to make mete and meal.

Yn that ſtyllneſs y knew not what would be done, but to myn relyef Loxſley fell to one dutyful knee, and we—wyth a clatteryng—dyd alſo. 'Y am certayn ye have heard, ſyr Abbot, of myn love y bear our ſovereygn—a greater love than y bear any man yn all the worlde. Welcome y hys ſeal, and ye hys honour'd fryend. Had y knowne howe cloſe hys truſt yn ye y maye have bene gentler ſtyll, and ſo y beg ye—by our ſhare'd love—to joyn yn dynner 'neath myn Tryſtyng Tree.' Bytterly y thought of howe yll he had treated ſheryff John, though he had bene bothe truſted and kyn of Edward. Yet, y ſhould no longer lyve had Robyn's morals bene yntact. He offer'd back no coyn and the abbot aſk'd of none, but followe'd us aſyngyng back through Barneſdale Wode.

Full wyth many merry men was the glade as we came upon, and at the ſyghte of Lorde Robyn leadyng the abbot on hys horſe great laughter ſpread throughout. Robert Hode bade Lyttle Jon the feaſt fore to prepare. He then drew out hys yvory whyte horne and blew yt loud. ſwyftly gather'd ſome ſeven ſcore men who knelt, ſmyleyng, at hys fete.

Y heard then the holy man mutter a moſte unholy thyng and ſaye, as yf unto hymſelf, 'ſuch a wonder y had not thought to ſee thys daye; y wene[62], by God's payn, hys men are more at hys bydyng than myn men be at myne!'

Yn lyttle tyme was the ſcene ſet to ſup and y ſat wyth myn famyly—ſtyll at the hyghe table though y was nowe lyttle more than any other of Robyn's men. As all were gather'd and the common ſyngyng ſubſyded the Hode ſtode, as was hys cuſtome, fore to delyver hys heretyc ryte (y had not had a true Catholyc ſervyce yn nyghe on a year at thys tyme, and when y was releaſe'd the very fyrſt thyng y dyd was to fly to a churche to be ſhryven), yet he dyd not begyn. Ynſtede, he turne'd and offer'd the duty to the abbot. Yet the abbot declyne'd (and glad am y that he dyd, knoweyng nowe what y dyd not then of hys nature), 'Naye, gode maſter, fore y have had much too much of formalyty yn Nottyngham. ſhowe me ynſtead the hoſpytalyty of the Grenewode!' Robyn Hode ſcowle'd bryefly at thys, but

62. Think

clap'd hys hands and call'd fore meat.

Venyſon was brought and clean whyte bread. Red wyne and all manner of ales followe'd. The meal was longe and loud and party to much exceſs. Maſter Grenewode ſpake longe of the joyes of foreſt lyfe, and tolde many tales—ſome made ynnocent by omyſſyon, yet many more unalter'd. The abbot commented on the exquyſyte taſte of the dere and Robyn laugh'd ſayeyng, 'Would a kyng's game produce meat any leſs dyvyne?' The abbot could not dyſagree.

Y ate yn polyte ſylence wyth myn wyfe, and playe'd worde games wyth myn daughters, yet found myn eye drawn ever to the black-bearded monke. He muſt have noted myn eye, however, fore ſone he drew up hys cowle.

At laſt y heard Robyn callyng fore the tables to be clear'd and y order'd myn houſeholde to retyre, leſt they wytneſs agayn ſome terryble myſchyef. Yet e'en as thoſe wordes left me y heard Lorde Robert cry, 'Nowe ſhall ye ſee what lyfe we lead, that ye maye ynforme our Kyng when next ye two mete!' Yn an ynſtant nyghe every man at table was afote wyth bowe ſtrung and drawn. The monkes they made the holy ſygne, and Edyth ſhe dyd ſcream.

But then Wyll ſcarlocke laugh'd, and tumble'd ynto vyew, 'Fear not, O man of Chryſte, thys byt of ſtagelyke whymſey, but watch the game ſet forthe, and ſmyle not ſo grymly!'

And yndede yt ſeme'd a game was promptly beyng ſet upon the ſward. Two yardes[63] were laye'd fore ſhoteyng and hung wyth garlands. 'Too far by fyfty pace are theſe bothe,' complayn'd Robyn's geſt, already recover'd of hys fryghte, but

63. Posts or rods

naught was done to change them. On each rod was ſet a roſe-garland, and ſone the monkes had bowes (and none amongſte them dyd refuſe).

'Whoſoever fayls of theyr garland hys tackle[64] he ſhould forfeyt. To hys maſter ſhall yt go,' and here Lorde Loxſley pauſe'd and held wyde hys ſmyrkyng arms fore prayſe, 'no matter the make of the man. And ſo ſhall all be won by Robyn, fore no greater maſter there be, e'en ſhould y take ale ore wyne!' As yf to prove hys worde, he toke then a meaſure of red wyne and drayn'd yt ſwyftly yn hys crawe. Belchyng, he contynue'd, 'And ſo too ſhall that man bear a buffet on hys head.' Thyſ laſt fearſome boaſt brought a great roar frome the crowde.

Myn daughters beg'd to ſee the conteſt, yet y ſtode fyrm and ſent them offe wyth Edyth; y would not have them expoſe'd to more of the Grenewode's barbaryty than y muſt.

There was lyttle competytyon to be had 'gaynſt Robyn, though all preſent ſeme'd of great ſkyll. When faceyng nyghe anyone elſe each was a myracle to beholde, yet once 'twas the Lorde of Loxſley they ſhot beſyde theyr aym was ever offe. And, true to hys worde, each man what loſte gave up what godes he carry'd and bore a terryble blowe upon hys head. Many men were bruyſe'd and made porer yn lyttle tyme, yet Robyn Hode—blodey-knuckle'd and whyte-tothe'd—ſhot on. Even the fyve brothers what joyn'd the abbot were beſted and clobber'd o'er theyr cowles. The only ſkyll y wytneſſ'd (deſpyte ſo many worthey bowemen) truely near the maſter's owne was Gylberte of the Whyte Hands, though y never ſaw the two face. Jon the Northeman and ſcarlocke bothe were ſhowne theyr place by the Wodelorde's myghty fyſt, and myghtey Much bore the blowe and ſtode. Y cry'd to ſee ſuch nedeleſs vyolence, and ſpuren'd a

64. Gear, in this case specifically the arrows of the defeated

bowe when lent.

But yn the laſt a ſtrange upſet occure'd. As he ſhot 'gaynſt the myſteryous abbot, who had yet wythſtode frome gyveyng a name, the churchman gracefully made the garland and Robyn's arrowe fayl'd of yt. ſemeyngly ſtrycken by hys owne faylure, he ſtode fore an ynſtant ſtyll, then began to rant and to rave. Yn hys fury he ſaye'd thyngs more foul than anythyng y have heard before, nore have heard ſynce (even ſpeakyng agaynſt hys beloved ſaynt). He threw hys bowe and march'd the fyeld towardes the poſtes, demandyng bothe ſhots be redone, yet gode Gylberte ſtep'd before hym and, wyth one pale hand on hys maſter's cheſt, bade hym ſtaye hymſelf. 'Maſter, thy tackle be loſte. ſtand forthe and take thy paye.'

Wyth ſome efforte Lorde Loxſley calm'd hymſelf and, ſtyll red-face'd returne'd to the vyctore as all watch'd yn blodey'd ſylence. 'The truthe be that y have loſte to ye, ſyr Abbot, and no amount of complaynt maye change that. Take ye myn arrowes, and ſerve me as y would have ſerve'd ye.'

'Yt ys not the manner of myn order,' ſaye'd the kyndely churcheman, 'to ſtryke ſo godely a yeoman as thyſelf, fore fear of doyng hym harme.'

'ſmyte me,' growle'd Robyn Hode. 'And do ſo boldely, fore y gyve ye leave. Y ſhall not be undone yn myn honour by the honour of another.' And ſo the abbot rolle'd up hys ſleve and, wyth a great fyſt of many ryngs, he dealt hys hoſte ſo myghtey a blowe that the Hode was taken e'en to the ſoyl. He roſe, no longer red, but wyde-eye'd and laughyng yn ſurpryſe. 'By a vowe to God, ye be a ſtalwart fryar! There ys pyth[65] yn thyne arm. Y trowe'd[66] ye could ſhote well, but—' Hys voyce

65. Spirit

66. Think or believe

279

trayl'd offe as he loke'd frome the ſtranger's face to hys ryngs and back agayn, 'fore fallyng to hys knee. 'Edward Kyng, Lorde of all England! Nowe y knowe ye well, though y have not ſene ye ſynce y was young!' A ſtun'd murmur ran through the crowde, and others began to knele. Y dyd as well, and at once y recognyze'd the black-hayr'd fryar (who ſat yn the graſs nurſeyng a bruyſed head) as ſyr Roger of Doncaſter who had once vyſyted and aſk'd of Robyn Hode.

'Mercy then, Robyn,' ſaye'd our Kyng, 'under thy Tryſtyng Tree, of thy godeneſs and grace, fore myn men and me!'

So ſombre was hys voyce that at fyrſt y was confuſe'd; why ſhould England's Kyng beg mercy of a yeoman? Surely no man would dare to ſlaye theyr owne kyng, even ſo outnumber'd. Then ſcarlocke's laugh ran through the glade and y loke'd up to ſee Edward's ſmyleyng face. A jeſt yt had bene, fore already Robyn's ſpell was laye'd.

Meteyng hys kyng's eye, Loxſley laugh'd alſo. 'Ay, by God. And alſo, God ſave me, y aſk mercy, thy Grace, fore bothe y and fore myn men.'

Edward Kyng ſtode grym afore laughyng full, 'Ay, by God!'

And ſo was the tenſyon relyeve'd and all laugh'd and drank together. Y ſent fore myn famyly ſo they ſhould mete the Kyng and y felt a weyght lyft offe myn ſhoulders. Yn that nyghte y was ſo relyeve'd to be yn the Kyng's comely company that y dyd not even pauſe to lament the ſpread of Lorde Hode's enchantments. Y made merry that nyghte—merryer than y had yn many monthes—and ſpoke freely wyth many there. Of thoſe wyth whych y met only two—yn myn ageyng mynde—were worthey of note: Edward Kyng and ſyr Roger of Doncaſter.

Fyrſt, once Edyth had come, y went to ſee our monarch. As can be expected, there were many who wyſh'd to paye reſpect to Hys Hygheneſs. Many more, y noted, than had wyſh'd to do ſo when he was yn the guyſe of an abbot. We wayted patyently, untyl Robyn noted us yn the queue and motyon'd fore us to ſtep ahead. Y proteſted, yet he would not be deny'd—thys was the pryde of Robyn Hode.

'Hayl Edward Kyng!' y ſaye'd, and fell upon myn knee. Y tolde hym of myn name, and thoſe to of myn three kyn.

'Rychard Veryſdale yt ys? Who has ſo vex'd and threaten'd myn mynyſters and captayns?' Yn fear y made to deny theſe clayms, yet was ſtyll'd by a wave of one kyngly hand. 'Be yt ye ore be yt Robyn what has kept thoſe lands frome me, yf Robyn ys made fryend—as fryend he ſemes—then to ye y gyft thy lands. Fore yndede ys yt not true that y offer'd them to he what brought me ye? And here ye crouch, e'en before myn fete. ſtand ye, Rychard Knyghte, and knowe thyne exyle to be undone.' Yn awe y ſtode as Edyth ſob'd and preſently myn lyege's hand was on myn ſhoulder. 'ſorely have ye bene kept by that late John of Yorke. 'Robyn has ynforme'd me well of the yll done ye, by noble and by yeoman. There be many more, y fear, what have bene wronge'd by myn dead couſyn. Yet he ys gone, and ye are free, ſo rejoyce and be once more a fryend to the Englyſh Crowne.' Hys eyes were kynde and myn heart weak, ſo y fear myn thanks was pore yndede, but once we had made our leave (after promyſe of legal documents to come) y allowe'd myn tears to fall.

ſo grateful was y that y dyd not fore longe tyme dwell on thynkyng that the kyng hymſelf had fallen prey to Lorde Robert's ſpell. Often yn the years ſynce have y bene thankful alſo (and equally ſurpryſe'd) that Robyn was trutheful of hys owne ſyns as well as ſheryff John's; he never came hymſelf to tell me what was ſaye'd, but a letter yn the Kyng's owne hand (whych y kepe dear even to thys daye) explayn'd a tellyng clearer than y ever could have preſumed of the rogue.

Fore all hys ſyns, y knew Robyn Hode to be a loyal man, and a lover of all fayr lordes.

After we had met the Kyng—and he had kyſſ'd myn wyfe's hand—y ſent Edyth and our chyldren to prepare fore bed. Y mynſelf dyd not at fyrſt leave, ſo enamour'd was y to be yn England's preſence, but ſtaye'd and drank ale ſpareyngly. Yt was only as y prepare'd at laſt to retyre that ſyr Roger dyd acoſte me.

'ſyr of Ryverſmotte,' ſlur'd he, fore drunk and ſtumbleyng was that darkeſome knyghte. 'Lyttle was y amaze'd to ſee ye here yn Robyn's ſynful care. Y thought perhaps when ſeeyng ye on Ermyne ſtrete that y maye be the one to pyerce thy traytore heart. But naye!' And here he drank once more frome hys tankard. Younger than y and ſtronger of arm was he, and he ſtode ſo as to trap me yn myn ſeat. 'Yt ſemes ynſtead that all ys foregyven, and we once more muſt be fryends.'

'Y had thought ye enjoye'd myn company when once ye came to Ryverſmotte,' y ſaye'd, and he fell ynto a chayr beſyde me. 'Ys yt ſo foul to be ſuch fryends wyth me?'

Hys gaze was darke though depe yn drynk, and yt toke longe fore hys wordes to come. 'Mayehaps not ſo foul had ye not throwne yn wyth the lykes of Robyn Hode. Y have a nun what ſhares myn love—of God and other ſuch ſacred thyngs—not far but at Kyrklyes. And ſhe has knowne of many a fryar—and of many a knyghte—who have fallen prey to Loxſley's games, and come awaye unman'd!'

'Unman'd?' y ſaye'd. 'Y have not ſene hym do ſuch vyolence.'

'Naye, not as ſuch, though vyolence does he do.' He wave'd hys hand dyſmyſſyvely. 'But ſtryp'd of coyn and ſometymes garb, and often a poynt of rydycule. Yt pleaſes me lyttle to ſee myn fryends ſo ſore offended, and y thought that to march wyth Edward Kyng would gyve me vengeance fore the ylls of Robyn Hode. Yet alack! He has charme'd England's Crowne, and nowe a rych man muſt nedes lyve yn fear when on theſe rodes he wends.'

'But Roger, fryend,' y ſaye'd, 'nowe wyth myn lands re-turne'd y am a rych man once more, and y wene y nede not fear hym.' Y thynk perhaps y ſaye'd thys only to mock hym, fore yndede would y fear hym fore the reſt of hys mortal lyfe whene'er y paſſ'd that waye! He gave me only a ſtartle'd gaze then ſtumble'd offe once more. Ne'er agayn dyd y ſpeak wyth that black-eye'd man, and y dyd not thynk much of our meteyng untyl y heard of the death of Robyn Hode.

Y retyre'd then to myn foreſt bed, and ſlept untyl the morne. And yn that morne y made myn laſt ryde wyth Robyn Hode.

Loxſley broke hys faſt that daye, as he ſometymes dyd, yn hys lowe ſaxon hall. As a man of means, wyth wyfe and chyldren beſydes, y had bene gyven a rome thereyn on myn fyrſt arryval, and had knowne better than to argue. Y roſe late, beſet by an unantycypated yllneſs whych churne'd myn ſtomach and pound-ed myn head. As y returne'd frome relyeveyng mynſelf y found the Kyng and hys party already depe yn joyeful converſatyon wyth Clorynda and her lorde. Y avayl'd mynſelf of a mug of bere and ſat ynconſpycuouſly at one end of the chamber, largely re-move'd frome the feaſtyng.

On ſome ſubject they had bene dyſcuſſyng wyth ſome

myrth before myn arryval (O that y could have knowne not to attend that meal, fore the embarraſſment theyr plotyng coſte me! Yet who can deny theyr ſovereygn?), and ſone after y toke myn ſeat the Kyng ſet aſyde hys mutton and ſaye'd to Robyn Hode, 'Have ye any grene cloth that ye wyll ſell nowe to me?'

'Ay, 'fore God,' laugh'd Robyn, 'Thyrty yardes and three.'

'Then ſell yt me, Robyn, to be paye'd when next y mete myn treaſurey. And yf ye ſell yt me already ſewn to fyt myn men y'll paye ye yet more wyllyngly.'

'Ay, 'fore God,' laugh'd Rob agayn, 'fore y am no fole. And another daye y trowe ye wyll clothe me fore to celebrate a Yule.'

'Ay, 'fore God,' joyefully echo'd Edward, and caſt aſyde hys cowle. Grene garments were brought ſwyftly fore the royal and hys men, and each was ſone full-garb'd. 'And y ſee Rychard ys fyt yn foreſt weft already,' ſaye'd our lyege as he caſt aſyde as well hys grey and ſtode yn Lyncolne ſhade. 'And fyt to followe us to Nottyngham! Awaye, y ſaye, awaye!'

Awaye once more y was ſwept by the ſtrange fates whych favour'd Robyn Hode, and ere longe y ſat ahorſe, once more headed fore the late ſheryff's towne. Forthe we went wyth bowes abent, and much ſhoteyng there was had. Y knew not what reaſon was yn our maſters' heads, but beyng yn the company of England's Kyng y thought mynſelf ſecure. And ſo y too ſhot and laugh'd beſyde ſcarlocke and Gylberte.

Robyn and Edward rode together, and made a forme of that game whych before they had playe'd; they ſhot and bet, ahorſe and afote, and whoſoever ſhould fayl the greater would fele the weyght of theyr fellowe's fyſt. Many a buffet our Kyng won of Robyn Hode that daye, and ſo too dyd nothyng ſpare gode Robyn of hys paye. Bothe ſhot and beat and laugh'd the whole, deſpyte theyr blodey browes. Had yt bene any man but Loxſley what ſtruck our Kyng a great pryce would he paye, yet Robyn was a ſpecyal ſoul, and no further punyſhment would he face. Y knew by the lokes on thoſe about that yn myn dyſcomfyt at thys conteſt y was not alone, yet none would challenge eyther man. And ſo we made ſlowe yet merry progreſs on the waye to Nottyngham.

And when we made thoſe Englyſh gates, a ſcene we dyd beholde. Yn confounded ſylence ſtode the folke of the towne, theyr eye's growne wyde wyth fear. Then crys went up and bells were rung and fete began to fly. 'The Kyng ys ſlayn! Comes Robyn Hode to towne! Our lyves are loſte! Alas and curſe thys daye!' Yeoman and knave and crypple'd old wyves all hurry'd out our waye. At fyrſt y knew not why the gode olde Kyng ſhould be greted yn thys waye. But then y ſaw hym ſmyleyng, hys bowe yn one great hand, and ſaw hym as they dyd ſee—naught but mantles grene.

The Kyng laugh'd loud as yn the ſquare he rode. Where once myn gallowes were he ſtop'd and watch'd the locals' flyghte. He ſhoke hys ſworde yn mock barbaryty, then call'd out happyly, 'Ye foles and peaſants are not fyt to plowe! Knowe ye not thy choſen kyng, what rydes thys noble roan?'

ſone Nottyngham's dores were once more unbar'd and a feaſt was had yn John Yorke's hall. Y thynk thys was a cruel joke (and wryte ſo nowe only knoweyng that that kyng has dye'd), and myn gode mode was then ſpoyl'd. The feaſt was fayr and rych—and full of dere brought by Grenewode men—but anon y felt myn mornyng's yllneſs returne. Robyn and our noble ſovereygn wyth noble men dyd joyn, and laugh'd to ſee the faces whych they themſelves had fole'd wyth death.

After the ſonges were ſung and ale ſerve'd dyd Edward call loud to me. To all he tolde myn name and lands, and full embrace'd he me. 'A gode man yndede ys ſyr Rychard at the Lee!' he dyd declare, and call'd fore lawyers, myn lands to gyve yn wryt to me. As y ſygne'd and ſygne'd agayn the two new fryends dyd mete nearby, and plot a ſtrange new tale (of whych y knew but lyttle fore y was ſafe then yn Veryſdale).

To Robyn ſaye'd the Kyng, 'Fore God, O Robyn Wode, promyſe me that ye ſhall be a man at home yn court. Y would have ye dwell wyth me and ſee what chere thy love maye bryng myn halls.'

'Ay, Edward,' ſaye'd Robyn wyth a kyſs. 'Y make myn avowe to God, and ſo yt ſhall y followe. To thy court wyll y to go, thy wyll fore to ſerve, and wyth me bryng of myn men ſeven ſcore and three. Theſe wyll be as thyne owne men, and fyghte to kepe the yſland free and ſtronge.' Hys mouth grew ſombre then, though hys eyes ſtyll gryn'd. 'Yet ſhould y lyke thy ſervyce yll, back up Ermyne ſhall y wend. To laugh and praye and ſhote thy dere, as ys e'er myn wyll.' The two great men dyd clap each other's backs and toaſt to theyr gode health, and y—wyth wryt yn hand—made haſte back home to wyfe.

Y ſaw naught agayn of Robyn Hode, yet heard much yn myn tyme. What common bond was 'twyxt hym and royal houſe y neytherknew nore care'd at all. Happy y was (and am y ſtyll) merely to have myn lyfe.

Yf Robyn tyre'd of Edward ore yf Edward of Robyn grew bored y knowe not, yet knowe y only that he ſtaye'd yn court but twelve monthes and three. On the fyfth monthe he ſtaye'd yn court dyd Much come to Veryſdale, and ſpoke that the lyfe was not fore hym, and ſo he to Grenewode hye'd. 'He

ſpends and ſpends,' ſaye'd that ſmallyſh man, 'e'en frome our—
hys men's—fee. Yn every place where he goes he layes downe
marke and pound. Y am no fryend to hym as once ys tolde y
was, and y ſhall not ryſk myn name and neck yf empty myn
purſe y fynde.' Y had heard eke that other men had fled that
waye, and after the dwarf came yet more.

When at laſt the Grenewode Prynce dyd leave once
more fore Barneſdale, 'tys ſaye'd he had but two men true—
Lyttle Jon and dyre ſcarlocke—and hys loveyng lady wyfe. Thoſe
three yt ſemes would love hym no matter hys ſyns nore debts.
Yet when he came back myn waye y heard hys men dyd come to
hym anew, and celebrate hys reygn. Ne'er agayn dyd he caſt lyghte nore ſhadowe on myn dore (and an half myn mynde thynks
thys abſence was yn hys waye a gyft, fore truely yt ſemes he knew
the trouble he cauſe'd me), but ſaxon Jon and ſcarlet Wyll came
ſometymes to dyne. They ſpake of Robyn's love of bowe and
ſaynt, and the joye yn all the Wode. Much came oftener ſtyll to
geſt and ſpake of hys travels, though grene he no more wore, and
the only geſt y wyſh'd fore more was myn loſte ſon (who, woe to
me, ſurely nowe has dye'd). Two and one ſcore years dyd
Loxſley ſtaye wythyn hys holte, and e'er thereyn hys myſchyef
cauſe. But ne'er agayn dyd our Kyng come (the one he knew
nore the next) and none ſeme'd to care of hym hys crew to
dyveſt.

Y hear he dye'd a fole's death, fore truſtyng much yn
kyn. 'Tys ſaye'd wyth colde ore flu he went to a couſyn at Kyrklyes. And there ſhe bled hym dry, that pryoreſs foul, on dynt of
lecheyng craft. Thys woman nun ys ſaye'd a lover had, and he a
full darke man. Though never y learn'd the blaggard's name, ſyr
Roger dyd y ſuſpect; hys hatred of ſyr Robyn Hode was well-
knowne to me, and oft had he ſpoke of that abbey. Doubtleſs
thys death was an adventure great, though of yt y ken gladly lyttle.

The tyme y ſpent yn Grenewode was as tyme ſpent yn Hell. Yet through that Hell y gayn'd myn lyfe and lands, and met fayr Edward Kyng. Gredey was that Maſter Wode, and full of troubleſome wyll. Yet deſpyſe'd he brybery and unfayr law, and love'd he feudal government. Yf only he had bene borne above hys yeoman caſte he maye have made a noble man. A fayr yet warſome lorde would he be (and perhaps, God foregyve, he would dye yn holy lands).

Myn daughters are fayr growne, bothe marry'd and wyth chylde, and myn coffers glytter endleſſly as myn peaſants worke the land. Myn wyfe growes more beautyful by the daye and, though ſtyll ſometymes y ſup wyth the Myller's ſon, adventure y have left behynde. Maye Robyn Loxſley reſt ſofte yn Hell ore— yf God foregyves hym, perhaps ſeeyng hym as another Davyd Kyng—A lowe ſeat yn Heaven maye he have; yf any man could charme the Devyl and have Chryſte eke yn hys hand, 'twould be that lorde of Lyncolne Grene what ſhot upon thys land.

And ſo here ends myn tale (and weary growe myn eyes) of thoſe trouble'd tymes yn whych y, ay me, knew Robyn Hode.

Afterward

Some books begin with a forward wherein the author (or an editor, etc.) speaks on the evolution of the work and why it is so important. But I am a relatively new face on the writing scene and as such don't imagine that many folks are looking to hear me ramble on aboutwhy my work is so enjoyable without my first having proved it. Besides, nobody buys a short story collection to read why it was written; they buy it to read what is contained therein, so putting the stories first only seems a logical course of action to me.

Of course, if you have made it this far you likely at least have some interest in the process which brought this little publication into your eagre hands. For years I had assumed that my first published work would be my long-in-production novel about a discontented psychopomp stealing the life of a mortal princess, but when I put out *Bone Orchard Gospel* last year I proved myself false, and this short story collection further separates my assumptions from reality. But life is full of surprises and discoveries, and this book, in many ways, has been a decade or more in production, so it deserves to be let out to breathe. It has taken me many starts, stops, erasures, and new beginnings to finally craft this afterward and ultimately I settled on the idea that it should serve as something of a brief, itemized overview of each of the pieces herein.

The first tale included, *The Lady of Salt and Shadows*, was the first story ever published on my Patreon back in 2019. It came to me as a sort of folk tale to further flesh out the expansive mythology of Eord—the fantasy setting I have been writing in for almost a decade but have yet to officially release. I did not want to explain too much, and wanted it to seem familiar enough in form that it could be read by anyone, without knowledge that there was a greater body of work attached. As for the content, it was inspired primarily by the statue *Medusa* by Luciano Garbati, which depicts the famous gorgon as the victor in the clash with Perseus, mirroring the classic statue by Cellini. I have written before on how I find the female perspective more engaging than the male in fiction, and saw the opportunity to flip the expected narrative of the gallant knight-saviour on its head (though, of course, it is not a complete reversal, for there are no true heroes in my story). This piece also displays, even though it is only a few pages long, my adoration for the concept of the story-within-the-story in storytelling, as I seem utterly unable to control myself once I begin rambling.

Old Master Wood began to germinate as I undertook my first read-through of *The Lord of the Rings* as an adult. Specifically, as I read the novel there was one particular page which stuck out to me as the hobbits were guests of Tom Bombadil and he told them of old tales of terrible trees and forgotten kingdoms (indeed, for much of its writing the working title for the novella was *Bom Tombadil* until I could think of something better). I wanted to tap into something more whimsical, and tell a story which, while still adult, felt more at home next to *The Hobbit* or *Moomintroll* than *The Dark Tower*. Writing it took me longer than anticipated (though this often happens and I should no longer be surprised), but I allowed myself to guide its progress in many ways through automatic writing, and allowed disparate inspirations to enter the tale as they came to me over the course of a little over half a year—not least of which being a continued dabbling into the Old English language. Ultimately, the result is a folk tale with its own voice, and the patchwork of influences have been blended together with the help of the diminutive wizard of the title. The little hermit himself is a character who has lived in my head in one form or another for ages, and will continue to do so for ages more—the wise recluse who gains more from beasts than books and yet, despite his age, is still very much a child at heart. I think that all of us should make an effort to cultivate our own small seed of Old Master Wood in our breasts; I know that for me at least it is a place where I can find peace.

The Hat Tree, though charming in its own way, has always been a sinister story. I began it late in 2019 after looking on a fir tree at a worksite I was on where a hat had been hung on a cut branch. At the time I was also reading Stephen R. Donaldson's The King's Justice, and doubtless the inquisitorial undertones of that tale also influenced it. The story is purposefully obtuse, and it is up to the reader to find it either charming or insidious; the story's protagonist ultimately chooses the former.

As the oldest of the tales in the book, The Beauty and the Beast is also an extremely important part of my development as an author. Written in early 2011 on a whim after watching the now classic Jennifer's Body I was geased, based merely on the inclusion of a painting of Nyarlathotep in the film, to write this story. Originally much shorter, I have revised The Beauty and the Beast many times, constantly adding, revising, taking away, and altering until it reached its current state. It marked the first short story I had written since middle school and, like a bolt of lightning, convinced me that perhaps I did have what it took to write for a living. Inspired by my love of Lovecraft and classic færie tales, as well as the strange dreams I treasure so dearly, this story has followed me through the years, and I have always known that it would be featured in my first collection (though what form that collection would take has changed as often as this story). In the final revisions for A Boke of Gests I made the conscious decision not to modernize the voice to my current style, preserving the author of ten years ago forever in paper—so if this tale reads differently than the others that is (a part of) the reason.

Initially written for a weird west zine which never materialized, *A City Man* drew upon my love of the western aesthetic, despite my relative inexperience with it (I have, to this day, never read a western novel—unless King's *The Gunslinger* counts—and have seen scant few western films in the last decade and a half). Not wanting to wade into territory I was wholly unfamiliar with (such as the real-world American West) I set it instead in the fictional faux-West of my *Bone Orchard Gospel* game (where this tale may also be found, though I believe it stands strongly independent of the setting). The dichotomy between the city and the open plains seems to me to be the most iconic struggle of the western genre, and out of this was born the unhappy Ernest Boragne. I, ironically, have no memory of how the idea of his disease came to me, but as for the ghoulish wendigo, I identified it as the only purely North American legend I felt familiar enough with to include (and the song *Red Fox* by *Tomahawk* was almost certainly playing in the background at some point during the writing process). The astute reader may also draw parallels between the cannibal herein and the infamous subject of *Pickman's Model*, and this was intentional; even though the references are less blatant than in *The Beauty and the Beast*, I consider this story my most ardent love letter to H. P. Lovecraft, to whom I owe so much on my journey towards becoming a writer. As for the little details—the fate of Valio, why so many unimportant characters are named whilst it takes until the very end for his wife to be labelled by more than a pronoun—I leave those assumptions up to the reader; its entirely possible that you have created a more fantastical answer than my own, and I would hate to speak out and inadvertently betray my own accidental triumph (though by all means, if you do want to discuss this, or any of my stories, send my an email).

Another example of a writing fervor set off by watching relatively irrelevant media, *At Eternity's Gate* was written in a single evening, about a decade ago, after watching whatever episode of *Doctor Who* featured Van Gogh. At the time, as a lovesick but depressed college student, I wrote this bleak bit of self-discovery. I tend towards writing protagonists who are self-defeating and far from heroic, and Balthus is an excellent example of this. Short but to the point, *At Eternity's Gate* is, in its narration, perhaps one of the most distinct of those which I have written, to my biased eye.

The Chalice and the Noble Blood began as an adventure I wrote for the *Pendragon* roleplaying game to play with my friends. It includes a few tie-ins and hints at things that had happened in other games I had run (many of which are now making their way into my writing), but also resulted in incredibly dramatic and memorable moments. Almost immediately after writing the adventure—before I had even run it—back in 2014 or so I began adapting it into prose, though I would not finish it until around six years later. Each of the characters in the tale (save Bryn, who barely made an appearance, if at all, either time I ran the adventure) are amalgamations of the two separate versions of the character played by different players and of my own intentions for the character. No scenes from play made it into the story per se, but there are many scenes influenced by the choices of my players, and for that I must thank those who played, both in 2014 and in 2019: Ell Viner, Kieran Kane, Laura Berger, Lillie Smith, Luke Murphy, Mike O'Connell, Nate Bakke, and Sam Grey. In many ways this story has become a lynchpin to my writing, tying all of my disparate stories together, and ardent readers should be able to find threads here which lead back to almost everything in my catalogue, eventually.

An unexpected favourite of mine, *The Hole Under the House* came to me as I was driving one day; I thought of a love story between a man and a ghost, but wasn't sure if I had the chops to pull it off. A few weeks went by and, while sitting at my computer looking for something to write, it came to me. I drew upon various northern European superstitions (specifically around burial) as well as the overarching dichotomy between civilization and the natural world present in *The Lord of the Rings* (which I was reading at the time; and yes, I wrote this while procrastinating on finishing *Old Master Wood*). The end result is something between sweet and nightmarish, and in those few pages I sought to capture the fierce loneliness of a man unloved and betrayed (though perhaps not the wisest nor purest of intentions).

Finally, the real star of the show, *Y Knew Robyn Hode.* The idea for this story came to me as I was reading Waltz's translation of *The Gest of Robyn Hode*, the oldest complete Robin Hood poem. I found the poem endlessly entertaining (and strongly suggest reading it before or after my own take on it), but also was stuck by how much it seemed like an incomplete version of a story told by someone unquestioning of Robin Loxley, no matter what deeds he perpetrated. Focusing on the character of Sir Richard at the Lee (one of many once-prominent figures in Robin Hood lore that have now fallen to the wayside and been forgotten), I began to fantasize what the story may be like from a less one-sided perspective, and how a more three dimensional character may react when replacing the original Sir Richard. The result came to me in gouts of clear verse, as if Sir Richard sat with me and recounted his own tale, yet still took me over half a year to complete. As for the unusual language, I have always loved literature which purposefully defied conventions in order to further a story's theme or story, and more and more as I've aged as a writer have enjoyed developing near-analogues to our familiar speech (a phenomenon which I have come to refer to in private circles as 'Unglish'). My intentions was to create a text which looked and felt Middle English, but featured more consistent rules and was approachable for a modern reader (after the initial shock wore off) - doubtless inspired in part by the incomparable *The Wake* by Paul Kingsnorth, along with hearty dashes of *Ivanhoe*. Additionally, I found that it encouraged the reader to recite aloud in order to better parse the meaning of the text; this was an unintended but welcome consequence, as I am a firm believer that *all* stories (especially mine) should be read aloud (so make sure you try that on a subsequent read of this collection, if you have not already). The downside to this exercise was the absolute nightmare which was editing and formatting the story—a task which took nearly as long as the task of composing it. In the end I swore that I would never approach a similar task again, only to— shortly after my edit was finished—fall down the rabbit hole of Beowulf and begin work on a novella of similar length, ambition, and uncomfortable legibility. Suffice it to say, *Y Knew Robyn Hode* is the beginning of many great things, and I have been glad to hear the varied reactions from my test readers.

Together these stories form a rather tightly themed collection in my eye (though in many cases I leave it to the reader to determine who is the guest and who is the host; in others it is fairly obvious), and one which was endlessly thrilling to work on. Already I am excitedly planning my next foray into the world of collected short fiction, a genre which I will never fall out of love with. I hope that what is held here is as enjoyable to read as it was to write, but that is your job to determine; my job here is done.

F. Killian

February 2021

Acknowledgements

There are too many influential people in my life to thank them all, but here are a few, some of which have been thanked before and many of which shall be thanked again.

My ardent test-readers: Luke Murphy, Wyatt Sander, Chris Pitner, and Em. Your input helped put the final touches on some of the pieces of this work which needed the most aid. There are others who have read some of the pieces in this book in the past (especially *The Beauty and the Beast*) and I am sorry that I do not remember every face who has seen parts of this book before its publication.

My Patrons, who have stuck by me and continued to support my art even as I sometimes am tardy to post new content: Brady Murphy, Carissa Herbrand, Dan Parke, Kate Jennings, Luke Murphy (thanked here for the third time in this book), Malilda, Ross Jennings, Samuel Claeys, S. Rintoul, and Terra Peach. You make it all worth it.

My professors who encouraged me in my explorations and pursuits deserve thanks as well, of which Dr. Timothy Decker, Richard Zinober, and Dr. Patrick Calder-Carriere deserve especial mention for inspiring me to continue my work as an artist.

I'd also like to thank my parents—both of whom encouraged my eagre exploration of literature—as well as my grandmother—who not only aided in my pursuit of literary enlightenment, but also has tried her hardest my whole life to make sure I stay on track. I would be remiss also in not thanking my friends who have helped me tell stories for over two decades, including (but not limited to, I could not list you all but know that I do love you) Andrew Ring, Bladerunner John, Colin, Dillan Folkerts, Ell, Hopper, Jake Myer, Ken Tollefson, Lillie, Nate Bakke, Ross, Sebastian, Shauna Basques, and Tori; each of you has inspired me and enlightened me, offering seeds which eventually grow into stories. Also I should thank Malachi Becker, who was the first to ever request I sign their book (a fact which, to this day, I am flattered by) and Boat Jon, who pre-ordered this book without knowing what it was or when it would be released.

Thank you.

About the Author

F. Killian lives with his dog Howard in an old parsonage in a small midwestern town. A lifetime of interest in myth, fantasy, and rumour has bred in him a healthy fascination with the spiritual, historical, and occult. When he is not rolling dice at the tabletop or drawing, he is walking in the expansive forests and hills near his home and writing fiction or keeping company with the various goblins, ghouls, and gnomes which follow him wherever he goes.

He can be contacted on his various social media pages via:

linktr.ee/F.Killian

www.ingramcontent.com/pod-product-compliance
Lightning Source LLC
Chambersburg PA
CBHW021036030726
47496CB00006B/1561